HOME FOR CHRISTMAS

Christmas is family time. Sons, daughters, grandchildren . . . what luck when they all come home to celebrate their favorite holiday. The house is filled with the sound of carol-singing and the smells of delicious Christmas cooking. Love is in the air. And Christmas is a time for tradition. The same recipe for the holiday pudding; the same lovingly collected ornaments for the tree; the same cookies and milk left on the hearth for Santa.

But sometimes Christmas is a time for surprises. Brand-new traditions. A brand-new way of celebrating a beloved holiday. Here are six heartwarming Christmas stories about six very different kinds of celebration . . . each with a very special Christmas love story of its own. Six stories — one by each of the first six Zebra To Love Again authors: Claire Bocardo, Marjorie Eatock, Marian Oaks, Garda Parker, Peggy Roberts, and Clara Wimberly.

Merry Christmas!

HOME FOR CHRISTMAS

Claire Bocardo   Garda Parker
Marjorie Eatock   Peggy Roberts
Marian Oaks   Clara Wimberly

ZEBRA BOOKS
KENSINGTON PUBLISHING CORP.

CONTENTS

A Patchwork Holiday

by Claire Bocardo

When Chloe's children are big enough to cluster around my knees and ask their grandma to tell a story, I'll tell them about the Patchwork Christmas and show them this quilt to prove the tale. It's got a block for every part: two hearts broken and mended for Roxy, the paper chains, and the Christmas tree; the black bull, a satin snake, and a scrap of white fur from Ashley's coat. There's gray for the skies, blue for the flood, and crackly white stuff for the ice. The mistletoe at the center was the final motif. I still can hardly believe it myself: one minute I was sitting in the parlor, listening to the story of a man's life, and the next I was on the sixth floor of

7

the old Crockett Hotel in San Antonio, looking down at the Alamo and picking rice out of my hair.

It began, I guess, that early December afternoon at Chloe's brand-new tract house in Wylie. I was sitting there among the boxes she hadn't finished unpacking. You could still smell the paint, the house was that new. Chloe is my only child and the light of my life, though a mite more conventional than I'd have had her. The house, for example: they'll be paying her entire wage every month for thirty years for the privilege of living in a house exactly like every other house on the block, when they could have snapped up any one of a dozen perfectly nice, individual, older homes in town with established trees and ready-made vegetable gardens for half the price, plus a coat of paint.

Chloe was the receptionist for a real estate agency; she even knew where those houses were and how much they cost, but no. All she ever wanted was to live just like everybody else, dress just like everybody else, *be* just like everybody else. I used to hope it was a phase, but I think it's in her genes: her father was straight as a ten-penny nail. She favors him in her looks, too: naturally curly blond hair, blue eyes, and a sweet little rosebud mouth. I must have married her father for his looks—can't think of any other reason, except I was just so young and silly.

Be that as it may, we were sitting there listening to the dumplings boil, smelling the simmering fricassee, and sorting through her and Dan's old clothes for anything old enough for the ragbag but still good enough to work into this patchwork quilt. Thanksgiving was past, and we were talking about Christmas and how they would share out the day between Dan's widowed father and me, when Chloe came up with the idea.

"I know!" she said. "We can have it here! You and Will can both come, and we'll have a real family party, my first party in my first house, to start patching our families together."

I knew right away she was talking about more than Christmas.

"Chloe, I've told you a thousand times: stop matchmaking," I said. "You've been trying to find me a husband ever since you learned to talk. Honey, I don't want one! All I need at this point in my life is to become some man's house slave."

Dan laughed.

"That's no problem," he said. "Just be sure and show him the house before you say yes. No man who wanted a house slave would take you, Livvy."

I reached out to give him a smack, but he dodged back, grinning.

"Oh, Mama," Chloe said, "just Christmas! I've never had a Christmas with both a mother and a father! You don't have to marry him — just eat dinner with him!"

Poor little orphan child. It would've been enough to bring tears to my eyes if I hadn't known better. Will Lockhart owned a couple of little hardware stores in nearby farm towns; Dan managed the Wylie store, and Will the one in Allen. He looked like a good catch to Chloe, who wanted somebody to take care of me in my old age. She thinks old age is lurking around the corner to snap me up the minute her back is turned, but I'm content to wait another twenty-five years before I start to think about it.

Will and I liked each other well enough — it wasn't that — but I've told you how I felt, and Will was beating off widow-ladies with a broomstick. . . Not that I hadn't found a stray fellow here and there along the path, but I preferred the sort who were just passing through and would be gone before the bloom was off the rose. A daughter's father-in-law is something different. He's not going anywhere.

Dan, who was standing behind me now, ruffled my hair and bent to kiss my cheek.

"Come on, Ma," he said. He knew I loved it when he called me that. I'd waited almost fifty years for a son to call me Ma. "It's our first Christmas as a married couple. Chloe's been so excited, and it's no fun all alone. Let your baby have her party."

I couldn't help smiling, thinking how proud she'd be, buzzing around in her dinky little kitchen like a real wife. I could just see her. Child of a single mother, Chloe'd never wanted anything but to be a wife; now she was doing her best to out-Donna Donna Reed. Then it occurred to me that if Chloe did Christmas dinner, I wouldn't have to.

"Well, if it means that much . . ." I said, and just then the phone rang and Chloe picked it up.

"Dan?" she said, holding it out with two fingers as if it might bite her. "It's Victoria."

Victoria Plummer is Dan's older sister, and I mean to tell you, in Victoria's presence, strong men quail. To those who meet her standards of wealth and culture Victoria is gracious enough to gag a goose. Her general demeanor toward the rest of us is that of a woman whom nature has formed to tame the unruly. Needless to say, Chloe's scared spitless of her.

Dan took the phone into the other room so as not to interrupt Chloe and me, but she wasn't talking anymore; her little ears were stretching around the door frame to listen. All she could hear was an occasional "uh-huh" or "I s'pose," and it was making her skittery as a lizard.

"Even if it is your husband, it's not nice to eavesdrop," I reminded her. Generally Chloe is a well-mannered young woman, but I still have to remind her sometimes. She's not but four years out of high school.

"Hush, Mama," she said. "It's *Victoria!*"

"Never mind," I said. "He'll tell you the minute he gets off the phone with her. Dan doesn't keep any secrets from you."

She chewed her thumbnail with a mordant air until Dan came back and replaced the phone in its cradle.

"Well?" she asked.

"Just checking in," he told her, innocent as an egg. "I told her about the Christmas party and asked if she wouldn't like to bring up Grady and the kids for the holidays. They're all alone down there, you know," he added to me. "No kin."

"Dan!" Chloe started, but I hushed her with a warning look. You don't go putting down your brand-new husband's sister when he's being so sweet.

"That was thoughtful of you," I said. "What did she say?"

"Said she'd think about it. They could stay with Dad in Allen. He's got that big old house with nobody in it but him, plenty of room for Vic and hers. I guess she wants to talk to him first, and maybe to Grady, see how he feels about it."

Dan was sweet, but never really on top of things where personalities were concerned. Any decision made in that house would be made by Victoria alone. I'd met Grady only the one time, but it was clear to me that he was as much in awe of her as Chloe was. He was a rough diamond, long on money but short on couth. A day in proximity to the pair of them would be interesting, even without their brood of vipers—Adrian, Ashley, and Alexander—to stir the mix.

For Chloe's sake, I told myself, I could mind my manners for one day. I spent about half an hour calming her down and—once Dan was out of the room—encouraging the wan hope that they wouldn't come.

* * *

After dinner I packed up the scraps she'd given me and went back out to my little white house on the hill to cut another quilt block. I live at the top of a perfectly round little hill, a nipple on the breast of Mother Earth, halfway between Chloe's house to the southeast and Will's to the northwest. Will's wife Patsy — Dan's mama — grew up not three miles from here, and she's buried in the graveyard across the way.

My daddy built this house before I was born on land his daddy and granddaddy had owned; it's been ours for almost a century, and except for the five years I was married, I've never lived anywhere else. The nearest paved road is half a mile away, counting the long, steep driveway up my hill.

The house had been quieter than I liked since Chloe left home. I still saw her and Dan several times a week, but it wasn't the same. They were newlyweds and I didn't want to be an interfering mother-in-law, but I have to confess I was lonesome sometimes. Still, when I was growing up, clinging and crying were not respectable forms of expression. Sturdy independence was the ideal, and I learned to take care of my own needs most of the time. I can't complain: it was good training. But Chloe and I had been a close pair, and her absence had left a hole in my life. Leaving the warmth of her kitchen for that cold and empty house was never easy.

The house is in the shape of a T, with the crossbar facing north toward the gravel road and the driveway spiraling up behind. The living room, a big bedroom, and the bathroom are on the crossbar of the T, and the farm-style kitchen, laundry porch, and smaller bedroom retreat down the stem. A long, covered porch runs down the east side of the house past the kitchen and back bedroom. When I was a girl, Daddy finished off the attic over the front of the house and made two more bedrooms and a bath.

I still sleep in my old room up there. Windows opening on three sides catch any summer breeze, and I love the sound of rain on the tin roof. In winter, if I burn a fire in the evening, the chimney holds the heat and keeps my bedroom warm. My folks used the big bedroom downstairs, and when they were gone I turned it into a guest room. The one at the back is my sewing room, its bed always piled with fabrics and patterns. I used to supplement my child support by taking in sewing.

Since Chloe turned eighteen it's been my whole income, excepting barter and the vegetable stand I run in the summer months.

I tossed Chloe's scraps onto the bed back there, meaning to sort them out the next morning, and sat down to read my book. I used to go to bed with the chickens and get up with the sun, but no more. With Chloe gone, I'd begun to stay up later and later at night, reading until my eyes got sandy and I knew I would sleep. No use lying there alone in the dark and feeling sorry for myself, I thought. Might as well use the time to advantage, learning.

Chloe called me from her office the next day to tell me Will and Victoria had both accepted the invitation, and it was a done deal: we were committed to Christmas at Chloe's. Victoria and Grady would arrive on the twentieth for a week. They would stay at Will's.

"Except you know she's going to want me to keep the A's while she goes shopping and looks up her old friends," Chloe said glumly. "I was going to take the time off anyway, but I sure didn't have baby-sitting in mind."

She'd got that right, I thought. Victoria had a live-in maid and baby-sitter at home. She was sure as by-God not going to drag those kids all over Dallas for a week.

"They're going to be bored," Chloe said. "There's nothing for them to do here but watch TV."

I hardly even hesitated, didn't even sigh.

"You can bring them out here for a day if you want. We can make cookies or something."

"Oh, Mama, thank you!" You'd have thought I'd offered to raise them. "A farm will be fun for them. They've never lived anywhere but the city."

Uh-huh. I had a large portrait in oils of those prissy-pants kids on my farm. It was not a pretty picture, but I wasn't about to tell that to Chloe. She already had enough on her mind.

"Too bad most of the animals are gone," I said. I still had two sheep, which I kept for their wool and as living lawn mowers, and a small flock of chickens, but I'd gotten rid of the big animals several years earlier. I never could get the hang of giving a calf a name, petting it, feeding it, hosing it down, medicating it, and keeping its stall clean and fresh for a year, and then sending it off to have its throat slit so I could have stew for supper.

"Lumpy had her kittens two weeks ago,

though," I said. "They'll be big enough to play with by Christmas." I probably ought to warn Lumpy. She might just as soon hide them in the barn. "Well, maybe it'll snow. It won't be Aspen, but I can always find a board for them to slide down the hill on."

Even Chloe knew that was a dream. Snow is a rarity here, and I could count on one hand the years it had snowed before the middle of January.

"Maybe we can make Christmas cookies," she said, her voice a little more hopeful. "Kids like to make cookies, and I'll bet the A's have never set foot in a kitchen."

"Well, it's only a week," I said. "We'll figure something out."

As she hung up the phone, Chloe said, "Thanks, Mama. You're a peach."

Her grandma used to say that to her: you're a peach. She'd looked like a peach when she was a baby, round and sweet and covered with red-gold fuzz. Every time I heard the phrase, it reminded me. I was glad Chloe seemed to feel better, but I myself was not much reassured. Well, it would not be boring. I could count on that.

* * *

I chose a quilt design called Family Album and spent the next week sorting and cutting scraps, only to find that I didn't have enough to make the forty-two blocks—seven down and six across—to complete it. So I set it aside, planning to get back to it after the holidays. I didn't know it yet, but by the time the holidays had passed, the family would have changed so much I'd have to start all over.

The next Monday night, long after I'd gone to bed with a good book, I heard a car crunching up the gravel on my drive. I put on my old pink chenille bathrobe with the roses down the front and went downstairs. As the car stopped out back, I turned on the porch light and saw a skinny young woman get out and hold the door open for two little kids.

They came up on the porch and I opened the door.

"Aint Livvy? Is that you?" she called, and I recognized my brother's oldest girl, Roxy Smoot. I hadn't seen her since her wedding almost ten years earlier, but her voice was one you could not forget. We used to say that if all other sources of income failed, Roxy could make a decent living calling hogs. The last I'd heard, she and Bud were living in Okmulgee, Oklahoma.

Roxy looked just the same. A halo of feathery, rust-colored hair surrounded her narrow face, which featured a prominent, curved nose over lips like quarter-inch pink grosgrain. She was wearing glasses with lenses as big as the palms of my hands, and the overall effect was of an anxious Rhode Island Red in goggles.

"Roxy! Come in this house, child! What in the world are you doing here at this time of the night!"

She shooed her children inside, and they stood staring at me with suspicion in their eyes. They looked licked to a splinter. The little girl, about nine, was wiry and freckled, with a mop of carroty curls falling about her shoulders. Her chin looked sharp enough to poke holes in a concrete sidewalk. The boy looked just like her, except he was a year or so younger, his hair was straight, and he had a strong, square chin and a stubbornly downturned mouth. Trouble walking, I thought.

The minute they were all inside, Roxy fell into my arms.

"Oh, Aint Livvy, I'm so glad to see you!" she cried, and started snuffling.

"Well, honey, I'm glad to see you too," I said, "but why don't you tell me who these two are?"

The girl was called Corky and the boy

Tooter. Please, God, I thought, let them be nicknames. I got their coats off and hustled them into the kitchen, where I put on some milk to heat for cocoa and poured them each a bowl of cereal. Roxy told me they'd been in the car for hours, been sleeping ever since Atoka, and I could see they were worn out and hungry. She went straight to the icebox for a beer, and I made it my business to get those kids fed and into bed in the big front bedroom before I let her tell me what the trouble was. I didn't figure they needed to hear it.

What it was, was, she'd left her husband to make a new life. It all came out in a rush once the kids were out from underfoot.

"There I am, working my fingers to the bone, keeping his house and kids and fixing his dinner and washing his filthy clothes, and he never says word one of thanks. I'm just another household appliance," she complained. I remembered feeling that way myself once upon a time. A woman needs appreciation, and it seems little enough to ask.

"And we're broke all the time," she added. "It's terrible, Aint Livvy."

"Well, honey, if there isn't any money, there just isn't any," I told her. "There's no sense in fighting over money you don't have."

"Well, we ought to have," she said darkly. "He's gone all the time."

"Working or playing?" I asked, and that set her off again.

"He works all day—I know that—but at night . . . Well, he calls it work, but it looks like play to me. Bounces drunks at the roadhouse out on I-75, and don't those old women think he's a hunk! They're on him like flies on a cow patty, and he's so damn dumb he thinks they're just being sweet." She snorted. "He's good-looking, I'll give him that, but he hasn't got the sense God gave a goose. I don't know what I ever saw in him in the first place. The world's full of better men than Bud."

Pacing the kitchen like a caged beast, Roxy dropped her whole "somebody done somebody wrong" song right in my lap bar by bar, but with one missing note. I just kept on nodding my head and saying "uh-huh" and "who'd have guessed?" till she sang that one too. It was a pip.

"The last straw was, we'd been saving up for three years for our own house, almost had enough for the down payment, and—Aint Livvy, you're not gonna believe this—that man let his three crazy friends talk him into investing it in a string of fried okra stands in

22

Oklahoma, Arkansas, and North Texas! *Fried okra stands!*" She was the picture of indignation, all pink cheeks and clenched fists.

"Those old boys said he had the money and they had the experience, and together they could go into business and make a fortune. He didn't even tell me, just did it. He knew I'd have a hissy fit, and didn't I just!" Her eyes were bitter as sloes. "They gave him the business, all right."

So now they had the money and Bud had the experience. Well, he wasn't the first. I was surprised she'd let it happen, though. Roxy didn't have any education, but she'd always been one step ahead of the world. It wasn't easy to put one over on her.

"How long ago did this happen?" I asked her.

"It happened about six months ago. I only found out about it this week, and we've been fighting about it ever since. He won't admit he was wrong, Aint Livvy! He keeps telling me to wait, that it'll work out, but you know as well as I do those cowboys have hit the trail. We'll never see that money again."

Poor old Bud. He wasn't any dumber than a box of rocks, but he didn't sound much smarter, either. But whatever made Roxy think he'd admit he'd been snookered? Even a box of rocks has its pride.

"And besides being broke," she finished off, "now he's mad all the time—and at *me*, not them!"

It was plain to see that Roxy felt unjustly driven from Eden—after all, it had been Bud who bit. I'd thought Bud was the perfect match for her ten years earlier, but of course things change: nobody knows that better than I do. Still and all, I could tell she still loved him. Hate's not love's opposite; indifference is, and she was a long way from indifferent. She was just trying to get his attention.

"I'll get a job and a place to live right after the holidays," she promised, "if we can just camp out here for a couple of weeks. I don't want to be a burden."

"You're not a burden. You're my niece," I told her, all the time thinking about Victoria and hers coming for Christmas. Chloe would flat have a fit when she found out about the new addition to the party. Well, there was nothing to be done about it. Roxy was already here, and she was family, and she was in trouble. We would just have to make do.

The next day was a Tuesday, Chloe's day off, and in the afternoon I took Roxy by her house to say hello. Chloe's face was a study when I walked in with her cousin. I never did find out what had happened to cause it, but Chloe'd been mad at her ever since we went to Tulsa for Roxy's wedding.

Roxy put her arms out to kiss my girl, and Chloe went stiff as a boot. It made Roxy nervous; you could see it. She knew something was wrong and couldn't figure out what, so she brayed on and on, congratulating Chloe on her marriage and asking to see Dan's picture and wanting to know all about Chloe's new life. She did have the good sense not to describe her own troubles to the new bride.

Even so, Chloe went all tight-jawed and answered Roxy's questions in words of one syllable, and as few of those as she could.

"Roxy's come to stay awhile," I told her, a warning in my voice. "She'll be out at the farm till after the holidays."

Tooter and Corky were poking into boxes and pulling things out to look at.

"You kids cut that out now," Roxy bawled. "Leave your Aint Chloe's stuff alone before you-all break something."

They minded like a pair of fish. Tooter found an old tin colander at the bottom of a box of kitchen things and put it on his head like a helmet, and Corky knocked it off with a broom handle. Roxy set her coffee cup down hard on the kitchen table and stood up, and the two of them scooted. She picked up the broom, I rescued the colander, and then we heard the back door slam.

"Good," Roxy said. "They can't hurt anything outside."

Chloe was frozen in place at the table. She hadn't said word one, not even blinked her eyes since I gave her the news, but I knew what was going through her mind, all right.

"Honey," I said, "I know you're worried about your Christmas company, but if it'll help, I'd be glad to move the party out to the farm. I've got more room to put people out there, and it'll save you doing for so many."

Her face got pink and her eyes real shiny, and then she gave herself a little shake.

"I want to do it here," she said. Stubborn. "It's my first Christmas in my first home, and I want to have the family here." She looked bleakly at her cousin and then turned her head to stare out the window. Tooter's little jack-o'-lantern head popped up over the sill and gave us all a start, and then my daughter looked back at me. "It'll be all right, Mama. I'll just borrow some chairs and an extra table. We'll work it out."

"Well," I said, "if it means that much to you."

"I can help," Roxy offered. "I make the best old corn bread dressing you ever did eat, if I do say so myself. It was my mama's recipe, and her mama's before her. And I make a mean lime Jell-O and pear mold too."

An expression of strained sweetness crossed Chloe's face. She shook her head.

"Thank you all the same," she said, polite but firm, "but I want to do it myself. I'll make Grandma's pumpkin pie recipe, the one she got from her mother. And I'm not making corn bread dressing. We prefer white bread."

She said it as if corn bread were the tackiest dressing known to man, and I could see the puzzled hurt on Roxy's face. It was time, I thought, to separate these two before they started saying things better left unspoken.

"Well," I said, rising from my chair, "it's your party, honey; we'll do it whatever way you say. Just let me know." I turned to Roxy. "Time we got those little toots home and fed, girl. Let's go on."

Roxy stepped out on the patio and hollered for her kids, and just as we were collecting our coats and all, Dan came in. As I was making the introductions, Chloe turned away and started for the bedroom.

"Dan, there's fresh coffee," I said. "You-all sit here and get acquainted. Excuse me just a minute, please."

I took off down the hall after my daughter, knocked at her bedroom door, and went on in. She was standing with her back to me, looking out the window, stiff as starched crinoline.

"What?" I asked, and she whirled to face me.

"Oh, Mama! Of all people!"

"Well, I know, honey, but what can we do? She didn't have anyplace else to go, and she and Bud are having a bad time. I don't believe for a minute she's leaving for good; she just needed to get away."

"But why *this* week? Why can't she straighten out her own life and leave us alone?" Chloe sat down on the bed and put her head in her hands. "I'm not surprised they're having trouble, no better sense than they've got," she muttered.

"What are you talking about, honey?"

"Never mind," she said darkly. "My mama taught me not to spread gossip."

"It's not gossip when it's family," I told her. "Not unless you're meaning to hurt."

She straightened herself up and looked me dead in the eye.

"Well, right now," she said, "I *am* meaning to hurt, so if it's all the same to you, I think the kindest thing would be for me to keep still. Only this: I don't like Roxy, never did like her much, and sure to God haven't since the wedding. I know Christian charity as well as the next one, so I won't try to get you to send her back. But if you want peace on earth, I suggest you keep her out of my path."

Well, I don't need to tell you I was astounded. Words like that coming out of the mouth of my sweet baby girl? Lord have mercy! But I gave her a stern look.

"Let me give you a bit of motherly advice, Chloe," I said. "Don't be a grievance collector. Those things get too heavy to carry; the sooner you put them down, the happier you'll be."

She didn't answer, and I didn't know what more to say, so I just picked myself up and walked back down the hallway to the kitchen. Roxy had her brood all jacketed up and ready to go, so I just kissed Dan goodbye and promised to see him over the weekend, and we went on home.

We got there after five, and as we passed the graveyard I saw Will's old truck parked beside the road. Putting Christmas flowers on Patsy's grave, I reckoned. He was awfully good about that, keeping the weeds down and putting out flowers on her birthday and holidays. Not a man who'd forget a woman the minute her back was turned, I thought, though he'd let go of his grief by now. He looked up as I drove by, and I waved.

Right at sundown a blue norther came through and dropped the temperature thirty degrees in an hour, and it hadn't been that warm to begin with. The weatherman said it wouldn't rise above freezing for two days, so I had Roxy bring in a load of firewood while I went around opening taps so the pipes wouldn't freeze. I started to call Chloe to warn her, and then I thought, shoot! Dan's in the hardware business; he knows how to prepare for a freeze! They'd only think I didn't trust them, so I let it go.

Chloe called me the next afternoon in a panic. Victoria was due in on Thursday, and Will had called to say he'd picked up some kind of quick-trot bug and didn't think the grandkids should come to his house till he felt better. He'd called Victoria and told her to go on to Chloe's, at least for the first night.

"Mama, you know what this house looks like!" she wailed. "I can't have company now, and especially not her!"

"Well, she's kin," I said. "You can't send her to a hotel. I'd squeeze them in here, but I already have a houseful." I couldn't help grinning at the idea of Victoria and hers roughing it at my place, even without Roxy's bunch, but I managed to keep it out of my voice.

"Tell you what, honey. You send Dan out to his dad's to get a bed for his sister and camp cots for the kids, and I'll run down tomorrow and help you get the house ready. They ought at least to appreciate a good hot dinner after six hours on the road, and by the next day maybe Will can take them off your hands."

Actually, I felt kind of sorry for Will. If it were my daughter and me sick, she'd want to take care of me. Victoria didn't take care of anybody; she felt generous enough giving folks the opportunity to wait on her. I told Chloe I'd be there first thing in the morning, hung up the phone, and dialed Will's number. His voice was deep and gravelly when he answered.

"Chloe tells me you're not feeling so hot," I said. "Anything I can do?"

"No, thanks, Livvy. I was just fixing to unplug my phone and go back to bed."

"Think you'll feel like eating later on? I could bring you something. It's not that far."
Lord, I thought, he'll think I'm like those pur-

suing widow-ladies. Then I thought, no, he knows better.

"Not likely," he said. "I'm living on Pepto and Seven-Up now, and it's all I can do to hold that down."

"Well, then," I said, "you take care of yourself. I expect to be at the kids' place most of tomorrow helping Chloe get it ready, but if you need anything I can do, you holler, hear?"

"Thanks, girl," he said. "I'll let you know."

I hung up the phone, shaking my head. First man I'd ever known not to leap at the chance to be waited on, even in the bloom of health—and Will's voice had cried out "sick" through the whole conversation.

"Girl," he'd called me. Huh.

We had that house shining like a new dime by the time Victoria and Grady and the A's pulled into the driveway the next afternoon. They were in a silver Cadillac that looked a block long.

The kids got out of the car first. Adrian— Lord Fauntleroy—was ten, Miss Priss was seven, and young Mr. Thumb-in-the-Mouth was barely five. Adrian, with his slicked-back hair and slavishly polite manners, gave the impression of someone studying to be a gangster or a politician. His sister was the spit of her mother, a long, narrow, Dresden-china child with golden curls, eyes as round and green as a Persian cat's, and a high, thin nose that always looked as if it were smelling something unpleasant. Alexander kept his thumb so firmly in his mouth that it looked like a benign growth. His cheeks were round and pink, just begging to be pinched, but he looked like a biter to me.

Their mother, Victoria, has taken too much to heart the advice that a woman can be neither too thin nor too rich. In her early thirties, she's taller than Dan and about as big around as my forearm. From the neck up she looks like a painted death's head in a champagne-colored wig. She solved the "rich" part by marrying a building contractor half a generation older than herself — Grady's almost as old as me — and now she spends her life queening it around Houston on his money, which is considerable. Grady's proud to tell you he's a self-made man, but you get the feeling Victoria thinks he's done shoddy work.

I just happened to be standing in the window, where I could watch Victoria and her daughter in matching white fur coats and hats, artfully "distressed" blue jeans, and matching leather boots. Watching Ashley follow her mother up the walk with her head at the exact same tilt, her shoulders at precisely the same angle, her little pelvis thrust forward in the identical high-fashion runway walk, gave me the chills. That poor baby didn't have a chance, I thought. Ruint before she started.

"They're here," I called, and Chloe jumped up to let them in. Grady and Adrian staggered up the walk loaded with enough luggage for a year's tour around the world. I counted seven bags before Grady went back for more.

Once the greetings were taken care of and the coats shed (I watched Ashley stroke that fur across her cheek as she took hers off and succumbed to a brief hope that she might be a real child after all), things got uncomfortably quiet for a minute.

"How was your trip?" Chloe asked them, and Victoria launched into a recital of complaints I didn't want to hear.

"Come on, kids," I said, picking up a bag in each hand. "Let's take these upstairs. I'll show you where you're going to sleep."

To his credit, Adrian picked up two suitcases and followed. Ashley stood there looking helpless and sort of insulted at the suggestion, but I nodded at her and she picked up one little overnight case and came

34

along. Alexander just plugged in his thumb and watched us go.

"You three kids'll be in this room," I told them, turning right at the head of the stairs. "Your folks'll be across the hall. That's the bathroom, in between."

"I can't sleep with them!" Ashley said.

"Oh? How come?"

"They're *boys!*"

"I'd noticed that," I told her. "A girl's brothers usually are."

She looked so baffled that I didn't have the heart to continue.

"Well," I said, "talk to your aunt Chloe. There's a little space out here on the landing. Maybe she'll let you move your cot out here to sleep. Chances are it's just for tonight, anyway. You can pretend you're camping."

That seven-year-old gave me the sort of withering look you don't expect from a girl till she's at least thirteen, dropped her case on the floor, and went back down the stairs.

"Ma-*maaaa!*" I heard her holler. "They want me to sleep with the *boys!*"

It was going to be a long week.

I knew it was Dan's night to lock up at the store; he'd be home for supper, but then he'd have to go right back and leave his poor, defenseless young bride with this crew. Even so,

I made my goodbyes and fled with the vision of that Barbie doll in her white fur mucking around my farm. No, I decided. She was a hothouse flower if ever I saw one. Little Ashley would decorate the couch while the others played.

I stopped at the bookstore on the way home and bought her Christmas present: *Understood Betsy,* the story of a spoiled city child humanized on a farm.

Roxy had dinner on the stove by the time I got there, a savory stew whose odor wafted clear out to the car shed. The temperature was still below freezing and would be for another day, though they were predicting a thaw for the day after. I was just grateful we hadn't had sleet with the freeze; dry cold I could handle. I clutched my big old sheepskin coat around me as I ran into the house.

"Well," I said as we sat down to eat, "did you kids have a good day?"

"Pretty good," Corky said. "How come you don't have a Christmas tree?"

"I was waiting for y'all," I said. "You want to go get one in the morning?"

Tooter broke into a grin so wide the ends of her mouth met at the back.

"You bet!" he said. "Can we make popcorn and cranberry strings for it? I already cut out a star for the top."

He showed it to me, a lopsided thing cut out of cardboard and covered with tinfoil.

"You did a real nice job, Tooter," I said. I believe in praising children when you can. "We'll go out tomorrow and buy a tree, and I'll get out my trimmings. You kids can start stringing popcorn right after supper, and maybe Chloe'll bring her niece and nephews out to help decorate it. One day between now and Christmas, she's going to bring them out here to make cookies."

"What niece and nephews?" Corky asked. "How old? What're they like? Where are they now?"

So that occupied the rest of the supper-table conversation. I described them as generously as I could, hoping Roxy's kids would see them as exotic specimens of humankind instead of objects of scorn and derision. Adrian's lord-of-the-manor air was not going to sit well with these two, and I didn't even want to think about the sparks that would fly when Corky met Ashley. God help us all, I thought. I'd have to keep an eye on that.

The next morning I took Tooter and Corky

into Allen to find a tree. We tossed it into the back of the pickup and proceeded to the dime store, where we bought red, white, and green construction paper, colored foil, a sheet of poster board apiece, stencils, and glue-on sparkles. The idea of a sweet-smelling, old-fashioned tree trimmed with hand-made decorations sounded good to me. Besides, making paper chains and glitter angels would keep those two out of worse trouble for at least twenty-four hours.

After the dime store—where I also picked up a Christmas coloring book for each of them and a big box of crayons—I pulled around the corner to Will's house and parked in his driveway.

"I've got to run in here and check up on Uncle Dan's daddy," I told the kids. "He's had the flu, so you can't come in. You sit right here and color in your books, and I'll be out in about five minutes." My voice was firm.

"Yes, ma'am," Corky said, and, "Yes, ma'am," Tooter echoed. They hadn't known me long enough to guess how much they could get away with yet. I thought I could trust them five minutes, but I didn't know how much more.

I went up onto the front porch, knocked loudly on the door, and walked in.

"Will?" I called. "You here? It's Livvy."

"Upstairs," he called back. His voice was still gravelly, but not as weak as before. "Stay there, Livvy. I'll be right down."

He wasn't decent, I thought, or else he didn't want to be found in his bed at eleven o'clock in the morning. I looked into the living room and saw it was neat as a pin. Will looked like a better housekeeper than I was, unless he just didn't use that room.

"I'm going to get a drink of water," I called up the stairs. "I'll wait in the kitchen."

Will *was* a better housekeeper than me. Three clean casserole dishes sat on the kitchen table with little slips of paper in them lettered "Martha," "Nonie," and "Leta." Aside from those, there was one drinking glass on the counter and a cup with a quarter-inch of coffee in the sink; even though he'd been sick for two days, everything else was spotless. Maybe he took his meals at the Main Street coffeeshop, I thought. That would explain it. I opened a cupboard and found vitamins and a prescription bottle and, out of perfectly normal curiosity, reached for the prescription to read the label.

"Right-hand cupboard," Will said.

I started like a peeping Tom caught in the bushes.

"What?"

"The water glasses. That is what you were looking for, isn't it?" He sounded amused. I couldn't look at him.

"Oh. Sure. Thanks." I opened the cupboard, got a glass, and turned on the tap to fill it, hoping he hadn't noticed my snooping. I knew better.

"I just dropped by to check on you," I told him, finally turning toward him and talking fast. "Didn't mean to get you up. My niece's kids are waiting in the truck, so I can stay only a minute. How're you feeling?"

He grinned.

"Able to sit up and take nourishment, anyhow."

Will was wearing an old woolly bathrobe of the same odd, mossy green as his eyes, and his thick, silvery hair was freshly brushed. Either I was shrinking prematurely or he was taller than I remembered. He'd grown a beard since I'd seen him last, and he looked downright distinguished even in his robe and slippers. Gave his face a whole new character.

"Anything I can do for you while I'm here?" I asked. I glanced over at those casserole dishes. "Looks like the local widows have you well in hand."

"They do their best. I'm over the worst of it

40

now, just getting my strength back." He cleared his throat. "Bad timing, I guess. Sure did hate having to tell Vic to stay away."

He was grinning, and it made me feel self-conscious. I couldn't tell if he meant it, or if he was playing with me.

"Especially since it dropped her family into Chloe's lap," I said a little severely. "That was no joke. She wasn't half ready for company."

"I should've told them to go to a hotel. Didn't think she'd really go to Dan, with all those fancy hotels not twenty minutes away in Dallas."

"Well," I said, "Chloe's a married woman now. She'll manage." I couldn't stop looking at that beard. Most men's beards are stiff and scratchy, but his looked like silk. I drank my water and put the glass in the sink beside his coffee cup.

"Well, if you're sure there's nothing I can do for you, I've got to get back to those kids," I told him. "You going to be all right by Christmas Day? Chloe's got her heart set on us both being there." Shoot! I thought. If she and Dan had been working on me, they must've been working on him too. He'd think I was after him too, just like Nonie and Leta.

"I'll make it," he said. "I'll be well enough to go back to work tomorrow." We paused at the door, and he put his hand on my shoulder. It was firm and square, a good, strong, useful hand. "It was kind of you to stop by, Livvy. Thanks."

It had been some time since I'd felt the touch of a man's hand, and it surprised me. I hoped he wasn't just humoring me. I reached up to pat it.

"Glad to see you're better," I said, and smiled. "I guess we'll see you on Christmas, then."

The kids were right where I'd left them. They'd taken everything out of the dime store bag and were arguing artistic matters concerning the decorations, but at least they'd stayed put.

"There's enough there for both of you to make just what you want," I told them. "No need to argue about it. Just put it away and keep it clean till we get back to the house."

We set the tree on its stand inside the front window when we got home, and Roxy strung lights on it while the kids cut strips for the paper chains. Then Roxy started sniffling and retreated to the kitchen, where she shed a few tears about her poor, brave, fatherless children making the best of Christmas so far from home. She made them sound like something out of a Dickens novel, but my heart was not touched. Bud might not be the brainiest man God ever made—if his brains were wool, you'd be hard put to find enough material to make longjohns for a gnat—but I hadn't heard her complaining about cruelty or the lack of love. It was Roxy, not Bud, who'd orphaned her children. But I didn't say a word. If I let her feel bad enough about them, I thought, maybe she'd turn around and take them home.

In the meantime I was enjoying having children in the house so much that I took a fit of domesticity, tidying up and putting away things that had lain for weeks and months around the house. To be perfectly honest, the sight of Will's spanking-clean house might have had something to do with that, too. I even cleaned out the back bedroom, which turned out later to be a blessing, and set to baking pecan pies and a big gingerbread cake. Whatever other faults Roxy might have, she wasn't afraid of hard work; I came out of the back room one time and found her on her hands and knees scrubbing dirt out of the corners of my kitchen floor.

We spent a nice, homey, quiet day that reminded me of my own childhood. It was a comforting demonstration of continuity: there I was, doing what my mother and grandmother used to do, in the same house on the same land where I'd grown up; there was my brother's girl, helping me out the way I used to help my mama; and there, running back and forth from living room to kitchen, were Roxy's children, making the same kinds of Christmas trimmings I used to make when I was little. I hummed old-time hymns as I worked—"Bringing in the Sheaves" and "Amazing Grace" and "I'm Gonna Let My Little Light Shine"—and got down my pruning shears to cut mistletoe out of the old oak that shades the west side of the house. The weather outside was bleak as a Russian novel, and the midafternoon temperature never rose above twenty-five degrees, but inside my house it was warm and cozy. I felt as full of contentment as an old cat in the sunshine.

When Chloe called after supper to say she'd bring the A's out the next day, it hardly put a nick in my pleasure. I just gathered Roxy and her kids around my grandma's old pedal organ, and we sang Christmas carols until bedtime. Later, I was glad I'd had that day. It shored me up for the next three.

* * *

Chloe and the A's came crunching up my driveway at ten o'clock the next morning. The sky was a brilliant, cloudless blue and the temperature already up to twenty-eight on its way to a promised forty-two when they came running in from the car, huddled in their coats. The boys were wearing leather bomber jackets over identical Levi jeans and plaid shirts, and Ashley looked like the Snow Princess in her white furs.

Corky took one look at that fur coat and hat, and her eyes turned green. Of the Ten Commandments, the one that punishes its own breach the quickest and most painfully is the last: "Thou shalt not covet." I could see old Number Ten having its way with my grandniece and wondered what other sins it would urge her into before the day was out. Well, I thought, surely three grown women could keep an eye on two little girls. How much opportunity for sin could she find on my twelve acres, anyway?

"Victoria and Grady went partying last night and spent the night at the hotel," Chloe said while we were getting their coats off. Pushing them ahead of her into the house, she lowered her voice to add, "I guess Grady got too drunk to drive, and you know Victoria'd always rather stay in luxury." If I were married to Victoria, I thought, I'd never get sober. Even so, I could tell Chloe was ready to share the burden of child care.

She made a little face.

"I don't know what's wrong with me. Feel as if I were the one hung over," she said. She did look a little peaked, and there were definite circles under her eyes. The stress must be getting to her, I thought.

We took them into the living room to see the tree, and you'd have thought it was Disneyland. Those kids had never seen an honest home-made Christmas tree in their lives, and they were as curious as monkeys. Tooter, who'd been too busy to get up when they arrived, sat with his tongue poking out of the corner of his mouth, cutting little stars out of posterboard; the glitter and glue were under his elbow, next to a roll of kitchen foil.

"What are you doing?" Ashley asked him.

"Making paper airplanes," he said. "What does it look like I'm doing?"

"Tooter," Roxy said, "mind your manners and say hello to Aunt Chloe's niece and nephews." She told him their names, but he hardly had a glance to spare them, let alone a word.

"May I help?" Ashley asked. She sounded downright humble.

"I guess, if you think you can be of any use," Tooter said.

"Show me," Ashley said, and I could see there wouldn't be any more out of her for a while. Unlikely as it might seem, Ashley was in love as quick as that. All it took for Miss Queen of the May, it seemed, was being roundly ignored and soundly put down. Some women have no sense at all.

Adrian took a cool tour around the room, touching things as he went: the animals my daddy'd carved into the mantelpiece, the big glass ball that stood on a stand made like a brass dragon, the painted pigskin box I kept old pictures in.

"This is beautiful, Mrs. Hardy," he said. "Where did it come from?"

"Honey, you don't have to call me Mrs. Hardy," I told him. "I'm your aunt's mama; call me Aunt Livvy, like the other kids do." I know they were only shirt-tail kin, but they were kids. It wasn't their fault they had Victoria for a mother. "My daddy brought that box back from the Philippines after World War Two. I always thought it was pretty."

I felt a little arm wrap around my leg and looked down to see Alexander gazing up at me. He took his thumb out of his mouth long enough to speak.

"Can I call you Aunt Livvy too?"

"Sure, honey. All three of you."

"Who are they?" He pointed at Corky and Tooter.

"They're Roxy's kids. They're all staying with me for a while."

"How come? Who's she?"

We did about five minutes on who belongs to whom and how before I realized what he was after: Alexander wanted to belong. So then I said, "Honey, it doesn't matter. We're all family; I'm an aunt and they're cousins."

"Will they play with me?" he asked.

"I expect they will. Corky, aren't there some more paper strips left? Why don't you teach Alexander to make a chain."

She gave me a look, but she picked up the paper and glue and spread them out at the other end of the table.

"Come on, Adrian," Alexander said, "you help too."

Adrian took a last glance into the curio cabinet and sat down at the table. So far, so good, I thought. All five productively occupied, the big ones teaching the little ones, and love in bloom, all in ten minutes' time. I could hardly have asked for more.

Except my Chloe's nose was out of joint for some reason I still hadn't been able to fathom. Just being in the same room with Roxy seemed to irk her; Roxy didn't even have to say anything. It wasn't right.

Before lunchtime I dug out my old cookie cutters and pans and we made sugar cookies. I'd forgotten how children cook — before they were through we had flour strewn from one end of the kitchen to the other and pans stacked to the rafters — but they had a good time, even the boys. Roxy'd made a big pot of soup, and we had that with grilled cheese sandwiches for lunch. By then it looked downright springlike outdoors, and the kids were getting bored. They were ready to go out and play, and I was ready to let them.

"You-all keep an eye on Alexander," I cautioned. "He's littler than you, and never been out in the country before. No telling what he'll find to get into."

Corky had formed a motherly interest in him during the morning — he really was a sweet little boy, once you got his thumb unplugged — and she was squatting in front of him to button up his jacket.

"I'll watch him," she said.

"There's new kittens in the barn," I told them. "If you're quiet and don't move too quickly, maybe their mama will let you touch them."

Tooter and Adrian weren't interested in kittens. They'd been eyeing each other all morning like a pair of bantam roosters, and my guess was that now they'd settle things. It looked like an even match to me: Adrian was older and bigger, but Tooter was tougher.

I watched from the porch as Corky led the smaller ones across the yard to the barn. She turned to caution them before opening the big door, and they slipped in behind her. Tooter swaggered over to a big, bare-armed pecan tree, swung himself up into it, and started scrambling for the top, hollering down some challenge. Adrian had to think about it for a minute before he followed. Looked like they'd spend the afternoon seeing who could outdo whom. I only hoped they could settle it without any bloodshed.

The house was blessedly quiet when I went back in.

"I'm going to take a rest," I told the girls. "Five kids for four hours has done me in. Can you keep a lid on things for an hour or so?"

"Sure, Mom," Chloe said. "You go on and lie down a bit."

I went upstairs and shut my eyes, and the next thing I heard was "Alexander! Alex-

*aaannn*derr!" I looked out the back window, and they were all out in the yard, calling that child. I slipped my shoes back on and ran down the stairs and out the back door.

"What's going on?" I demanded.

"We can't find Alexander," Chloe said. "He was with Corky and Ashley in the barn, and then they turned around and he was just gone. We can't find him anywhere."

"Oh, Lord!" I said. "How long has he been gone? Corky?"

She came to me, her little face pinched and white.

"I don't know, Aint Livvy. Not very— maybe ten minutes."

Ten minutes! A child could get anywhere at all in ten minutes, from the barn loft to the road to the neighbor's pasture. . . . The pasture! I ran around the back of the barn and down the hill, wishing it were muddy so he'd have left tracks.

"Alexander!" I yelled, and then I saw him.

Once, when I was little, my older brother playfully jerked away my chair and left me to sit on thin air. For more than forty years the memory has remained fresh. Now I experienced the same sensation, as if I had been hit by a blunt instrument at the exact moment of slipping on a banana peel.

Alexander had gone to visit the neighbor's bull, as friendly as if he were at a petting zoo. Unfortunately, the bull—his name was Hector—didn't know anything about petting zoos; solid black and big as a boxcar, he was not a friend to man. Hector was standing with his head down, chewing thoughtfully on some dried grass. Alexander stood in front of him, his boots almost touching the bull's nose. As I watched, the child leaned across Hector's face and dropped his arms around the bull's neck in a trusting and affectionate hug.

Such a danger to myself would have been less terrifying. That would only have left me staggering, white as a bone, with a rattling windpipe and knots in my stomach, but in this peril all that seemed a complete waste of time. Seeing the child already broken in a tree-top or spitted on Hector's horns, I was cool. I might, I thought, react later. The next time I looked in a mirror, I might see hair like drifted snow and skin like gray crepe paper. But for then I was unnaturally calm.

I turned around and held up my hand in a "stop" sign to the others, who were trailing down the hill behind me, and put my finger over my lips before I pointed. One unexpected noise might be all it would take: Hector would lift his head and throw that child halfway to Dallas.

The others slunk silently down the hill and formed a knot around me.

"Not one sound," I whispered to them. "And don't move."

"Aint Livvy," Corky whispered, "let me go get him. I can do it." I shook my head, and she pulled on my sleeve. "Please. I was the one watching him."

"No sense in losing two of you," I said. "The bull knows me. I'll go." I didn't tell them Hector liked me no better than any other human. Why he hadn't yet trampled Alexander was a mystery to me, but I was willing to let it ride so long as Hector kept his head down grazing.

I nodded to Roxy to hold up the lowest strand of barbed wire and rolled under the fence into the field. Circling around behind the bull, where he was less likely to see my movement, I stole silently to within a few feet of his hindquarters. Alexander had released his grip on Hector's neck, but he was still leaning across the broad face to stroke his ears.

"Alexander," I said softly, "it's time to come in now."

He looked up at me, his eyes shining with love.

"Isn't he beautiful, Aunt Livvy?" he said. "I was just talking to him."

"He is," I conceded. "But I need you at home now, honey. Tell Hector goodbye, and let's go on."

Alexander kissed Hector between the eyes, straightened up on his feet, and reached to give him one more pat. The bull lifted his head a little, staring at him, and I held out my hand.

"Come on, now," I whispered.

Hector turned his head to watch Alexander go, and when he caught sight of me he gave a snort. Animals are like children—they know who loves them—and I knew by then that Hector wasn't going to hurt Alexander. I was another matter: I didn't hate Hector, but I didn't love him either. Alexander slipped his hand into mine and, under the bull's thoughtful gaze, we backed slowly toward the fence and slipped underneath.

Chloe grabbed Alexander and felt him all over to be sure he was in one piece, and then she started to cry. Corky and Ashley hugged him, and the big boys stood in awe while he told them about his adventure. Now that he was safe and at the center of attention, my legs turned to noodles and my stomach lurched. I plumped down on the frigid earth and dropped my face into my hands.

"You all right, Aint Livvy?" Roxy asked.

"I'm fine," I said. "Let's just get those kids back into the house, where we can watch them. I'm about done in."

It wasn't very long till Chloe packed up the A's and took them home. She said she wanted to get them there before their mama came back; I think she was hoping they'd go on to Will's that night and she'd be shut of them. But not fifteen minutes after the gate closed behind her the phone rang. I knew before I answered that some new catastrophe had struck, and I was right. She was hysterical

"My house, Mama! My beautiful new house!" she kept saying. When I finally got her calmed down enough, she added the kicker: "It's all full of water! I'm ankle deep in my kitchen, and it's pouring through the ceiling! Mama, there's water everywhere!"

"Call the city and get it turned off," I told her. "Then get ahold of Dan and tell him to bring you a water vacuum. We'll be right over."

Roxy and I collected kids and mops and cleaning rags, and we were there in about twenty minutes. The house was a disaster. Chloe's sunken living room was a pond, and the ceiling had collapsed, dropping chunks of sheetrock, plaster, and insulation onto her wall-to-wall carpet. Chloe was standing in the entry hall, staring goggle-eyed at the damage.

Dan drove up right behind us and ran in with the water vac. He took one step inside and I could see he was as undone as she was. Dan hadn't any more than come in the door than the silver Cadillac pulled up in front and Grady and Victoria stepped out and came up the walk. Victoria, dressed all in black, looked like something out of a traveling company of Macbeth; all she lacked was a cauldron to stir.

"Shee-*yit!*" Grady said, looking into the house. "This is some swimming pool!" He surveyed the damage for a minute and then took charge. "Call your builder, Chloe. Right now. Have you called the insurance?" She nodded. "Victoria, you take the kids and get out of here. Go on to your daddy's house and let us clean this up."

I guessed Grady knew useless when he saw it. My only question was, why had he married it?

"I don't even know where to start," Chloe said.

"I guess the living room's as good a place as any," Dan said. He just stood there, heartsick and dumbstruck, and then turned back to Chloe. "Honey, we can't stay here."

"You'd better come on home and stay till you get this fixed," I said. "Somebody ought to call Will and let him know. We're going to be moving furniture around and sucking up water all night long."

Tooter and Alexander were out in the middle of that carpeted pond, stamping their feet and splashing the water around.

"Get out of that water!" Roxy bawled. "Honest to God, don't you kids have any sense at all?"

Victoria glared at her.

"I'll thank you not to raise your voice at my child," she said.

"Well, excuse the hell outta me! You planning to wade out there and haul him in yourself, are you? Tooter, you get your skinny little ass out of there *right now!*"

"Yes, ma'am." Tooter gave it one last stomp and sent a sheet of water against the already ruined wall before he waded reluctantly back to join us.

"Alexander," Victoria cooed, "come to Mommy now."

The little imp looked up with a wicked light

in one eye and mischief in the other, turned his back on her, and started to sing and dance.

"Come on, sweetie," she wheedled. "You're ruining your brand-new boots."

"Rain, rain, go away," Alexander chanted, grinning like a chimp and scooping handfuls of water to throw into the air.

Victoria clapped her hands prettily together.

"I mean it, Alexander. Come out now." Her voice was like sugared honey. "I swear sometimes I don't know what to do with him," she told me. "Isn't he cute, though?"

Under different circumstances I might have seen the humor, but I was not amused; if it weren't for child-abuse laws, I'd have taught that child a quick lesson with the flat of my hand. I don't approve of hitting—it teaches children a bad lesson, that might is right—but it surely can relieve frustration. Still, a child does what his folks let him get away with. What his mother needed, I thought, was about one fluid ounce of weed killer, scientifically administered.

"That's enough, Alexander," I said firmly. He looked up, still grinning, but when he saw my expression, the grin faded. Alexander might be mischievous, but he isn't stupid.

"Oh, all right," he sighed.

"Tell you what," I said. "Since you're already wet, go open the patio door before you come back."

He did, and water started flooding into the backyard. I let him watch the river run for a minute, and then I called him back.

"You-all kids go on upstairs and help pack," I said, "and then you can carry stuff down to the cars."

Victoria followed them up the stairs, whether to escape or to supervise I didn't know or care, and left the rest of us to survey the damage. What we finally figured out was, the kids had turned off the water taps upstairs the night before and the pipes had frozen solid during the night. Instead of telling Chloe that the water wouldn't run, they'd just skipped their showers and come down to breakfast in the morning. Then, while they were at my place, the pipes had thawed and burst.

I sent Roxy and Chloe to the kitchen to start mopping up while I helped the men get started. There's nothing to resolve a quarrel like help in time of trouble, I've always thought. Sure enough, by the time I went to join them, they were talking to each other.

"That little Ashley reminds me of you when you were little," Roxy was saying. "You seemed so citified that first time you came to our place, we hardly knew what to do with you."

"I don't know what you're talking about," Chloe said. "I was raised on a farm just like y'all. Just didn't have any sisters and brothers to play with, so I was quieter. Y'all scared me, you were so rough and noisy."

"Well, Jimmy and LuAnn thought you were prissy. I thought they were real mean to you, but I couldn't stop them." Jimmy and LuAnn were Roxy's younger brother and sister. LuAnn was a year younger than Chloe, and Jimmy a year older.

"*They* were mean!" Chloe said. "It was you and Bud rigged that bucket of ice water over my door!"

"What water? When?" Roxy sounded honestly surprised. I stepped quietly through the kitchen door, just in case they might need me.

"The night before you got married, at the motel. Surely you haven't forgotten half drowning your own cousin the night before you got married!"

"So it was your room," Roxy said. She made a sound halfway between a cough and a laugh, and I could see the effort it cost to straighten out her face. "It wasn't us, Chloe. I promise it wasn't. I didn't even know about it till a week later. I never even knew who it happened to, just somebody from out of town."

"Jimmy said it was you," Chloe insisted. "I thought it was them, but they said no, said you and Bud did it." She squared her shoulders. "I'll bet you-all had a good laugh about that. Ruined my hair, soaked my clothes, like to gave me my death of cold . . . You ought to be ashamed."

Roxy snorted, trying not to laugh, and then lost it and brayed like a mule. Chloe looked as if she might be contemplating a right cross to the jaw and then turned her back.

"It wasn't us," Roxy repeated when she could talk again. "Aunt Maisie told me when we came back from Eureka Springs, told me how Jimmy and LuAnn set it up and watched it fall. It was an awful funny story, but nobody ever told me it was you. I'd have broken their necks." She took a big gulp of air, trying not to laugh again, and then pulled herself together. "I'm real sorry, Chloe. Is that why you've been so mad at me all this time?"

Chloe nodded, her back still turned, and Roxy crossed the kitchen and put an arm around her shoulders.

"I reckon it's too late now to bust 'em, isn't it," she said, leaning her forehead against Chloe's head. "But I'll tell you what: next time

I see 'em, I'll put snakes in their beds. How'll that do?"

Chloe's head lifted.

"Snakes in their beds?" she said. "Would you really do that?"

"Maybe not to LuAnn. She's turned out okay. But I can't think of one thing that would make me happier than putting a snake in Jimmy's bed, unless it was hiding in the closet to see his face when he crawled in with it."

Chloe snickered.

"What kind?"

"Well, a copperhead would be nice, but I'd be afraid to handle one. How 'bout a big old kingsnake?"

Chloe started to giggle, and I left the kitchen. They were going to be all right, I guessed.

Well, it was a long night. Victoria took her kids and left right away, of course—catch *her* cleaning somebody else's house! I sent Dan down to Grandy's for chicken-fried steaks all around, and after a couple of hours I made Roxy drive her kids home in my truck. It was near midnight before Dan and Chloe and I gave up. I was about as ready for bed as I'd ever been.

"What'll we do about Christmas?" Chloe asked in the car.

"Have it at my place, I guess," I said. "There's no reason we can't all be together just because we can't be at your house, and I wouldn't drop a party like that in Will's lap at this late date. Just bring everything to the farm, and we'll do it there."

"Oh, Mama, I wanted so bad to have it this year!"

"I know, baby, but there's years and years to come. And don't think I plan to do this all by myself; you sure can help."

But of course that meant I had to organize things at my place. It was only two days to Christmas, and I'd gone from Christmas at Chloe's to a dozen at my own table in one minute flat. Tired as I was, I made lists in my sleep all night long: an extra table, chairs, the turkey and trimmings, pies, presents — you can't have people at your house for Christmas and not give them presents, even if you're not crazy about them all. And there wasn't time to make the gifts: that meant shopping, and if the Taj Mahal had gone on sale for a quarter that week, I'd have had to pass on it. Well, I'd think of something. I always had.

Will spent all the next day hauling stuff from Chloe's place to mine. Chloe tried to help, but she woke up sick to her stomach again and wasn't much use till afternoon. She was going to have to have new walls and carpeting, and they'd be out of the house for a couple of weeks, so what wouldn't fit upstairs at her house came to mine. On one trip Will asked for a list of what I needed for the party, and on the next he brought a little electric oven from the store, some spare dishes and cookware, and extra tables and chairs.

"You're working pretty hard for a sick man," I told him.

"That was last week," he said. "I'm okay now."

I believed him. He looked strong and well, not like somebody who'd been down two days earlier. We were standing in my kitchen, and he glanced over at the coffeepot.

"I could do with a cup of hot coffee if you've got it, though."

"It won't take a minute," I said. "Take your coat off and sit down. How about a bowl of Roxy's soup to warm your innards while you wait?"

"I'll take it," he said.

In all the years I'd been single, I never had brought men to the house. My mama didn't recognize divorce; in her mind married was married till somebody died, and fidelity beyond the grave was the more respectable path. She kept waiting for my husband to come back, and she could be real snippy to any other men who came around. And poor little Chloe was just the opposite: she'd been wanting me to find a new husband almost since she could talk. When she was little, Chloe used to fall in love with them before I did—any old thing in pants, no matter how useless. Keeping my men friends away had always seemed the best policy, so it felt real strange to have a man who wasn't kin to me sitting at my kitchen table waiting for a cup of coffee.

"Grady went and talked to their builder for them," Will told me. "Him being another contractor and all, he knew just what to say. Told him he'd be checking in through the week to see how it was going, let the builder know he wouldn't put up with any more shoddy work. I think they must have slapped that place together in three days, foundation to shingles."

"Well, I tried to tell her," I said, "but you know kids. She had to have brand-new, never mind how flimsy it was built."

"Don't blame Chloe," he said. "Dan should've known what to look for, but he was in as big a hurry as the builder. Should've been more careful."

"Dan's just young," I said, "and used to

people being honest. It's not his fault." My voice was sharp. I didn't like anybody picking on Dan, not even his daddy.

Will laughed.

"I think each of us is sticking up for the wrong kid," he said, and I laughed with him. "Why don't you tell me about your niece instead?"

I told him the story, watching the laugh lines build up around his eyes while he expressed sympathy for her troubles.

"Well," I said, "Bud is pure-D goof from the soles of his brass-toed alligator boots to the button on his green gimme cap, but he's a sweet man and she loves him. They'll work it out somehow. I just wish it had been Fourth of July instead of Christmas."

"I've got kin like Roxy," Will said. "You can't help but love them, but they surely do create a three-ring circus wherever they go." He looked up and studied my face for a minute. "How are *you* doing, Livvy? Seems to me you've had enough excitement this week to last you some time, and it's not over yet. You holding up okay?"

Nobody'd asked me that question for years and years. They always just assumed I would hold up, because I never did let them see when I fell down. It touched me, you know?

"I'm fine," I told him. "Christmas is just the day after tomorrow. And, of course, a body can do only what a body can do. I'll work it out the best way I can and then just hope for the best."

He smiled. Will has the sweetest smile; it just lights up his whole face and makes you want to touch him.

"Well, if we live long enough, that's a lesson we all have to learn," he said. "You can't have somebody else's good time for him; certain things, they have to do themselves."

Lord, he looked good! How come I never had noticed it before? It was that silky beard, I decided, and the way that thatch of near-white hair framed his face, and a certain . . . goodness that shone through his eyes. Will was about six years older than me, the same age as his wife Patsy'd been. She'd been my neighbor, but enough older that I didn't know her all that well, and of course after she moved to Allen I'd more or less lost track of her. The kids had gone to school together, but I never had known Will until they started dating — and then his being Dan's dad had made that kind of interest seem improper. I just never had really looked at him before, not to see who lived behind those moss-green eyes. I was beginning to like him in spite of myself.

Still, I thought, he wasn't likely to take that kind of interest in me, a blowsy old farm woman with hands like leather and sun wrinkles around my eyes, with half the women in Allen after him. Except for weddings and funerals, I hadn't worn a dress in years; I didn't even feel much like a woman anymore. The last man had been more than two years earlier, and I'd sworn off after him.

Of course, my hair was still black and my teeth were still strong, and I hadn't let myself get as fat as my mama'd been. A good haircut and little makeup could do wonders, I reminded myself. No harm in admiring a good-looking fellow when he struck my eye. I wasn't dead yet.

The next day was Christmas Eve, and we were still preparing like crazy. Chloe was sick again and blamed it on her upset about the house. Roxy, a demon housekeeper, turned my place out from one end to the other while I grocery-shopped and baked, and Chloe helped all she could. They even had the kids helping. Corky worked as hard as her mother, and even Tooter didn't complain too much.

"I don't want to hear one word about 'women's work,' " Roxy told him. "Work's work. It doesn't care who does it." She set him to vacuuming, showed him how to work all the attachments so he could clean the drapes and under the couch and the corners of the ceilings, and she had Corky washing baseboards—I mean, they *cleaned!* By the time they were through, I hardly recognized my own house.

The radio had been forecasting another norther, this one with sleet, and I was nervous about it. A serious sleet storm makes this hill a prison. Ice can sheet an inch deep on the roads, so even the gravel is no protection; the whole world becomes a skating rink, and travel is impossible. In the winter of '83 we had two sleet storms in ten days and the temperature never rose above twenty-eight degrees. I felt real lucky to have firewood and a cellar full of canned goods then. So I kept watching the sky, waiting for it to fall.

Will dropped by a little after noon to see if we needed anything more, and I fixed him a plate of leftover stew and some fresh biscuits. I was starting to feel more comfortable with him; he was so much at ease with himself, it was hard not to. After he'd eaten, without my asking he went outside and checked around the place to be sure everything would stand up under a cold spell—we were all a little antsy since Chloe's disaster—and chopped more firewood to pile up on the porch.

"Clouding up out there," he said, coming into the kitchen. "Getting cold fast, too. You got coffee made?"

I poured him a cup and sat down with him. I had sweet bread rising and pies in the oven, and it was time for a short rest.

"Where's Victoria and hers?" I asked. I'd invited them all out for the evening, planning to serve supper and sing carols. Victoria wanted to go to Dallas to attend midnight services at the Episcopal cathedral, and then they'd go to Will's for the night and come back the next day.

"They're coming by here around four," he said. "She had some shopping to do."

"Lord, what more could those kids want?" I asked. "I went out and bought Ashley a book, and I'm giving the boys trinkets they've been admiring in the house. Couldn't think of one other thing they'd like to have and didn't yet."

"God knows," Will said. "That girl's a mystery to me, always has been. Her mother wasn't like that. Maybe she got it from my grandma; my grandma always wanted to be carried on a satin pillow, just fold her hands and act like a lady."

We heard Roxy hollering at Tooter in the other room, and Will smiled.

"Roxy's more like the daughter I expected than the one I got," he said. "I admire a certain toughness in a woman. Spare me the clinging vine and the hothouse flower. They're nice to look at, but not much use for anything else."

He gave me a special look as he said it, and I looked down at the table.

"Well, it's not like we choose our children," I said. "All we can do is take what we get and love them. God sits up there and says to himself, 'Let's see what I can do for fun today. I'll send the boy violinist to that football coach, and this tree-climbing girl can go to that dainty little woman with the lace gowns and the fainting spells.' Then he holds his sides while he watches us try to raise them."

Will laughed.

"I suppose he's got to do something to entertain himself," he said. He went out to the porch and craned his neck to look at the sky.

"Flat as a ceiling," he said, "and gray as gray. It doesn't look good."

"Maybe it'll hold off until tomorrow," I said. "I've had the radio on all day, and they don't seem to know when it'll hit."

* * *

Victoria's family pulled up the hill later in the afternoon, and Dan followed at five. Dan and Grady plopped themselves down in the living room and started putting themselves on the outside of a fair amount of Southern Comfort to guard against the cold, with Will to watch. He doesn't drink much; it upsets his stomach. By then Chloe and Roxy were in the kitchen, resting for a few minutes before we started fixing dinner for a dozen. Victoria was in the living room with the men, watching TV.

"Hey, Dad," Dan said. "The playoff game started five minutes ago!"

I heard the TV switch to the football game, and in about a minute Victoria came out to sit in the kitchen, watch the rest of us work, and tell us what we were doing wrong. The Bible tells us no one is beyond salvation, and I suppose miracles do still happen — and of course, she was a guest in my house. Besides all that, my mama always told me that those who seem to deserve love least generally need it most, and I never can forget it even when I want to. So I was as patient with her as I could be. Still, I don't mind telling you, Victoria was a trial.

The little girls were laying the table for me,

and Ms. Manners set about teaching Corky the proper way to set out the silverware and place the napkins and drinking glasses, asking about bread-and-butter plates and salad forks. Ashley seemed to be used to it, but I could see Corky growing restive; an explosion was in the making, and I needed to defuse it. We'd had enough excitement in the past day or two. I didn't need any more just then.

"Young ladies?" I said. "Would you-all do me a small favor?"

"What is it, Aint Livvy?" Corky said, dropping the silverware in a pile and running to my side.

"Put your coats on, take the basket and that flashlight you'll find on the back porch, and go on out to the smokehouse after some vegetables. It'll take the two of you to carry. I want three pints of green beans, two of pears, and a dozen potatoes, please. The potatoes are in a bin on the floor, and the canned goods are at eye level on shelves to the right."

"Yes, ma'am." She threw her arm over Ashley's shoulders like her oldest friend. As they stepped through the door, I heard her whisper, "Can I wear your coat?"

Victoria went on setting the table, and I stood at the stove with my back to her. I'd just turned around to ask Roxy a question when a prolonged shriek of absolute and unmistakable terror sailed like a Bowie knife into the kitchen.

Victoria reacted as if it had sliced off her ear. I froze, and the next thing I heard sounded like a Comanche war party resurrected to attack my smokehouse. Then, after a bit, the shriek trailed off into a sound like the last fluttering breath of a dying duck, leaving only the war whoops.

Suddenly aware that I hadn't breathed in more than a minute, I sucked in a lungful of air and raced for the smokehouse with Roxy and Chloe on my heels. Victoria, recognizing that protocol had failed completely, was only a moment or two behind us.

We found Corky rolling on the dirt floor in Ashley's white fur coat, alternately howling and holding her belly, and Ashley standing ashy-faced and frozen by the canned goods shelf. The lantern was on the floor, shining up into Ashley's face and making her look like something out of *Friday the Thirteenth, Part Four.* Jars of vegetables lay shattered at her feet, and the child was winding up for another shriek.

"What?" I asked, grabbing her shoulders and staring into her face. She was shuddering like a plate of Jell-O.

"Ss-ss-sss . . ." she whispered. "Sss-ss-sss."

Her eyes were like dinner plates, and she pointed a ghostly hand toward the shelf. Victoria stood outside the door with her nose in the air, disapproving of the noise and commotion. My mama'd taught me the same as hers, that a lady doesn't call attention to herself, but this seemed like a special circumstance to me.

"Honey, what happened?" Chloe knelt to look into Ashley's terrified face, and Roxy bent to pull Corky to her feet.

Ashley made another series of sounds like drops of water on a hot griddle, still pointing at the shelf, and then shook her head helplessly. She was sucking wind as if she'd been steam-rolled.

"Corky, what did you do to her?" Roxy demanded. "Did you hurt Ashley?"

If Ashley was sizzling, Corky was doing her best to imitate maracas: "Ch-ch! Ch-ch!" She shook her head, grabbed her middle, and let out another holler.

"Chicken snake," she finally got out. "On the shelf. Old Ashley reached for the beans and caught a chicken snake barehanded." She whooped again. "That old snake musta been six foot long if it was an inch! Oh, Mama, you should've seen it!"

"Did it bite you?" I asked Ashley. She

shook her head. "Show me your hand."

Just as she reached it toward me, I caught a quick, sinuous movement out of the corner of my eye and then heard Victoria out-shrieking her own child. The snake, unwilling to accept such loudly unappreciative company in its dark and quiet home, had made a break for it and slithered out the door right between Victoria's feet. Ms. High and Mighty was dancing a tarantella in the moonlight, right there in my barnyard.

"Lord, have mercy!" I muttered, and strode out the door. I grabbed Victoria's bony shoulders and gave her a stiff shake.

"Stop that this minute," I said. "Not another sound. You're scaring the children."

About that minute, five men and boys came tumbling down the porch steps to find out what all the hullabaloo was about. Victoria gave me a look that would have blistered the paint off a battleship, turned, and fainted into her husband's arms as gracefully as Little Nell in a Victorian melodrama.

"What's going on?" Grady demanded. Distracted by her mother's performance, Ashley found her tongue and told him. Corky, wiping tears from her eyes, added to the tale, and I told its finish.

"Damn," Grady said sorrowfully, looking

down at his conked-out wife. He relaxed his lower jaw fully, the better to consider the situation, and then sighed the sigh of a disappointed man. "God, I wish I'd been here to see it."

Will started to laugh, and then Dan did, and then the rest of us couldn't help joining. Even Ashley was tittering in a minute. Grady turned to Will.

"You want the head or the feet?" he asked. "Let's take her inside and pour her a stiff drink. I think she can use it when she comes to."

For the rest of the evening Victoria suffered from a sort of cosmic twitchiness, starting at every sudden sound or movement. She paced most of the time, and every time she was about to sit she turned the cushions to be sure they weren't hiding any stray wildlife. About nine o'clock she sent Grady out to the car for their good clothes to get the kids ready for church.

"You're not going anywhere," he announced when he came back in. "Nobody is. Livvy, I'm afraid we're stuck here."

If I'd been upstairs, I could have heard the sleet ticking against the windows, but the porch roof and the fire's crackle had kept the sound out below. We'd been so cozy and relaxed inside, with the older kids playing Go Fish at the kitchen table, Alexander curled up in my lap, and the adults sitting around the fire, we hadn't noticed the storm. I grabbed my coat and went out on the side porch to see the whole world glazed with ice: ice on the roofs, ice on the ground, ice covering up the cars till you couldn't open their doors. Their windshields looked like pebbled glass, and the porch light showed a glassy path to the barn. Will came out and stood beside me, his hand on my shoulder.

"What do you want to do?" he said. "We can try to dig ourselves out and go home."

"I wouldn't hear of it," I said. "You'd be in the ditch before you ever got to the road. No, I'm afraid you-all are here for the duration." I turned and gave him a tired smile. "Merry Christmas, Will. Like it or not, here you are."

He gave me that sweet smile back, and then dropped his arm around my shoulders in a friendly little hug. Will was warm and solid, and he smelled of a mix of wool and good soap. Man-smelling. I leaned briefly into his shoulder, grateful, before I straightened up again.

"Well, it'll be entertaining," he said, his arm

still around me. "Five kids and seven grown-ups, half mine and half yours, in a four-bed-room house—it's a rich mix, Livvy. Where'll you put everybody?"

I started counting. Roxy'd been sleeping in Chloe's old bed upstairs, but she'd already moved down with her kids to make room for Dan and Chloe. I could put the A's in the little back bedroom, and Victoria and Grady could have mine.

"I've got beds for everybody but you and me," I told him, "and I can make up the couch for you. I'll make pallets on the floor for Victoria's boys, and I'll sleep in the bed with Ashley. It's tomorrow morning I'm worried about, all those kids waking up to no presents."

"Victoria's spent the day shopping; I reckon her trunk is full. Mine are at my house, but I brought Dan's and Chloe's out yesterday, and yours are here. They'll have packages to open."

We went back into the house, where Victoria was having a hissy fit. She wanted out, and right now—wanted to take that silver Caddy down my hill and make poor, half-crocked Grady drive those narrow, winding, sheet-iced roads back to her father's house, where she had clean clothes and plenty of space. Dan was trying to reason with her, and Grady looked about ready to cold-cock her. Will took a firm hold on her shoulders and looked straight into her eyes.

"Stop it, Vic," he said, quiet but firm. "Livvy's offered her hospitality, and we've accepted. We're staying here—every last one of us, like it or not. You can go outdoors and scream at the sky if it'll make you any happier, but inside this house you will mind your manners and act like the lady you pretend to be."

Shocked, Victoria gaped at him like a fresh-caught bass, her eyes goggling and her mouth sucking air.

"Daddy!" she said. "How can you be so mean?"

"Bull," Will said. "How can you be so rude? Didn't your mama teach you anything at all?"

I wanted to applaud. If I ever had seen a grown-up child who needed a quick refresher course in decent behavior, Victoria was it.

"Get busy, now," he told her, "and help your hostess prepare for unexpected company. It's the least you can do."

To my great surprise, she helped me make up the back bedroom. I sent Dan to the attic after the space heater and a couple of sleeping bags for the boys, and I lent Victoria a flannel nightgown and even found a pair of my daddy's old pajamas for Grady. All five of the kids were racing around like wild things, excited at this new adventure, and it was a job to calm them down. Finally we did what I'd planned to do in the first place, only earlier: gathered around the organ and played Christmas carols.

It was close to midnight before I finally started "Silent Night," and then we made the kids bed down. I brought my toothbrush downstairs, laid my gown across the foot of the bed, and bent to kiss Ashley good-night.

"When are you coming to bed, Aunt Livvy?" Alexander asked.

"In a little bit, sugar. I just want to sit down and be quiet for a few minutes first. You-all go to sleep now, and I'll be in soon."

"You can't stay up too late," he said, worried. "Santa won't come down the chimney if you're still up."

"I'll sit in the kitchen, honey. He won't mind if I just stay away from the tree." I bent to kiss him. "Roses on your pillow, Alexander. I'll see you in the morning."

Dan and Grady went out and brought the gifts in from the car, and Chloe and Roxy got out theirs, and I brought down mine, and we arranged them all under the tree. By then everybody else was ready for bed, but I was too wound up to rest.

"You-all go on," I said. "I'm going to sit up for a little while and listen to the silence."

The house settled down in a few minutes, and then I sat in the kitchen and listened to the sleet against the north window, the occasional snap of boards contracting in the cold, the hum of the heater from the kids' room. Will had brought in another load of wood and built up the fire just before everybody went to bed, and it crackled gently. Snow was mixing with the sleet now, and I looked out and watched it cover my hill like a goosedown comforter. I got up to look at the outside thermometer—seventeen degrees—and decided to turn on the oven and leave its door ajar. The kitchen would be an icebox by morning otherwise; I could take it, but I didn't know if the others could. My body was worn to a nub, but my mind was whirling like the snowflakes outside.

"Long day," Will rumbled softly, padding into the kitchen in his stocking feet. "Let me make you a toddy. Got any herb tea?"

"Over the range," I said. "Right-hand side." He got out a pot and brought some water to a boil, and then poured in a little lemon juice. Then he put a spoonful of sugar and a shot of bourbon in one mug and a tea bag in the other and added the water.

"Good for what ails you," he said, setting the mugs on the table and sitting beside me.

I felt my eyes fill up. I never cry, and it embarrassed me, but I was so tired, I was starting to cave in. And I'm not used to being taken care of. It was just such a kindly thing to do, I couldn't keep the tears from welling.

"Thank you," I said, and lifted the cup. It smelled so good, the steam rising off the top. Made my throat feel thick, and I couldn't say any more.

Will sat there quietly, studying me while I pulled myself together. He had sense enough not to try to make me talk, and that was a blessing; one more word and I'd have been boo-hooing like a baby. I wiped my eyes with the backs of my fists and took a deep breath and then a swallow of that sweet hot toddy. It warmed me all the way down.

"You look like you could use a rest, girl," Will said after a while. "From what I hear, it's been more'n a week since you had any time to yourself. That's a long time for somebody who's used to living alone."

"It is," I agreed. "I've enjoyed it, but a little

goes a long way. I'm about peopled out."

"Well, I'll get my bunch out of here tomorrow afternoon, one way or another. I'm sorry for the imposition."

I smiled.

"I don't hold you responsible for acts of God, Will. You-all are welcome as long as you need to stay." After a moment I added, "Anyhow, it'll be nice to have children in the house on Christmas morning. It's been a long time."

Will reached across the table to pat my hand and smiled that sweet, sweet smile.

"I miss that too, and it must be worse for you. You only had the one child; I had two. But that's what we brought them up for, isn't it? So they could go out into the world and make their own way? So it's no tragedy when they finally do; it's just a little lonesome."

I didn't know what it was about Will: I'd been strung up tighter than baling wire, and he'd calmed me down in nothing flat. We went on talking for a little while, and then that toddy did its work and my eyes started to close.

"It's two o'clock in the morning, and those kids are going to be up with the birds," Will said. "Think maybe you can sleep now?"

I smiled.

"I do believe I can," I told him. "And thanks, Will. Now I know where Dan gets it."

Before I left the kitchen, he surprised me under the mistletoe. That beard was just as silky as it looked; added a whole new dimension to kissing. It was such a nice kiss that I just wanted to melt into it and stay there, but the house was full of people and I had another big day coming. After it I looked into his eyes so long I all but drowned. It made me dizzy.

"Sweet dreams," he said at last, and turned me toward my bed with a little shove. He could bet on that, I thought. "See you in the morning, girl."

Morning came early. It seemed I'd hardly shut my eyes before I heard whispering, and Tooter and Corky were shaking the A's awake.

"Did Santa find us?" Alexander asked. "He wasn't expecting us to be here. Santa didn't leave all our presents over at Paw-paw's, did he?"

"Just come look at the tree," Corky said. "Old Santa must've been driving a dump truck!"

I pretended to sleep, wishing they were part of a dream, till I heard Will give them permission to go upstairs and wake their folks. When he started bustling around the kitchen I gave a groan, rolled out of the bed, and pulled my clothes on.

He grinned when I came into the kitchen and started to sing: " 'Good morning, merry sunshine/What makes you wake so soon?/ You've frightened all the little stars/And scared away the moon!' "

"Hush," I told him. "No singing till the coffee's ready."

I wandered out on the porch to survey my winter wonderland and check the thermometer. It read ten degrees. Icicles hung everywhere, and fog lay like a ruffled petticoat around the bottom of my hill. Bare trees stretched icy fingers against a pearl-gray sky, and four inches of snow lay on top of last night's ice. It was the first white Christmas I'd ever seen in my life.

Will stuck his head out the door.

"Coffee's ready," he said. "For Lord's sake, Livvy, come inside the house before you turn into a Popsicle!"

He'd filled two mugs with fresh coffee, and between its smell and the chill air, I started to revive. Will brought in a few more logs, and he had the fire blazing before the family assembled itself around the tree.

I wouldn't have believed it possible, but Victoria looked more deathlike without makeup than she did with it. Grady's hair was standing on end, and he was rubbing sleep out of his eyes. Chloe came down in her gown and robe, tousled and sleepy and faintly green around the gills, and she and Dan sat together in my daddy's big old armchair. Roxy was the last to appear, showered and combed and dressed for the day.

The kids had been poking around the tree and rattling packages for half an hour already when Will pulled out a big red Santa hat and put it on.

"All right, you little toots," he said, "find yourselves a place to sit, and I'll play Santa Claus."

Before long my living room looked like a toy store, and fancy papers were strewn from one end of it to the other. Even the grown-ups had gifts. Chloe'd found me a beautiful flowery soup tureen in an antique shop, and Roxy'd crocheted me an afghan in a rainbow of zigzag stripes.

"When did you make this?" I asked, and she said, "I been working on it when you were gone or asleep." She'd done it in less than a week.

As soon as the presents had all been

opened, I headed for the kitchen to see about the turkey. I'd bought a twenty-pound tom, planned to be up at oh-dark-thirty to put that bird in the oven, but I'd slept like the dead. Now it wouldn't be out of the oven till after dark, I thought. Even if the roads did thaw, they'd freeze up again by then and all these people would have to spend the night again. But when I opened up the fridge to start, old Tom wasn't there.

I shut the door and turned around to see Chloe grinning like a Cheshire cat.

"I set the alarm and got up at five," she said. "That bird was stuffed and in the oven by six o'clock this morning. We can eat at three."

"Honey, that's wonderful!" I said. "I didn't know you knew how to dress a turkey!"

"I had a little trouble trussing it, but I did okay." She was as proud as if she'd given birth.

"Well, honey," I said, "if you can stuff and truss a turkey, I guess you're not a little girl anymore. My goodness, what a surprise!" I looked around my spotless kitchen. "And you cleaned up, too! I guess there's nothing left for me to do but go back to bed!"

I didn't, of course. What I did was, I beat up a big batch of buttermilk pancakes, fried a couple of dozen eggs and two pounds of bacon, and served that crew breakfast. Those kids ate like they'd just come out of hibernation, and the grown-ups weren't far behind with their appetites. Then Roxy shooed me out and cleaned the kitchen while I played cards with the men.

The kids got along all day like any other set of cousins: two or three minor spats, a little teasing, a lot of sharing. Ashley trailed after Tooter till he was ready to knock her down, but you could see he was flattered. Adrian and Tooter, after their original banty rooster act, had settled into a sort of macho conspiracy against the little ones. As the oldest girl, Corky made herself the mama and defended them. The house was about to burst with all that life.

Along about noon the skies cleared and the temperature rose enough that we bundled up the kids and sent them outdoors. I found them a couple of cookie sheets and a breadboard to slide down the hill, and I watched out the window as Corky taught her charges to make angels in the snow. Wrapped in her white furs, Ashley almost disappeared.

The men went outside with pots of boiling water and melted down the cars enough to open the doors. They scraped the ice off the windshields, and started the motors, but it didn't look to me like anybody was going anywhere right away. Dan and Grady chipped the ice off the steps so nobody'd break a neck going in and out, and I set Roxy to making hot cocoa for the kids and went to take a lie-down before we started the dinner.

Just before three, when we were getting the tables set and the food dished up, I heard the sound of a big truck whining up my driveway. What in the world? I thought. Who could be coming here now? Who else *is* there!

I stepped out onto the back porch just in time to see a great big shiny-black Ford truck make the last turn and pull to a stop about six feet from the steps. The door opened, and out stepped Roxy's Bud with the biggest grin you ever saw and his finger over his lips to shush me.

I shrugged on my coat and hot-footed it out to greet him. Bud is built along the general lines of Cowboy Stadium, and his hug all but smothered me.

"Merry Christmas!" he whispered. "Where's my sweet wife and babies?"

"In the house," I told him. "Bud, I'm so glad to see you! What are you doing with that beautiful new truck?"

"You'll find out quick enough," he said. "I

got a surprise, and I want to tell Roxy first of all. Where is she?"

"In the kitchen," I told him. Bud reached into the cab and brought out a black leather valise a little bigger than a bread box, quietly shut the door, and started up the walk with me on his heels.

Roxy's face was something to see when he walked in. You could see she wanted to throw herself into his arms, but her pride was in the way; she needed an excuse. Before she could say a word, Bud grabbed her in a bear hug, and she started hollering and beating him off with her fists.

"Sit down, baby," Bud said. "I got something to show you."

He sat her in a chair, set the valise in her lap, opened its zipper, and put in his hands.

"Ready?" he crowed. "Merry Christmas, Roxy!"

He brought his hands out full of money, held them high over her head, and let those bills flutter down on her head like rose petals in the wind: twenties, fifties, and hundreds filled the air along with Roxy's screams.

Of course the whole family was there in about two seconds to see what was up. We hadn't had enough screaming and hollering in the past few days; they needed more. Roxy and Bud worked at cross purposes for a minute or two, she scrambling around on the floor picking up money and Bud standing over her throwing it in the air, till she just gave up and clutched his knees.

"What in the world?" and "I'll be damned!" and "Will you look at that!" and "What the hell's going on?" filled the air in voices from soprano to baritone, and I heard Will ask, "How'd he get up that hill?"

Finally Bud said, "Well, Rox, you ready to come back to Okmulgee now?"

It was the first time in her life I'd ever seen Roxy speechless. She was sputtering like a rusted waterpipe, her arms around Bud's legs and her head tipped back to look into his face.

"Get up, girl!" he said, hoisting her off the floor like a toy and swinging her around the kitchen in his arms. When her ankle hit the leg of my mother's dinner table, I put a stop to it.

"Put that girl down and explain yourself," I said. "I can see you're almost too happy to live, and I can't say that I blame you, but we all sure would like to know what's going on here."

Bud set Roxy on her feet and gave her a hug that hid her from view. Then he kissed her, and then he just stood there, grinning at her like the great goof he was.

"I told you they'd come through," he said. "Those old boys came by yesterday afternoon with three times the money I gave them. Sold the damned *idea,* Roxy! Never even built one stand, just sold the idea to some Yankee for a hunnert thousand dollars and their 'business expertise!' " He laughed. "I guess they're expert enough for me!"

Roxy's no fool. Eyelashes a-flutter and bosom heaving, she gave him the sort of look a damsel in distress might have given a knight errant as he set his foot upon the dragon's head and dusted off his hands.

"Oh, darlin', darlin'," she breathed, "how could I ever have doubted you?"

"Never mind," Bud said. "Just come on home and help me pick out that house, and we'll start all over again."

"Well, before you do that," I said, "suppose we set another place at the table. Christmas dinner's ready to serve, and you're as welcome as flowers in May."

Well, it was a good dinner and they did it justice. The minute it was over, Roxy and Bud and the kids started loading their belongings into that brand-new pickup. The men rigged a tow rope to drag home Roxy's car, and they were out of there.

"Thanks for lookin' out for my little family, Aint Livvy," Bud said as they kissed me goodbye.

"No thanks needed," I said. "I'm just glad everything worked out all right."

I watched them drive down to the road before it hit me that if they could make it out, the rest of them could too. Let me tell you, that was a happy moment, and what made it even happier was that Victoria had the same idea at the same time. It wasn't half an hour till they were on their way to Will's house to open the rest of their presents.

That left Dan and Chloe and Will and me. I went back into the kitchen and saw Will at the sink with his sleeves rolled up above the elbows, washing my dishes, so I grabbed a towel and started drying. Chloe gave Dan a meaningful look and hauled him off into the other room, and in about two minutes they came out in their coats and said they had an errand to run, and they left us.

"Shouldn't you be going back to the house to be with Victoria and them?" I asked him.

"You trying to get rid of me?" Will said.

"Of course not! I just thought . . ."

"Never mind. Victoria can look after herself, and if she can't, it's time she learned. I'm not walking out of here and leaving a mess for you to clean up."

So we got that kitchen chromed down and shining, and then we sat at the kitchen table and talked. Chloe and Dan came back and went upstairs, and Will and I just kept talking.

"How come you never remarried?" he asked. "You've been alone as long as I've known of you."

"Didn't like it much the first time," I said. "Staff Sergeant Michael James Hardy drove me up a wall. Mike was so tight-assed, he didn't use but one square of toilet paper at a time, and I like things a little more relaxed. And then my mother had a snit fit every time I looked at another man, from the time I came home until she died. By then I was too set in my ways. There just weren't any men worth changing for."

Will laughed.

"Don't you know the right man wouldn't want you to change?" he said.

After a while we moved it into the front room, sat together on the couch, watched the fire burn, and talked some more.

"How come you're such a prickly thing?" he asked one time. He'd taken my hand in his and I'd pulled back, but he sounded more amused than hurt. "I been watching you ever since the kids got together. You don't let much of anybody close enough to offer any help, let alone touch you."

"I don't know," I said. "Just too used to doing for myself, I guess. I wasn't brought up to ask for help, and touchers make me nervous."

"Don't you get lonesome?" he said. "I do sometimes, miss having somebody to do things with."

"Shoot, you don't have to miss that. What about Martha and Nonie and Leta?"

He chuckled.

"It's not the same, Livvy. They're looking for a good catch. I want to do my own catching." He dropped his arm around my shoulders and pulled me closer, and that time I didn't pull away. We talked some more, and after a while he kissed me, soft and sweet but with a real power behind it that aroused my curiosity. When the power started surpassing the sweetness and I felt something stir within myself, it halfway scared me. I got up to make us some tea.

When I came back, he'd taken the sheepskin throw off the back of the couch and spread it on the floor, and we lay on that fur rug and watched the fire burn and exchanged a few more of those sweet, sweet kisses and talked, slower and slower, about what we wanted out of life now that our kids were grown and gone, and what we hoped for them, and places we'd been or never been but wanted to.

"I always wanted to go to Hawaii," Will said. "My uncle was stationed there in World War Two, and he's never stopped talking about how beautiful it was."

"Not me," I said, yawning. "My travel ambitions lie closer home. You'll laugh."

"No, I won't. Tell me."

"I've always wanted to see the Alamo," I confessed. "I've lived not three hundred miles away from it all my life and never been there. I've got a great-great-grandaddy's name on that memorial down there, and I'd just like to slide my fingers across those letters once." I snuggled back against him, and he dropped an arm over my waist. "Well, I paid the last bill for Chloe's wedding last month," I said. "Maybe next summer."

We got more and more comfortable, and sometime after midnight I went to sleep right there beside him. I woke up when the sun rose and found he'd covered me with a big feather comforter and gone to sleep on the couch. I knew he hadn't taken any liberties, and I appreciated it. I never did have any respect for a man who'd take advantage.

By the time I was out of the shower, Will had the coffee going and was sitting at the kitchen table, waiting for me.

"I've got a real good idea," he said, and I said, "What?"

"Aren't you tired of all this cold? Why don't you pack a bag, and we'll go by my place and I'll pack one, and we can go to San Antonio. Do you know, the temperature's in the sixties there? We wouldn't even need coats."

A man doesn't ask to take you out of town for nothing. The question was, how much did he want? My brain, which up until then had been working perfectly, seemed to have been replaced by a large, overcooked cauliflower.

"You ought to be at work in half an hour," I told him. "I always heard December twenty-sixth is the biggest day in the year for retail stores."

"Not so much for hardware," he said. "You don't find many people giving sets of wrenches for Christmas, and even fewer returning them the day after." He sat there gazing at me, and I could tell there was more he wanted to say. I just waited, tongue-tied.

"It's awful pretty in San Antonio this time of year," he said. "Colored lights strung all over, and mariachis playing those Mexican carols . . . We could visit the Alamo." He cleared his throat and looked down at his coffee cup. "Though I suppose we ought to get married first. No use scandalizing the children."

"What's going to scandalize the children?" Chloe demanded, coming through the door behind him.

"Going to San Antonio without being married," Will told her. "I'm trying to talk your mother into a wedding trip. What do you think?"

Well, it was all over then. Dan heard Chloe squeal and came to see what was up, and they all three ganged up on me. Chloe ran up the stairs and packed me a bag while I was still arguing, and when she came down again they hustled me into my coat and into the car, and there I was, on my way to the JP down the road. Dan and Chloe stood up with us, and it was she and the JP's wife who threw the rice. Five hours later Will and I checked into the Crockett, and I'll leave the rest to your imagination.

It's working out real well, thank you very much. We're still in my house on the hill—Will gave his to Dan and Chloe, and traded stores with his son. He's made Dan his partner, and the kids will buy him out in about ten years, when he's ready to retire. Chloe's twins will be born at the end of the summer, and we'll start another generation. And after all these years, I've learned two things.

One is, an old dog *can* learn new tricks, some of them pretty amazing. And the other is, if it's the right man, it's nice to have a man around the house.

A New Life of Her Own

by Marjorie Eatock

No dismal ravens croaked as Susan Gray left home for work that afternoon. No dark cloud slid across the pale December sun, as it certainly would have in the very best novels. In fact, glancing back at her square old house, she thought it had never looked so handsome with the newly painted white against the evergreens and that blazing red poinsettia wreath on the door.

No sign appeared to warn her of impending disaster. Nothing!

Her gray-frosted head full of Christmas plans, she drove the six blocks to the small town library almost on automatic. She did wave at the postman staggering beneath his load of holiday mail, and the flashing sign at the supermarket also cued part of her brain into remembering to pick up more horse radish for the ham sauce, but beyond that she was oblivious of everything. It was Wednesday. The family would come on Friday, Christmas Eve, and stay — she hoped — until Monday at least. After all, the grandchildren were on vacation, and surely that job of Bill's could do without him a few hours! She hadn't seen any of them for a month!

What a shame, she thought for the zillionth time, parking her old dark green Chevy beneath the stark branches of the sweet gum trees, that children had to move away when they grew up! With Lloyd passed on five years ago it was so lonely! This part-time job not only augmented a rather fixed income, it kept her from going right out of her mind!

A frosty wind hit her face as she slid out. Colder tonight, the TV weatherman had said. Perhaps snow for Christmas. That would please the kids. Gathering up her bag and the new Katherine Hepburn biography she was supposed to review for book club, she huddled her collar around her rather stately nose. ("Look out," her grandkids always said, "Grandma's got her snoot up!") No need to lock the car. If there was anything anyone wanted in this heap, they were welcome to it — dicky alternator, slick tires, and all! Besides, her son-in-law, Bill, had promised he'd look into trading vehicles for her when he came.

There weren't many other cars around, she noted, hurrying across the frozen lawn of the handsome old brick edifice and up the regal flight of stone steps. Christmas vacation was on, and both the school crowd and the community-college kids had other things to do. Most of the college bunch had, as a matter of fact, gone home — at least she knew the dorm was closed. The out-of-county plate on the Buick meant Cliff Crane was inside, working on his commissioned genealogy research — and she had a quick mental picture of the broad-shouldered stocky frame hunched intently over the microfiche machine. Quiet. Gentlemanly. He'd endeared himself to the whole staff the three weeks hc'd been in town — but he certainly hadn't given any of the available local ladies the time of day. She almost giggled, thinking of Roberta Glosson's determined effort to engage him in casual conversation with an eye to establishing much more than rapport. Everyone in town understood Roberta. (She'd taught three-fourths of them their high school math!)

As she reached the massive doors, somewhat out of breath, they opened, and Melissa Parks came out into the pale sunshine, her long blond hair shining brightly over a bulky red anorak. She said, "Hi, Mrs. Gray! Thank you for running down that stuff on Indian coppersmiths. It really helped me."

"You're welcome, honey. Ready for Christmas?"

"I guess. My mom sent me my presents—some really neat stuff. Of course, it's not like going home. But if I keep my job at the jeweler's, maybe I can do that next year. Your family here yet?" And she was smiling again; everyone knew Susan's world revolved around her kids.

"Friday. Oh—hi, Kenneth. Steven." More college kids were coming out, shrugging carelessly into bulky coats. "I thought you guys were gone!"

"Right now. We're on our way!"

Big Kenneth bent, gave Susan's round cheek a smack. "Have a neat Christmas. Thanks for everything. You've really been a doll this quarter."

"You're welcome, sweetie."

Susan waved and went on in. A rush of heat poured at her from the foyer. It was obviously Edna's shift; she had the chill tolerance of a tamale.

Bobby Simotovich's gangling frame was draped against the pillar by the copy machine inside the door. She knew instinctively he'd been watching Melissa depart, seeing with *whom* she departed. The two of them were both on private scholarships, living with townspeople reimbursed by the state. Bobby got his support from the Society of Foreign-Born Citizens. She wasn't certain about Melissa's. They were nice kids. Well mannered. A joy to have around. Quite a contrast to some of the high school brats. Unzipping her coat, she said, "Hi, Bobby. It is getting colder. I hope you brought your woolies from Chicago."

He was helping her out of her heavy jacket, and he smiled—an expression that lit up the broad Slavic face, the dark eyes.

"I'm fine, thanks," he said. The machine ground its last copy and he turned back to it.

Of course her glasses had steamed over. As she pulled them off she saw Cliff at, naturally, the microfiche, slouched down with sturdy blue-jeaned legs extended and shoving thick gray hair back with clutching fingers as he frowned over a sheaf of notes. He looked up and waved.

" 'Afternoon! Is it snowing yet?"

"Not yet."

Suddenly aware of how she'd miss that smile when he left, she tossed her glasses on her desk, a little perturbed at herself. That sort of reaction was juvenile and did not enter into Susan Gray's list of necessities. A Roberta Glosson she was not, for heaven's sake!

"Good!" said her coworker, Edna, popping up from behind the tall checkout desk with a handful of videocassettes. "I need to buy groceries before I go home. Mind if I leave a scootch early?"

"Heavens no, run along," Susan answered, casting an appraising eye over the books to be shelved as she headed for the back office closet to hang her coat. "Not busy today?"

"Oh—in flurries. You know. You had a call—from your daughter. She said she'd call back." Edna reached past her, plucked out her own coat. "I put the hotpot on. Cliff looks like he could use a break. It will be ready in a minute."

"Thanks." Coffee sounded good—even instant coffee. "What's my shift tomorrow?"

"Nine to two if you can. Then Connie won't have to come in, and we close for Christmas."

"Sure. No problem."

Susan glanced briefly at the closet door mirror, fluffing the short, frosted hair into place. She straightened the strand of pearls over her blue pullover sweater, sucked in her stomach, noticed no appreciable difference, sighed, thought briefly about giving up morning waffles, then surveyed the premises. Cliff. Bobby. A pair riffling magazines. That was it.

She sat down to tackle the Baker & Taylor stuff stacked on her desk and smiled at the picture of Diane, Bill, and their three kids, Patrick, Marilyn and little Susie. Then sadly her eyes went to the one of herself and Lloyd, taken a year before he died. What a sweet man he'd been — so patient, so understanding. Certainly no Greek god, and definitely not well versed in the romantic arts, but a girl couldn't expect everything!

The top of Cliff Crane's head could be seen above the level of the checkout desk. Retired from a university. A pair of sons somewhere. No mention ever of a wife . . .

For Pete's sake, Sue! she said to herself suddenly — angrily! What has gotten into you today? The man's life is his own!

Put yourself on a positive thought: Edna said Diane had called.

Why?

Something trivial, no doubt, such as could she bring the dog? Diane had always tended to get lost in details.

The hotpot was beginning to bubble. She

hurried down the back stairs to the basement supply room, picked up a stack of paper coffee cups. On the table by the cutting board the microwave caught her eye, its door ajar. She shut it—then opened it again, looked at the definite smear of pizza topping, and laughed. Edna had heated her lunch, which was standard when one was doing the day shift alone—but she obviously was also off her diet again—really off, Susan amended, noticing the Snickers wrapper in the wastebasket.

Upstairs the sun was beginning to shine darkly gold through the west windows. As Susan put down the cups and adjusted the blinds, she saw Bobby winking at her from behind his stack of research books. An expensive fur wrap was tossed carelessly across a reading table, an expensive perfume filled the air, and Roberta, newly coiffed to a crusted and expensive perfection, was riffling through *The Wall Street Journal.* Cliff was nowhere to be seen.

Answering her raised eyebrows, Bobby dipped his head toward the closed rest room door. They both smiled. Roberta said in her well known you-are-the-servant voice, "Oh, Susan, there you are! Don't you have that new Danielle Steel book yet? I know I asked for it weeks ago!"

With great pleasure Susan went behind the desk, thumbed a list, and answered, "Yes, of course we have it. You are—mmm—let's see here—almost next on the reserve list."

"Almost!"

"It's a very popular book," Susan said calmly. What she was thinking was not so calm: If you want it so badly, you old witch, go buy the sucker!

Roberta flounced back to the magazines, replaced the *Journal,* glanced at the rest room, then at her watch, then back at the rest room again. Susan had a sudden hilarious picture of Cliff crouched down, watching her through the keyhole. With an audible sniff Roberta threw her wrap across her chubby shoulders and stalked out.

Not until Bobby saw the Cadillac drive away did he say, "Okay, Mr. Crane—it's safe."

"Coward!" Susan laughed as the rest room door opened.

Cliff didn't even look sheepish.

"That woman is a horror!" he said without compunction. "She tried to nail me on her investments—as if I'd give her advice! I don't even presume to advise my kids!"

The telephone was ringing at Susan's desk.

She said, "There's the jar—make your coffee," and went to answer.

It was her daughter. Diane said, "Oh, Mom, I'm so glad I caught you."

And that was when the roof fell in on Susan Gray's Christmas plans.

Diane said, "We can't come this weekend."

Susan sat down faster than she'd intended. She croaked, "Can't come — but — but why? Sweetheart, it's Christmas!"

"I know, Mom. I know. But Bill's won a cruise — for all of us — the kids, too. We leave Friday morning. For the Caribbean, Mom! Isn't that exciting?"

It depended on your point of view. From Susan's it was not exciting. It was the end of the world.

She found herself mumbling, "But — but — all that food in the house — and your presents — "

"I know. I know, Mom. You'll eat it. Have someone in. And mail the presents. We'll be gone almost until New Year's. Of course, this is our turn to go to *Bill's* folks for New Year's, but we'll get back home in time to maybe see you in January — "

If Susan had been really listening, she'd have known her daughter was gabbling, desperately rattling on and on. She wasn't listening. She was in shock. She said, "But Diane — but Diane — "

110

"I know it will be different, Mom, but Bill simply can't pass up this chance — the company is letting us go because of the contacts he'll make during the cruise — you do understand — don't you, Mom?"

What Susan understood was that she had just been abandoned. For Christmas. She said the obvious: "Sure. Sure. It's okay." And despite herself, her voice broke.

She heard her daughter gulp and drop the phone. Then there were a number of jumbled sounds in the background, and the telephone was picked up again and her grandson Patrick's voice said angrily,

"Grandma?"

"Yes. Yes, Pat."

"You just made my mother cry. I really don't appreciate that, Grandma. This is a chance of a lifetime for them — something they could never in the world afford by themselves!"

"Yes, Pat, I know, I just — "

The cold sixteen-year-old voice went on inexorably. "And I just have one question for you, Grandma. We love you dearly. We all do. But — isn't it about time you got a life of your own?"

If someone had doused her with ice water, the effect could not have been more paralyzing. She gasped, "What?"

"Remember — we love you. We do. But coming back there *every* holiday, *every* time one of us spits — it's getting to be a drag! Susie's too little — but Marilyn and I miss all sorts of neat stuff with our friends — please, Grandma — get real!"

Then the phone was obviously wrenched from him, and her son-in-law's voice said, "Patrick, that's enough! Go to your room! Sue dear, I'm sorry — "

Sue dear was finally getting it together, albeit a little late! She said with a remarkable degree of steadiness, "Bill, it was my fault. I was just — surprised. That's all. What a grand thing to happen to you all — cruising the Caribbean! Of course you'll go. Tell Diane and Pat I understand. I really do. And don't come down on Patrick too hard. He may have given me some very good advice."

Then she talked to Diane again, and Marilyn — whose voice was cautious — and small Susie, who just knew she was going on a boat — a big boat — with Santa Claus! When she hung up she found tears streaming down her cheeks — and Cliff Crane looking at her over the low office partition with concern in steady gray eyes beneath lowered bars of brow.

He said, "Hey — bad news? May I help?"

112

She mopped with a tissue and answered ruefully, "I think I just made an ass of myself with my family."

"Nothing to it. I've done that for years."

The remark was just chatter. His eyes hadn't wavered. They stayed keenly on her messy face while he stirred enough instant coffee into her cup to serve three people with strong palates, and handed it over. "Here. Good for what ails you."

That remark was also moot. She took an incautious gulp, thought she was going to die, had a second thought that perhaps it was better than being alone for the holidays, then rallied back.

"My—my kids can't come home for Christmas. It's the first time ever. I was—caught by surprise."

"Because you had a lot of plans. Right?"

"Right."

She took a deep breath—but not another drink of coffee. Later, she might plant a geranium in it if it wasn't too thin to plow. Putting the cup down carefully, she went on. "And my grandson—maybe—told me a home truth. I guess one never—never likes to hear those things. Do they?"

"Nope."

"He said—he said that it was time I—I got

a life of my own."

The iron bars of brow suddenly beetled. *"That* sounds a little smartass!"

"No. No. He didn't mean it to be. I know my Patrick. But"—she swallowed—"but how awful—to hear the truth from a sixteen-year-old kid."

"If it was. You haven't struck me as such an—inept person."

"Not—inept." She swallowed again, then said it honestly: "Thoughtless, mostly. And selfish—wanting things never to change."

"But they do."

"Yes. They do. They have."

Her eyes went to Lloyd's picture. He followed them with his, and asked quietly,

"How long has he been dead?"

Dead! He *was* an outlander, this man. Local people said, "Passed on." It was considered a gentler phrase. But she answered it anyway: "Five years. Five years last October."

"Coincidence. Irene and I were divorced five years ago."

She spoke before she thought. "Divorce is different."

"Only if you've never had one. Divorce can be like death."

That caught her. She looked up at him and

saw pain in his eyes. She said, "It was for you?"

"Then. Not now. I'm free. Scot-free. But it took a little doing."

"So does death." And she went on slowly. "Perhaps that's been the problem. Perhaps I'm my own victim. Or my kids have been. The victims, I mean. God. I never thought of myself as selfish — or grasping — or clingy."

Softly he quoted Robert Burns. " 'Oh wad some power the giftie gie us — to see oursels as others see us.' "

"Thanks a lot. I needed that." But she did smile, and it was watery but genuine.

He drained his cup and tossed it into the wastebasket. "So what are you going to do now?"

Ruefully she answered, "I don't know. Not yet. God! I have all that food — stuff I'll never eat!"

Then suddenly Patrick's angry young voice came back to her, saying, "Isn't it about time you got a life of your own?"

Perhaps it was. Perhaps she should.

She swallowed, and said tentatively, "I — I just may — give a party. A Christmas party. Would you like to come?"

Mistake. That was a Roberta Glosson speech. She could almost feel him back away.

"Thanks but no thanks," he said, and glanced at his watch. "But it sounds like a good idea. Call up some friends. Have a ball. And may I use the phone? I was supposed to check in with my office before five."

She waved him to it. Her mind was already going click-click-click. "Call up some friends." What an easy phrase—if one had friends. What Susan Gray had were acquaintances.

Wait a minute. Whoa. What about Elvira Williams in the next little town. They'd taught school together twenty years ago. And Elvira had no family, only her little craft shop full of lop-eared bunny rabbits—busy work, she said, since she'd retired. And Martha Coles— Martha had retired from the college faculty last year, but she was still around. Susan had seen her at the grocery store just a week ago; they'd chatted briefly—and Susan had always liked Martha. And May Belle Jefferson— she'd taught school with her too.

Why not get those girls together? It could be fun!

Just don't ask Roberta. All the girls knew she was still the same opinionated, overbearing bossy type she'd been when they all were faculty members.

Three people came to the desk to return

books, four more went back to the stacks, wafting a breath of fresh, cold air, and Mrs. Axton, a regular, bee-lined for the evening paper. The closing-time flurry had begun.

Between checkouts Susan got on the phone.

Elvira was delighted. Her bus trip to Nashville, she said, had fallen through—but could she bring Walter Cox? Surely Sue remembered Walter—he'd taught chemistry the year Jim Dooley's boy almost blew up the bell tower.

Susan remembered. "Sure," she said. "But he may have to sleep on the couch. I have only three bedrooms and I thought Martha could go in with you."

Elvira giggled. "Martha can sleep on the couch," she said, and Susan asked incredulously, "El, are you serious?"

"Sue dear, I'm not dead, and I'm certainly not going to get pregnant. If it bothers you, we'll sneak."

"It won't bother me." At least she didn't say so.

"Good. And one thing more."

"You want male strippers."

"No, no, no. I just don't want you to invite Roberta. We really don't need her at Christmastime. Once a year at homecoming is quite enough."

117 –

"I'm not inviting Roberta." Fat chance of that!

"Good. We'll see you Friday midday."

"Even if it snows?"

"Even if it snows. It's ice I'm scared of."

"All of us," Susan said, and hung up to dial again.

Martha accepted—without reservation. So did May Belle. They both lived in an adjoining town and said they'd drive down together. They also both said, "Don't ask Roberta."

Not that she ever in the world would!

By closing time she had six acceptances—her quota—and was a little stunned at how many people she knew who were also going to be alone at holiday time!

She checked in and shelved the last books, happy to leave Edna a clean slate for morning, turned down the thermostat, and glanced around. Bobby was nowhere to be seen; he'd gone without her noticing. Cliff Crane stretched long arms above his head, turned off the microfiche machine, grinned, and said, "All right, all right! I know—closing time."

They walked down the stately steps together through a lightly falling veil of snow, making the streetlamps almost ghostly in their pale shining.

Susan had a flat.

She said a word of definite bovine derivation. Caught by its unexpectedness, Cliff wheeled around and came back to her, making big black tracks in the snow. He said, "Got a spare?"

"Yes."

No. When they looked, the spare was flat also.

Susan said, "That's that. I'll go back in and call the gas station. Johnny will come and fix it — he's just a block away."

He rolled up his eyes. "The amazing small town! But then what?"

"I'll wait."

"Suggestion. Have a cup of coffee with me." And he grinned. "I'll let someone else make it."

She placed her call, noticing again as she went through the foyer that pizza smell from the basement. But her mind was really on Cliff Crane.

She hadn't gone anywhere — alone, with a man — since Lloyd died.

Died! That caught her. She came to a full stop, in the foyer in the dim half-light.

Died! What a final word! Was that why she'd avoided it for five years? Was that why she was saying it now? Because he *was* dead.

Because it *was* over?

Hold it, Sue, it's getting too deep around your ankles, she muttered to herself, and went on out into the twilight.

Johnny Schultz was already hauling himself from his pickup, his gimmecap reversed on his head and his St. Louis Cardinals jacket zipped over grease-stained coveralls. He nodded to Cliff, eyed the problem, and said " 'Bout an hour, Miz Gray. Give or take."

"We'll be back at six," Cliff said, and opened the door of his Buick.

Susan got in. The inside of the car was as neat as the man himself, except for a topcoat thrown over the seat back and a box of files in lieu of an armrest.

"My traveling office," he said with a grin as he slid in beside her. "Champaign isn't all that far away, especially with access to a fax—but it still takes a lot of data."

As he started the car, the garage attendant tapped on the window.

"Hey, Miz Gray," Johnny said, "did you accidentally leave a light on in the basement?"

Susan frowned. "Why—why I don't think so."

"Oh, well—I don't see it now anyway. Must

have been a car light on the intersection. Sorry. Catch you shortly."

Cliff rolled the window back up and said, "Brrr! Okay—do you have a favorite watering place, madam, or shall we embrace the local fast-food joint? I'd ask you to dine, but my evening is committed."

Well—that drew a nice line, Susan thought, and didn't know if she was relieved or not. Or appreciative. What an odd day she was having! "Hardee's is just around the block. That's close."

"Hardee's would be fine. Then I can have some of those curly squiggly things."

And at this time of day no one is in there but kids. Perhaps he wasn't thinking it, but she was.

While he went to the counter she chose a booth away from the windows and behind the potted plants, sat down, got up again, sat down on a seat near the catsup bar. And stayed. Enough of that nonsense. While she waited, Melissa Parks came from the rest rooms, paused, and said, "Hi, Mrs. Gray. Have you seen Bobby?"

"No . . . not since late afternoon. I'm not even sure when he left the library. What's the matter, dear, he stand you up?"

They were both laughing. Melissa said,

"No—I'm just—sort of concerned. His host family is gone for Christmas and they didn't want to leave him alone in the house—and I'm just not sure where he's staying. I hope he's okay."

"He's not going home?"

"He can't afford it. He doesn't have a generous sponsor like I do. Mine's a doll. Even," she added wistfully, "if I don't know who she is. With the crazy family hosting me, I'd go nuts without extra cash." At Susan's puzzled look she explained. "They're very nice—don't misunderstand me—but they just don't believe in holidays—or birthdays—or fast food—and sometimes, like tonight, I get a real fry attack. I'd kill for a burger. And Lark gives me money for it."

"Lark? I thought you didn't know who she is."

"I don't. She deposits extra cash in my account—or sends it to me in an envelope—and just signs herself with the picture of a flying bird. It's lovely. Really. She must be a gifted artist—the sort I intend to be. Oh—hi, Mr. Crane."

"Hi, Melissa." Cliff slid in opposite Susan, carefully placing his tray between them. "Want a squiggly curl?"

"No, thank you. I pigged on fries. Besides,

I have to get back to the house; my host family has prayers at seven."

She gave them both a bright smile and went out the door. Susan said, "What a lovely child. And she's worrying about Bobby."

"Bobby? Why?" He was munching a squiggly, and pushed the tray over to her. "He seemed fine to me."

She took one, too, and crunched. Hey. Good. "He is fine. She just doesn't know where he is."

She explained. He nodded. He said, "I have the definite impression things are tough for Bob in Chicago. No parents. An illiterate uncle who loves him when he's sober but beats him when he's drunk. That sort of thing. Anyway," he went on, and smiled. Susan suddenly became aware of how attractive his smile was. "Enough of that. Tell me about yourself."

Three junior high kids drifted by, slurping sodas, all of them saying, "Hi, Mrs. Gray."

Cliff added, "You seem to get along with youngsters okay."

Susan laughed wryly. "All of them except my own," she said, thinking of Patrick's angry voice. "I taught at the community college years ago. And loved it."

"How old are you, Susan Gray?"

The question caught her by surprise. The silvering brows over those dark eyes drew down briefly. "A—a—fifty-five. Oh, gracious, no. Fifty-six." And she flushed a little. "That's not an affectation. Really. I just forget."

He munched another squiggly. "Let me quote old Satchel Paige to you: 'How old would you be if you didn't know how old you were?' "

She considered it. "That depends. On the day."

"Right. I'm sixty. Some mornings I'm a hundred and sixty. This evening I feel sixteen." And suddenly he flushed a bit also, the color tinting the lean cheeks already showing silver beard beneath the yellow lighting. A tad hastily, he went on. "I retired my university post this spring and took on the genealogy research job. It's fascinating, it keeps me moving, and it also keeps me from handing out unwanted advice to my two grown and very capable sons. Although," he added, and grinned again—a rather boyish grin, "when my present client—who is rather hoity-toity—discovers her triple-great-grandfather did not bother to marry her triple-great-grandmother, she is not going to be too pleased. But those are the breaks when one starts digging into family archives."

Susan giggled. "What will you do?"

"Absolutely nothing. I just present the facts, ma'am."

She took a slow sip of her coffee, suddenly presented with an immutable fact about *this* man. "But—*you* have—got a life of your own."

"I'm trying. Oh—I see your drift." He frowned. "Look, Susan Gray, don't let that loudmouth grandson throw you. He's not around every day. What does he know—really—about his grandmother? That she makes good cookies on holidays and likes to see her kids? That's a crime?"

"Only if he's right," Susan answered painfully. "And I rather suspect—that he is."

Cliff said shortly, "I find that hard to believe."

But Susan didn't. She shrugged, trying to look insouciant, and sipped her coffee. He crunched the last squiggly. Over the muted recording of Christmas carols, Hammer suddenly started to rap as one of the kids slipped coins into the jukebox. There were squeals from the side door as another cornered a fluffy-haired waitress beneath a bunch of plastic mistletoe. Cliff abruptly balled up the paper tray and said, "Let's get out of here."

125

Snow sifted down silently on their bare heads as they left, and there was a wet feeling of damp cold to it. Susan shivered.

Cliff shut the car door for her, and loped around to the other side. How long had it been since a man had helped Susan Gray into an automobile? Lloyd had given up the practice in their second year of marriage. . . .

He slid in to his side, wiping snow off that thick silver crest of hair. "I don't like the feel of this stuff," he said, starting the car. "It could turn to ice real fast—and that will mess up a lot of Christmases." He gave her a sideways look. "Are you going to plan a party?"

"Yes. I've already asked six people."

"Old friends?"

"Yes. Very old friends."

"So you'll spend two days looking back."

Sudden inexplicable anger flared. Through gritted teeth she said, "Yes. Yes! Now, get off my case!"

"Sorry."

But he wasn't, and she knew it.

They pulled onto the parking apron beneath the naked sweet gum trees and saw Johnny standing by her car. He made a thumbs-up gesture. She opened her own door, hesitated, then said, "No. I'm sorry. Thank you for the coffee."

"You're welcome," he said, and drove away. Not fast, but decisively.

"Wow," said Johnny. "Spat with the boy-friend?"

To her amazement, Susan heard herself answering, "Sort of. Something like that."

"Poor timing with Christmas coming on," the young man said cheerfully. "Cuts down on the loot. I think the car's okay, but let me follow you home."

And he did, trailing her in his red pickup truck, across the south side of the small town square with its bright lights and hurrying, huddled shoppers, and the public address system blaring "Silver Bells." As she pulled into her driveway among the evergreens, he tootled his horn and went on by.

She garaged her car, punched the automatic door closer, and shivered her way up slick steps into the dark kitchen.

Never, never had she been so aware of how empty and still her house could be!

Shape up! she told herself angrily. "Get real!" Isn't that what Pat had said?

It's the same house. I'm the same person who left it this afternoon. Or—

Or am I?

Not quite ready to deal with that, she snapped on the light, made herself a ham

127

sandwich, shoved some hot chocolate in the microwave to heat, and flipped on the overhead TV set.

Then she remembered, and said the bovine derivated word again. She'd left her damned glasses on her desk at the library. That was the problem with being nearsighted; you didn't need them for anything but the faraway stuff. Like TV.

And driving a car.

Oh, boy. She really had been screwed up! She must have made it home on conditioned response!

Tightlipped, Susan rummaged in a kitchen drawer, found the old pair Scotch-taped together where the earpiece had come loose, put them gingerly on her nose, pulled her coat back on, and made the return trip to the library.

She'd unlocked the heavy door, and was halfway up the carpeted foyer steps to the main section when it hit her.

The pizza smell.

And that couldn't be right. Edna had eaten her pizza at noon.

If it had been any other smell but pizza, Susan might have had sense enough to be scared. But it wasn't. And she didn't.

She quietly crossed the small foyer and followed the next flight of stairs in the dark to the basement.

The supply room door was closed, but there was a small sliver of light beneath the bottom crack.

Okay.

Because she thought she already knew the answer, she pushed open the door and said, "Hi, Bobby!"

—And found a knife at her throat.

It was dropped in a moment, and a very sheepish Bobby Simotovich was saying, "Oh, God, Mrs. Gray, I'm sorry—"

"Put that thing away!" she whispered.

He did. He said, "I heard you coming. You scared me!"

"*I* scared *you!*"

But, still shaking and trying not to, she was looking around at the pizza on a paper napkin, the bedroll on the floor by a stack of books, the large flashlight propped up on a chair. She added, "I must say, you've made yourself at home."

He sighed and nodded. "I haven't hurt anything, Mrs. Gray. Honest I haven't."

"What did you tell your host family?"

"That I was staying with friends." He pointed to the stack of books. "These *are* my friends." Then his young, broad-planed face sharpened. "Who told you — Oh. Melissa."

"Yes. She was worried. She didn't know *where* you were."

Susan had made up her mind. She went on crisply. "Gather up your gear."

"Oh, Mrs. Gray — let me stay tonight! I'll find somewhere else tomorrow — I promise."

She shook her head. "Bobby, I can't. If something happened, our insurance would be zip."

"I've been careful — I never touch the heat, never turn on the lights, never even go upstairs! — well, only to use the john."

In amazement she asked, "How long have you been down here?"

He swallowed and grimaced. "Since last week. It's easy, really. I'm out before the custodian comes, and I'm very careful with the door locks—"

"Do you have a key?"

"No, ma'am. I haven't needed one. I get everything I need before closing, and you ladies lock me in. Then I don't leave. Honest. Oh, Mrs. Gray, let me stay just tonight. I don't know where to go!"

"I know." And Susan smiled. "You're going home with me. Come on, come on, move. Get your gear. I'll go up and find my glasses, then meet you at the front door. Okay?"

"Okay," he answered in a daze.

But when she came back down the foyer steps, he was there, bedroll, books, and all, a tall skinny Waldo shape in the muted gleam of the streetlight.

He asked a little huskily, "You really mean this? Gosh, it's so great!"

"Of course I mean it. You can have Patrick's room—he's my grandson."

"I'll find something else tomorrow. I promise."

"We'll deal with tomorrow when it comes. Where's the damned knife?"

"Put away."

"Be sure it stays there—I am not a side of beef."

"Yes, ma'am."

She drove across the south side of the square again, although the music had changed from "Silver Bells" to what Susan recognized in amazement as vintage Bing Crosby.

Bobby asked, "Who the heck is that?"

Without comment she told him.

"Wow. The old guy could sing."

"Yes," Susan answered dryly, and garaged her car again.

Back in the house she showed Bobby Patrick's basement room with its basic bath adjoining. "Oh, God," he exclaimed. "This is so

131

neat. May I use the stereo?"

"Of course. Just keep it down. When it bounces off the ceiling, bucko, you're out of here."

She was smiling. "Get comfortable, then come up in the kitchen We'll get a bite to eat."

"I—I had the pizza."

"Then top it with a ham and cheese. Okay."

"Wow. Sure."

The hot chocolate, predictably, was cold. She made another, and set the timer on both of them. She was briskly shaving ham off the big hunk intended for her kids on their first evening home, when she heard him behind her. Over her shoulder she said, "Get the plates. There, on your right, second shelf. If you stay here, you have to carry your weight, buddy."

And there was hesitation—as palpable as sound.

Susan turned around. The gangling kid was standing stock still in the kitchen door, his young face a mask of misery. He said, "Mrs. Gray—I gotta say this. Please don't misunderstand me. But—but I don't—" He hesitated, in abject wretchedness, knowing the street word, knowing it would offend her, searching desperately for a substitute, finally blurting out: "I don't screw with ladies."

Her mouth dropped. It must have clicked. He backed away. And suddenly—because this situation summed up the entire damned day— she began to laugh helplessly, hanging on to the back of the nearest kitchen chair.

"Oh, Bobby," she gasped finally. "Bless you, child! But listen, sweetie—listen to me! I'm fifty-some years old! I'm a small-town grandmother, not a big-city one! And I don't screw with anybody either! Trust me, Bobby. And I'll trust you. Then we'll get along just fine. Come on, child. Eat your ham and cheese."

There was another long, heart-wrenching moment. Then Bobby Simotovich grinned. "Okay," he said, "Grandma."

Susan slapped the pile of ham on a plate, put it on the table, and said, "Find the mustard in the fridge. Horseradish, if you like. I'll slice bread."

"Mayonnaise." But his head was already inside the appliance. His voice came back muffled. "Wow. Are you expecting a siege? I haven't seen so much chow since I got invited to Minnie Todavich's confirmation party."

"My kids were coming for Christmas. They aren't."

"Oh. Sorry." He was hauling out jars, putting them on the table beside the ham. "That's a bummer for you, I bet."

"Things happen."

"Yeah. Tell me about it."

He towered over her, all long young bones. "Holy mac! Homemade bread? I don't believe it!"

"Believe. And get a plate." But she was pleased, and inexplicably felt better. About everything.

The boy had Patrick's hollow leg. Susan sat across the table from him, sipping hot chocolate and watching him eat. Pizza, she realized, was obviously not very filling. If that's all one ate.

She knew his college major: archeology. She asked, "What do you want to be, Bobby?" really curious that a kid from the Chicago slums would choose so esoteric a subject.

He swallowed, his adam's apple bobbing. "In the end? A museum curator. I think that would be so neat. Before that I'd like to get in on some digs somewhere. But I guess that will have to wait. No one on the community college level seems to have much information. Great ham!"

"Have some more."

He did, finishing up with a massive slice of fruit cake, then tidily putting his dirty dishes in the sink. He said to her, sighing, "That was wonderful. You have no idea — well. Anyway.

Now, what can I do for you? Got some chores?"

Patrick had never asked that. Patrick, as a matter of fact, might be considered just a bit spoiled.

Since the girls were coming, she might as well finish the holiday decorations, she mused. As she remembered, they all had nice homes—not as nice as Roberta's, but she'd inherited money—and she didn't want to appear a slob. And without the children around with their heaps of stuff, the house might actually stay decorated. Last year, with Pat's computer-word processor mess and Marilyn's clothes and Susie's Barbie-doll beach house, it had been hard to discern even where the chairs were.

She marched Bobby into her living room.

The house was of the wrong vintage to have a fireplace—something she and Lloyd had always regretted—but it did have ample walnut-framed arches and a handsome staircase. In the curve of the stairs sat the artificial Christmas tree, surrounded by boxes of decorations.

Bobby said the predictable, "Wow." Then he reached out, touched a branch, and gave her a reproachful look.

"Jeez. You make your own bread but you have a pretend tree?"

This was not the time to tell him the bread had been originally long frozen lumps in the grocery freezer. Instead, she answered wryly, "When real trees went to twenty-five bucks a piece, child, the time had come for pretend. Would you like to decorate it? I can't reach the top branches without standing on a chair."

"Oh, sure. Sure! But—will you show me how?"

"How?"

"I—I've never done a Christmas tree. My grandma did. I guess. But Uncle Anka never—never cared for American holidays."

There was an entire sad story in that speech. Wisely, Susan ignored it. She said, "Honey, just get out the stuff and hang it on. Here." And she sat down on the floor to open boxes. "Lights first. And icicles. Then ornaments. I'll hand."

Nothing. No response. She looked up and saw the indecision on his face. Carefully he said, "Mrs. Gray, could I—would you mind if I—I called Melissa? She knows about this stuff—and she's just missing it awfully. She can't afford to go home—her dad's stationed in Europe somewhere—and I've seen her cry."

"Why, Bobby! What a good idea!"

"Would—would you call?"

"Of course. But why?"

"Her host family—they're really nice. But they're so afraid she'll get—raped, or something. You'd make it official."

"Safe," she amended, reading an extension of his thoughts. "Okay. But the responsibility is yours, Bobby."

"Yeah. I know."

She glanced at her watch. Almost nine, and she could feel the familiar signs of a tension headache behind her eyes. She said, "I have another suggestion."

"What?"

"It's getting late. Why don't you and I just hang the evergreen swags over the arches and up the stairs? Then in the morning I'll call Melissa's hosts. Tomorrow she can come for dinner and you two can do the tree. Okay?"

"Wow," he said, and his face was like sunshine. "Okay."

She held up her hand. "Boost," she said.

He hauled her to her feet and impulsively kissed her cheek.

"Thanks," he said. "Show me what to do."

They were done by nine-thirty, and even if it was her house, she thought, as always, that it looked lovely with the green and red wreathing wound around the staircase and draped gracefully from atop the doors. As Bobby bent to nest the empty boxes, something fell

137

to the carpet and lay there sparkling beneath the chandelier. Susan pounced.

"My Christmas tree pin!" she cried. "That little widget, Susie! I *knew* she had it last year! But she was only three, and no one could get a straight answer from her. My husband gave it to me years ago, and I wear it every Christmas — oh." Her happy voice tapered off as she looked at the miniature tree shining green and red in the palm of her hand. "Oh, dear. It's broken. The pin part is gone. Oh, well" — and now her voice was both hurt and weary as the headache was really starting — "the kids aren't coming anyway. I'll just put it away and get it fixed after the first of the year." Turning her back so Bobby couldn't glimpse the tears, she dropped the brooch in the drawer of Lloyd's desk near the telephone.

But he was watching and he knew.

"It's been such a great evening," he said. "Why don't you sit down and I'll bring you something. A little tea? I heat a fantastic cup."

He was trying to be helpful. Why did she suddenly feel a hundred and ten years old? Was it because he was so *young?* She shook her head.

"No, thanks, hon. I think I'll just go on up

to bed and read. Snack if you like before you turn in. Breakfast is at seven-thirty. I open tomorrow at the library, and it's invoice day, too. Good night. There are extra blankets in the closet."

He answered, "Okay. Thanks. Thanks for everything."

She was suddenly aware of rain pattering against the window as she mounted the stairs. Too emotional to deal with whether that was good or not for the ensuing holiday, she brushed her teeth, creamed her face, pulled on a flannel nightie, took two aspirin, and fell into her side of the empty double bed.

Downstairs, the TV lasted for about half an hour, then was followed by the noise every mother knows — the fridge opening and shutting — and the sound of Pat's stereo in the basement.

The house, Susan acknowledged dully, felt a lot less empty. How Patrick would feel about someone else using his equipment she didn't at the moment precisely give a damn. He certainly wasn't here to bitch!

She flounced over and closed her eyes for the thousandth time.

Nothing. Just whirling stars where her hands pressed and a hundred disconnected thoughts grinding against each other in her brain.

Get your own life! Patrick had said.

Doing what? She was fifty-six years old; she should take up bungee-jumping?

And that damned Cliff Crane — bad-mouthing her party. Six old broads — he might as well have said that. What was *wrong* with that? It was a start, dammit!

The rain was now really beating against her windows, making black streams that shimmered in the light of her bed lamp. Flopping over, she reached for the telephone. Didn't every gray-haired old broad make an hourly check on the temperature?

But the phone lines were down, a fairly frequent local happening. Happy she wasn't a telephone lineman, she pounded her pillow, shut her eyes, and finally went to sleep.

Then she dreamed. Crazy dreams. She was on the cruise with her family but Patrick locked her in her stateroom because her company wasn't desired. When she bawled about it they dumped her on a desert island with two crocodiles and a chimpanzee wearing Roberta Glosson's fur wrap. Then Cliff Crane swung in on a bungee cord and said he'd rescue her if she'd marry his client's triple-great-grandfather.

Morning was a blessing.

The sun was trying to shine, the rain had melted the snow, and there was a lovely smell of coffee in the hallway.

Just like the TV ads, she thought, and although she felt as if she hadn't slept for days, there was a thin band of happiness around her discontentment. It *was* nice to have someone else in the house!

Going downstairs, she met Bobby, freshly shaven and in a clean plaid shirt, just coming up from the basement.

She said, "The coffee smells wonderful. Thank you."

"I made it last night."

"Oh. You what?"

"It's got a timer. Or—don't you use it? Should I have not?"

She grimaced. "I'd forgotten. And that's one of the things that sold me on the pot. I set it twice. I think. A gadget user I am not. Pour me a cup, and we'll have some breakfast. Oh—and the telephone's out. I have to report it from the library. Where do you go from here?"

He shrugged. "I carry out groceries from the Shoppers' Shed from ten to two—but I'm free right now. Want me to stay here awhile in case it's *your* phone?"

"Why don't you? It might be they'd want inside. Sometimes they do."

An hour later, leaving him contentedly putting laundry in the washer, she left for work, conscious of being a somewhat different person from the one who had thus departed yesterday.

Cliff Crane's Buick was already parked under the bare trees. As she got out, she saw his strong legs swing out also. He stood up, facing her, the padded coat making him appear as massive as a Green Bay Packer.

She said cheerfully, "Good morning. The rain has stopped."

He said, "Your phone's out."

"I know. I've got to report it."

"I already have."

"Oh. Thank you." And inasmuch as that meant, *ergo,* that he'd obviously tried to call her, she said, "Was there something you wanted?"

And unexpectedly he grinned—that charming grin that lit up his lean face. "Yeah," he said, "but we'll not go into that just now. How about dinner tonight?"

And she'd said she'd fix it for both Bobby and Melissa. Was she glad or sorry? Dodging that issue, she told him the bare facts, adding, "Why don't you come over, too?"

It wasn't exactly what I had in mind."

He waited, holding her book bag while she fumbled with her key. "How in the world did you get both Bob and Melissa?"

She went inside, and while she snapped on the lights for the basement and foyer, she told him about finding Bobby camping in the supply room. When she looked back, he was still standing outside, looking absolutely stunned. He said, "Susan! My God! He could have killed you! I've checked his record. He did detention for armed robbery when he was thirteen! And you've taken him into your house?"

The remark about armed robbery was a bit of a poser, but she answered sturdily, "Well— that was six years ago!"

"Seven. He's twenty now. Even so—look, Sue, let's figure out something else. This worries me."

It had worried her a bit, too, but trust had to start somewhere. And somehow the Bobby she knew didn't equate to the one he was talking about, unless—

And Cliff said it for her: "What if he's setting you up?"

She answered, "Come inside."

It was fifteen minutes before opening time. She locked the door again, leaned against it. Her knees felt weak. She said desperately, "I can't turn him out. I've promised."

"Then ask me to your damned party."

"What?"

"Ask me to your damned party. And I'll come early. Like tonight."

She had this sudden, wild, left-field picture of her elderly neighbors Mrs. Fitch and Mrs. Onnes, both peering through their blinds at the people going in and out of the Gray house. "Look at that!" they'd say to each other on the telephone. "A boy—and a girl—and a strange man. Who is he? That's not Diane's husband. . . ."

Did she care?

No.

What she did care about was the angry, bewildered, and almost pained look on Cliff Crane's face. He bent, put the book bag on the step, straightened up again. It was as if he'd given himself a moment to think.

"Maybe I'm jumping the gun," he said. "Is there anyone in town—preferably male—who *would* come and stay?"

"No." It was an honest answer. "I have no family with the kids gone. But the girls are coming tomorrow—for Christmas Eve."

"That won't do."

"But it's just a day!"

"How long does it take to get a clop on the

head?"

"He didn't do it last night!"

"He hadn't looked the place over! Now he's had a chance!"

"Oh, I don't believe this!"

"Small-town people! Christ in a night-gown!"

He took a deep breath and lowered his voice. "Okay. Let me tell you something. I was going to do it tonight, but now will do."

She was standing on a step, which made her eyes level with his. And suddenly her heart started beating faster at the look in his eyes. He was saying simply, quietly, "I told you I had another commitment last night. I did. We went to dinner. Again. And—and she still didn't cut it, Sue. I'd known it before, but last night I kept looking at her and—and seeing you. That's why I was trying to call you this morning. To ask—ask if you would give me a try. Please. And I don't want you bonked on the noggin before you do."

And what does one say to that? What does any woman in her right mind say?

The phrase "right mind" was moot—but somehow Susan wasn't going to quibble with it. In a daze with sparkles on it, she put out a shaky hand. She said in a whisper, "Yes. I will give it a try. Please do come to my party."

145

"Tonight?"

"Tonight."

"No strings, Sue. I'm not asking for strings. Not yet. Believe it or not, I'm rather new at this. I've been—choosy."

"I'm glad."

He was going to kiss her! She knew it, she could see it in his gray eyes—but suddenly three library patrons were tapping imperiously on the locked doors. The fifteen minutes were up and the moment was gone.

She felt as if something precious had been snatched away. But it couldn't be helped. And he knew. That was the scary part: he knew. The man could read her like a book: the small-town patsy.

He was smiling, and stepping aside.

"Next time," he said. "Now unlock the door. Let the unlettered masses in. I'll be in Springfield all day. When do you close?"

"At two. For Christmas. But I'll be home."

"With Bobby? And Melissa?"

"Yes."

"It's probably a good thing," he said, and winked at her! "When's dinner?"

"About—about six."

"Set a plate."

And he was gone, loping back down the steps, getting into his car. Mrs. Watson, looking for the new *Antiques* magazine and Mrs. Caylor, defying anyone to beat her to the new *Wall Street Journal,* surged up the stairs, taking Susan with them, and that was that.

Until—about six.

It seemed years before she got a moment to herself. The library system man came in with three canvas bags of loaner books; Mr. Billings wanted help with the copy machine; three fourth-grade boys, holed up in the nonfiction stacks giggling over the pictures of the female anatomy, had to be gently shooshed over into the children's department; and Mrs. Black inadvertently dumped the entire A to BE file card drawer.

However, perhaps it was a good thing. At least it was something with which she knew how to deal.

When Abercrombie (Fitch), Abner (Felix), and Absenteeism (Military) blurred before her eyes, she realized she still had her glasses on, plucked them off, put them somewhere, shoved the rod back through the drawer (from which it should have never been removed anyway) and shoved the drawer in the cabinet. She would have liked to shove Mrs. Black back out the door, but that was against library policy. Fortunately Mrs. Black went anyway, and Susan at last had a lull in the action.

147

She used it to stare at the cassette tape rack as if she'd never seen it before. She could make a tape herself. It would be called "From Despair to Complete Insanity in Twenty-four Hours." She should at least spend the next twelve moping about being abandoned by her family—but no one was giving her time!

"A—a—Mrs. Gray?"

A young man in a very well cut topcoat was standing by the checkout. When she nodded, he held out his hand.

"I'm Dean Willard, of the college. Bobby's just told me about you. We're very appreciative. If you can find room to keep him until Monday, you'll be reimbursed, I assure you. Then the office is open and we'll try to make some different arrangements."

Bobby? Bobby who? Oh!

Hoping she hadn't made the impression of a total ass, Susan returned the handclasp and said, "Bobby is no problem. As a matter of fact, he's welcome. My family is unable to come for the holidays—and somehow I suspect he can help me with the—the overabundant food supply."

He laughed. "*I* suspect you are right. You enjoy our youngsters, Mrs. Gray? I hear nothing but good reports—on this library, and especially you."

"Why, thank you. Yes, I do enjoy them. It's the eternal schoolteacher in me, I suppose."

"You're full-time here?"

"Oh, no. Part."

"Ah. Well. They're fortunate to have you."

He said a few more nice things both about Bobby and herself, then decamped. Susan was left still standing in the middle of the floor, a little perplexed. What was that all about?

Oh, well.

The lusty sounds of "Jingle Bells" began to filter up from the lower-level children's library, indicating that Mrs. West was winding up her annual Christmas party. This was underlined by the fourth-grade boys marching out through the double doors of the foyer, arms linked, singing cheerfully, "Jingle bells, jingle bells/Granny's got a gun/She shot a deer in the rear/And watched that bastard run."

Whatever, Susan thought ruefully, happened to wide-eyed innocence and a firm belief in Santa's elves?

Two o'clock was marked by locking the doors, posting the closed sign, and searching in bemused resignation for her glasses. She finally found them perched atop the exchange paperback rack, put them on her face, and wondered again, briefly, about a chain — except that when she'd worn a chain, the glasses had kept swinging into whatever she was doing at the time. She recalled once having them totally immersed in tomato juice.

Oh, well.

All of this was sheer persiflage to obscure the fact it was four hours until dinnertime. And Cliff Crane. In her house. *Staying there.*

In a sudden panic she thought, *If Bobby and Melissa try to leave, I'll tie them up!*

Oops! She had to call Melissa's host family.

She did. After a short conference they agreed to allow Melissa time at the Gray house if she was at home by ten for evening prayer.

Gracious, Susan thought, hanging up. I thought they had that at seven! Well—never mind. Bobby will be pleased.

Bobby was. As he helped her unload two sacks of groceries, he reported that the telephone repairman had found a small wire broken where it entered the house beneath the living room window. It was repaired. All was well.

As she went upstairs to change, she heard rain begin to drum on the windows again. So much for a white Christmas.

Briefly she indulged in remembering little Diane and her friends, bundled to the eyebrows, rolling in the snows of past holidays, of driving out to Lloyd's folks' farm and hitching up the old sleigh behind an amazed old Clydesdale who thought he'd retired, of the pungent smell of bread stuffing on Christmas Day and small Patrick sneaking into the kitchen and eating an entire chocolate pie.

But that had been yesterday. It was over.

Over, Sue Gray. Listen to your head, not your heart!

Get your own life! Pat had said. *Get real, Grandma!*

I'm trying, Patrick. I'm trying. . . .

The girls will help. Tomorrow. Elvira and May Belle and Martha—and dear old Walter Cox. Well. Not so old, according to what Elvira had said.

And the kids will help tonight. Bobby and Melissa.

And Cliff Crane.

Would he help?

Suddenly Susan realized she was scared. But ready.

She looked at herself in the mirror, standing still in her white slip, and thought again briefly about waffles and syrup. She pulled on nice slacks and a comfortable, deep red sweater. There was, after all, work to be done. She was having a houseful tomorrow. The welkin would ring. Or it better ring, dammit,

151

she thought, snapped off the light and started back downstairs.

At the storeroom door she was caught short by the large stack of carefully wrapped, bright and shiny Christmas presents. Diane's set of crystal. Bill's camouflage hunting gear. The lovely pierced earrings she'd so looked forward to seeing Marilyn unwrap. Susie's Queen-of-the-Jungle set. Pat's new sweater . . .

Oh, well. She'd bundle them all off in the mail Monday.

If she wasn't too busy to remember.

Then tears came, partly at her own surging bitterness, and partly in shame. God, she really *could* be insensitive! She had to get over that! She had to do it!

From the bottom of the stairs she suddenly saw Melissa's bright face looking up, and Bobby on a ladder, setting the golden angel on the top of the tree. They turned and waved, saying in chorus, "Hi! Come look! Isn't it gorgeous?"

Abruptly she knew that there was an altered destination for the earrings and the sweater. She smiled at them, and said, "It's lovely. I'm so glad you found the angel. She's my favorite."

"She looks old."

"She is old. My mother brought her from England when she was six. That was about 1902. Now, Bobby — don't forget: lights first, then ornaments. If you don't, you'll have a terrible time."

"Yes, ma'am," he nodded, grinning.

"And I will go start the mac and cheese, and zap the green beans," she said. "Brownies or angel cake for dessert?"

"Do we have to choose?"

"Not as long as you leave the mince pies for tomorrow."

"What is a mince pie?" Bobby asked, frowning.

"Tell him," Susan said to Melissa's startled face, and went on into the kitchen.

Cliff Crane was sitting there on one chair, his feet on another, and clasping a coffee cup with the succinct lettering, SHIT HAPPENS. He looked as if he'd been there forever. He grinned and said, "Hi."

"Hi. When did you arrive?"

"I didn't go. I called over and arranged to meet my boys for breakfast tomorrow. That way we can spend some time, they can still get back to their girlfriends for Christmas Eve — and I can get back over here. For whatever." He grinned even more broadly at the last term.

"They're — not married?" she said.

"Not yet. Their mother and I didn't set a very good example."

She certainly wasn't going to touch that. She poured herself a cup of coffee and ran water for the macaroni and cheese. She had, after all, urgent things to do.

To her busy back he said, "I put my suitcase behind the couch. I was making a statement to the children."

Dryly, she answered, "Thanks."

"I also said I was lending my motel room to Christmas transients. Which is true. I thought the manager was ready to kiss my feet. Bobby suggested we hang out a sign: ALL HOLIDAY DERELICTS REGISTER HERE."

"Thanks a lot."

"Oh. And shall I make the salad dressing? I mix a mean roquefort."

"How did you know there was roquefort? And a salad?"

"I peeked."

Suddenly she started laughing, and turned around, shaking her head. "I *am* on a roll!" she said. "This is going to be a fun Christmas. Isn't it? Cliff, I am so grateful!"

"So," he said, "am I."

He did slice the ham, looking at her dull knives with horror, and making, she felt, al-

154

most a fetish out of sharpening one. Bobby set the table, handling her old china from the sideboard so reverently, she had no courage to tell him she ordinarily used plastic, and Melissa poured water into the thin-stemmed cutglass goblets her aunt had brought across the ocean from Gloucester wrapped in her husband's underwear. After all, Susan told herself, perhaps this *is* a special occasion. And she knew it was indeed, when Bobby looked from Melissa to Susan to Cliff and said almost shyly, "This is what a family is like. Isn't it?"

After dinner Melissa opened the lid of the piano bench and fell into ecstasies over the old, yellowing sheet music there. Seeing the two males' dismayed faces, Susan sent them to the basement to watch whatever manly necessity was playing on TV while she polished silver for the next day and reveled in a cascade of music from the old upright piano and Melissa's fingers—the *Moonlight Sonata,* and *Clair de Lune* and the demanding concertos of *Rhapsody in Blue.*

Before they knew it, it was almost ten.

Melissa left, running to her car through the drumming rain, saying, "I'll see you all tomorrow!" The three of them watched the news, Cliff sitting comfortably slouched in Lloyd's chair. Susan didn't mention it. After all, Bill sat there. And Patrick.

Then they went to bed. Bobby to the basement, Susan upstairs, and Cliff on the blanket-heaped expanse of the sofa bed.

"I don't think it's very comfortable," Susan said.

Cliff answered, "It will be fine. Now, run along. You have a big day tomorrow, and I must get going by five o'clock. Shoo!"

She did — but sleep was a long time coming. The basement stereo went off at twelve, and then she was charmed to hear from small, staccato whispering noises that Cliff tended to snore. Apparently, she thought with satisfaction, he'd given up thinking about Bobby's evil intentions.

The two kids up the street pulled in at two, parting company with their friends as they noisily chorused some rudely accompanied "Ho-ho-ho's" and another chorus of the "Jingle Bells" crudity she'd heard at the library. It must be the popular one for the year, she thought drowsily and drifted away herself.

Something woke her up — perhaps the sound she'd not heard for so long: other bodies moving in her house. The rain had lessened to a gentle hiss. Rising up on one elbow, she looked at her clock. Five of five.

That's what she'd heard! Cliff, leaving.

Suddenly, inexplicably compelled to see him go only if it was glimpsing his car driving away, she struggled from the warm covers, tugged on her old white flannel robe, and stumbled on base feet down the quiet stairs.

He hadn't gone. He was standing in the shadowed living room by the tidily made-up sofa, heavy coat zipped, looking upward.

When he saw her he hesitated — then held out his arms.

She ran down into them.

"Oh, God, oh, God," he whispered into the top of her tousled head, "if you could have seen yourself standing there, that white robe flowing behind you like a — a Christmas angel — "

Blindly, eyes shut, she held up her face and he kissed her, gently at first, then with mounting heat. His hands found the rising swell of her breasts, the soft curve of her beneath the molding flannel, and on a tide of longing she felt herself answering his need, binding herself to his length, the solid warmth and strength of him.

"Oh, God," he said for the third time, and she sensed his stiffening, his mind taking command. "No. No, not yet. Not yet, love. This is to be no one-night stand, no snatch, grab, and run. Not this. I've waited too long for someone like you. No. No."

And he stepped away, leaving only his big hands cupping her face. One finger flicked the "grandma snoot." Then he kissed her one more time, gently, lovingly, and turned her back to the stairs.

"Tonight," he said. "Tonight, love. Christmas Eve. We'll start properly—and see where we can go from there. Okay?"

"Okay."

It was a bare whisper, but he heard. He chuckled, said softly, "Attagirl." And went out the door into the rain.

She didn't watch him drive away. She went blindly back to bed, hugging herself beneath the warm blankets—and dreamed incredible dreams.

Morning came much too fast.

The rain changed to sleet and the sleet to ice. Before she even got her turkey into the oven, the entire world was sheathed in treacherous glass. The calls began to come in at noon, as the skies darkened to a heavy, threatening gray.

It was Elvira first, saying, "I'm sorry, Sue—but I just can't ask Walter to drive in this. It's really bad up here. Maybe tomorrow. I'll phone you."

158

Then at one o'clock, May Belle: "No way, hon. I can't even get out of my drive."

Then Velma: "Sorry, Sue. We're just not going to try. My neighbor says there are cars in the ditch all along the interstate. Maybe we'll see you tomorrow. If not — Merry Christmas."

"You, too," said Susan wryly. She hung up just as Bobby walked in from his supermarket job.

"It's mean," he said, pitching his jacket down the basement steps. "Have you heard from Melissa? I don't want her driving her car."

So you'll bring her piggyback? Susan thought, not being in the most cheerful state of mind to begin with. But the entire situation resolved itself when Melissa herself came in the door like a ray of sunshine.

"I decided to walk," she said with her usual perky smile. "The shop is staying open — there's always someone who impulse-buys jewelry on Christmas Eve, Mr. Lossner says, but he let me off. He is so nice to work for. Gosh, Mrs. Gray, I hope Mr. Crane made it to Springfield!"

That was very much on Susan's mind, also — as well as "When will he make it back?" Because it mattered to her — it mattered very much.

159

"Oh, he made it all right," Bobby said, channel-changing rapidly on the living room television. "It's just the return I'm worried about. If he'd only just sit tight right there in Springfield—jeez Louise!" he interrupted himself suddenly. "Look at the pileup on the interstate! One—two—three—nine cars! Oh, God."

"What?"

"What?"

Both asked it simultaneously, rushing for a view, Susan with the portable phone still in her hand, and Melissa with her coat on.

"Nothing. Nothing—I'm not sure. Maybe they'll show it again—I'll try Channel Ten."

Susan found herself ready to scream at him, "What did you see? What did you see?" Because it was Cliff. She knew he'd seen Cliff's car. Instead, she leaned against the end of the sofa and took a deep breath. Two of them. Three.

Melissa slipped out of her red jacket and covertly handed something to Bobby in the palm of her hand. Cigarettes? Neither of them smoked—or admitted they did. She went on calmly. "I got the loveliest letter from my Lark today, guys. And an oil portrait of me—imagine—she said she painted it from our freshman yearbook. I'm to send it to

160

my mom. She is just the sweetest thing—there, Bobby! There! The Springfield channel! Stop!"

On the screen the storm-coated shoulders of the newsman moved aside, and behind him could be seen the flashing lights of ambulances, a jackknifed tractor-trailer, and cars scattered like toys from the highway to the ditches. The reporter was interviewing a state trooper, but Susan wasn't listening. One cold hand clutching the sofa back, she was scanning the crumpled cars—red ones, black ones, white ones, blue ones—

Oh. Oh, God. That man being slid into an ambulance—that stocky man with the thick silver thatch of hair, one arm clutching the other and blood on the front of his coat—

Susan's throat closed convulsively, but the picture changed and the man was gone. She looked at Bobby and Melissa, almost begging them to say "No, it wasn't. He was too tall—(or too short—or too *anything*) for Cliff Crane!"

But they weren't going to say that.

Bobby said, "Well, at least we know he's still alive."

And Melissa said, "He'll call. When he can. I know he will. Or his family will."

They'll not call me. They don't even know

161

me!

She couldn't say that either. Besides, there was no point. And at least he was alive . . . and his sons would be there. They'd look after him.

She hadn't felt so—so *out* of it, so helpless since Diane's call Wednesday night. It must have shone in her face. Bobby glanced over at her, hoisted his gangling frame erect and threw an awkward arm around her shoulders. He said, "Don't worry, Grandma. We'll take care of you."

And he and Melissa exchanged significant glances over her head—a look Susan sensed more than she saw.

Suddenly it hit her: she was alone in her home with two young people she hardly knew—and Cliff Crane, who had worried about such a thing happening—Cliff was gone. When the doorbell rang just then, she would have answered had it been Frankenstein's monster.

It almost was.

Roberta Glosson stood there.

She held a covered baking pan in gloved hands, her heavily made-up face was wearing a rigid smile, and she was saying brightly, "You need more salt on your steps, Susan. I almost fell. I hope I'm not late; I had to drive very slowly. Have the rest of the girls arrived? My telephone has been out, but of course I knew I was invited. *May* I come in? I'm freezing!"

Numbly, Susan stepped back, and the apparition swept inside. Mascaraed eyes flicked the room.

"Pretty. Nice tree. You do have taste, Sue. Where is everyone?"

Beginning to function again, Susan thought nastily, *Who is "everyone," Roberta? Because if you're using the girls for an excuse to find Cliff here, you've just struck out! And so have I,* she added, blinking to hide sudden, useless tears. A little huskily, she said aloud, "They're not going to make it today. Because of the ice."

"Really? What a shame. But we'll manage. Bobby—it is Bobby, is it not?—take this to the kitchen, and look out—it just came from the oven. My nut roll you girls used to like so much." Despite her discomfiture, Susan had to bite her lip to keep from smiling. *Liked so much,* indeed! Elvira used to say she saved her piece to patch her tire, and May Belle always murmured, "Nut roll, indeed. It takes one to know one!"

Roberta was rasping on. "But I thought I should bring *something.* Manners, you know.

Have I met you, young lady? Your face is familiar."

Melissa was smiling politely, but her quick eyes had already grasped the situation. "I'm Melissa Parks. An art major at the college. My family is with the military overseas, and Mrs. Gray has been kind enough to ask me for Christmas eve. May I take your coat—or—are you staying?"

Bless the child. It was a good try. But of course Roberta didn't bat an eye.

"Yes, you may, thank you. Of course I'm staying. I'd hoped to have a lovely chat with my old teaching buddies—we did have such good times, didn't we, Susan—and I'm sorry to hear the others can't make it. But friends don't leave each other alone at Christmas, do they?"

The woman was incredible, not only for the faculty battles now recalled airily as "good times," but for so neatly evading the fact she'd hardly been a pal in the ten Christmases since then!

She was briskly shrugging her chubby self out of the heavy fur coat, revealing dark green jogging pants and a red sweatshirt appliqued with the antlered head of one of Santa's deer. Melissa said, "Oh—that's neat!"

Roberta grinned, and touched the deer's

164

nose. A Christmas tune filled the room. "Only," she said, "if you are not at the communion rail and hit the button accidentally. Father McCully thought I was singing 'Rudolph the Red-nosed Reindeer' to him. He was not pleased. No sense of humor, that man."

She suddenly put up a surprisingly long-fingered hand and touched the golden angel at the top of the Christmas tree. "Lovely," she said in an almost gentle voice. But in a flash the old rasp was back. "Is that right? Art major. Old Pete Macklin's classes.

"Yes ma'am," Melissa answered, a little surprised at the pudgy little woman's knowing. "He's such a good instructor. I'm learning so much."

"It's there if you listen." (How many times has Susan heard *that?*) May I sit down, Sue? That chair looks right. (Lloyd's recliner.) I do hope no one is smoking; I find the habit totally reprehensible. Now then, Susan. Let me get my breath back, and we'll decide what I can do to help. Is dinner planned?

Bobby had appeared with a cup of coffee in a saucer — the good china, Susan noted. He rolled his eyes up at Susan behind Roberta's back, and then bent over her with an almost courtly gesture. "Here you are, Mrs. Glosson.

Mrs. Gray, your oven timer is about to go off."

"Excuse me," Susan murmured, and fled, blessing the boy. Melissa followed.

"Bobby's shift," she said in a whisper. "Mrs. Gray, why is she here? She could see no one else was! is she—is she just—lonely?"

Susan thought, bingo!

"Yes," she said soberly. "That's probably it. And I'm this year's solution. Go on back in and help him. I'll be there in a moment and we'll figure out something."

"Maybe she isn't *so* bad," said Melissa hopefully, and obeyed.

"And maybe Rome *was* built in one day," said Susan to herself, and checked the oven timer. It still had ten minutes on it, which Bobby had known, of course. He'd bought her time to think.

And what she thought was: What can go wrong next? Her family wasn't coming, her party was spoiled because of the ice, what may have happened to Cliff was too frightening to contemplate, and Roberta was here!

If *this* was getting a life of one's own, she'd take vanilla!

And then she thought, whoa! Back off, lady. Say a prayer for Cliff—oh, please, God, let him be all right—and for your kids that they do enjoy themselves, and they do miss you just a little bit — oh, no, God, sorry, scratch that! — baste your turkey, and get back into the living room to help Bobby and Melissa.

She opened the oven to baste the turkey; the outside of the breast was a little crisp. Wryly quoting to herself, " 'Other than that, Mrs. Lincoln, how did you enjoy the play?' " she did what she could with more butter and a damp cloth, then returned to the battlefield in the living room.

The long shadows outside were giving way to darkness through which the icy sheath on the world shone beneath the streetlamps like iridescent glass. The three were standing at the large front window — gangling Bobby, slender Melissa, and in the middle Roberta, blocky and shapeless in her joggers and sweatshirt. As Susan snapped on the table lamp by the sofa she heard Roberta say, ". . . and the glass shines like that. Shimmers, really, so the entire stained panorama is a mosaic of rainbows. Everyone should go in the cathedral at night — then they'd realize what a gifted artist the man was."

"I'd just like to see Vienna," breathed Melissa.

"And perhaps you will, dear. Perhaps you

will."

As the lamp came on, they all turned. Then, suddenly, the lamp and the Christmas tree flashers dimmed.

Bobby said, "Wow. Is the power going off?"

"It may," Roberta answered, and she was back to her old bossy self. "Lines are overloaded, I imagine. Better get out the candles, Sue. Where are they? I'll help."

"I've some right here in the desk. Run and find the kitchen matches, Bobby — left-hand shelf beneath the dry goods. Melissa, bring the candleholders from the sideboard to the table. We may as well be prepared."

Susan was opening the desk drawer as she spoke, scooping up the long, half-burned assortment of tapers saved from many other occasions. Red ones from last Christmas, blue from Susie's birthday party, yellow ones from Easter, along with some fat, stubby blocks that used to be fashionable but weren't anymore.

Gosh, the drawer was messy. She was glad she hadn't let Roberta see it — but she'd not been in that drawer for weeks.

Wait. Yes, she had. Wednesday.

Wednesday, when she'd opened it and dropped her Christmas brooch inside.

And the brooch was gone.

Really gone.

And so were the lights.

She stood like a stone in the abruptly dark room, unable to move. From behind her Bobby's voice said, "Hand one to me, Grandma. I don't want you falling over something." And she felt his arm, reaching, the soft warmth of the old sweater with that young tensile strength inside, and the comforting shoulder pat as he found the clutch of tapers in her cold grip, took one, and lit it.

"There! Here, Melissa, we can start the others from this. Gosh, light is nice. You don't realize how nice until you don't have it anymore."

Numbly, she shut the drawer.

Who? Who had taken it? Oh, God, please, not Bobby! Not Melissa!

The telephone repairman — he'd been here, he'd used the telephone on the desk when he'd repaired the wire!

Please let it be the telephone repairman!

Stonily she thought, I'm not going to mention it. I'm not going to ruin this evening for the innocent. It's Christmas Eve!

And one I certainly will remember — if not in the way I planned!

Shutting her lips tightly against their quiver, she turned and looked at her living room, now bathed in the roseate glow of candlelight that even sparked flashing peaks of ruby and gold from the ornaments on the tree.

Her three guests stood in the middle of the floor. Melissa had slipped one arm casually through Roberta's. Giving it a little squeeze, she giggled and said, "It's beautiful! I like it better this way!"

The look on Roberta's aging face was one of longing.

But it was gone in a flash as Bobby leaned down to punch the deer's nose on her sweat-shirt. As the tinkling song began, they all three laughed. And some of the hurt and shock and sadness slipped from Susan's shoulders.

If the brooch was missing, there was a reason. She knew there was a reason. And she'd wait until later to find it out. That much she could do. It might be the dumbest decision she'd ever made. Roberta would probably say so. . . .

Roberta, as a matter of fact, was saying something now, trying to penetrate her fog: "Sue! Susan!"

"Oh. Excuse me."

"What about the turkey? The power *is* off, you know,"

"It was just on *done* twenty minutes ago.

The oven heat should finish it. Of course, unless the power comes back again, we're up the creek for gravy."

"Make the gravy tomorrow. If these dear children don't mind, we can sandwich it tonight."

From what Susan had seen yesterday, Bobby could eat a sofa cushion if it had catsup on it.

And so could Cliff.

She shut her eyes briefly, trying to sweep away the memory of last night, of the chandelier shining down on that thick thatch of hair, of his munching thin-sliced ham lathered with horseradish, of Bobby saying suddenly, "This must be what a family is like!"

Tears blurred her eyes again. Turning swiftly so no one could see, she said, "Okay, troops. Bring the candles in the kitchen and we'll see what we can do."

What they could do was certainly different from any other Christmas Eve in Susan's memory—even those back on the farm when everyone had gathered around the kitchen table also—but then it had been in the glow of smoky old kerosene lamps. Grandfather would bring out the one bag of store-bought candy he'd been able to save for, Grandma would pop corn, shaking it in a blackened pan over the stove burner, and Daddy would read

" 'Twas the night before Christmas . . ." to three drowsy little girls in homemade flannel nighties.

How long ago that had been!

Roberta's black, pencil-thickened eyebrows were raised at the sudden silence. In answer Susan said, "The ghosts of Christmas past."

Bobby said nothing. Only Susan knew he'd never had a Christmas. Melissa said, "Three of mine were in Japan. Those were different. Then one on Okinawa. Four in the Philippines. The rest of them stateside. But this was going to be the most lonesome. I am so grateful to be here!"

Unexpectedly, Roberta said, "So am I. You see — I never had a Christmas either. I always had to stay at boarding school. My parents sent me gifts that didn't fit and went to Europe every year. In college my father insisted that I major in math — what I wanted was too — too trivial for the family image. And I could never go home unless I was on the dean's list."

Melissa was staring at her, wide-eyed. "Why — why that was so cruel!" she said. "How could they say they loved you?"

Roberta shrugged. "They didn't," she said. "I was a mistake in the first place because I wasn't a boy. Then my mother couldn't have any more children — and they always felt it was my fault. It does," she added, "do something to you. As a person. But, my dears, I was so lucky, teaching in a school where I did and making such dear friends as Susan." She beamed at Susan, who was feeling roughly the size of a bug, and said, "All right. Now let's slice the nut roll."

And I will eat it if it tastes like driveway gravel, Susan vowed silently, and reached behind her on the counter for the knife.

It almost did, but she wouldn't have said it for the world. Not this night. Bobby and Melissa were bravely washing theirs down with mountainous drafts of milk — and Roberta was eating none at all, saying in a return of her old imperious manner, "I never touch it. Gallbladder problem. It hits me just like dear Elvira's meat loaf used to do. How I dreaded being served that meat loaf!"

Bobby had quietly dropped his second slice of nut roll on the floor and was covertly shoving it beneath the table with his foot.

"What would you have been if — if your father hadn't insisted on mathematics?" Melissa asked Roberta.

Roberta hesitated. "An artist," she answered quickly, and almost reluctantly, adding, "Of course, he was right — I didn't have enough

173

talent and would have made just an ordinary hack. There's enough of them in the world. I assume you have a dishwasher, Susan. I'll rinse if you'll load."

Bobby said, "No, no—we'll do it—'Lissa and I. You two ladies go on into the living room. I'm sure you have a—a lot to talk about."

The condemned woman ate a hearty meal, Susan thought, handing over her bare plate. There were in the world a few more things she'd rather do this evening than go have a heart-to-heart with Roberta Glosson—despite her rather astonishing revelations at dinner. Like forty pushups. Or reading aloud two chapters of *Plutarch* in the orginal Greek.

Or find out about Cliff.

Or where the brooch went.

No—no—perhaps she'd rather not know about the brooch. At least, not yet.

Roberta went to the front window and stood looking through it. She said over her shoulder, "The sanders are finally out on your street."

Susan found her glasses on the piano, where she'd left them last night, put them on, and glanced out. "So they are. Perhaps tomorrow will be better."

After all, it wouldn't have to go too far to

top this one.

Beside her, Roberta said quietly, "Perhaps. Perhaps so will I." As her hostess started in surprise, she went on. "I don't have too many illusions about myself, Sue. But I do try to do a few good things in the world." She sighed. "Isn't Melissa a lovely child?"

Susan answered, "Yes. She is."

Then suddenly something clicked inside her. Things matched. And paired. She *knew* why Roberta was here — and it wasn't because of Cliff or because she thought she'd been invited to a party. Very quietly she said, "You're Lark."

"You know about — Lark?"

"Of course. Melissa is so grateful — and so pleased. Roberta — now that you've met, you *are* going to tell her!"

"No. I don't think so."

"Roberta! Why not?"

"Look at me — a raddled, fat, bossy old woman — hardly a beautiful bird! How can I tell her?"

"Then I will."

"No. I forbid it."

"Well, I would," said Susan, and gave up. She had enough on her emotional plate already. "One thing I wish you would do."

"What's that?"

"Drive her home. She walked here—and she was to be back in her host family's house by ten for prayers. I promised."

"She what?"

Susan repeated herself.

"Why?"

"Oh, they're in one of those church groups who find celebrations worldly."

"That's absurd. I'll have to change that."

"I'm afraid you won't change them."

"But I certainly can find something more accommodating for that poor child!"

That poor child was entering the room, hand in hand with Bobby, faces aglow. Hmmm, thought Susan. A bit of hanky-panky among the soapsuds. Roberta was rummaging in her large bag, perched on the piano bench.

"Pill time," she said, trotting toward the kitchen. "Then I'll drive you home, dear. It's almost ten."

Susan glanced down into the bag. Then with a gesture almost vaudevillian in its fakery, she brushed by and managed to knock it over. Articles spilled. Melissa said, "Oh, my— here, let me help!" and began scooping things back inside.

Then she saw what Susan had seen: a small crystal medallion. On it was etched the bare, soaring lines of a flying bird. Her breath caught. She looked up at Susan and her heart was in her lovely eyes.

Susan nodded, with no repentance whatsoever. And Melissa smiled.

"Thank you," she said softly. "It's been such a good Christmas Evc!"

Susan accepted the kiss on the cheek, glad it had been so for someone.

They said their good-byes, and Susan watched through the window as Bobby carefully helped both women across the icy lawn and into Roberta's car. Then he picked his way slowly back into the house.

A candle had just guttered on the desk. Susan was replacing it with another when she heard his voice behind her:

"Well—I guess it's just you and me, Grandma."

The tone was strange. She was almost afraid to turn and look. But she did.

And she saw two bright tears streaking his broad young cheeks. He was saying huskily, "Would you do me one more favor?"

"What is it?"

"Loan me your car for just an hour? They're saying Mass at St. Mary's and—and I think I have something to go for."

"Of course. Be careful."

"But first—first I have something for you." And he held out a small package.

"But, Bobby—"

"Open it. Please."

She did. And her brooch lay glittering in her hand. With the clasp repaired.

Proudly he said, "Melissa got it fixed. She works at the jewelers, you know."

Now she understood—the exchange of glances, the article in Melissa's hand. Her brooch. Her own eyes brimmed. She said, "Oh, Bobby, thank you. Thank you so much—for more than you'll ever know!"

He had loped off, was retrieving his jacket from its heap on the stairs. Some maternal part of her brain said silently, Bucko, you'll learn to hang it up if you stay here! Aloud, her voice sounded funny: "The keys are on the fridge."

"I know. Oh—oh, golly! I almost forgot!"

Jacket half on, he came back, handed her a bent envelope from one slash pocket. He said, "Dean Willard said be sure and give you this. He says he'll call Monday morning."

Puzzled, she took the envelope, then was suddenly completely distracted by an enormous bear hug that knocked her glasses askew.

"You are the greatest!" said Bobby Simo-

178

tovich. "See you about twelve. And don't worry. I'll say a prayer for Mr. Crane."

How simple life seems to the young, she thought, taking the glasses off and opening the envelope.

As the kitchen door slammed, she was staring incredulously at the short note in her hand.

Dean Willard was asking her to be house mother at the college dorm next term.

House mother! To sixty-five kids in a coed dormitory, where the problems would never end! He must think she was out of her gourd!

She *knew* she was. Because she'd *take* the job. Somehow.

Footsteps on the kitchen floor: Bobby must have forgotten something.

She turned around—and saw Cliff Crane. There was a bandage taped to the right side of his forehead beneath his thick silver hair. His left arm was in a sling. The other he was holding out to her.

A few long, lovely moments later, he said to the flushed lady cradled against his good side, "For a girl of fiftyish, you run pretty good."

"For a guy of sixty, you kiss pretty good. Perhaps," she added impishly, "you've had practice."

"Perhaps," he said. "Or—I've just never had

179

such nice material to work with. Merry Christmas, Susan Gray."

"Merry Christmas, Cliff Crane."

And the damned telephone rang! Why in the world had she thought it a good idea to have the thing repaired!

"Answer!" he said, planting a last swift kiss on the stately nose beneath his chin. He limped off to find his SHIT HAPPENS cup, and she obeyed.

Through a strange, shimmering static, she heard her daughter say, "Merry Christmas, Mom!"

"Diane! Merry Christmas, honey! Where are you?"

"At Grand Cayman. It's lovely here. Mom, I wish *you* were!"

"Maybe. Sometime."

"Are you okay?"

"I'm fine, hon."

"I've been so worried!"

"Then stop it. Just have a good time."

"Bill and I have been talking. Perhaps I can get back home after New Year's — just for a day or two."

"Good. If I'm not here, you know where to find the key."

"Are you working full-time?" Translation: You won't be home when I want you?

She was, after all, human. And just a teeny bit of revenge can be sweet. "I may be. We'll work it out. Listen, doll, this is your nickel. Give the kids my love. Tell them Merry Christmas for Grandma! And enjoy yourselves."

"We will. We are. Goodbye, Mom. See you soon!"

"Bye, honey. Thanks for calling. And don't worry."

She put down the phone. Cliff was leaning against the counter, feet crossed, sipping coffee and smiling at her. He looked battered, tired, dirty—and happy. He said, "That's what I told my boys a little while ago."

"What?"

"That I was fine, have a Merry Christmas, I'd see them soon, and don't worry. Our minds fit as well together as—the rest of us. Come here. I can drink coffee anytime."

She went. Into her soft hair he said, "I promised I'd come back. Christmas Eve. And we'd see where it would go from here. So we shall, love. One step at a time. I don't really know much about you at all. Do you like Cajun cooking? What books do you read? How do you feel about driving a Buick? What's your favorite color, who's on first—"

"What?" she said, glancing upward

in surprise. She met two very amused gray eyes.

He said, "All right. I'm driveling. What I do know, lady, is that with you in my arms I feel like I have the whole tough world by the tail. And I think that's a damned good start."

So did she.

And there were about forty-five minutes left before Bobby came back, in which to prove she did. Time enough. For a start.

After all, she had the rest of her life. Her new life.

A Family for Christmas

by Marian Oaks

Jessie McCormick pushed her way through the crowded mall and eyed the ubiquitous tinsel and glitter with disfavor. It seemed almost indecent that with Thanksgiving leftovers still in the refrigerator, the Christmas decorations were already looking shopworn. Or maybe it was just that for the first time in her life, she dreaded the approach of Christmas.

She paused to study her reflection in a store window. Her months of widowhood had aged her. She looked every one of her fifty-five years. And felt them at least twice over.

She caught her breath and whirled to stare across the mall as another face appeared beside hers in the glass. As always, she was too late. The face had disappeared into the crowd.

Or, more likely, had never been there at all.

She drew a deep breath and tried to fight off the depression that gathered around her like a thick fog. How many times had she seen that face — or thought she'd seen it — over the years? Six? Eight? Maybe a dozen times all told. And always from a distance, a half-seen shadow or reflection that disappeared when she tried to see it more clearly.

It could have been anybody or nobody, a case of mistaken identity or a figment of her imagination. Easy enough to explain. But how to explain that although it was the face she'd remembered these thirty-six years, it wasn't the way she'd remembered it. It had aged with the passage of time, even as hers had.

Resolutely, she put it out of her mind and hurried around the corner to the restaurant, pausing as she always did to admire the graceful, curving letters of the sign that read *Jessie's Place*.

She found her son Michael in the office, working on the payroll, and watched him for a minute, looking for similarities between his face and the one in the mall.

He turned to greet her, his quick smile, as always, warming her heart and her day. The smile gave way to a look of concern. "Are you feeling all right, Mom? You look tired."

She set her purse down and dropped into a chair beside the desk. "I'm okay. I just realized how close Christmas is, and I'm having a little trouble coping with it. I keep forgetting that Pat won't be here, and that's bad enough, but then I remember, and that's worse. And as for planning the Christmas Eve party this year—" She broke off abruptly, before the tears gathering in her eyes could spill over into her voice.

The Christmas Eve party was a tradition started by Pat years before, when the restaurant was still Pat's Place, and more bar than restaurant. Pat had lost his wife and only child in an automobile accident, so he eased his loneliness at Christmastime by making a family of his employees.

The bar was always decorated for Christmas, with a big tree and other trappings. On Christmas Eve Pat gave his employees a party—not the usual "office party," but a family affair, with spouses, children, dependent parents, visiting cousins, everyone welcome. Pat himself cooked and served a holiday meal, gave each child an individually selected present, and when business was good, had gifts for the adults as well.

After Pat's Place was replaced by Jessie's Place, the tradition continued, with Jessie, and later Michael, taking part.

Michael studied her soberly. "Surely you aren't planning to have the party as usual? I'm sure everyone would understand if we skipped it this year."

"They might understand, but they'd be disappointed. And so would I."

"It won't be the same," he warned her. "Not without Santa."

"I know. I know, but . . . I thought perhaps you could . . . you could watch the reindeer this year." It was Pat's whimsical way of explaining why he always left the party just before Santa arrived. He had to go and watch the reindeer.

Michael stared across the room for a few minutes, then said quietly, "I don't know if I could do that." He glanced away from her, but not before she saw the pain in his eyes and knew he was remembering last year's party.

A bout with the flu had left Pat weak and tired. Jessie and Michael made all the party preparations and limited Pat to "watching the reindeer." It was his final appearance as Santa. A few minutes after they said goodbye to the last guest and started cleaning up, he collapsed, clutching at his chest and whispering Jessie's name. He died at the hospital scant minutes before the night turned into Christmas morning—still dressed as Santa.

Jessie had spent the past eleven months thinking how ironic it was that Pat, who loved Christmas more than anyone else she'd ever known, should have died on Christmas Eve.

Michael turned back to face her again. "I don't know if I could do that," he repeated.

Sounds filtering into the office from the kitchen and dining room told her that preparations were underway for lunch, and she'd be needed soon. She stood up and studied Michael for a moment. "We don't have to decide right now," she told him.

She slipped out of the office, leaving him alone with his memories of the man who had been the only father he'd ever known.

For the rest of the day the face in the mall kept drifting between her and whatever she had to do, bringing thoughts of Christmas vividly into her mind. Not the Christmas that was about to happen, or the one last year, or even the wonderful ones they had shared for almost four decades. She remembered instead the Christmas before Michael was born.

She hadn't even known Pat then. The man in her life had been Tom Elrod. Man? Boy. As alone in the world as she was, and not much older.

They'd been so happy, so thrilled by the miracle of finding each other, so sure of their future together. They had it all planned out. As soon as he got the raise he expected, they'd get married. She'd keep her job until they saved enough to have a baby, then she'd be the full-time wife and mother neither of them had ever had.

But fate, or their own foolishness, had turned things around. She got pregnant first, then lost her job — and then lost Tom, who, it turned out, wasn't ready for the responsibilities of fatherhood.

She'd broken the news to him on Christmas Eve, naively thinking it was the most precious gift she could give him. He hadn't agreed, and when she swore she would have the baby, whether he wanted it or not, he'd told her to go ahead, but she'd have to do it by herself. And he'd left.

She'd spent the next week afraid to leave the apartment, afraid he'd come back and she wouldn't be there. And when the landlord came to collect the rent, she couldn't pay it, and she'd had to leave the apartment for good.

She'd never seen Tom again, never knew if

he came back, if he looked for her, if he was even still alive.

It no longer mattered. She'd long since gotten over her anger, long since forgiven him. Maturity had given her understanding. They'd been so very young, both alone in a hard world, clinging to each other for comfort and security.

And she'd been happy over the years. She'd found Pat, who'd given her a job, a roof over her head, a name for her baby, and finally, a warm and wonderful love. It hadn't mattered to either of them that he was more than twenty years older than she was. They'd loved each other, and he'd cared for Michael as he would have his own son, until last Christmas Eve, when his seventy-six-year-old heart had failed him.

Now all she had left was the son she adored, and an occasional imagined glimpse of an oddly familiar face, a face that came when she least expected it, and always disappeared before she could see it clearly.

She found the day alternately creeping by one slow second at a time, or leaping past in great chunks that were gone before she realized it. Lunchtime faded into the dinner rush, which in turn gave way to a few late diners and the regulars who gathered in the bar for

189

an after-dinner drink and good conversation.

"Mom?" Michael's voice brought her out of her fog. "Do you think you can manage for the rest of the evening? I thought I'd take Andrea to a late movie, but if you need me here, it's no big deal. I can cancel."

"Don't you dare. At the moment Andrea seems to be my only hope of ever becoming a grandmother. Don't keep her waiting. Give her my love. Ask her if she'll be my daughter-in-law, the mother of my grandchildren. Go!"

He laughed, bent to kiss her on the cheek, and disappeared through the door.

Harry, the bartender, grinned at her. "The hours he works here at the restaurant don't leave him much time for a normal social life, do they?"

"No. I worry sometimes that that's why he isn't married and producing the grandchildren Pat and I always wanted."

"I think you're worrying over nothing. He probably hasn't caught a wife yet because he's been so busy dodging the ones trying to catch *him*. But it is kind of a shame. Pat would have loved grandchildren."

Jessie felt her eyes grow misty again, and turned away quickly, before Harry could see.

The rest of the evening dragged on as if it would never end, but eventually, the last customers left. She was about to lock the door behind them and help the staff with the closing-up routine, when someone stepped out of the shadows and reached for the door handle.

"Wait. Don't lock it yet."

She was startled, but not alarmed. "I'm sorry," she told him. "We're closed."

He took another step into the light spilling through the glass door so that she could see him clearly. Her heart seemed to slow and stop as she recognized the face from the mall, the face she had been seeing over the years.

"Please, Jessie. Don't turn me away. I need to talk to you." His voice was deeper, more resonant than she remembered it.

She tried to speak, but all that came out was a nearly inaudible croak. She cleared her throat and tried again. "Tom?"

"Will you let me in, Jessie?" He spoke quietly, as if he didn't want to startle her further.

She pushed the door open and stepped back as he entered. They studied each other silently for a minute, then she drew a deep, unsteady breath. "We can talk in the office," she told him.

In the office—not her own cluttered little cubbyhole, but what Michael called the VIP office—she rejected the intimacy of the comfortable sofa and chairs that turned one end of the office into almost a living room, sat instead at the desk and offered him the other chair. Was it really only this morning that she had sat in it? It seemed like a lifetime ago.

She studied him, not a figment of her imagination, but real; not the nineteen-year-old boy she remembered, but a grown man with the passage of time as evident in his face as it was in hers.

There were so many things she probably should ask him, but the only one she could think of was "How did you find me after all these years?"

His voice was gentle. "Jessie, I found you thirty-six years ago, when Michael was born."

"I don't understand."

"I read the birth announcements in the paper every day for months. At that, I almost missed you. I was looking for Jessie Martin. It took me a little while to realize that someone with better sense might have married you, or that the Jessie McCormick in the paper might be you." His lips turned up in a faint smile. "It took me another good while to realize that if you hadn't married someone, there might not have been any announcement for me to find. It's common enough today, but back then unwed mothers didn't usually advertise it."

He leaned back in the chair, seemingly at ease, but his hands gripped the arms hard enough to squeeze the foam padding out of shape, and she realized he was as tense as she.

"Why are you here, Tom? What do you want?"

He lifted one hand and rubbed the back of his neck, a gesture she remembered meant he was puzzled or thinking deeply. "I'm not sure," he said slowly. "Maybe to see if you need anything, or if I can help you in any way. Or maybe I just need to know if you can ever forgive me for the way I behaved that night."

Some of the tension went out of her. "Oh, Tom, I forgave you years ago. It was my fault too. I hit you with something you weren't expecting and then lost my temper when you didn't know how to handle it. No wonder you panicked and ran off."

He leaned forward suddenly. "Jessie, I *didn't* run off. At least, I didn't mean to. I'd lost my temper and was saying things I didn't mean, but I meant to stay away only a little while, to give us both time to cool down. But I was upset and I was angry, and I was a damned fool. I ended up in a bar. By the time I'd gotten my fill of drinking and sobered up, and got up enough courage to come back home, it was more than a week later.

"But I *did* come back. Only . . . by then, *you'd* gone."

The guilt and pain in his voice brought back her own hurt and despair. "I didn't leave the apartment for a week," she told him. "I was afraid if I did, you'd come back and I'd miss you. But the landlord had friends who needed a place. The minute the rent came due, and I couldn't pay it, he put me out."

She shivered, remembering how frightened and desperate she'd been. "But I made him promise that if you came back, he'd find out how I could get in touch with you." She blinked back tears. "I called him every day for weeks, but he never told me you'd been there."

Tom shook his head. "I never saw *him,* only the people who were living there, where you should have been, and they didn't know where you were, or even who you were. I looked for you for months — asked all our friends if they'd seen you, checked all the places we used to go together. Finally, it occurred to me to check the birth announcements in the paper."

He leaned back in the chair again, and his voice was thick with unmistakable regret as he added, "But I was a day late and a dollar short again. You'd already married Pat Mc-Cormick. I watched you for a while, from a distance, and you seemed happy. I didn't think I had the right to spoil something else for you. Besides, I knew he could do so much more for you and the baby than I ever could."

Her thoughts went back to the early days of her marriage to Pat. "Yes," she agreed. "We were happy." Her voice softened. "Pat was alone in the world, too, and so lonely. He needed somebody to look after, somebody to love. And I needed a father for my baby. But we fell truly in love, and Pat was a better father to Michael than—"

"Than I could ever have been?" Tom interrupted.

Jessie shook her head. "No, I was going to say, 'a better father than most real fathers.'"

"Sorry," Tom said. He sighed. "I guess I'm hypersensitive on the subject. You'll never know how hard it's been for me, watching my son grow up, calling another man father."

"Watching?"

He nodded. "Oh, I don't mean I was always here, but I looked in on you often enough to make sure you were all right, that you never needed anything. I tried never to let you see me, but I thought . . . once or twice . . . You'd turn suddenly, and stare in my direction, and I'd wonder what you were thinking, or feeling."

"I thought you were a figment of my imagination," she said honestly. "Or a trick of my memory. Only . . . your face didn't stay the way I remembered it. It grew older, just as mine did. Now I understand why."

Someone knocked on the office door and Harry called out, "We're through closing up. Are you ready to go yet?"

She glanced at Tom, then told Harry, "Go on home, Harry. An old friend dropped by to see me, and we're not through talking yet. He'll make sure I get to my car safely. I'll see you tomorrow."

"All right, then. Good night."

Jessie waited until she was sure he was out of earshot, then turned back to Tom. "But you still haven't answered my question. Why are you here? Not just here, but here, now, after all the years when I never knew if you were alive or dead?"

He grinned unexpectedly, showing a flash of the young Tom she remembered. "I guess that does take some explaining, doesn't it? Well, to begin with, my wife died a couple of years ago." At her involuntary exclamation of surprise, he nodded. "Yes, I married someone else, too, and heaven only knows what a psychiatrist would make of it, but I married a widow with two daughters and helped her raise them."

"Oh, Tom. I'm glad. I always thought you'd make a great father—if it wasn't forced on you against your will." She hesitated, then added, "Were you . . . were you happy with her?"

"Yes." His voice was soft with emotion. "Yes, I was. But I never forgot you, or that I had a child of my own, even if he didn't know it. And when I found out, not long ago, that your Pat had died, too, I thought . . . I thought, if you're as lonely as I am, maybe we could . . . see each other occasionally, just friends, you know? And maybe I could get to know Michael a little. Jessie, does he know? That Pat wasn't his real father, I mean?"

"Yes. When he was old enough to wonder why his father was so much older than the other boys' fathers, we told him the truth."

"How did he take it?"

"Pretty well, I think, although I can't be sure. He's never talked much about it. But maybe that's why he and Pat were always much closer than most fathers and sons. There was a special bond between them."

"He probably hates my guts. Are you going to tell him I was here tonight?"

The question startled her. "I . . . I don't know. He's still having trouble dealing with Pat's death. I'm not sure how he would react if I told him. And I'm not sure there's any reason to."

"Jessie, I know I haven't the right, but . . . I'd like to get to know him. And I'd like to get to know you again, too. Michael doesn't have to know who I am if you'd prefer it that way. You can let him think I'm just an old friend, or someone you met recently — just a casual acquaintance. But please, let me see the two of you. Let's try to be friends again, get to know each other again."

She suddenly wanted very much to know more about this quiet, mature man her young sweetheart had grown into. "I'd like that, too," she told him.

He walked with her to her car and they said good-night. As she pulled out of the parking lot and headed for home, she could see him in the rearview mirror, still standing where she had left him, watching her drive away. It gave her a strange feeling.

At home she undressed and crawled into bed, then lay awake for hours, puzzling over the twists and turns her life had taken. It hurt to know that she and Tom had lost each other for such senseless, unimportant reasons, that they had failed to find each other again by such a tiny span of time.

But if they hadn't, she would never have

met Pat, never have shared thirty-six years of happiness with him.

And that, she understood as she finally drifted into a troubled sleep, would have been a far greater loss.

Jessie made her usual last-minute check of the ladies' lounge before the restaurant opened and paused to study herself in the mirror, assessing the damage her restless night had done. She looked tired, but no more than she had any other morning since Pat's death. Michael probably wouldn't even comment on it.

But he did, and added, "Harry said you had a visitor last night. What did you do? Sit up all night, talking?"

"Well, we did talk a lot. We . . . we hadn't seen each other in years."

He grinned. "You manage to do a lot of talking even when it's someone you've seen the day before. Who was it?"

"No one you know. Just an old friend." She hesitated, then told him, "If you can spare me tomorrow evening, I'd like to take the night off. We still have some catching up to do."

"No problem. You need to take more time off, get out of the place more often. But I'm curious. I wasn't aware that you and Pat had any old friends I don't know."

She smiled faintly. "You'd be surprised." And then, to forestall any questions she might not know how to answer, she added, "It's someone I knew before you were born. Before I met Pat."

"Ah-ha! It must be an old school chum."

She knew she should tell him the truth, but the truth was still so new and unsettling that she wasn't ready to share it yet. She drew a deep breath and changed the subject. "Michael, I've done some more thinking about the Christmas Eve party, and I've decided to go ahead with it as usual. Giving it up would be like . . . like giving up a part of Pat."

"I've been thinking about it, too," he admitted. "You're right, as always." He put his arm around her shoulders and hugged her gently. "I'll help with the cooking and decorating, and buying the presents, the way I always do, and if I can bring myself to take his place as Santa, I will."

"I hope you'll be able to do it, but if you can't, we'll think of a good excuse and just pass the presents out ourselves. The adults will understand, and the children will be too excited to care."

"The problem is," he said slowly, "I don't know if Pat would understand." He grinned suddenly, "I don't know if you ever noticed,

200

but it wasn't always easy, being Pat's son. He set standards that were pretty hard to live up to sometimes. But I'll do my best."

She blinked back the moisture that filled her eyes. "That's all he ever asked. That we do our best. Now, we'd better get to work. I hear customers coming in."

As Jessie hurried to the dining room to cope with the lunch crowd, she remembered how many times she had wished that Michael had truly been Pat's son. How silly she'd been! In every way that mattered, he was.

Later, in the lull between lunch and dinner, she admitted to herself that she hadn't done her best. She hadn't told Michael the truth about her visitor the night before. She wasn't sure why, except that telling him might have given Tom's presence and her agreement to see him that night an importance they didn't deserve. She was only going to satisfy her curiosity, after all, and then Tom could go back to wherever it was he'd sprung from so unexpectedly, and Michael would never need to know that his father—his *biological* father, she amended hastily—was alive and well, and watching over them.

Maybe she was making a mistake, but she couldn't see any reason to upset Michael needlessly.

At any rate, it was too late to call him back and tell him now.

Jessie found Michael in the bar with Harry and told him, "I'm leaving now, Michael."

"Well, where's this old friend of yours? Aren't you going to introduce us?"

Not until she had to, she thought, aware that the longer she waited, the harder it would be. "I asked him to pick me up at home," she said finally. "I wanted a chance to spruce up a little."

"You look fine the way you are," he assured her.

He was right. She'd come a long way from the maternity slacks and smock she'd worn her first few months at Pat's Place. As co-owner and hostess of Jessie's Place, she was accustomed to dressing well, and had standing appointments with her hairdresser and manicurist, but . . .

Harry grinned. "Don't bug her, Michael. She wants to dress up in something special. After all, this is her first date in—how long, Jessie?"

"Almost forty years," she said. "But it isn't really a date."

"Pretend it is," Harry advised, "and before

the evening is over, maybe it will be."

"And you pretend you're still going to have your job tomorrow, and if you don't make any more wisecracks, maybe you will."

She slipped away before he could answer her, but the warm laughter of both men followed her as she left.

At home she showered, dressed, and applied fresh makeup quickly but with painstaking care. Silly, she thought. She was behaving as if this really were a date instead of just dinner with an old friend. And not even an old friend, really, but just someone she'd once known, and hadn't seen in years. Never mind that she'd loved him, planned to spend her life with him, created a child with him. The feelings she had had for him then were a girl's feelings, and she had long since become a woman—a woman who had enjoyed a full and happy marriage to someone else.

If it weren't for the bond of Michael between them, she would feel only mild anticipation about the evening instead of fretting over how she dressed, and what would happen, and how she felt.

How she *should* feel, she told herself firmly, was that she was having dinner with someone she'd known a long time ago, who might have meant something to her then but in whom she could have only the most casual interest now. And that was most certainly how Tom felt.

She paused with her lipstick halfway on and stared at herself in the mirror. Was it? Then why had he kept watch over her all these years, and why had he revealed himself now that Pat was gone?

She hastily finished applying her lipstick and pushed the questions to the back of her mind as the doorbell rang. They popped right back to the front when she opened the door and saw the look on Tom's face. He'd looked at her that same way the first time they'd met.

He took both her hands in his and leaned forward to kiss her cheek. "You were a pretty girl, Jessie. You've turned into a beautiful woman."

It occurred to her that she was probably gawking at him, too. She tried to hide her discomfort with a warm smile and a quick "Thank you."

He offered her his arm, and as they walked down the porch steps he told her, "It hadn't occurred to me until just now that dinner at even the most elegant restaurant probably wouldn't be much of a treat for you. If you'd rather do something else . . ."

The question was harmless, impersonal,

and her voice was fine as she told him, "Don't be silly. I always welcome a chance to check out the competition."

He laughed, not the quick, brash display of amusement she remembered, but a richer, more sophisticated sound.

They chatted amiably as they drove, about things of no special importance—the weather, the approaching holidays, the impersonal things that two people who barely knew each other would talk about.

He waited until they were halfway through dinner in what was certainly one of the city's most elegant restaurants to ask her soberly, "Jessie, where did you go when you had to leave the apartment? You didn't have much money. What did you do?"

Her throat closed up and she couldn't answer right away. How could she possibly sum up those hours of grief and terror with nothing but words? Finally, she said, "Do you remember that diner at the end of the block? I went there, with everything I owned packed in that old cardboard suitcase. I must have looked like death warmed over. The waitress let me sit for hours in a booth toward the back. She even brought me a bowl of chili and a glass of milk—on the house. She said it was left over from the day before, and if I didn't eat it, they'd only throw it out. I didn't argue."

He had grown pale as she talked, and she realized the words weren't important after all, except to evoke Tom's memory of his own grief and terror. She tried to sound comforting as she continued.

"I found a two-day-old newspaper someone had left and read the help-wanted ads. I lucked out. Pat's barmaid had just quit, and he was looking for a replacement. In those days it was Pat's Place, instead of Jessie's Place and it was a bar, not a restaurant. I had just enough change in my purse for bus fare and, probably because no one else was reading help-wanted ads over the holidays, I got there first. Pat didn't really think I'd make a good barmaid, but I persuaded him to give me a try." She grinned. "It turned out I made a terrific barmaid, and the customers thought so, too." This was the part she didn't mind talking about, the happy, upbeat, new-beginning part.

"Good God, Jessie! You weren't old enough to *be* in a bar, much less work in one."

She laughed at the shock in his voice. "Well, I fibbed a bit about my age. I think Pat probably guessed I was only eighteen, but he didn't know for sure until we applied for a marriage license and I was afraid it wouldn't be legal unless I gave my real age." She glanced down at her plate, waiting for the memories to recede so she could speak normally again. "We were married a few weeks before Michael was born, so Pat would be Michael's legal father."

"He was quite a bit older than you, wasn't he?"

She nodded. "And he was very much aware of it." She looked up at him again, wanting him to understand. "Tom, he treated me like a princess, took care of me, loved me and my child . . . and gave me my own bedroom. Finally, when Michael was about three months old, I told him I didn't want to spend the rest of my life married in name only, and either we made it a real, one-bedroom marriage, or I was going to leave." She felt warmth and contentment, remembering. "I was bluffing, of course. By that time I was so head over heels in love with him, I think I'd have died if he hadn't felt the same way about me."

"Then you really were happy with him?"

"I really was. And when he died last year, I wanted to die with him."

He reached across the table and laid his hand over hers. "Thank God you didn't."

They were quiet while the waiter brought

their dessert. Jessie found herself comparing the man across the table from her with the boy she remembered, and she liked what she saw. Much of the old Tom was still there—a gesture, an expression, the quick boyish grin.

Back then he'd been what today's woman would call "a hunk." Allowing for the years, he still was. His hair had silver at the temples and he'd gained weight, not too much, just enough so that the rangy teenage body was now solid and mature—and even more appealing.

She pushed that thought away as quickly as it had come, and asked, "What about you, Tom? Where did you go that night? What did you do? And what's happened to you in the years since then?"

He was silent so long, she had begun to think he wasn't going to answer. When he spoke, his voice was sober and filled with pain. "Jessie, I don't want to sound as if I'm making excuses for myself, but I want you to know I loved you with all my heart. I wanted to spend the rest of my life loving you and making you happy. But I bungled it."

He pushed his uneaten dessert away and signaled the waiter for more coffee, then left it untouched in front of him as he told her slowly, "I knew you wanted to get married, and that no matter how much you loved me, you felt we were—how did they used to say it?—living in sin. And I wanted to marry you. In fact, I was planning to propose to you that Christmas Eve, as soon as I got home from work."

His shoulders sagged and he looked suddenly decades older than his fifty-six years. "I figured there'd be a Christmas bonus in my pay envelope, and maybe the raise we'd been expecting. Either way, I thought we could get married, and get out of that crummy little apartment, and all our hopes and plans, all our wonderful dreams, would start coming true."

His voice had dropped to a murmur she could hardly hear. "Only there wasn't any bonus or raise in my pay envelope. Only a notice that because of a cutback in production, some people had to be laid off, and I was one of them. That's what I had to come home and tell you. And that's when *I* wanted to die."

She drew in a quick, ragged breath. "And then I made it worse by announcing that I was pregnant. Oh, Tom! If I had only known! If I could only take back all those awful things I said to you."

"I said some pretty awful things, too, as I recall. I accused you of getting pregnant to
209

force me into marrying you. And, God help me, I told you if you really wanted to have the baby, you'd have to do it without me." He let his breath out in a long, slow sigh. "Of all the stupid things I said that night, that's the one that's haunted me the most all these years. I didn't lose just you that night. I lost—threw away—my child, my future, everything I cared about.

"I looked for you, but by the time I found you, you belonged to Pat McCormick. I knew that if I interfered, I'd only hurt you again. But I kept watch over you. If he'd ever done anything to hurt you, if he'd ever stopped deserving you . . ."

There was no doubting the sincerity in his voice. Or the pain and grief. She realized suddenly how much harder the years had been on him than on her. She could only imagine the guilt he had lived with.

She touched his hand gently. "Tom, it's over. We can't change it now, and it's useless to blame ourselves. We were the victims of circumstance, or perhaps fate simply had other plans for us. Either way, all we can do now is go on with our lives and be as happy as possible."

He caught her hand in his and kissed it. "You're right, Jessie, as always." He signaled the waiter for the check. "If you're through, let's leave now. Maybe we can go somewhere else and talk some more. We still have a lot to say."

They paused outside the restaurant, savoring the unseasonable warmth of a Georgia night that was more like early autumn than the beginning of December. Jessie studied Tom again, admiring the maturity, the quiet self-possession, in his face and bearing. They boosted him to a whole new level of attractiveness. The years might have been difficult for him, but he'd used them well.

"Where would you like to go?" he asked.

Jessie said impulsively, "It's such a wonderful night. Let's just walk, and maybe window-shop a little."

Tom looked pleased. "The way we used to do when we didn't have money for gas?"

She nodded. "Or when that beat-up old jalopy of yours wasn't running, which was most of the time."

"Don't criticize old Bertha," he told her. "She was a wonderful car."

Jessie took the arm he offered and they began to walk slowly, not going anywhere in particular, just going together. "The backseat was pretty great, as I recall." The words were out before she could stop them. Tom turned

211

to grin at her, and she knew her face must be as colorful as the Christmas decorations all around them.

"They don't make backseats like they used to," he agreed.

Clearly, it was time to change the subject. "Tom, you seem to know what my life has been like over the years, but I have no idea where you went, or what you did, or whether you were happy."

"Oh, I was happy, Jessie. I really was. It just took a little longer to happen for me than for you. I spent a while wallowing in guilt and self-pity before I rebuilt my life and my self-respect enough to realize I still had a life and the right to live it.

"For several years I kept a close watch on you. I wanted to make sure you were all right." He stopped, so suddenly she took another step or two before she could stop, too, and turn to face him. "No, I have to be honest. Jessie, I spent those years secretly hoping your life with Pat would fall apart and I'd be there to pick up the pieces. That didn't do much to relieve the guilt I was wallowing in." He took a deep breath. "The truth is, I still feel ashamed when I remember it."

The pain in his voice and face made her reach up to touch his cheek. "I told you, Tom, it's over now, and blaming ourselves isn't going to help. "

He smiled at her, the warm, loving smile that had always made her heart skip a beat. "Bless you, Jessie. Lila would have loved you."

They began to walk again, and Jessie asked, "Lila was your wife?"

He nodded. "She was a wonderful person. You'd have liked her, too. She was a lot like the two of us — lonely and all alone in the world, except for the two little girls she was trying to raise after her husband died." He seemed to relax a little, and smiled.

"Actually, it was the girls I met first, when Dorothy was five, and Susan was only three. I was sitting on a park bench, feeling sorry for myself, as usual, when they ran up to me. The little one climbed into my lap and hugged me, while the older one leaned against my arm and buried her face in my sleeve.

"Lila ran up a minute later, out of breath and looking as if she might burst into tears at any minute. I thought I was about to be accused of child molestation, but she only wanted to apologize and tell me my shirt was like one their father had often worn. I almost burst into tears myself."

He paused, and when he continued, his

voice was gruff, with more than a hint of tears in it. "I hugged those little girls, and I thought of you and Michael, and how Pat was being a better father to him than I could ever be." He paused again, and when he continued his voice sounded almost normal. "I bought us all chocolate ice cream cones, and Lila and I talked. And talked. We talked through Big Macs and fries, we talked while we were tucking the girls into bed, and we kept talking until the sun came up. I knew, one way or another, I was going to help raise those two little girls, and earn the right to be hugged by them."

He slowed his steps and came to a stop again. "I could hardly believe it, Jessie. Lila and I, alone, needing each other, and managing to find each other, the way you and I did. It seemed like a miracle. A few weeks later I persuaded her to marry me."

"And you fell in love with her," Jessie said softly. "The way I did with Pat."

"I tried not to at first," he admitted. "It seemed disloyal to you. But she was so sweet and loving and . . . like you in so many ways. And it didn't take me long to understand that I'd not only been given a chance to do for Lila what I should have done for you, I'd been given another chance to be happy.

"And we were, Jessie. But now she's gone, and your Pat is gone, and however much we miss them and grieve for them, you and I . . . you and I are alone again. But maybe we don't have to be. Maybe the old feelings have died away over the years, but there must be something left. No blazing coals, of course, but maybe . . . warm ashes?"

He looked so anxious, and hopeful at the same time, that she could only laugh softly and say, "Warm ashes? Oh, at least that."

His relief was obvious. "Then can we continue to see each other? Just because we're both alone again and need someone to ease the loneliness? I promise, I'm not asking you to pick up where we left off or to try to rekindle what we once had, although I wouldn't turn away from it if it happened. But I'll settle for just being friends. Do you think we could try it?"

She studied his face, reading the loneliness there, feeling it echoed in herself. "Yes, Tom. I think we can try it."

The face that looked back at Jessie from the mirror in the ladies' lounge wasn't the same one that had looked back at her the morning after Tom had come back into her life. This one looked rested and relaxed, and even a little bit happy.

Michael noticed it, too. "You must have had a good time last night."

"Yes, I did."

"What did you do?"

"Not much. We had dinner, talked for a while, then took a walk and looked in store windows. I went home nicely tired — not hard-day-at-work tired, but relaxed tired — and had a good night's sleep."

"Glad to hear it. And you'll be glad to hear I'm making a list and checking it twice." He held up a memo pad. "Here are the names of all the children who'll be coming to the party, along with suggestions for what each one would like."

She took the list and studied it. "These look like pretty reasonable requests. I guess we'd better get on with the shopping before all the good things are gone."

"This Wednesday?"

Wednesday was the day Jessie's Place was closed, the day they ran errands and tended to the personal sides of their lives. But this Wednesday? "I'm sorry," she said before she stopped to think. "I already have plans."

Michael looked surprised, and no wonder. It was the first time in nearly a year when she'd had anything planned but her regular shampoo and manicure. "But I can change them," she added quickly, and knew by his puzzled expression that she sounded as flustered as she felt.

"No, that's all right. We can come in early a couple of times during the week and do it before we open." He hesitated, then asked, "Are you seeing this mysterious old friend of yours again?"

Now was the time to tell him, she thought, but all she could say was, "Well, yes. I am."

"But don't you think . . ." He didn't meet her eyes, and she realized he was ill at ease about something. "Don't you think it's sort of soon after Pat's death? To be getting involved with someone else, I mean."

"Oh, Michael! You make it sound like some sort of . . . I don't know what. He's just an old friend, and we haven't seen each other in many years."

"Sorry. I didn't mean that, exactly. I just meant . . . well, don't you think it's strange that this old friend of yours didn't show up until now?"

"What do you mean, until now?"

"I mean, since Pat died."

"But that's exactly why he showed up now. Michael, his wife died recently, and when he found out about Pat's death, he thought maybe it would help us both to get together after all these years, and just talk to each other. And it has."

"Maybe you're right," he admitted grudgingly. "But be careful."

"Of what, for heaven's sake?"

He looked embarrassed, but said, "Oh, come on, Mom. You know. Don't you remember all those customers who were hitting on you after Pat died, thinking they had a chance at an attractive woman and a thriving business besides?"

Some of her guilt at not telling Michael who Tom was vanished under a wave of amusement. "Don't be silly, Michael. I'm not a complete twit. I've known this man for years. He's not out to take advantage of me—businesswise, or otherwise."

"Well, if you're sure," Michael agreed reluctantly, and added, "But be careful anyway." He went to supervise the preparations for the salad bar while she dealt with the fact that once again she'd failed to be honest with him.

And with herself. If all that was left between herself and Tom was "warm ashes" and the desire to comfort each other, why was she suddenly feeling happier, freer, more vital and alive than she had since she'd lost Pat?

* * *

Jessie hurried through her Wednesday errands and chores, added a facial to her shampoo and manicure, and indulged in a rare spree of grocery shopping. Except for breakfast, she seldom cooked at home. It wasn't worth it for one person, one day a week, but she liked to cook, and tonight she was cooking for Tom.

She'd dithered all week over the menu, and finally discarded the idea of anything fancy or gourmet in favor of the kind of plain, stick-to-the-ribs, workingman's food Tom had always liked. By the time he rang the doorbell, she had a simple tossed salad in the refrigerator, pot roast with vegetables simmering in a rich, thick gravy on the back of the stove, and fluffy, homemade biscuits ready to slip into the oven as soon as the apple pie came out.

She knew she'd made the right choice when she opened the door for Tom. He sniffed deeply and exhaled in a long, slow "aaaah" of pleasure. "I guessed right about the wine," he said. "Red." He handed her the bottle, label up, and she saw with pleasure that it wasn't the expensive wine she might have expected, but a cheaper one that had been all they could afford years earlier.

"Just right," she said softly. "Come in, Tom."

He stepped inside and glanced around the living room with unconcealed interest. "This place looks so friendly and comfortable from the outside. I've always wondered what the inside was like."

"You watched me here, too?" He'd invaded her privacy, she thought. She should feel angry, outraged. She didn't. She felt warm, and safe, and somehow less alone.

He nodded. "And sometimes I stood across the street from Michael's school and watched the children at recess. I never spoke to him, of course, or even let him see me. I didn't have the right, and it wouldn't have been fair to you, or to him."

On impulse she asked, "Would you like to see his room?"

"His room? I thought . . ."

"Oh, of course, he's had his own place for years. He offered to move back in when Pat died, but I persuaded him not to. But the room he had as a boy is pretty much the way he left it. Well, maybe a little neater."

"Then I'd like to see it."

She showed him to the room that had been Michael's and watched for a moment as he glanced around it, trying to soak up the character and personality of the son he'd never met, then left him alone and went to the kitchen to finish dinner.

A few minutes later he joined her in the kitchen, where she was setting the table. He watched as she took the pie out of the oven and slid the biscuits in. "You haven't told him yet, have you? Who I am, I mean."

She shook her head. "No. I just told him you were an old friend."

"That's not like you, Jessie. You were always so forthright and direct."

She took two wineglasses from a cupboard and held them out for his inspection. "Will these do? I don't seem to have any paper cups."

His quick grin told her he remembered, too. "They'll do fine. Jessie, why haven't you told him?"

She set the glasses on the table and stared down at them. "At first I thought that you and I would only talk, and you'd go away again, and I wouldn't have to upset him. Then, when I agreed to see you again, I couldn't tell him without admitting I had kept it from him before. And I knew he'd wonder why, and . . . and I didn't really know why myself."

"You're going to have to tell him sometime,

Jessie. Beyond the fact that I want to know him, he has a right to know about me. About us."

"Tom, you're going too fast. There really isn't any 'us.' "

"Maybe not yet, but . . ."

She glanced up at him, startled by the husky, intimate tone of his voice. She hadn't noticed how close he was standing, or realized how inevitable it would be for him to take her into his arms and kiss her, gently at first, and then with a hunger that roused an answer in her. The years slipped away, and she was eighteen years old again, in the arms of the nineteen-year-old boy who was the most important person in her lonely world.

Without warning the years rolled forward again, and the loneliness that had been with her day and night since Pat's death began to ease a little. Then Tom's warmth, the feel of his body against hers, the taste of his lips on hers, began to have an impact of their own. A quick rush of desire swept over her, and whether it was a memory from the past, or newly-kindled in the present, she didn't know.

They continued to stand together, their arms around each other while they soaked up the joy of being close, and warm, and together.

Then the hot smell of biscuits browning in the oven brought Jessie out of her fog. She pulled away from Tom and grabbed a pot holder.

He let her go with obvious reluctance, but obediently opened and poured the wine when she told him to, then sat opposite her at the table and let her make small talk as if the kiss had never happened.

But it had. Her whole system reverberated with it, and her assurance to Michael that she was merely seeing an old friend might have seemed laughable now if she could have laughed. It wasn't, she assured herself sternly, that there was anything left of what she and Tom had shared before. Warm ashes, he'd said, and warm ashes was what they had.

And maybe just a tiny spark of memory that remained, like a bit of yeast, to start a whole new ferment if she wasn't careful. And that would never do.

She missed Pat. His absence left her with a vast emptiness inside her that didn't seem to be shrinking noticeably with the passage of time.

That didn't mean she was going to fill it with empty memories or anything that might spring from them. With her mind firmly made up, she smiled warmly at Tom across the table. "More pot roast?" she asked. "Another biscuit?"

When the evening was over and it was time for him to go, she walked to the front door with him but kept her distance. One kiss had been enough. She didn't want to risk her reaction to another.

"Does it really have to be a whole week before I can see you again? Surely, you can take a night off now and again."

"Yes," she admitted, "but I don't like to. Although either Michael or I can handle things with the help of our very excellent staff, we have a lot of regular customers who like to see us there. So we don't take time off very often, except for emergencies or special occasions."

"That must make for a pretty limited social life."

"Well, actually, it *is* my social life."

"Not anymore. Let me pick you up after the restaurant closes at night. We can have a cup or two of coffee, an hour or so of conversation and visiting, and I can still have you home at a reasonable hour."

"I . . . I don't think that's such a good idea, Tom."

His eyes narrowed slightly and his jaw thrust out the tiny bit that told her he was going to argue. "Why not?" It was more of a challenge than a question.

She tried to think of a plausible reason, but he had reminded her that she'd always been forthright and direct. She couldn't be less than that now, and she certainly couldn't duck his challenge.

She looked squarely at him. "We found each other irresistible once. I don't intend to take the chance that it might happen again."

The stern thrust of his jaw softened to a grin. "That kiss got to you, too, huh?" He waved away her beginning protest and caught her hands in his. "Would it be so terrible if it did happen again?"

He leaned forward and she braced herself for another kiss, but he only brushed her cheek with his lips and told her, "Jessie, we've been given a second chance. Let's not blow this one."

He released her hands and opened the door. As he stepped out onto the porch he glanced back, grinned, and said, "Tomorrow evening. After the restaurant is closed. Coffee and conversation, and . . . who knows?"

He was gone before she could gather her wits enough to protest.

Jessie spent the next day alternately wishing

it were evening so she could see Tom again and dreading the inevitable moment when she'd have to introduce him to Michael. It wasn't going to be easy, explaining to Michael that she'd been seeing his natural father for nearly a week and hadn't bothered to mention it to him.

She found it hard to explain to herself and was grateful when Michael decided to take advantage of a slow evening to leave early and do some Christmas shopping.

"I always intend to get it done sooner," he explained, "but I never know what to get. What do you suppose Andrea would like?"

"Never mind what she'd like," Jessie said. "Get her an engagement ring."

He laughed, and she sighed with relief when the door closed behind him.

"When are you going to tell him?" Harry asked.

She exhaled slowly and braced herself against one of the barstools. "Tell him what?"

"That the old friend you've been seeing is his father."

Her quick denial died on her lips. She'd never been able to fool Harry. "How did you know?"

"I got a glimpse of him that first night. He and Michael don't look a whole lot alike, but the resemblance is there. And that's the only reason I can think of that you haven't brought him in for us to meet."

"I wasn't sure how Michael would feel about it. I'm still not."

Harry shook his head. "I think the real reason is you're not sure yet how *you* feel about it."

"I know perfectly well how I feel about it," she snapped.

"Okay, how's that?"

She slipped onto the barstool, and propped her elbows on the bar and her head in her hands. "Confused," she admitted after a minute. "I loved Pat with all my heart; you know I did. But . . ."

"But you loved Michael's father, too, and either some of the old sparks are left, or you're striking new ones, and you aren't sure where your loyalties lie. Is that it?"

"I guess so. Oh, Harry, what shall I do?"

"You're the only one who can decide that, Jessie. All I can tell you is that your loyalty should be to *yourself,* not to Michael, or some misguided sense of what you *should* do. Just remember that you're still very vulnerable, and don't let yourself be stampeded into anything that doesn't feel right to you."

"Maybe you're right. Maybe it's just too

227

soon for me to be seeing anyone, much less someone I have such mixed feelings about."

"Maybe. And maybe later would be too late. Besides, just seeing this guy doesn't commit you to anything, does it?"

"No, it doesn't."

"Then why don't you just relax and see what happens?"

Impulsively she reached across the bar and clasped his hand in hers. "Bless you, Harry. I don't think Pat and I ever had a better friend."

Tom came a little early, as she'd known he would. She introduced him to Harry, who greeted him politely but not effusively, and told her, "Why don't you go on and leave? I'll tend to closing up."

"What shall we do tonight?" Tom asked as they stood outside Jessie's Place, watching the throng of late shoppers that swirled around them.

"Why don't we just stroll through the mall and window-shop? The crowds will be thinning out soon, and there'll be plenty of empty benches where we can sit and talk, if you like."

"Sounds good to me." He offered her his

arm and they began walking. "I take it Michael isn't here."

"No, he left early."

"Then you haven't told him about me yet?"

"No," she admitted.

"Afraid of how he'll react to having me back in your life?"

"That's part of it." She stopped to study a display of dolls in a toy-store window. "The other part is, I need to know how *I* feel about having you back in my life before I have to cope with how Michael feels."

He sighed and they resumed their stroll toward the center of the mall and the brightly-lit Christmas tree that rose through the open area and almost brushed the skylight two stories above. "As much as I want to meet him face-to-face, I think you're probably right." He glanced down at her and grinned. "I want to be sure you're a hundred percent on my side before I take him on too."

They rode the escalator to the lower level and found an empty bench with a good view of the tree. "Isn't it beautiful?" she said. "It was one of the things Pat liked most about being here in the mall—all the Christmas fuss and furor. I always liked the Christmas decorations, but I haven't had much heart for them this year."

"Neither have I," he said, "until now."

She studied his face as he sat relaxed and quiet beside her, and wondered why she hadn't seen, over the years, how much Michael was like his father. She decided finally it was a form of denial, a way to put aside the hurt and pain, and to keep from remembering that Michael wasn't truly Pat's son.

"Tom? How do you think—" She reached back into her memory for the names. "How do you think Dorothy and Susan will feel when—I mean if—they find out about Michael and me?"

"Jessie, they've always known, just as Lila did, that I lost the first woman I ever loved, and that I had a son I'd never met. It wouldn't have been fair not to tell them. And I think it brought us a little closer for them to know that I'd suffered a loss, too. I understood how they could love me and still miss their father."

He reached for her hand and laced his fingers through hers. "And now they understand how I can grieve for Lila and still miss you. When we found out that Pat had died, it was their idea for me to come to you and let you know I was still here, if you . . . if you needed me."

She felt her eyes sting with sudden tears. "I'd like to meet them someday."

He lifted her hand and pressed it against his lips. "You will. I promise."

The hurrying throng began to disappear and the lights grew dim as shopkeepers closed for the night. Jessie and Tom sat together, contented just to be with each other. Jessie knew that Tom was remembering, as she was, how badly they'd needed each other. He had grown up in an orphanage, she in a series of foster homes. They'd believed that finding each other was no lucky accident, but a sign that fate had brought them together.

And now? Not an accident, of course, but . . . fate? Or simply two lonely people faced with making what might be the most important decision of their lives?

Why don't you just relax and see what happens? Harry had said, and how many times had Pat laughed and told her you should always listen to your bartender? She stood up suddenly and tugged at Tom's hand. "Let's walk some more, and talk some more. We still have a lot of catching up to do."

They walked and talked as the mall emptied, reliving the past, sharing what had happened to them since. Jessie found herself admiring this strong, quiet man her childhood sweetheart had become, and wondering how she would have responded to him if he'd been a stranger, someone she'd just met.

She'd have liked him, she decided. And so would Michael. She drew in a deep breath and let it out slowly, wondering whether the past she and Tom shared would bring them together or drive them apart.

When the last customer had gone, and the last shop closed, they sat close together on a marble ledge near the fountain. She made no protest when Tom took her into his arms and kissed her, gently at first, then more urgently as she began to kiss him back.

It was the sound of approaching footsteps that pulled them apart finally, and a man's voice, saying, "I'm sorry. The mall is closed for tonight. I'll have to ask you to leave now. Oh! Sorry, Mrs. McCormick. I didn't recognize you."

Her face grew hot and she knew she must be blushing furiously. She cleared her throat and managed to say, "I'm sorry, James. We didn't realize it was so late."

She and Tom began the endless walk to the exit nearest her car. She fought the urge to run, and maintained a steady, dignified pace until the exit door swung shut behind them. They glanced at each other, then, and burst into laughter.

"Poor James," she said when they were sober again. "Only a couple of weeks ago he complained to me about having to round up and chase out young people who thought a deserted mall was a great place to neck, and now—I can just imagine what he must be thinking."

"So can I," Tom assured her. "He's thinking what a lucky so-and-so I am, and wishing he'd been in my place."

"Tom!" She tried to sound shocked, but spoiled it with a sudden giggle.

He walked her to her car and unlocked the door for her. "It's awfully late. I'll follow you home to make sure you get there safely."

"There's no need for that. I go home later than this sometimes. But maybe we shouldn't meet here again. At least, not until I think it's time to tell Michael about you."

Tom nodded. "As long as there's going to be an 'after this,' I don't care where we are, just so we're together."

"Tom, I didn't mean . . . that is, I'm not making any promises. I just . . ."

"You just talk too much," he said. "But you're right. Tomorrow I'll be waiting for you at home. Until then . . ." He slipped his hands inside her unbuttoned coat and slid his arms around her waist. The coat fell open and when he drew her close to him, she could feel every inch of him pressed against her, from shoulder to knee, with only his suit and the soft fabric of her dress between them. Worse, she couldn't stop the decades-old memories of how wonderful he'd felt against her with nothing at all between them.

She tried to pull away, but her car was too close behind her, and when he eased his knee between her legs and brought it up to press firmly against the juncture of her thighs, and moved it slowly back and forth—only an inch or two, but enough, enough!—she stopped trying to pull away and let herself relax against him. She parted her lips at the urging of his tongue, savoring the well-remembered taste of him, and when he brought his hands up to cup her breasts, she shamelessly wrapped her arms around his neck and pressed herself closer to him.

Again it was the sound of approaching footsteps that separated them. While she fought to keep her knees from buckling under her, he smiled and touched her cheek with one finger. "Another good reason not to meet here. I hate saying good night in a parking lot."

Jessie took a minute in her office to freshen her makeup and comb her hair, and paused to study the face that looked back at her from the small pocket mirror. The past week had made a tremendous change in her. She looked rested and relaxed, with a sparkle in her eye and color in her cheeks. The gray depression that had plagued her all year had lifted, and she woke each morning looking forward to the day ahead. No, she thought. Not the day. The night, when she'd go home to find Tom waiting to spend a marvelous hour or two with her.

It had been awkward at first to see him sitting in Pat's chair at the table as they sipped coffee or ate some goody she'd brought home from the restaurant, or sitting in Pat's rocker by the fireplace, but gradually she'd grown accustomed to it.

Sometimes they talked — about Michael, about Tom's stepdaughters, about the upcoming Christmas party, or the terrible time he'd come and found only an empty burnt-out shell where Pat's Place had been.

Other times they just sat quietly, sharing unspoken memories of what it had been like between them — not just the passionate, uninhibited sex they'd found, together, because by some miracle, they'd both been virgins, but the wonder of having a place to belong, and someone to belong to.

235

But the sex was there, too, implicit in the good-night kiss that was all the physical contact she allowed, all she dared to allow, because as loyal as her heart was to Pat and all that he had meant to her, her lonely, traitorous body wanted Tom.

She folded the mirror and dropped it into her purse, slipped into her coat, and went to find Michael or Harry to walk her to her car.

She found them together, in the alcove off the main room, where the bar was located. She paused before she went into the bar, as she often did, to glance around the room and soak up the aura of Pat that still lingered, would linger forever.

"Oh, Pat," she whispered. "Help me. Tom's already thinking about the future, and I'm still trying to cope with one day at a time. What shall I do?" She listened intently, as if he might help her solve the problem, as he'd solved so many problems for her over the years, but all she heard was Michael's voice as he spoke to Harry.

"Well, you've been one of the best friends we've ever had over the years, and I know that since Pat died she talks to you sometimes. I just thought she might have said something."

Harry was silent for a moment, and she could picture the look of discomfort on his face at being put on the spot by Michael's question. "I'm sorry," he said finally. "You'll have to ask Jessie about that."

Jessie hesitated briefly, then stepped around the corner and into the alcove. "Ask me about what?"

Harry looked up with obvious relief and put down the glass he'd been polishing. "Guess I'd better be on my way. Michael, you can walk your mother to her car tonight." He picked up his coat and disappeared before either of them could even say good-night.

The silence stretched out until it began to be uncomfortable, and Jessie asked Michael gently, as if she didn't already know, "What is it you want to ask me?"

He hesitated, clearly uncomfortable, then cleared his throat. "I'm sure if this were any of my business, you'd already have told me, but . . . you've been so different this past week. Younger. Prettier. More relaxed. If you're feeling better, of course I'm glad, but . . . I have to wonder why. I thought, maybe . . . that old friend of yours . . . Are you still seeing him? Is he the reason for this change in you?"

It was out in the open now, and all she could do was answer him honestly. "Yes. To both questions."

"You said he was just an old friend. You

237

weren't going to get involved." It sounded like an accusation. She hoped he hadn't meant it that way.

"I didn't intend to. It just happened. That is, nothing has really happened yet, but . . ."

"Are you in love with him?" he asked abruptly.

She shook her head. "No. I don't think so. Not yet, anyway."

"Why haven't you let me meet him?"

"I don't know, exactly." It wasn't really a lie. Her motives had been confused, and confusing. "At first it didn't seem necessary. And then I wasn't sure what to say, because . . . because I didn't know how I felt, or how he felt, only that I liked him, and felt less lonely with him, and I was willing to wait and see what would happen. But I didn't want anybody watching me and also wondering what was going to happen, if you know what I mean."

He was silent briefly while he thought about it. "I guess I do, sort of. It would be about like giving you a blow-by-blow account of whether I'm going to propose to Andrea before I even make up my own mind."

She felt a tremendous surge of relief. "Exactly. And I guess I was afraid you'd object."

He glanced away from her and stared across

the room briefly, then looked back at her. "I have to admit, I'm not exactly crazy about the idea of any man but Pat in your life, but the important thing is for you to be happy.

"But I want to meet him anyway." He caught her face between his hands with the long, sensitive fingers that were so much like Tom's and told her, "Don't worry. I'm not going to storm in and ask him what his intentions are. I just want him to know you aren't alone, and that there's somebody looking after you who'll tear him limb from limb if he hurts you in any way."

"Oh, Michael!" She put her arms around him and held him close. "I love you!"

He circled her with his arms and kissed the top of her head. "I love you, too, Mom. Now, when do I get to meet this other man in your life?"

There was nothing to do but bite the bullet and get it over with, but the words still wouldn't come out. All she could say was "Why don't I ask him to come over tomorrow and help us decorate for the party?" and pray she'd think of a way to tell him before then.

Tom finished the last bite of his apple pie and pushed his plate back. "Great pie. My compliments to your chef." He accepted her offer of another cup of coffee, but instead of drinking it set it aside and studied her soberly. "Something's bothering you tonight. Want to tell me what it is?"

She folded her hands on the table in front of her and stared down at them. "Michael wants to meet you."

"You finally told him we were seeing each other?"

She shook her head. "He guessed. It seems I've been looking happier than usual lately, less . . . lonely."

"How did he seem to feel about that?"

"Glad, but concerned, too. He wants me to be happy, but it upsets him that I might be forgetting Pat—as if I ever could! And he's concerned about why I haven't introduced the two of you already."

"Then you still didn't tell him who I am."

She shook her head. "I know I should have, but . . . I guess I was worried about how he'd take it. And I still don't know what to tell him."

"We'll be honest with him, Jessie."

"That's what I mean. What is honest?"

"Honest is that at least part of what we had once never died. It's still there, coming back to life, and there's every chance that we're not

240

only going to have a past together, but a future together, and a future that includes not just us, but Michael, and my daughters, and their children." His eyes sparkled as he grinned at her. "Jessie, I'm a grandfather. Marry me, and you'll be a grandmother."

Grandchildren? It was more than Michael had done for her, but . . . "Don't try to bribe me," she exclaimed. And then, "Marry you? Oh, Tom, it's too soon to talk about marriage."

"Well, I was going to wait until Christmas Eve, but I tried that once, and look what happened. Jessie, it's fate. We found each other once, two people alone who needed each other. Fate tore us apart, but now it's brought us together again, given us a second chance. Let's not blow it this time."

"But we aren't alone this time. There's Michael and your daughters. We have to consider them, too."

"I am considering them. I want them, and us, to be part of a family again, a whole family instead of two half families. But most of all, I want *us* to be together, the way we were once, the way we can be again. Jessie, I need to be part of something as much as Pat did, and I want to be part of something with *you*."

"I can't promise you that, Tom. Not until I

talk to Michael and find out how he's going to react." She stood up and piled their dirty dishes in the sink, rinsed out the empty coffeemaker, and went into the living room to stand in front of the fireplace and stare down at the blazing logs.

He followed her. "And if he doesn't approve, what then? Jessie, my love, this isn't a decision you can let anyone else, not even your son, make for you. You have to go with what *your* heart wants, not his."

"Maybe, but right now I don't think I know what my heart wants."

He had moved closer while she was talking, and she thought he was going to touch her, kiss her, use the growing physical attraction between them to sway her, but all he used was his voice, low and intense as he said, "Yes, you do. You want what I want, for it to be the way it was with us before. Just the two of us against the whole world. And sometimes just the two of us and no world but us. Do you remember how it used to be? I do. I can't forget it. Not ever. I don't see how you can forget it, either."

She looked away, afraid her face would reveal too much of what she was thinking and feeling. He caught her chin in one hand and turned her back to face him. "I was never with another woman after I lost you, Jessie. Not until I met and married Lila. How could I have wanted another woman when I kept remembering you, and how it was with us, not just those wonderful nights together, but everything."

He moved closer still and put his hands on her shoulders so they were as close together as they could be without actually touching. "And during those long, lonely years, I remembered and relived everything that happened between us, every time I touched you, or you touched me, every time we made such wonderful, passionate love.

"I remembered all the way back to our first time. I'd never done it before, and I was scared to death that I'd do it wrong and not please you. Or worse, that I wouldn't be able to do it at all, and you'd know I wasn't really a man but just a scared and clumsy kid. Then you cried out and I knew I'd hurt you, and I almost died. I thought it was something I'd done, and I tried to tell you how sorry I was, and when you told me it was the first time for you, too, I almost died again from sheer joy."

He paused and studied her face, as if he'd never seen it before, or was afraid he'd never see it again. "Sometimes I think back and try to decide which time it was that we conceived Michael. It seems incredible that I can't pick that time out from all the others. How could we have committed such a miracle and not even known we were doing it?"

She came back to her senses abruptly and tried to stop the flood of words by pressing her hand to his lips. He caught the hand and kissed it, and then the words started again as he made love to her with his voice, arousing her as surely as if his hands were stroking and caressing her most intimate and sensitive places.

"I remember all the things that pleased you most, and the way you enjoyed making love in the daytime, or with the lights on."

His words stirred a flood of memories she couldn't stop—of herself, eighteen, passionately in love with Tom, newly awakened to the wonders of sex, joyously aware that Tom found her lush, ripe body beautiful and exciting, and that showing herself to him thrilled and aroused her beyond anything she had ever known before. And she remembered Tom's naked body—young, strong, virile—so eager to love her. She had loved watching him become aroused and ready, knowing it was because of her.

Unable to help herself, she whispered, "I

liked looking at you, and I liked having you look at me."

"I remember more, Jessie." His voice had sunk to a husky, intimate whisper that sent spasms of raw desire through her. "I remember all the places you liked to be touched, and the way you enjoyed touching me. I wonder if you still like to be touched in those places, and how it would feel to have you touch me again."

She tried once more to hush him, but the memories were too strong, her loneliness too great, and her need for him too overwhelming. And then he wasn't using just his voice any longer, but his hands, and his lips, and she couldn't bring herself to stop that, either, or to stop herself from using her own hands and lips.

He undressed her quickly, then himself, never taking his eyes off her naked body, still lush and firm from the years of loving she had shared with Pat. He pulled her down onto the soft rug in front of the fireplace and knelt beside her, quickening her body with his eyes, making her flesh tingle wherever his gaze traveled. She felt her breasts grow heavy with desire, her nipples stand erect and firm, felt the welcome rush of moisture between her thighs as she watched his body respond to her.

But when, as she had done so many times in the past, she spread her legs apart and held her arms up to him, he shook his head and lay beside her instead. "It takes me a little longer now. The spirit is ready, but here—" He caught her hand and guided it down until he could wrap her fingers around him, and added, "This needs a little help."

And while she stroked and caressed him, pleasuring him in the ways he had loved all those years ago, he touched and fondled and delighted all her secret places, until she was shaking with need and he was ready to kneel between her thighs and slide eagerly into her.

This part took him a little longer, too, and she reveled in every glorious minute of feeling him against her, inside her. They moved together in the wild, free rhythm she remembered so well, until he shuddered violently and she cried out in joyous response.

They lay together for a time longer, while their breathing slowed and the frenzy inside them quieted to a gentle pulsing. "Oh, God, Jessie!" he whispered. "It feels so good to be inside you again."

They dozed finally, their naked bodies warmed by the glowing logs in the fireplace, then woke as hungry for each other as before.

It was even better the second time. They

still had the excitement that had brought them together those years ago, the youthful zest and energy, the raw desire, but laid over that was a new maturity, and years of experience. That they'd both gained that experience with someone else only added a touch of spice, a new excitement as they discovered each other again.

But long after Tom had fallen into a satisfied sleep beside her, and the tumult inside her had died away enough for her mind to start working again, Jessie lay awake, wondering if she had just brought disaster on herself for a second time.

Michael had warned her against letting herself get involved so soon after Pat's death. Harry had warned her that she was vulnerable, and not to let herself be stampeded. She'd ignored both of them and listened only to her loneliness and her eager, love-starved body.

Had she made a mistake? Did she really love Tom, the Tom who lay beside her now, or was she remembering the Tom who used to be? Was it the adult Jessie who responded so completely to him, or was it the naive teenage girl she had once been?

Worse, had she betrayed the memory of the man who had married her, raised her son as his own, and given her thirty-six years of love and happiness, for a few minutes of mere physical gratification?

If so, how could she face Michael in the morning? And how could she tell him the man she had been seeing, the man she was so ready to let come back into her life—into their lives—was the father he believed had deserted them so long ago?

Jessie slept, finally, and when she woke again, the fire had burned out and the sun had climbed high enough to spill through the patio doors. Her body felt relaxed and satisfied; her mind was still a jumble of doubts and worries. After a moment she eased away from Tom, still peacefully asleep beside her, collected her discarded clothing, and carried it into the bedroom.

She slipped into a robe and returned to the living room to find that Tom was awake. She glanced away, unable to meet his eyes.

"Jessie? What is it?" He didn't wait for her answer, but came to his feet and laid his hands on her shoulders. "Having regrets about last night? Did I . . . did I disappoint you? Not live up to your expectations?"

"No! Nothing like that." She hesitated, trying to sort out her thoughts enough to put them into words. "Last night was wonderful.

Maybe too wonderful. It always was, and I can't think any more clearly about us now than I could then."

"What do you need to think about?"

"About whether I really care about you, or just . . . wanted you, last night. About whether whatever this is between us is worth betraying Pat's memory for. And about what to say to Michael when we see him today."

"Whoa. Hold it right there." He caught her chin in his hand and tipped her face up. "You aren't betraying Pat's memory any more than I'm betraying Lila's. They loved us and we loved them, and we'll never forget them, but they're gone now, and we're still here."

He paused, then added slowly, "As for whether you care about me or not, that's something only you can decide. But I want you to know that I love you. I loved the girl you were when I first met you, and I love the woman you are today. I think you love me, too, but your fear of being disloyal to Pat and your worries about Michael are keeping you from seeing it."

"Maybe you're right," she agreed after a minute. "But just now I'm too confused to think straight. Let me fix us something to eat while you dress. I have an appointment to have my hair and nails done in about an hour.

Maybe sitting under the drier for a while will help me sort out my feelings and decide what to tell Michael about us."

"We'll tell him the truth, Jessie. That we're two lonely people who were right for each other once, and would have been right for all time if I hadn't been so stupid. If he's half the man I think he is, he'll understand. And even if he can't bring himself to forgive me, surely he wants you to be happy."

While Tom gathered up his clothes and began to dress, she went to the kitchen. As she set the table and started the coffee, she admitted to herself that Tom was right about one thing. It wasn't just the memories of their past love that had drawn her down onto the rug with him. She had fallen in love with him again, with the man he was now. But would Michael understand? Would Pat have understood?

She took bacon and eggs from the refrigerator and turned around just as the back door swung open and Michael stepped inside, a bulky box under his arm.

"Look what I have." He set the box on the counter and pulled it open. "I didn't think Pat's old Santa suit would fit me, so I bought a new one." He seemed to notice for the first time that she wasn't dressed yet. "You're running a little late this morning, aren't you?"

He glanced at the table, set for two, then back up at her, a puzzled frown starting to furrow his forehead. "Do you have a guest?"

The door to the kitchen swung open and Tom came in, still knotting his tie. He stopped short at the sight of Michael, and Jessie thought she heard him whisper, very softly, "Oh-oh."

She tried to speak, to explain, but her tongue had become stiff and unresponsive, and her lips felt as if they were frozen together.

Michael glanced from one to the other a time or two, his bewilderment turning to comprehension and then to disgust. "So this is the old friend you've been seeing. No wonder you're looking more relaxed. For God's sake, Mom, how could you let him take advantage of you this way? Don't you have any respect for Pat's memory at all?"

"Don't speak to her that way," Tom said sharply.

"And who the hell do you think you are," Michael demanded, "coming in here and taking advantage—"

"I'm your father," Tom said. His voice held enough authority to silence Michael briefly. "And I already know that doesn't entitle me to anything from you. You can hold me in all the scorn and contempt you want, but don't speak to your mother that way. She doesn't deserve anything but your love and respect."

Michael's anger gave way to astonishment. *"My father?"* He and Tom stood face-to-face, almost toe to toe, in nearly identical poses, and Jessie wondered how she could ever have failed to know how much like his father Michael was, or how Michael could fail to see it for himself now.

She forced her lips apart, managed to get her tongue in motion. "I tried to tell you, Michael, but . . ."

"Well, you didn't try very damned hard, did you? Mother, how in hell could you do such a thing? After all Pat did for us, for *you,* you can go back to *him?* And *here,* for God's sake, in the home Pat made for us."

"Michael, you don't understand."

"The hell I don't. Pat's dead, and instead of mourning him properly, you're playing around with the man who deserted you when you needed him."

"No!" Tom's voice held an almost desperate vehemence. "I didn't desert her. I came back. I never meant to leave for good."

"That's right," Jessie said. "We were having

a terrible fight. He only left to give us both a little time to calm down."

"When I came back, *she* was gone."

"And by the time he found me, I had married Pat."

"And she was happy," Tom said. "I'd hurt her once. I couldn't do it again. And Pat was doing so much more for you — both of you — than I could ever have done."

"But he kept watch over us, over *both* of us. Michael, he cares about us, and about you. Won't you at least give him a chance? He's your *father*."

He turned away from her. "Pat McCormick was my father. My *only* father. I'm not going to forget that and let someone else take his place, the way you seem so eager to do."

He grabbed the box with the Santa costume in it, jammed it under his arm, and slammed the door behind him on his way out.

Tom caught Jessie's arm as she started after him. "Let him go, Jessie."

"But he's so upset."

"He won't listen to you now. We'll talk to him later, together, when he's had a chance to calm down, and think it over."

"No, Tom." She blinked back the coming tears. "All the thinking in the world isn't going to calm him down or change his mind. Because he's right. It isn't going to work for us this time any more than it did last time."

"Jessie, you can't let Michael—"

"This isn't for Michael, Tom. It's for myself. Michael is all I have. And I'm all he has. We're what's left of Pat's family. If I lose Michael, I'll lose everything I have left of Pat, and I won't risk that, even for you."

"Jessie, you don't mean that. You can't possibly mean it."

The tears spilled over and rolled down her face, but she met his gaze without flinching. "I do mean it, Tom. It hurts, because you're right; I love you. But I loved Pat, too, with all my heart. I'm going to remember him the same way."

"I don't want you to forget him any more than I want to forget Lila, but—" He stepped forward as if to take her in his arms. Then he shook his head and dropped his hands to his side.

"I keep remembering the last time I argued with you, and what happened as a result. I promised myself that I'd never again do anything to hurt you, and I won't. I certainly won't try to come between you and your son—our son—or between you and your memories of Pat. So I'll leave you alone and not try to change your mind, no matter how much I want to.

"But I won't be far away. I'll still be watching you, making sure you're all right and that you don't need anything. And maybe, when a little more time has passed, you'll be able to see that we do still belong together, that we do have a future together."

He leaned forward and kissed her. "Just remember. I'll always be there, watching and waiting." He let himself out the back door, closing it quietly where Michael had slammed it, and her heart ached at the way the spring had left his step and the joy of living that was what she had loved most about him was missing from his face.

Surprised at how old habits held, Jessie kept her regular beautician's appointment, and welcomed the drone of the hair drier as a way to block her mind as well as her ears.

She went to Jessie's Place afterward, not knowing whether Michael was decorating for the party or had called it off. He and Harry had just finished setting up the big tree when she walked in. "Michael, I need to talk to you. Will you excuse us, Harry?"

For a moment he seemed about to refuse, then he nodded and followed her to the office.

Michael took a deep breath and words began to tumble out of him before she had a chance to speak. "You don't have to say anything, Mom. I know I owe you an apology. You've never interfered in my life, and I have no right to interfere in yours. But I have to be honest about my feelings. If it were any other man, I might not like him, but if you loved him, and I knew he'd treat you right, I'd accept him somehow. But *him!* No. When I compare him to the kind of man Pat was . . ."

The pain in his voice was almost as raw as it had been the night Pat died. "He's not worthy of you, Mom. If you want to keep seeing him, I guess that's your right, but I don't want to be a party to it, so please don't expect me to."

She drew in a deep breath and let it out slowly, hoping it would ease the cramped, painful feeling in her chest. "No, Michael. Pat's death diminished our family enough. If you and I go our separate ways, there won't be anything left. I won't let that happen. I've told Tom so."

Michael drew a deep breath and put his arms around her. "Good girl. I can only guess how hard that was for you to do, but for what's it's worth, I think it was the right thing."

She buried her face against his chest. "I

suppose so," she said. She leaned against him a minute longer, while he held her gently and stroked her hair, almost as if she were the child and he the parent.

But she couldn't help wondering bleakly why, if she had done the right thing, she felt so totally and completely miserable.

Jessie got through the next week somehow, painfully aware that her life had once again collapsed around her, and that Christmas would forever after be a time of grief and sorrow for her.

Michael was unusually solicitous, trying to lift her spirits, fretting that she wasn't eating properly, becoming more and more distressed as the circles under her eyes deepened.

They ran over the checklist one more time on Christmas Eve morning, to make sure that everything that needed to be done for the party had been done.

Michael took the Santa costume out of the box and shook it out. "It won't be the same without Pat," he said, "but he'll be with us in spirit."

"I suppose so." Her voice sounded as dull and lifeless as she felt.

"Of course he will. He wouldn't miss it.

You know how he loved his party, and his 'family.' "

His words hit her like a spear thrust through her heart. She clutched her clipboard to her chest and bent over it as the pain spread through her body, and the fog that had clouded her mind all week vanished suddenly. She straightened up and sucked the air back into her lungs. "No, he won't be. We drove him away."

"What are you talking about? Drove who away?"

"Pat. When we drove Tom away. Michael, *think*. What was it that Pat always cared most about? To be remembered through grief and loneliness? No! The most important thing to him was us, his family. He cared more about our welfare and happiness than anything else in the world. We could never betray Pat's memory by loving again, only by closing ourselves off from the love and life he cared so much about."

Her eyes filled with tears. She let them spill over and roll down her cheeks. "Oh, Michael, we had a chance to be happy again, to be a whole family again, and we blew it."

He stared at her, his face expressionless, and she added fervently, "I loved Pat, you know I did. If Tom had come looking for me while Pat was alive, I wouldn't even have seen him. But Pat's gone now, and we need to know that we're alive, and it's all right to be alive. It's all right to get on with our lives, and be happy again. Not doing so is the real betrayal of Pat, and everything he loved best."

She put the clipboard down and laid her hand on Michael's arm. "Maybe you won't understand this now, but I hope you will later, when your grief at losing Pat has had time to heal. *I* need healing, too, and I'll find it faster if I don't shut myself off from all that Pat loved and would have wanted for me—for us." She brushed the tears from her face and took charge of her life—for the first time in a year.

"I don't know for sure what, if anything, will happen between Tom and me, but I do know I'm not going to turn my back on it. I hope you'll be able to forgive me, and someday even forgive him, but today I'm going to find Tom and tell him—"

The office door opened and Tom said, "Don't shoot. I only came to say goodbye." He listened to the silence for a minute, then added, "Michael, if you ever have children, I know you'll be a better father than I was. I only hope that someday you'll realize that I'd have tried to be a good father to you if fate hadn't intervened. Maybe then you'll be able

259

to forgive me. I truly never meant for things to turn out the way they did."

He took Jessie's hands in his and looked down into her eyes. "I meant what I said. I'll always be there, in case you ever change your mind. Meanwhile, I love you. Oh, God, I love you!"

He dropped her hands and turned to go. She glanced once at Michael, saw that his whole body had gone as still and rigid as his face. She wanted to take him in her arms as she had done when he was little, and soothe the hurt away. But Tom was hurting, too, and the door was about to close behind him.

Oh, Pat, she pleaded silently. *What shall I do?*

And then she knew. With a quick prayer that Michael would understand and someday forgive her, she called Tom's name.

He turned back, and she cried, "Don't go, Tom. We were wrong, Michael and I, and you were right. We have a second chance. We mustn't waste it."

They stared at each other for a moment, then they met in the middle of the office. Tom wrapped her in his arms and she clung to him, until she remembered that they weren't alone. "Michael? Can Tom stay for the party? Will you welcome him to Pat's Christmas Eve party?"

Michael stared down at the Santa costume on the desk as if he couldn't remember what it was. After a minute he picked it up. "If he comes, I guess I won't be wearing this after all."

Tears filled Jessie's eyes again, but before they could spill over, he held it out to Tom and added, "We're about the same size. This ought to fit you." When Tom only stared it at, not understanding, he said, "I may not be happy about it, but I love Mom and I want her to be happy. And I guess she's right. Shutting you out, no matter who you are, or what you did years ago, would be the real betrayal of Pat. If you're going to come to the Christmas Eve party, and be part of the family, I guess . . . I guess Pat would want you to wear this today."

Tom took the suit. "Thank you," he said. "Thank you, son."

Jessie's tears spilled over again, but they were happy tears this time, for the love and the family and all the Christmases that had been given to her again.

She put one arm around Tom, pulled Michael closer so she could put the other one around him. "*Now* Pat's with us," she said, her voice firm and confident. "And we're a family again."

Michael nodded. "Right." He cleared his throat and added, "Pat would have liked that. It's what he always wanted—a family for Christmas."

Snow Angels

by Garda Parker

"Fools rush in where angels fear to tread."

— Alexander Pope

Mary Madigan stepped out of the snowfall of a gathering Montana storm into a dark slab-sided cabin.

"Well, this here's your own Holiday Inn." The man she could describe only as Gabby Hayes's twin, right up to his battered black cowboy hat that looked as if a wildcat had taken a bite out of it, dropped her two pieces of luggage on the bare wood floor. He touched a palm to his aching back and turned to her.

263

"You need anythin', you know where I live. You won't find me, though. Me and the missus is goin' on vacation." The tone of his scratchy voice told her he felt pretty puffed up about that event. He leaned toward her and scrutinized her face with gray gimlet eyes. "You gonna be all right here, ma'am?"

Mary nodded, squinting her eyes. "Would you turn on a light, please, Mr. Robinson? It's very dark in here."

"Ain't but one light bulb. 'Lectricity's pretty unreliable in these parts."

Robinson scuffed in his battered knee-high boots to the other side of the cabin and flipped a switch. A shaft of yellow light illuminated the space in which Mary had all too hastily chosen to spend the Christmas holidays.

Robinson must have caught the shock registered on her face as she scanned the room, for he said as quickly as his western drawl would allow, "You did say you wanted to be alone, right?"

"Yes, I did say that," Mary acknowledged, pulling an ivory lamb's-wool cowl hood from her head and running her fingers through her shoulder-length hair.

She'd sought complete solitude at Christmas for the first time in her life, and "these parts" certainly offered that. She hadn't noticed another cabin in the more than ten miles of undetermined road they'd traversed since leaving the main route.

"Well, ya' got that here. Won't be bothered 'cept maybe by an animal lookin' for food. Keep the doors and windows bolted at night and they won't bother ya' none. You're sure a long way from Chicago, ma'am."

"I'll say," Mary concurred, her eyes darting over her surroundings. "That was the idea."

In front of the huge fieldstone fireplace that dominated the room, Robinson knelt down onto a shaggy bearhide rug and dropped a box of wooden matches onto the massive head. He shaped, then ignited, a stack of wood and papers supported by the largest grate Mary had ever seen.

"That there's your kitchen," he said, rising slowly and pointing to a corner that showed a small four-burner gas stove and a deep sink in a wooden cabinet. "Icebox is stocked for two weeks, cupboard, too, and deep freeze out back."

Mary spotted the ancient metal refrigerator by following the vibrating whir of its belt-driven motor. "What happens to it if the power fails?"

"Generator keeps that and the deep freeze

going. That there's your bathroom." She followed his outstretched finger to what appeared to be a closet with a curtain drawn across the opening. "And up there's your bedroom." He pointed to a log-built ladder leading to a loft that was enveloped in blackness. "But you might rather stay down here near the fireplace. Sure be warmer. Well, that's the tour. Plenty of seasoned firewood," he gestured with his head toward a bolted door under the loft. "Woodshed's attached so's you don't hafta go out in the wind. More wood out behind the shed under the tarp. Don't let the fire go out. Extra matches under the sink. Got everything ya' need here. Blankets, pillows, dishes. Flashlight on the table. Any questions?"

"I'm sure I will have later, Mr. Robinson, but I'll figure things out for myself."

"Call me Smokey. Don't stand on formality here. Well, I'll just be gettin' on, then. You have a Merry Christmas now."

"Smokey, did you say?" When Robinson nodded, Mary thought with amusement that it was a "Miracle" they'd found this place. "You have a Merry Christmas, too."

He tipped his battered hat and left the cabin, leaving a blast of cold air and a small snowdrift inside the door. Mary heard his

266

four-wheel-drive vehicle rumble away, the sound of its faulty muffler swallowed by the intensifying storm.

With the aid of the flashlight she searched under the sink and found a big box of wooden matches. She lifted the glass chimney of a nickel-plated kerosene lamp on the pine table behind the couch, struck the match, touched it to the wick, and replaced the chimney. The lamp's light didn't help much, owing to the black soot coating the inside of the glass.

"Merry Christmas, old girl," she said to herself, and walked around to the fireplace, avoiding the bear head with the permanently open jaws.

She looked back into the room, the corners of her mouth tipping in a wry smile. "And I've just been standing here talking out loud to myself in this empty cabin. Don't tell me I'm stir crazy already!"

Within an hour the cabin had warmed to an almost comfortable range, and Mary busied herself settling in. She lit a green Coleman lantern and climbed to the loft. There she discovered a deep feathertick bed raised on a square wooden frame, fitted with flannel sheets and covered with Indian blankets in earthy tones of sandstone and muted greens.

Not bad. She smiled to herself. It looked cozy and inviting.

She hauled one of her suitcases up there, pulled out heavy Ragg socks and a deep blue woolen sweater, and slipped them on with her jeans and black turtleneck.

Down in the great room she pulled a wood stand under the light bulb and set her portable combination radio and cassette tape player on it, then plugged it into the light socket, adjusting it to a wavering station from somewhere near the mountains. She refrigerated a bottle of wine she'd brought. She figured out how the stove worked, heated a pot of chicken noodle soup from a can found in the cupboard, and boiled water for tea.

Then she dragged the small couch covered with a scratchy red and white striped blanket closer to the fire, propped her feet up on the log-hewn coffee table, and sat sipping the soup from a tin bowl.

Less than a week before Christmas.

Two weeks after her fifty-second birthday, and her break-up with Phil Garrett, nice, safe, boring insurance salesman Phil; four years after her divorce from David Madigan, dashing, philandering television reporter David; about a thousand miles from her four grown children and grandchildren, and her boisterous O'Neill Irish clan of a family. And light-years away from her office in Chicago's Midwest Cattlemen and Stock Growers Association.

" 'Oh, there's no place like home for the holidays,' " came a crackling rendition of Perry Como's voice over the radio. Mary got up and twisted the single antenna and adjusted the dial.

"Hurry on down to Dillon's for your last-minute Christmas shopping!" a male voice shouted. "All those items you forgot. Can't let the kiddies think Santa didn't come, now, can you? We've got it all! Computer games, audio- and videocassettes, those all-important basketball shoes for under a hundred and thirty dollars! Open every night until midnight! We'll even do the wrapping!"

Mary snapped off the radio. In case she grew lonely and morose and needed reminding of all she'd left behind, she'd turn it back on. She searched her bag for the tapes she'd packed, and popped in one of soothing guitar music by Segovia. She picked up the kerosene lamp from the kitchen table and set it on the stand near the fireplace, then dropped onto the sofa and curled her hands around the mug of tea.

God, it was quiet.

"This is the way Christmas ought to be," she said into the flames, then patted a stack of books she'd piled on the floor, and arranged her sketchpad and pencil box on the log coffee table. "Quiet. No thousand dollars' worth of toys under a tree that cost two hundred dollars. No shouting at each other over the din of a packed room of family members. No inevitable arguments. No credit card bills stretching into summer. No office parties where somebody makes a fool of himself over the new cutie from the temp agency." She ticked off the pluses of the Christmas holiday she'd chosen on a whim and made a done deal amid protests (mild at best, she remembered now) of her family.

"No holiday headaches, no overeating, no overdrinking, no depression over worrying that I may not have a job by the middle of January because of some unknown hatchet man they're bringing in. No being reminded of the fact that I can't remember what it feels like to be in love at a romantic time of year like Christmas."

Suddenly surprised that her voice sounded deeper than she'd ever imagined, she smiled. She'd get used to it. At least in this cabin she should be able to hear herself think.

The wind raged outside, rattling the walls

and making the wood creak. Mary's eyes skimmed over the room, searching for something in it, she guessed, that would help to calm the fear of isolation that threatened to overtake her. Her eyes fell on a pair of carved dogs on a shelf below a side window.

She picked one up and blew dust out of the intricately worked animal's coat. She couldn't identify the wood, nor the breed of dog, which resembled a lean shepherd, but the workmanship was exquisite in its detail. Her thumbnail traced the contours of the hair along its throat. She picked up the other one and compared the eyes, the open jaws, the set of the ears. A sensitive artist had captured a look on the faces of both that suggested . . . what? Wistfulness, she thought at first.

No. Loneliness.

She wondered a moment about the carver, then replaced the carvings in the exact position she'd found them on the shelf. She took in a long, slow breath, and tried to concentrate on the cozy smells of the burning wood in the fireplace and the remains of the chicken soup still in a pot on the stove. Her gaze slid around the cabin again, resting on the hanging handmade quilts that proved a woman had touched these walls and attempted to soften their rustic surfaces. Her auditory sense caught the sound of the fire crackling out warmth as the wind, steadily gathering strength and velocity, almost drowned it out. All that she was aware of underscored one blatant fact.

"Boy, is this ever alone."

Alone.

Mary stretched out on the couch, propped the pillows behind her back, and pulled a ragged afghan over her legs. She picked up the book at the top of her pile and cracked it open. For the first time in years she'd have the time to do all the reading, all the sketching, she wanted.

She sighed in contentment at the thought.

Bang!

Something hit the door with a suddenness and intensity that nearly lifted Mary off the couch.

Her heart pounded against her chest wall and thrummed in her ears. No wild animal ever knocked on a door. Maybe it was Smokey Robinson—she couldn't get over that name—back to bring her something. She rose quickly, and for a fleeting moment was certain her knees would buckle and let her fall to the floor in a heap.

The pounding came again, harder, more rapid, insistent.

Mary shut off the tape player. She edged to the door and placed her ear against it. Nothing. No sound of a panting, growling, slavering beast waiting to rip her to shreds.

"Is . . . someone there?" she called timidly.

"What?" a deep voice said. "Of course someone's here. Open the door!"

She unlatched it, telling herself she probably shouldn't, and peered through the narrow crack she allowed. It wasn't Smokey. Smokey was short and bent. This was someone or something very tall and large enough to fill the doorway. Wind-whipped snow swirled around the shape and blew into the room.

Mary guessed it was a man, a big man dressed in heavy clothing. Before she had time to think about slamming the door, he roughly pushed past without looking at her and headed for the fireplace. She peered out into the thickly falling snow, saw no one and nothing, except . . . something sharp protruding from the slowly rising snow on the front porch.

She peered closer.

Antlers! A wide rack of sharply pointed antlers resembling a bramble bush perched atop a furry velvet-eyed face with a long black-tipped nose.

Stricken with horror, Mary clutched the

door handle. "My God, there's a dead reindeer out here!" she breathed.

With her shoulders backed by her weight, she pushed the door shut against the sight. She turned into the room, narrowed her eyes, and scrutinized the back of the intruder. In the glow she saw he wore a thick gray fur hat and a thigh-length dark brown range jacket with the collar pulled up over his ears. He'd dropped a heavy backpack on the floor at the end of the couch and leaned a rifle on the wall beyond the fireplace.

"What took you so long?" he said into the flames. "I nearly froze to death out there! I swear you're going deaf, Smoke." He stripped off hefty cowhide gloves and warmed his hands. "I was surprised to see lights. What are you doing here? You didn't back out of taking Bertie on vacation, did you? And why'd you bolt the door, anyway? You haven't done that in the forty years I've known you."

Mary swallowed hard to steady her voice, and said evenly, "I was concerned a lost sasquatch might wander by. I see I may be right."

The big man spun around, leaving a trail of melting snow around him. Mary saw his dark eyelashes and brows, mustache and closely-cropped beard glisten with melting snow crystals. He squinted a surprised gaze at her, but stayed put in front of the fireplace.

"You're not Smokey," he said.

"Neither are you."

"You're a woman." His deep voice sounded almost breathless.

"You're not."

He dragged off his hat, revealing collar-length dark hair with silver threads running through it.

"Who the hell are you?"

"I might ask the same of you."

Mary amazed herself at her calm demeanor. Had the quiet density of a Montana winter already numbed her nerves and intuition?

Back in Chicago, if he'd barged into her office like this, she'd be profoundly suspicious of him, certain he was the newly-hired vice president ready to fire half the division employees, herself included.

"Name's Nick Chase," he offered. "Friend of Smokey Robinson. He owns this cabin."

He opened his jacket and shook ice particles and snow chunks from it, letting them fly wherever they would. They melted into little pools upon contact with the warm floor.

"I know," Mary said with controlled calm, "I rented it from him."

"Rented . . . ?"

"For the holidays, yes."

"Well, I'll be damned. He did it."

"Excuse me?"

"Smokey's been a bit hard up for cash. His wife was after him for a vacation to Florida. In over forty years of marriage they've never been anywhere. I told him he could rent this place to some city slicker for a bundle, then he'd have the money to take his wife on vacation." He scratched the back of his head, then burst out laughing.

"What is so amusing?" Mary watched him as he took his time shrugging out of the heavy coat and draping it over the back of a chair. His big size in a navy funnel-necked sweater and jeans did not appear diminished in the slightest by the removal of the coat.

His blue eyes sparkled with gold glints in the kerosene lamplight as he spoke. "I never thought he'd do it on his own, so I gave Smokey's wife, Bertie, some cash and told her a story about how I'd rented out the cabin to a friend for a month. She was thrilled! Said they were going on a real vacation and he'd have nothing to say about it being too expensive." He chuckled. "But, say, how'd you get into this place? I didn't see a car."

Mary moved from her spot near the door for the first time since Nick Chase had entered. "Seems your friend Mr. Robinson took your suggestion seriously. He ran a newspaper ad, and I called and rented the cabin. He brought me up here in his four-wheel-drive, and said he'd pick me up the day after Christmas. That's our agreement. He did say he was going on vacation for a few days."

"Disney World. That is, if the airport isn't snowed in."

Mary couldn't say anything. The vivid picture of Smokey Robinson in his battered Gabby Hayes hat, hurtling through the strobe-lit caverns of Space Mountain consumed her mind for a dizzying moment.

Nick turned back and rubbed his hands together over the fire. "You need more wood or this thing is going out."

He bent over the wood box and picked out a couple of shaggy bark-covered logs. Mary noticed the length of his legs and the height of the leather shaft of his thick-soled brown boots, both much more than she remembered seeing on a man other than in a magazine.

He turned back toward her. "Did you happen to notice you didn't give me your name?"

"Yes, I noticed," she said evenly.

"Not very Christmas-spirited," he responded.

"Oh, is it Christmas? I was trying not to notice that." She shifted into a friendly mode, realizing he didn't seem menacing, even if he was a big man. "Mary."

"Now, that's Christmasy," he said with a broad smile.

"I have four children, so you can keep the virgin jokes to yourself." She sat down on the couch and drained the cold contents of her mug.

"Wouldn't dream of saying anything like that. Got any more of whatever's in that mug? I'm chilled to the bone."

"Tea. In the can on the back of the stove. There's some soup in the pot if you want it."

"Thanks, I do." He set about getting down the tea can, reheating the soup, and searching for a spoon.

"Have you known Mr. Robinson very long?"

"For years. He's the only family I have, except for a distant uncle out of state."

"How did you get here? I didn't hear a car." Mary eyed the rifle propped against the wall.

"Walked."

"You *walked* here?" Mary shifted her eyes

278

toward him, incredulous at such a response.

"Yep."

She watched him pour steaming water into a mug, and dangle a tea bag in it. He carried the mug and the long-handled soup pot, a spoon sticking out of it, to the coffee table. When he sat down on the other end of the short couch, she felt it give under his weight. In the firelight his beard showed a heavier sprinkling of silver threads than his hair.

"Just out for a stroll on such a pleasant evening?"

"Out for a trudge is more like it. I've been cutting wood most of the day. Sorry for the intrusion. I use this cabin often when the weather gets rough and I've skied or logged too long. Easy to lose track of time out here. And it got too dark and the snow's too deep for me to get back to my own place." He gestured toward the front door.

"You *live* out here?"

"Don't sound so skeptical. Montana is inhabited by actual human beings, you know, not just those errant sasquatches you were concerned about."

"Yes, I know. I didn't mean to sound insulting. I do feel compelled to ask you something. I hope it's not too personal," she ventured.

"Go ahead."

"There appears to be a dead reindeer on the front porch, and I can't relax thinking Donder or Blitzen is out there stiff as a board in the snow. Or could it be Rudolph, and his nose went out or something?"

He laughed. "You've been around little kids a lot, haven't you?"

She studied his face. "It's a legitimate question. I've never seen you before. I mean, you barge in here out of a snowstorm, rifle in hand, leaving a reindeer lying in a heap, and then calmly pour a cup of tea. How do I know you haven't murdered Santa Claus?"

He began eating the steaming soup directly from the pot. The heat of it didn't seem to bother him, and not a drop landed in his beard.

"I'm returning that rifle to Smokey. That's an elk, not a reindeer. And it's not even a whole elk."

"I'll try to take comfort in those thoughts."

"And I'd never hurt Santa Claus. I love Christmas."

"Bah humbug. What did you do with the rest of the elk?"

He gave her a lingering sidelong glance. "I didn't do anything with it. Smokey shot it last year and had the head mounted. I'm finally getting around to bringing the rack up here. Thought I'd surprise him and hang it over the fireplace while he's away. Four kids, hunh? How old?" he asked without skipping a beat.

Mary picked up the rhythm. "How thoughtful of you. My oldest is thirty-two and my youngest is twenty-five. And I've got six grandchildren."

"Grandchildren! You certainly don't look like a grandmother."

"This is what grandmothers look like. Something tells me you get snowed in here rather often."

He didn't react to her slight barb. "Sounds wonderful. Grandchildren, I mean. Why aren't you home with them during Christmas?"

He certainly is direct, Mary thought. No cagey questioning like city men. She decided she liked it, and would answer him with her own kind of directness.

"I have energetic parents who are pushing seventy-five but think they're still in their forties, six gregarious brothers and sisters who are all married and have children, the four of my own and my grandchildren. My name is Mary O'Neill Madigan. Every monogrammed piece I own is emblazoned with MOM. I have a big-city job full of big-city stress that I may

281

not have when I get back. The job, that is. The stress goes without saying. I've had the same secretary since I started there, who has a better social life than I have, a philodendron in my office I'm managing to kill painfully and slowly, and a couple of dozen positive-thinking slogans plastered on the walls. At my age, new jobs are hard to come by, new secretaries hard to get used to, new plants difficult to start, and the positive-thinking slogans are starting to take on negative meanings. I was getting jaded and needed to get away from everything and everybody for a few days to think. And I didn't have the energy to go through a Christmas-as-usual."

She skipped the other personal thoughts about wanting to find out who she was now and what she expected from the rest of her life. This mountain man, Nick Chase, appeared to be the kind who was probably put off by introspection.

Nick listened attentively. "You picked the right place," he said simply in his charming drawl.

"Think so?"

"Nothing but nothing around here, far as the eye can see. Isn't it wonderful?"

"That's what I thought, up until a few minutes ago." She stood up. "Well, don't let me keep you. You must have your own family waiting at home. I'm sure you'd like to get back to them now that you've dried out and warmed up."

"Nope."

"Excuse me?"

"I have no family to get back to, and I couldn't leave even I wanted to, which I don't."

"What do you mean?"

"I guess you haven't looked outside recently, have you?"

"Not since I checked for a miniature sleigh and eight tiny reindeer when you arrived."

He let out a nice rich laugh that affected Mary in a gently disturbing way. "I like your sense of humor. There's a blizzard out there. This place will be practically buried by morning."

"A blizzard! Buried?"

"Yep."

"Mr. Chase, I don't like *your* sense of humor whatever, and your Gary Cooper vocabulary is starting to get on my nerves."

"So soon? Too bad, since it's likely we'll be spending a lot of close time together."

Mary sank back onto the couch. "What . . . what do you mean?"

"Like I said, I'm not going anywhere in this weather. No telling when it will let up. And I'm finally getting my wish."

"What's that? To be buried in a snowdrift as high as Trump Tower?"

"No, but that's pretty amusing. Ever since I was knee-high to a yearling, my wish has been to spend the holidays with a big family. Well, at least you're someone who has a big family even if you didn't bring any of them with you. I'm looking forward to it. I hope Mr. Madigan won't mind too much, although I don't recall hearing mention of him."

"Well, I don't want to spend the holidays with you. No offense, Mr. Chase. I thought I made it quite clear that I don't want to spend the holidays with anybody. And there is no Mr. Madigan. I'm divorced."

"Now, there's something we have in common," he said, and Mary thought he sounded sad.

She sucked in a breath. "Mr. Chase, you can't stay here. My wish was to spend the holidays with peace and quiet, not with someone I've never met. And besides, I rented and paid for this cabin."

"So did I. I planned to drop out of society for the holidays, get away from meddling friends and the dates they lovingly refer to as

284

'digging up' for me, and do some quiet thinking about a problem I'm facing. I rented and paid for this cabin, too, so I'd say half of it's mine."

"Yes, but you were dishonest about it," she pointed out, "I wasn't."

"I had to be. If I'd told Smokey and Bertie what I wanted to do, they'd have thought I needed them and wouldn't have gone away."

"Mr. Chase, you have to leave. There's no room for you at this inn."

"That's mighty inhospitable of you."

" 'Tis the season."

"Well, if you feel you can in all good conscience throw me out into the freezing weather, it being Christmas and all, I suppose leaving would be the gentlemanly thing for me to do. Of course, if I open that door, it's unlikely I can close it again. There's about five feet of snow against it already."

"That's not possible!"

"Raise the front window quilt and look out there."

Mary stood up quickly and went to lift the heavy fabric that was drawn over the window. "I can't see a thing."

"That's because the snow is over the window."

"No." She drew out the word in an elongated *O,* and turned around slowly.

"Aw, you're not one of those claustrophobic types, are you?"

"No, I'm the Greta Garbo type. I want to be alone. With you here, I won't be." She suddenly realized the gravity of the situation. She was trapped in a small cabin somewhere in Montana. And worse, she was trapped with a strange man. She pulled into her five-foot-four-inch height. "I warn you, don't try anything. I know karate."

"Well, now, there's another thing we have in common."

Wide-eyed, Mary pictured herself suddenly spinning over his head with a flick of his powerful arm. Yet, strangely, she still wasn't feeling overly fearful about him. She was experiencing the kind of feeling she might have if the real Santa Claus suddenly dropped down the chimney—he'd certainly be a strange man, but she'd know she didn't have to be afraid of him.

She took a closer look at Nick Chase's face. He could hardly be called Saint Nick. She could tell that by the devil dancing in his Montana bigsky-blue eyes.

"You're enjoying this, aren't you?" She leveled her assessment with narrow-eyed scrutiny.

"I sure am, ma'am," he drawled.

"How long can this storm possibly last?"

"Unfortunately, it could be over too soon."

*"Un*fortunately?"

"Yep, like I said, I'm enjoying this. Might last two, maybe three days, if we're lucky."

"Lucky? Three days—? Then you can leave?"

"If I can dig out. It'll probably take two or three more days to do that. Then my own place'll be snowed in. Might as well stay here till the weather gets better."

He stretched his long frame to the end of the couch and pulled his heavy backpack onto the cushion. He zipped open the pockets and pulled out several packages of cheese and bread and canned foods, and extracted a six-pack of beer and a bottle of champagne. Mary watched him gather things in his arms, rise, and lug them all to the rumbling refrigerator. He hummed as he rearranged things inside, clinking cans and bottles together.

"Now, look, Mr. Chase . . ."

"Call me Nick. Long as we'll be living together, it has a friendlier tone, don't you think?"

"Living together!"

"Yep. And isn't it great we have so much in common?"

Mary sighed and sank back down on the couch. "Oh, yeah, just great."

". . . such fantastic tricks before high heaven as make the angels weep."—William Shakespeare, *Measure for Measure*

Mary's frustration mounted. She rose, paced the length of the cabin, twisted in several directions, looking for something. What? Anything she could use to solve this problem of being forced to share a snowbound cabin with a strange man. In a corner near the door that led to the woodshed, she spotted a pile of coiled rope.

An idea struck her.

She strode resolutely to the pile and tried to pick it up. The thick rope was much too heavy for her to haul. She searched through the coils until she found an end, picked it out, and slung it over her shoulder with both hands.

"All right," she puffed. "We're going to divide this place right down the middle. You have half, and I'll have half." From the wall on the far side she dragged the rope across the cabin toward the fireplace, scraping it over the floor, then draped it over the middle of the couch and table and across the bearhide rug. "Whew! What's the smell in this thing?"

"Horse."

"What?"

"Horse. Smokey used it on his team when he was drawing logs. Got horse sweat and probably manure on it, too."

"Horse manure?"

"Yep." He picked up a length of rope and held it under his nose, breathing deeply. "I love the smell of horses. Different from cattle. Did you ever notice that?" He thrust it under her nose.

"Nope." She affected his drawl and turned her grimacing face away.

"Well, now," he said, scratching his head and following the rope from wall to fireplace, "as I see it, you want me to stay on my side of this rope and you stay on yours, is that right?"

"Right. Will you agree?"

She watched him turn around infuriatingly slowly, surveying his designated area. "So then, if I've got this right"—he scratched his head—"this side is mine and that's yours." He gestured toward the couch which the rope sliced into districts like the Continental Divide.

"Right."

"That means you think you paid for the half with the bed in the sleeping loft, is that right?"

"Right," she said triumphantly. "Do you have a problem with that?"

"Oh, no, ma'am."

"Good."

"I can sleep anywhere. I'll just stretch out here on the floor in front of the fireplace. No problem for me. I've done it a thousand times. Long as you don't have a problem with me having paid for the half with the kitchen and bathroom."

Mary's eyes shot toward what she'd just decreed as Nick Chase's part of the cabin. Suddenly aware of her need of that bathroom almost immediately, owing to her consumption of soup and tea, she realized she'd spoken too hastily.

Pride would have to crumble in the face of need. She took in a deep breath and considered giving in to him, something she was loath to do. This moment was a thorny reminder of what she was facing in her job, being forced to give in to a stranger who had suddenly appeared and taken control.

"I can see that distresses you," Nick said before she could speak. "Appears like we have to arrive at another solution."

"I'm willing to listen to any *fair* method of working this out," she said with an air of superiority.

"Then there's only one thing to do."

She inclined her head and said with the voice of a skeptic, "What?"

"Take this dilemma by the horns . . ." When she grimaced and shifted her eyes toward the door beyond which the head and antlers of a dead elk lay buried in snow, he apologized. "Sorry. What I mean is, if we discuss this . . . ah, situation calmly and rationally, I'm certain we can arrive at a fair resolution. Don't you?"

Mary placed a hand at her waist. She wasn't certain she had much time or inclination to discuss the problem rationally. Or calmly. She had to go to the bathroom *now*. She frowned.

"Would you like to offer the first round of solutions?" he asked.

No, she wouldn't. She'd like to push past him and hit the john. She drew in an uncomfortable breath. "We can share the sleeping loft. I mean, take turns," she added quickly.

"Fine." He thought for another moment. "I'll cook supper every other night."

"Fine." It didn't take her half a second to

say, "I'll clean up the dishes those nights if you'll clean up on my nights to cook."

"Fine." Again he took a long, pondering moment without taking his gaze from hers. He must have known what she was thinking, for he said evenly, "And you have to promise that when I go outside—if I go outside—you'll let me back in."

Mary hesitated long enough for him to raise his eyebrows in question. "Fine," she said at last, "turnabout being additional fair play?"

"Of course. Fine." Nick nodded.

"Fine. Is that it, then?"

He scratched his head. "Let me think a minute."

Mary frowned at him. "While you're thinking, would you mind if I . . . ?" She pointed toward the bathroom with an agitated finger.

He turned slowly in its direction, then even more slowly back to her.

"Fine!"

"Fine!" She stomped past him and into the dark closet of a thing Smokey Robinson had referred to as the bathroom. She could find no light, but frantically felt around until she found the open commode. It was metal, and when she at down on it the coldness startled her.

"Oh, I forgot to tell you there's no light in there," Nick called from the other side of the curtain. "Good idea to take one in with you."

"I've discovered that," she called back with more than a hint of aggravation creeping into her voice.

"One other thing we should have settled on."

"And what is that?"

"Whenever either of us uses the commode, we take it immediately out to the holding tank in the woodshed and empty it."

Mary propped her elbows on her knees and dropped her head into her hands, visualizing herself slogging through the cabin with a commode in hand. "Fine," she groaned,

By the time Mary had unpacked her things and piled most of them at one end of the sleeping loft, the cabin seemed transformed. Almost homey, she thought as she looked down into the great room. Nick had brought out more lanterns, lit and placed them strategically so that the space fairly glowed. The wind howled outside and the walls of the cabin creaked, yet still this friendly stranger had managed to make the place cozy. She marveled at it. And at him.

Don't get too comfortable, she warned herself sternly. *Don't let your guard down. After all, you know nothing about Nick Chase. You've never seen him before. He seems all right but . . .* She started down the ladder.

Nick had unrolled a blue nylon sleeping bag and stretched it out at the end of the fireplace where the bear's head lay. He'd zipped it open partway down the side and pulled the end back envelope-style over the bag, revealing a blue plaid flannel lining.

Mary stopped at the bottom rung. "Oh, I'm sorry. Were you planning on going to bed now?"

"No, not yet. I like to do a little carving before I turn in. Relaxes me."

She watched him untie the rawhide thongs on a canvas pouch and pull out a cotton-wrapped roll of carving tools. Then he took out another cotton-wrapped package and carefully removed a wood object. Mary couldn't tell what it was.

"Carving?"

"Yep. Been doing it since I was a kid. My grandfather taught me. These are his tools. You'll find a few things of mine around this cabin."

She turned her head toward the window shelf. "You carved those dogs?"

294

He nodded. "Except they're coyotes."

"It's a lost art," she observed quietly, crossing to the near end of the fireplace.

"That's because it takes time and patience. People are moving too fast to take the time to feel the spirit in a piece of wood and know that if they take care and use their tools just right, an animal, or a tree, or something from nature will uncover itself. Kind of like getting to know a person, I think."

Mary listened to his voice, deeply rich against the sharp crackling of the fire. The warmth of both reached her in a sensitive place that hadn't been touched in dim memory. "You make it sound as if the wood has a life of its own," she said, drawing nearer to where he sat on a low stool at the other end of the fireplace.

"Spirit of its own," he said simply. "It will show how to bring it to life if the carver allows enough time."

Mary let his answer settle somewhere comfortable inside her. A calm she hadn't felt in a long while drifted languidly through her, and she spent a few silent moments just feeling it. That was the sense she hoped to achieve by being alone, without being surrounded by people, not something she expected to feel in the presence of another

295

person, especially a man.

"Will I bother you if I sit here and read for a while?" she said at last.

"Not at all. I'd enjoy your company."

Mary liked the sound of those words. He was having a rapidly profound effect on her.

"Like a little background music to carve by?" The sound of her own voice helped ease her tension.

"That would be a luxury."

Mary pulled herself away from the fireplace with some difficulty. Her limbs felt heavy. At the cassette player she started the Segovia tape again, then walked back around Nick, inching her way between where he sat on the stool and the couch. The side of her thigh brushed lightly against his shoulder. He looked up at her and smiled.

Soft strains of Spanish folk music settled around Mary and Nick. They sat quietly, each absorbed in personal concentration.

Nick absently rubbed his thumb over the piece of pine he'd been shaping over the last few weeks. This particular piece, the length of which equaled the width of his flattened palms spread side by side, seemed reluctant to give forth its spirit. Perhaps because his own spirit hadn't been open to much of anything the past couple of years.

He'd been plagued by questions he couldn't answer. Should he please his uncle and take over family company responsibilities in a city out of state? Should he please himself and stay right where he was, doing the same things, feeling the same things in Montana, on the land he loved and where he'd grown up? And why hadn't he found a way to soothe his spirit, wounded in the divorce?

He heard Mary turn a page. All he'd wanted to do was drop out of civilization for the holidays so he could *think* in the everlasting quiet of this familiar remote cabin. The last thing he'd expected was to be snowbound with a woman he didn't know. Here they were, their acquaintance only a few hours old, sitting together in companionable, not strained silence, as if that were the most natural thing in the world for both of them, as if they'd been doing it for years. He pondered the notion for a moment.

A couple of logs, burnt through to glowing ash, caved in on the grate, breaking into his thoughts. Nick set his carving paraphernalia on the couch, then hunkered down to replenish the wood. He finished with a brushing of the hearth with a homemade broom.

Mary turned a page of her book, then turned it back again. For some reason she couldn't remember what she'd read in the past half hour, and the story was making no sense to her. She glanced now and then at Nick. Watched him staring into the fire, watched him rebuild it when it fell in, watched his hands over the piece of wood carving, aware that he seemed to be almost idly caressing it. There was no use trying to read this book. She couldn't concentrate.

Later that night, settled in the featherbed under a mountain of blankets and wearing Ragg wool socks and long underwear under flannel pajamas, Mary pondered the turn of events. Her declaration of her desire to be alone over the holidays—she could honestly admit it now—had seemed a relief to her family, who immediately had plans of their own.

Her parents had taken a Hawaiian cruise. Her eldest daughter and her family were in Disney World right now. Maybe they'll even stand in line at Space Mountain with the Robinsons, totally oblivious to their connection. She thought of all the others happily engaged in an alternative Christmas, as her eldest son, the computer programmer, referred to it. She missed them, but this kind of separate Christmas would be good for all of them. She believed that wholeheartedly.

Soon it would be Christmas Eve, but she was not alone. She was with a strange man. He'd meant to be alone, too. Somehow Smokey Robinson and a Montana blizzard threw them together with the promise of keeping them together against their wills for several days.

She ought to be livid with anger that her plans had been thwarted, annoyed beyond reason that she wasn't alone.

She wasn't.

What did that mean?

Mary awoke to the mingled aromas of coffee and the rich smokiness of meat. She stirred in her feathered nest and drew her knees up to her chest, then stretched her legs out straight and her arms overhead. This must be what a cat on the hearth feels, she marveled, and thought briefly that a cat's life was probably not all that bad. At least they didn't have to deal with uncontrollable corporate upheavals that could alter their nine lives, or even one of them.

The warmth surrounding her beckoned her to stay, but the smell of the most important thing to her in the morning, that first cup of coffee, forced her out. Coffee already perking! A reminder of mixed blessings — she wasn't alone.

She peered over the loft rail down into the kitchen area. His back to her, Nick Chase in a burgundy plaid flannel shirt and jeans, wool socks but no shoes, was whistling as he flipped something in a cast iron skillet.

Now what? Mary was not good in the morning. She knew she looked like the wreck of the *Hesperus* upon arising and most of the time she didn't care. She'd never let Phil stay over on the rare occasions he'd initiated sex. Besides, it was always over in a precise thirty minutes, and she was glad to see him leave.

Whatever brought that to mind?

This morning she didn't want to look like that. Not with Nick Chase cooking breakfast. And there seemed to be a form of daylight in the cabin. What time was it? Had the snow been blown away by that mighty wind? She struggled with her jeans. She couldn't stand up in the loft, not without being visible, and it was impossible to zip them in the position she was in on the featherbed.

"Hey, up there in the cheap seats!" Nick called. "Breakfast is near done, MOM. You gonna roll out, or what?"

Mary shook away wonder about the *or what* alternative. She slipped on a pair of loafers, pulled a sweatshirt over her pajama top, made a vain attempt at doing something

300

with her hair, and wished she had a toothbrush. She'd left that in the so-called bathroom the night before.

"I'm . . . I'll . . . in a minute."

"If you're worried about proper dress, don't bother," Nick called.

What did he mean by that remark?

"I'm no day at the beach in the morning either," he added. "Not worth much before coffee which I had two hours ago. Got a fresh pot. Shall I hand you up a cup?"

"No! I'll be right down."

Tentatively she descended the ladder and tried to sneak behind Nick's back into the bathroom. No luck. He spun around just as she was about to duck behind the curtain.

"Good morning. How'd you sleep?" He gave her a smile as dazzlingly crystal as the light in the windows.

He lied about not being a day at the beach. He looked like a week on Waikiki! And she felt like a month in a cave.

"Um, I'll tell you after I . . ." She nodded toward the bathroom.

He turned his head. "Oh. Of course. Sorry."

When Mary emerged from the bathroom, a bit fresher from toothpaste, deodorant, and a splash of glacier-temperature water, Nick was sitting on the couch in front of the fireplace, perusing her stack of books. She poured a mug of coffee from a speckled graniteware pot. Small steaks sizzled in a cast iron frying pan next to a covered pan she assumed held eggs. All of it smelled heavenly, fit for the gods, or at least a couple of lesser angels.

"It was nice of you to cook breakfast," she said behind him. "Talk about room service! You run a nice hotel."

He turned and dropped an arm over the couch back. "Least I could do, since it was my turn. You cooked last night."

Last night. Last night. She struggled with the memory. "Oh, yes, a mug of tea and left-over soup. Not my best culinary effort."

"You weren't prepared for drop-in company."

"Why is it so bright? Have we had a melt-down?" She squinted around the great room.

"Nope. I just lifted the window quilts. Last night's wind drifted the snow away from the windows a little. That's sun reflecting off it. Wonderful, isn't it?" He stood up and headed toward the stove.

Mary had to agree. She could see stark blue sky over the drift at the front window, but nothing else. "Is the door still blocked?"

"I haven't checked, but I will after break-

302

fast. Sit down." He pointed toward the couch. "Stay warm. I'll bring us both a plate. Got biscuits in the oven, too."

"What oven?" She looked around the stove area.

"The one over there by the fireplace."

Mary turned and started toward it, then stopped cold. "Oh, my God, how did he get in here?" The elk head with its five-foot spread of rack lay propped against the end of the couch, inches from the jaws of the bear head.

Nick spun around. "Who?"

Mary pointed and said tremulously, "H-him."

"Oh, you mean Blitzen, there?"

"I hoped you wouldn't name him."

"I didn't. You did. I brought him in last night before he got frozen to the porch. Had a devil of a time digging him out. Snow piled in as fast as I could shovel it away from the door. Would you get the biscuits, please? Pot holders there on the table."

She picked up the pot holders and figured out how to unlatch the oven door. Inside were the lightest, fluffiest-looking biscuits she'd ever seen. This Nick Chase was certainly a talented man. She hauled out the tray and set it on the table.

Gingerly Mary lowered herself onto the couch as far away from the elk head as she possibly could. She heard Nick getting out plates and utensils. When had she ever been served breakfast by a man? "I can't remember when I last . . . had steak for breakfast," she said, trying to sound relaxed.

"You probably never had this steak. It's elk."

She twisted around. "Elk . . . ? Not . . ."

Nick laughed. "Blitzen? No. At least I don't think so."

Mary's eyes widened. "You don't think so? Don't you know?"

"Not certain of it, no. Smokey keeps a supply of things in the freezer box. But I'm sure he changes them regularly."

"You're sh-sure."

"Relatively."

She heard utensils scrape over tin plates. He came back to the couch with knives and forks sticking out of his shirt pockets and two plates of food held in dishtowel-covered hands, and set them all on the coffee table. Steam rose in gently moving curls over an inviting and deliciously aromatic meal.

Mary peered into her plate. She avoided lingering over the steak, and was surprised to see chunks of green pepper and onion dotting a perfectly formed omelette.

"Vegetables? Where'd you get the fresh vegetables?"

"Smokey keeps a kind of a root cellar here. Taste it. See if it needs more salt, or anything."

She sat back. "I don't think so. I'm not very hungry." A bold-faced lie. Her stomach was growling, letting her know the soup and tea from the night before had not been enough. "Besides, my mother told me never to eat wild animals or compost."

"Compost?" He laughed again. "It'll take some work, but I'll get used to your sense of humor. You seem awfully squeamish for somebody from a large family, I'd think you'd eat practically anything."

"I'm not squeamish. I'm selective."

"You'll like the breakfast, I promise."

"But . . . are you just going to leave *him* there, staring at us like that?"

"Not for long. Later I'll get him mounted up there." He pointed to an empty space in the fieldstone above the fireplace. "Soon as he's thawed out, that is."

Mary stared into the glassy black eyes in the elk head. "He will rather quickly, I imagine, once he sees you eating the other part of him."

"Nice pajamas," he said over his shoulder as he picked up his knife and fork. "You were smart to bring them. Some women might have packed some lightweight frilly thing, and then complained about being cold."

That was sort of a compliment, wasn't it? It wasn't a tease, was it? Or was he pointing out she was a frump? Wouldn't a highly sensual woman have brought the frilly thing?

This was all so strange. Waking up to breakfast of elk steak cooked by a man she didn't know, being forced into conversation, not her forte before breakfast, and then having to tax her mind with questioning the meaning behind everything he said. This only underscored her desire to be alone. She could get out of bed, be ugly and grumpy, eat nice normal things like Cheerios, and who the hell would be there to notice?

"I'm going to work on mounting Blitzen this morning. I didn't want to wake you too early by pounding nails into the stone, but I'll get at it right after breakfast so I won't disturb the peace you came out here to find any longer than necessary. I may need your help, if you don't mind." Nick cut a piece of steak and sucked it off the end of his fork.

Silently, Mary watched him chew as he cut another piece, her eyes riveted to his strong jaw as it moved. *Okay. This must be a dream, or a past-life regression, or an out-of-body experience. I'm not sitting here in front of a fireplace in a snowbound cabin with a bearded mountain man calmly discussing the mounting of a stuffed elk head over a fireplace that belongs to a man named Smokey Robinson who looks like Gabby Hayes. What was in that punch at the office Christmas party? Tequila? That's it. I have never been able to drink a drop of tequila without disastrous results. I'll just blink now . . .*

"Is the omelette cooked enough for you?" Nick asked without looking. "I've never liked it too dry, but I know some people don't like it runny."

So it wasn't a dream. Quickly Mary cut into her omelette and placed a small piece in her mouth. That was a dream. Light and fluffy, tasty. How did he do that in that makeshift kitchen? And the biscuits were heavenly.

Based on their agreement, her turn to cook was next, and Mary knew she would embarrass herself with her culinary efforts. She was used to putting on big plain meals to "fill 'em up," as her mother always said. Constructing perfect omelettes in the wilderness was not her talent.

She made an effort to find a voice not used to early-morning conversation. "The omelette is perfect." She sounded rather husky, as if she'd been in a smoky bar drinking whiskey the night before.

"What about the steak?"

"I've been thinking about becoming a vegetarian. Maybe this is a good time to start."

"Oh, go on, taste it. I think you'll be surprised."

That's just what she was afraid of. She cut the tiniest sliver she could manage and placed it back on her tongue as if trying to avoid the sensitive taste buds on the tip. She was surprised. It was actually very tasty, or maybe she was hungry enough to eat cardboard. She might have enjoyed her second piece more if it hadn't been for those glassy eyes staring up at her from the elk's face, where it lay at the end of the fireplace. They made her feel guilty.

"About . . . Blitzen," she ventured. "Maybe Mrs. Robinson won't want him hanging over the fireplace. Maybe we should just give him a decent burial or something. . . ."

"She'll love him! Besides, we need some decorations in here. Looks a little bare for

Christmas." He chewed a last piece of steak. "Oh, I forgot, you're trying to avoid Christmas. Well, it's just about here. Might as well make the best of it. Blitzen will enjoy being part of the festivities."

Mary drained her cup. "I'm sure he didn't say that in so many words when you gunned him down in cold blood."

Unfazed by the barb, Nick picked up their plates and took them to the sink. "I don't hunt for sport. I'll get the hooks set in while you do the dishes."

She twisted toward him over the back of the couch.

"That's not a sexist remark," he said quickly. "You do remember our bargain? I cook, you clean. You cook, I clean. Right now we have to get ready for a hanging."

Mary grimaced. He was right. Christmas — and the Blitzen-hanging — was happening no matter how much she resisted. She'd have to grin and bear it. At least bear it.

"I don't think this cabin is big enough for the three of us," Mary announced when they'd finished mounting the elk head over the fireplace. "Blitzen looks hostile to me."

"You think so?" Nick stroked his perfectly

groomed beard thoughtfully. "I think he's rather pleased with our handiwork."

"How can you say that? Look at his eyes! Those are the eyes of an accuser. He makes me feel guilty."

Nick turned toward her, still stroking his beard. "Something tells me your guilt feelings have nothing to do with the looks from a dead elk. You're worried about what your family would say if they knew you were holed up in a remote cabin with a man you've just met."

Mary looked down at her loafers. "God, will my generation of women never get over feeling guilty about such things?"

"Probably not. Just like my generation of men has a hard time. We never know how we're supposed to act anymore. My father would have had a lot to say about me cooking breakfast and you laying abed half the morning. Ain't manly, he'd say."

"And my mother would have agreed with him." Mary smiled. "I was almost afraid to enjoy the fact that the man of the cabin was preparing breakfast. I've worked very hard at becoming a modern woman. Home, family, high-powered job. Sometimes it's exhausting being all things to all people."

Nick picked up the graniteware pot and

poured a mug of coffee. "I know. I thought by the time I got to be this age I wouldn't have to worry about my duty as a son anymore. Or, in my case, as a nephew. I thought I could do what I want and not have to worry about family obligations. But that just isn't so." He lifted the mug toward her with a questioning look.

Mary nodded. "Is there enough for both of us?"

He laughed. "There's enough in here for Blitzen, too, if he had the stomach for it!"

Mary grimaced and took the mug. "Maybe we should give ourselves a Christmas present and just be who we are the way we want to be for the rest of the week."

"Great idea. After all, just a couple of days after Christmas, real life will start all over again."

Mary dropped down on the couch with a sigh. "Don't remind me. I haven't figured out what I'm going to do when it all hits me next week."

Nick leaned against the fireplace and took a long swallow of coffee. "I know what you mean."

Mary's eyes raised in quick surprise to his. "You're struggling with a problem, too?"

"I am, but I shouldn't be."

"Want to talk about it?"

"Do you want to talk about yours?"

Mary sipped her coffee thoughtfully. "Maybe. Not yet."

"Right."

Nick returned his coffee mug to the sink, then added logs to the fire. He picked up the pouches containing his carving work, and settled in a chair near the side window, where the light was strongest. His eyes rose for a moment to Blitzen, who appeared to preside over the room from his lofty position. A smile tilted one corner of Nick's mouth. He reached in the pouch for the wood piece and a tool, and held them thoughtfully.

He felt something, looked up, and caught Mary's quick glance in his direction, and the even quicker lowering of her hazel eyes. Her dark auburn hair seemed to move with the firelight shining on one side and the shaft of sunlight on the other, lending it an aura that seemed to glow dark red from within. The sprinkling of silver-gray among the waves that brushed her shoulders added a note of dignity to the restless earthiness he sensed about her. He was beginning to wonder about her, wonder about her a great deal.

The other corner of his mouth tilted up, and he lowered the tool to the wood.

Mary took her mug to the sink, then picked up a book and settled back on the couch. Her glance had caught Nick with one of his carving tools poised above the wood. A moment later she stole another furtive glance, watched him as he gazed at the piece a long time. Then he made a slow, blurred gouge in the wood, then another, and another, slower than the first.

And then she saw his face change, saw the hewn crags of it, looking for all the world as if another master craftsman had carved it, soften and take on a burnished glow in the sunlight. He began to carve now with a purpose. She could feel it exactly the way he'd explained it to her. He'd taken his time, waited, and sensed the moment when the wood gave forth with the knowledge of the spirit inside it.

And Mary knew the moment when Nick felt the spirit, and the intensity of sensing that in him unnerved her.

The two grew quiet, absorbed, and the only sounds in the cabin were the crackling of the fire, the turning of a page, and the soft rhythmic scrape of knife against wood.

"And young men glittering and sparkling
Angels, and maids strange seraphic

pieces of life and beauty!"
— Thomas Traherne

After almost three days of cabin confinement, Mary felt ready to break through the walls. She'd read until her eyes ached. She'd sat with a pencil poised over her sketchbook, doodling absently at first before she actually began drawing anything recognizable. Her body screamed for exercise and fresh air.

And her mind begged for a scene other than the disturbing one of Nick Chase moving in the center of it. His presence drew her focus away from the subjects she'd meant to concentrate on when she'd chosen this remote site as a retreat. But there was no retreating from Nick Chase. Where would she go in this small space that hadn't been touched by him? Even the strongest-minded woman bent on immersing herself in her own pursuits would be unable to ignore him.

For an outdoorsman, Nick seemed surprisingly relaxed to her, not at all tense about the closed-in nature of the time they'd been forced to share. In fact, Mary observed, he often appeared lost in thought as he sat carving or leafing through some of her books.

Something was becoming blindingly clear. Nick Chase was growing increasingly more attractive to her, personably as well as physically, and she struggled with the intensity of it.

This was not the Mary Madigan she'd been living with in recent years. That Mary had been going out only with men who were unchallenging. She'd felt safer that way. No concerns about losing him to a more exciting woman, no work molding herself to his desires and perceptions. But this man was something else entirely. He'd caught her in the act of being herself, had seen her in every state except naked, and never once had she read displeasure in his eyes. She knew if she allowed herself to hold eye contact with him for very long, she'd almost be capable of reading his mind, so expressive were his eyes. The thought overwhelmed her, and she always lowered her gaze before there was the chance of it taking her further.

She'd read about people, complete opposites who, when forced together in close quarters for a length of time, eventually fell into a relationship. Fiction and fantasy, she thought, yet after being snowbound all this time with Nick Chase he was fast shaping her reality, a reality that could go no farther than this cabin. He's G.U., as Meg, her secretary, had said about one of her own last flings with a man from New York City. Geographically unsuitable. Nick Chase was definitely G.U. Her life was in Chicago, and his was in Montana.

Try as she might, Mary couldn't dislike him, couldn't maintain a division of space, a division of duties, though the rope had long been recoiled and relegated to its own corner of the cabin.

Slipping inside his sleeping bag the second night had given her the unnerving feeling of having slipped into his arms. And picturing him enveloped in her featherbed nest in the loft served to effect an internal unrest she couldn't ease. She wondered if his body molded into the impression hers had made in the feathertick.

By the fourth night they'd abandoned the alternate sleeping arrangement. She preferred the featherbed and he preferred the sleeping bag, rather like a couple who'd early in their relationship unspokenly chosen their own sides of the bed. In the waning firelight she caught a glimpse of his naked hip flank as he crawled into the sleeping bag. She closed her eyes and quickly looked away, but then stole another glance and saw him settle onto his stomach.

She'd begun to wonder more and more

about him, and now she wondered if he always slept on his stomach. She'd never heard him snore. Even in a raging snow and windstorm was he sleeping in the nude? Did he wear boxer shorts or briefs? What did he read? What did he like to do for fun? Was he all work and no play, as he'd suggested? What was his ex-wife like?

"We work together well, don't we?" Nick observed as he filled the woodbox while she cleaned up pans from the next morning's breakfast preparations.

Mary had observed the same thing, but hadn't the courage to voice it. She felt nervous just thinking it. She smiled at him.

"I'm surprised at how easily a compatible living arrangement has evolved. Still, no matter how relaxed it's been, I have a wicked case of cabin fever."

Nick nodded. "Me, too. I guess, then, since you're in the midst of morning house chores, it's my job to shovel us out of here so we can at least get some fresh air." He dropped the last log in the woodbox, then started to pull his boots back on.

Mary looked around the room. "I'd rather be outside, if I could get there."

"If—" Nick paused, then plunged on. "If we both shovel, we can get outside sooner.

Then we can both clean this place later and get that over with quicker. What do you say?"

"Fine!" Mary went immediately for her jacket and gloves and boots.

"Fine!" Nick shrugged into his jacket.

The diamond-hard winter's day flew by as together they dug the snow away from windows and doors. Nick pulled Mary through waist-high drifts to show her a breathtaking view of mountain peaks piercing the clearest blue sky she'd ever seen, and pine trees poking through a blanket of sparkling white like pins from a cotton pincushion.

By midafternoon they'd worked up a sweat in their heavy clothes, something that surprised Mary. When she'd first stepped outside, the raw cold cut through her like the sharpest of razors. But she hadn't wanted to complain. As she and Nick worked together, she'd grown warm and invigorated, and loved every minute of it.

Later, back inside the cabin, Mary prepared a hot lunch.

"Mmm, soup," Nick murmured, breathing deeply over a tin bowl as he sat on the low fireplace stool.

"A specialty of mine," Mary responded with feigned pride, "and of the house, as I'm sure you've discovered." She pointed to the double row of soup cans on the shelf above the narrow kitchen counter.

Nick spooned it and took a taste of the thick concoction. "Clam chowder?"

Mary nodded, stirring her soup to cool it. "New England style."

"Yes, but different, and good. Must be your own secret recipe."

"I could let you in on the secret if you promise to keep it to yourself."

"I swear," he said, crossing his heart.

"I added a can of whole kernel corn and some garlic powder and pepper."

"You truly are amazing."

"I know." She flipped a lock of hair off her forehead. "It's an everything-to-everybody thing."

"You'd have felt guilty if you hadn't added the corn."

She raised her eyes to his. "Now you're amazing. How did you know?"

"Just an uncanny sense. If you'd simply opened a can of soup and heated it, somehow you'd have failed in your womanly duty."

"Somehow I think my mother would have known. That is, after she was through being appalled by the fact I'm even in this cabin with you in the first place."

"Yep."

"Yep."

They finished lunch. Nick washed the dishes, then dressed for outside again. "I'll be back in a few minutes," he said with a smile in his voice. "I have a surprise for you."

"What is it?"

"Well, now, if I tell you, then it won't be a surprise, will it? You do like surprises, don't you?"

"That depends." She thought of the surprise that the chief executive officer of her company had dropped on her just before the holidays.

"You'll like this one. I promise." He went outside.

Mary picked up her sketchpad. She felt a new enthusiasm for her work, and went at it with a determination to make it her best.

Bang! Something hit the door. Mary got up quickly and opened it just a crack.

"Oh, I hope it isn't a sasquatch," she whispered loudly with feigned terror.

"It is, woman. Open up!" he puffed, and pushed against the door.

Mary opened it wide and Nick struggled in, pulling a balsam fir tree, bottom end first, behind him. Mary watched him struggle to the corner, where the rope lay coiled. He leaned the tree against the window, rushed past her, went out, and returned with a bucket full of rocks. She watched as he dumped the rocks onto the floor, then set the tree into the bucket.

"Come hold this steady, will you please?" He started picking up rocks and dropping them into the bucket around the tree trunk. When she didn't move, he looked up at her. "It would be a good thing if you closed the door. Perhaps you haven't noticed that snow is blowing in."

As if snapped from a trance, Mary shut the door. "You've brought a Christmas tree," she said evenly.

"Are you surprised?" he asked through ragged breaths as he struggled, holding the tree and picking up rocks.

"Yes, of course. Especially since I'd been trying to avoid all that Christmas stuff."

"Can't. It's upon us. Come hold this, please."

Mary put her hand through the long-needled branches and held the trunk straight while he secured the tree. Its piney aroma caused total Christmas recall in her mind. Nick moved the whole lot to the corner, filled the teakettle, and poured the water into the bucket, then grabbed the colorful afghan from a nearby chair and draped it around the bottom.

"There. What do you think?" He stood back, admiring his work.

"A bit bare, but that's fine with me." Mary stepped back, too.

"It needs something. Look around for decorations." Nick headed for the kitchen.

"Nick, it's fine the way it is." Mary had successfully avoided the heavy-handed work of tree decoration when her mother dragged out box after box of ornaments every year and made everyone, even the mailman, hang a few until the tree groaned under the weight and its branches were barely recognizable. Something about this plain green Christmas tree, if she was forced to have one at all, was refreshing.

"Just a little something to make it festive. Ah-ha!"

"What?"

"A bag of yarn. Bertie never throws anything away. Here's the leftovers from the afghan." He threw a bulging paper bag to her.

When Mary saw the excitement in Nick's eyes, she couldn't keep herself out of the fun of decorating the tree. He turned on the radio and found a station that was playing upbeat Christmas songs, and they decorated the balsam while belting out a lusty rendition of

"Rockin' Around the Christmas Tree." When they finished they both stepped back for a look. Yarn bows in red, green, yellow, orange, and blue bobbed among green branches. Mary had fashioned a star of sorts from a skein of thick red yarn, and Nick had climbed on the stool and positioned it at her direction.

"Another great job, partner," Nick said, his right hand held out toward her.

Mary took it and immediately felt hers grow warmer. She withdrew slowly. "That's the most beautiful Christmas tree I've ever seen," she breathed. And she meant it.

An awkward silence hung between them. Mary was the first to ease away. She picked up the book she'd been reading and settled on the couch. Nick picked up his carving things and moved back to the chair by the window. He looked over at her now and then, unable to concentrate on his work.

Her skin took on a transparent sheen dotted with a few freckles. She had a strong profile. He liked seeing the corners of her eyes fan upward when she laughed or smiled. Her eyes fascinated him. Sometimes they seemed stormy blue, like the sky before a rainstorm, sometimes earth-brown with flecks of green like a pine-dotted hillside, and sometimes shot with gold like pebbles in a sun-dappled crystal stream.

Without makeup and in her jeans she looked like a young girl. He wondered how she looked in her office. Did she wear dresses or stylish suits? What did she look like dressed up in high heels and makeup? Did she wear her hair up off her neck, or all loose and moving about her shoulders? He pictured her in a full-length black low-neckline dress covered with sparkling jet beads that made her body shimmer like a night of stars.

Did she take baths or showers? Did she wear lacy underthings or cotton? What did she wear to bed? Always flannel pajamas, or a silk nightgown, or nothing?

What was happening to him?

Whatever it was that was happening to him, it was happening fast. He wasn't used to speed like this where a woman was concerned. Maybe she could stay longer. Maybe he wouldn't have to leave so soon. Could he ask her to come back? He'd thought he'd never feel like this again — young, alive, with all his senses collectively sending messages to his brain and confusing him beyond belief.

As the day waned toward evening, Christmas Eve, Nick grew increasingly restless and unable to concentrate. Carefully he rolled up his carving tools, then checked the woodbox for firewood.

"I'll get us some more wood for in here," he said into the air, "and then bring some into the woodshed from outside. It needs to thaw out before it'll burn."

Mary put down her book and stretched. "You can't sit for too long without finding work to do, can you?"

"Is it that obvious?" He smiled a bit sheepishly.

"When was the last time you played?"

"Played?" He cocked his head toward her.

"Yes, played."

"With toys?"

"Or not. Just let loose a little."

"I've worked on a ranch ever since I was a kid. It's in me, I guess. But I like it. I like to work."

"Yes, but you need some play, too."

"Well, I do have the carving . . ." He donned his outerwear and started into the woodshed.

"I'll help you," Mary offered, and started putting on her boots. "I can carry some logs."

After they'd filled the woodbox inside the cabin, Nick went out and brought in heavy-frosted logs from under the tarp. Mary held the tarp up so he could move under and out more easily.

"You really do work too hard," she said. She dropped the tarp over his head.

"Hey! Some help you are!" his voice echoed from underneath.

He backed out from under the tarp and turned around just as she threw an armful of snow over his head. The act startled him, and Mary thought for a stabbing moment that she'd gone a tad too far. What had possessed her to throw snow on his head? What possessed her to start giggling like a prankish kid? She saw the devil's own light in his eyes kindle and flame and knew she'd started something she hoped she could finish.

"So that's the way you want it, eh?" He scrambled away from the pile of logs. "You think I can't play, do you?" He started toward her.

He picked up a gloveful of snow, formed it into a ball, all the while inching closer to her. "Hmm, good packin', as we used to say when I was a kid."

Mary backed away. She reached for a gloveful of snow and formed it into a ball. "Sure is good packin'. Did you ever build snow forts?"

326

"Invincible ones. You?"

"Impenetrable. I was good at it."

"Yeah?"

"Yeah!" she shouted, and lobbed the snowball for a direct hit on his shoulder. She felt as shocked as he looked for a split second, then burst out laughing.

"You think that's funny, don't you?"

"Wild-ly!" She could barely get out the word. She was laughing so hard, her breath had taken leave.

He lobbed his snowball, but she ducked and he missed her. She was good, he agreed, and quickly formed another.

Mary tried to run behind a tree, but she wasn't used to snow up over her knees, and every step demanded a great amount of strength and energy. She tripped over a tree stump and fell on her back. He was over her in a moment, and together they rolled as one in the snow.

"We used to like washing the girls' faces when I was a kid!" He was laughing so hard, it made him almost too weak to pin her arms down with one hand so he could rub snow in her face with the other.

"And we girls used to love to drop snow down the boys' pants!" she puffed.

"Just try it, sister!" he laughed.

327

"Just watch me, brother!" she hooted.

They struggled against each other, but the depth of the snow and the depth of their laughter made each of them almost powerless to achieve their goals. They were forced to accept minimal success at best. Mary struggled to her feet. Nick scrambled to stand. They were still laughing.

"That was fun!" Mary said between gasps for breath as she wiped her face with the end of her scarf that had been inside her jacket.

"Yes, ma'am," Nick coughed, spitting snow out of his mouth.

And then they weren't laughing anymore.

"Your nose is running," he said quietly.

"I know," she answered, "but my mother told me not to wipe it on the sleeve of my snowsuit."

He reached into his back pocket and extracted a red bandanna. He walked up to her and held it under her nose. "Blow," he said.

Holding her gaze steady with his, she did.

Silently Mary turned and started back for the cabin. The moon was already on the ascent, and a light dusting of crystallized air seemed suspended around them. Nick followed.

"Look at that," Mary breathed, and stopped walking.

Nick stopped behind her and followed her gaze across a pristine clearing, alive with what resembled the glitter of rhinestones as the moon cast its silver touch.

"Beautiful," he whispered.

Mary stepped carefully into the clearing. "Let's make angels," she said in hushed excitement.

"Make angels?"

"Yes. Didn't you ever make snow angels?"

"No. I was into forts. It's a boy thing." He watched her back.

She turned around and faced him. "Snow angels aren't a girl thing or a boy thing, they're a . . . spirit thing. When you make an angel, you leave the imprint of your spirit in the snow. Watch."

She positioned herself with studied perfection, then dropped flat on her back, hands at her sides. He watched as she twisted her head from side to side, raised both arms high over her head and both legs wide at the same time, then brought them down. She repeated the process, then raised both arms in front.

"Help me up so I don't ruin my skirt," she commanded.

He reached for her hands and pulled her to her feet. She stepped away.

"See?"

He could see. A perfect silhouette of an angel shining in the moonlit snow.

"Now you."

Mary moved him to the side a bit and turned him around. He dropped back into the snow as she had done, and emulated her movements, then held out his hands. She grabbed them and helped him to his feet. He turned around and looked down.

"There we are. Angels." Mary's words puffed into crystals.

Nick stood still for a long time, letting his gaze drift over their joined images in the snow. She wondered what he was thinking about the childlike thing he'd just accomplished. She didn't wonder long.

"The last thing I'm feeling right now is angelic."

She held his gaze a protracted moment before tearing hers away from his face and back to her snow angel. She felt a small stab of irony herself. She wasn't feeling one bit angelic either.

The moon climbed high and the stars came out. Mary and Nick stood side by side, a narrow shaft of brittle cold air separating them, and saw their spirit images in a pair of snow angels joined at the tips of wings and the hems of skirts sparkle with the crystals of what they both knew had already become a special Montana Christmas Eve.

> "There was a pause—just long enough for an angel to pass, flying slowly."
> —Ronald Firbank, *Vainglory*

"Tell me about your family Christmas Eves," Nick asked, handing her a mug of hot buttered rum. Behind them the radio played seasonal music, their Christmas tree gave off its distinctive balsam fir aroma, and Blitzen gazed upon them from his elevated position.

"Chaotic," she said, settling down on the couch in front of the fire and propping her stocking feet on the low table. "But fun."

She yawned, then spun him the tales of homemade gifts that graduated to computer games, used plastic Christmas trees from garage sales that grew into towering perfectly-shaped real ones that cost hundreds of dollars. The Christmas she'd spent in the hospital having her third child, the Christmas Eve she'd spent crying all night when David left them, her first Christmas as a single mother and grandmother. The mountain of gifts in her parents' home and in her own. The food, the everlasting food. And through it all, the fun.

"Sounds great," he said with a hint of wistfulness.

"Sounds tiring," she said with a laugh. "My family makes a celebration out of everything. They'll make up holidays if it isn't soon enough between the normal ones. I remember one memorable Saint Swithin's Day when . . ."

Nick leaned forward and rested his chin on his upturned thumbs. He was gazing into the fire, or someplace beyond it, and Mary drew back from telling family tales. He got up and took down a long-handled corn popper from a peg on the wall, filled it, and held it over the fire.

"What about you?" she asked, watching his back as he hunkered down in front of the fire, shaking the popper.

The fire crackled and the corn popped as he told her about the first Christmas after his parents had died when he was seven years old and his uncle told him Santa Claus hadn't been able to find him. The first Christmas he was married to a girl he met at the University of Wyoming, and five Christmases later when she left him. The Christmases alone or with Smokey and Bertie. The Christmases without children. The first Christmas with his uncle again, who'd become wealthy in the cattle business and took him on as partner. The Christmas he found his wife again and she told him she wanted a divorce.

"I take it you didn't want the divorce," she said as they shared the bowl of popcorn.

"I knew it was inevitable. You?"

"I didn't really want it, but finally I knew it would be best for all of us. I have no regrets."

"Did he?" Nick stared into the fire.

"Some, I guess. Divorce is supposed to be harder on women than it is on men, or so they tell me."

"Don't believe everything they tell you," he said, turning back to her. "I think it's as difficult for men as it is for women. Men just have different ways of hiding it."

"I'll say! Dates with multiple women and a whole new wardrobe!"

"That's so they can hide from themselves the way they're hurting."

"You really think so?" She studied his face.

"I know so."

"Did you date lots of women?" That was really none of her business, but the question came out before she had time to think about it.

"Date. Sounds like school."

"If only it were that simple." She laughed.

"I'll say. Another reason I wanted to come out here now was to get away from well-meaning friends who want me to meet this cousin or that friend of a friend so neither us will be alone over the holidays."

"I know. Especially New Year's Eve. Have your friends ever insisted on taking you with them to a New Year's Eve party and then brought someone along to be your date?"

He winced. "Yes, and it was painful for all of us."

"Me, too. I hate New Year's Eve. It's my least favorite holiday. A bunch of people all trying to have a good time because they think they're supposed to. All I want to do on New Year's Eve is curl up with a good book and avoid it all."

He flung his arm up over the back of the couch. "I do, too! The only thing that might possibly make it nicer would be to be with the right person. And the right book. And maybe read to each other."

Mary didn't know how to respond to him. An emotion-laden pause hung between them.

Mary dropped her head back on the couch. She felt his arm under her neck. Her eyelids grew heavy and closed. The exercise, the air, the fire, and, she supposed, the rum contributed to the languor flowing through her limbs, yet her heart slammed against her chest with all the subtlety of a bass drum. There was only one thing she wanted at this moment, and she felt embarrassed to be thinking it. She wanted Nick Chase to kiss her, kiss her thoroughly and satisfyingly. And she wanted to kiss him back.

Nick set his mug on the table, then let his eyes roam over Mary's face as her head rested in the crook of his arm. He pictured their angel images in the sparkling snow and remembered how the tips of the wings had touched. She looked like an angel stretched out next to him, relaxed from the rum and the fire. And he felt just the opposite inside. He was *on* fire with a heat burning out of control. He wanted to take this enticing woman into his arms and make love to her and then he wanted to wrap them together in his sleeping bag and hold their mutual warmth together until first light.

His hands tightened into tense fists. Holding back was tough as hell. She looked inviting. Her lips looked inviting. He couldn't stop himself from wanting to know their taste and feel. He wanted to kiss her deeply, satisfyingly. He lowered his mouth to hers and brushed it lightly. She didn't pull away. Was she asleep? Her lips had responded ever so slightly, he was certain of that.

Mary felt Nick's kiss, the softness of his beard as if the brush of an angel's wing had fluttered over her face. Before she could give more than the merest hint of response, his lips had come and gone, leaving behind his scent of pine and sharp air, and his taste of sweet rum and salty popcorn.

She tried to open her eyes but hadn't the strength. And then his lips were back again softly, lingeringly. She parted hers slightly and fit them against his. And then his arm gathered her shoulders close; his other hand cupped her jaw and fitted her mouth farther into his. Her tongue reached out and met his and they explored the warmth and rum-sweetness behind their lips.

He lifted his mouth. Their eyes opened slowly. He took her mug and set it on the table, then gathered her into his arms. She slipped her arms around his wide shoulders. Their mouths came back together in fierce longing, and they each fulfilled their Christmas Eve wish with a thorough and mutually satisfying kiss.

When the kiss ended, they didn't move from the embrace of each other's arms. Mary wondered how she would feel, how he would feel when they opened their eyes and let reality come between them. They didn't know each other, who'd they'd been, who they were now. Never mind what they would become. She'd never engaged in one-night stands. Regardless of how incredibly and powerfully attractive Nick Chase was, she couldn't let that happen now. If she did, she knew she'd never be able to forget him, and since she'd never see him again, she didn't want that kind of painful yearning to dominate her life.

Be sensible, she warned herself. *Stop this now, while you still can. It's too risky. It's just that it's Christmas and you're far away from home, and you're lonely, and . . .*

Nick watched emotions cross and change her expression several times over. He shouldn't have kissed her like that, shouldn't have let himself get carried away. The chances they'd ever see each other again were remote. Yet they still had two days together. How would they get through them now without an awkwardness that hadn't existed before they'd kissed?

Mary carefully extracted herself from the circle of Nick's arms. "I . . . I'm too tired to eat any supper. I think I'll go to bed now."

Nick nodded in agreement. They were silent in their bedtime preparations, and when

337

Nick extinguished the last lantern, Mary believed she'd never been suspended in so deeply black a night.

Christmas morning Mary descended the ladder from the loft, steadying herself along the rough-hewn log wall with the palm of her hand. Her legs felt watery and her head full of cobwebs from lack of sleep. Nick was not in the cabin, but coffee perked merrily on the stove and a fire blazed in the fireplace. She'd heard him stoke it up very early in the morning right after she'd crept down from the loft and done something she hoped she wouldn't be embarrassed about.

She poured a cup of coffee and breathed in the aroma of something cooking in a big iron pot on the back burner. Nick had been creating again.

She heard him gathering wood out back, and ducked behind the curtain to take care of her morning ritual in the tiny bathroom. When she emerged, Nick was standing over the pot, stirring with the longest-handled wooden spoon she'd ever seen, shaking the contents of a glass jar into the concoction, and singing softly, " 'It's beginning to look a lot like Christmas . . .' "

"Whatever you're cooking smells wonderful."

"Why, thank you, ma'am. Christmas dinner. It's a specialty of mine. Elk stew." He held out the wooden spoon toward her, dripping with a dark brown liquid. "Here, taste."

Mary stepped back. "Elk . . . ? Oh, I couldn't." She looked toward the fireplace.

Nick laughed. "Blitzen? Nah. If it was him, I think I'd be feeling a lot more guilty than I do."

Mary took her coffee and stood by the fireplace.

"Sleep well?" he asked brightly, as if nothing disturbing had happened the night before.

She muttered something incoherent into her cup and said, "You?"

"Like a baby. I always sleep well out here."

Just like a man, she fumed inside. Typical! Why was it that men reacted to earth-shattering events so calmly? Good thing it wasn't too late to change what she'd done that morning so she wouldn't have to be any more embarrassed than she already was over her behavior the night before.

She watched Nick. He seemed to be puttering around the Christmas tree. He was withdrawing something from behind it. Oh, no . . .

"I see Saint Nick must have dropped down the chimney last night. There's a present here with your name on it." He moved toward her, holding out a newspaper-wrapped package tied with red yarn.

"For me? But . . ."

"I know, you're avoiding Christmas. But I guess it was inevitable."

He placed the package in her lap, and she noticed the pleased smile playing about his mouth. His mouth. The one that had kissed her so wonderfully the night before Christmas.

"I guess," she said quietly, setting her cup down.

She untied the yarn and drew away the newspaper. Nick's old cotton pouch lay there, and she felt a hard, strange-shaped object inside. Her hands shook as she unrolled the pouch and opened it. She reached inside and her fingers fell over a wooden object. His carving! She withdrew it and breathed in a long "oh."

She held in both hands a perfect replica of Blitzen, precise rack of antlers and full body intact. A red yarn bow tie encircled his neck.

"I didn't have time to oil and smooth it, but I'll get that finished before you leave." Nick's voice was thick and a little nervous.

"That is, if you . . . want to take it. Maybe it isn't appropriate . . ."

Mary found her voice over the lump in her throat. "Want . . . want to take it? Of course I want it. It's wonderful, beautiful." She turned it over and over in her hands, surveying every detail, running her fingers over the nose, the tail, the rack. "Appropriate isn't the word. It's . . . it's the most wonderful present anyone's ever given me."

Nick smiled. He felt something inside. What? Happy, that was what. Mary actually had tears in her eyes. His gift had been right. He busied himself stirring the stew and let the steam hide the tears that had built in his own eyes.

Mary rose from the couch and went to the Christmas tree. He watched her go to the other side of it and reach under the afghan tree skirt. She pulled out something.

"Looks like Santa left something for you, too. Will you come over here and open it?"

Nick couldn't move. He hadn't expected a present. How? When?

"I don't see any other boys here named Nick, so I guess you're going to have to take this present whether you want to or not." Her voice was as nervous as his had been.

He moved slowly to the couch and sat

down. When she placed the package in his lap, he stared at it for a long time. It was wrapped in a square blue-printed silk scarf, and tied with white yarn. He placed his hands over it and felt its contours; he couldn't imagine what was inside.

She was watching him closely. He felt her gaze pinned on him, felt her concern as much as his own had been when he gave her his present. Slowly he untied the yarn and pulled the scarf away. Mounted between two squares of white cardboard was a sketch of the landscape outside the front of the cabin, the trees surrounding the patch of snow where they'd set down their angel images, and those images faintly drawn in almost ethereal strokes. Her initials, MOM, and the date lay discreetly in the drawn tuft of winter grasses in the lower right-hand corner.

Nick was moved by the sentiment expressed in the drawing, but the words written below the drawing touched his senses and left him speechless.

The onset and the waning of love make themselves felt in the uneasiness experienced at being alone together.

— La Bruyère

He looked up at her, and through the tears clouding his own eyes saw those clouding hers. He knew what was happening. They were each wondering what might have been, knowing there could be no more than this week, and telling each other not to forget one memorable Christmas.

And he knew if he even uttered a word of thanks to her, his emotions would spill over. He couldn't let that happen. He heard his uncle's voice telling him to act like a man.

Carefully Nick replaced the drawing inside Mary's scarf and retied the white yarn. He rose and set the package on his rolled sleeping bag. He caught her gaze and held it for a long and heavy moment, then donned his jacket and boots and went outside.

It was late afternoon and Nick hadn't returned to the cabin. Mary wondered if he'd decided to go to his own place and stay there. She was growing frantic with worry, when she heard his familiar step on the porch. Relieved, she busied herself stirring his simmering stew. Something had changed between them; the companionable coexistence had been replaced by awkward stepping around each other.

343

She read his face the moment he came through the door. He almost looked angry. She thought he'd be pleased with her gift, as pleased as she was with his. How curious that they'd both thought to give the other a gift, and that it had been something from their own hands and hearts. Mary prided herself on being organized, capable of sorting out problems. But this . . .

"What do you plan to do with the rest of your life?" His question, his hard-edged voice, startled her. He was standing at one end of the couch.

"What?"

"It's a mature question, timely, I think," he said, cutting his words. "Didn't you come here to sort things out? Figure out where you're going?"

"Yes, but it's too soon to . . ."

He reached down and picked up four books from the pile on the floor. "I'd say you were on a power trip."

She cocked an inquisitive eye. "What do you mean by that?"

"Maybe I should say empowerment trip. That's the new buzzword, I understand." He displayed the books as if they were exhibits A, B, C, and D in a courtroom, then waved a thick paperback over his head. *"Native*

American Spirituality by Eagle Man. That means you're searching for a connection to a power greater than yourself." He put that book down and picked up the next, again waving it over his head. *"Your Rights in the Business World* by Stella Ramshaw, the way to handle the heavy burden of your own present, or absent, corporate power."

"Now, just a minute." Mary was growing heated. "You don't know anything about what I'm handling in my professional life."

That book went down and the next one went up. *"Daring Gamble* by Maria Greene. The portrayal of hard and fast rules that gave power to Victorian relationships. No need to wonder how to behave. Someone else has made that decision for you." He set that one down and picked up the last. *"Twilight Phantasies* by Margaret Benson." He leaned toward her and huskily whispered, "The erotic power and excitement of forbidden love."

Nick looked like a prosecuting attorney making closing arguments. Mary was not about to pronounce herself guilty by his rather accurate assessment. She sat down on the couch without looking at him.

"Just lucky guesses," she acquiesced. "I thought you were a cowboy. What do you know about female empowerment?"

"I'm a cattleman," he answered quickly. "But I read a lot, too." He sat down next to her and searched her face. "I'm not ridiculing you, you know. I'm searching, too, and I'm on some kind of trip I didn't buy a ticket for. I've learned something very important about you. And about myself. I suppose I came off like some male chauvinist . . ."

She held up her hand to stop him. "No, you didn't. I guess I'm just sensitive about . . . things that are going on in my life right now. My emotions seem to be hovering just under the surface, and I've been afraid they'd come skittering out like an open bag of marbles. Especially with someone I hardly know and will most likely"—her voice grew hoarse—"never see again."

"Sometimes that's the very one who will understand what you're going through the most," he said quietly, and leaned his head against the back of the couch. "I've been feeling like I've been losing my own marbles these days."

It was her turn to search his face. "Should I try for a lucky guess?"

"I don't think you could, no matter how lucky you are."

"All right." She thought for a moment. "Something or someone wants you to leave this big-sky country, and you're not sure if you want to do whatever it is they want you to do."

He rolled his head sideways and looked at her. "You're pretty lucky, too," he said evenly.

"You're easy to read—at least where this was concerned."

"I suppose now you'll just add me to that stack of books."

Mary thought he was volumes apart from any book she'd ever read, but she couldn't say it without dissolving. "Only if you think that would give me more empowerment."

"I'd never admit to it if it did."

"Ah-ha!" She lightened the mood.

"Ah-ha?"

"Yes, ah-ha. I know even more about you now."

He sat up. "Oh, yeah? And just what is that?" His voice held a slight challenge.

"You can't have a woman either besting you in anything or wielding more power than you, or . . . being your boss. That's it!"

"What's it?"

"Wherever you're expected to go, there's probably going to be a female over you, and you can't handle it."

He smiled enigmatically. "I'm going to take a chance here, and hope I don't injure your newfound empowerment by showing you that your luck just ran out." He ran a hand through his thick hair and let the strands sift through his fingers. "If I do take this job, I'll be the boss of a staff of all women. What do you think of that?"

She stared at him for a moment. *"That* bothers you?"

"Hell, yes. I don't . . . I'm not . . ."

Mary understood more than he knew. A painful divorce could sometimes chip away at one's self-confidence. Enough to make it difficult to interact with the opposite sex.

"Don't worry, they'll teach you."

"That's what I'm afraid of."

She knew what she and Nick were doing now: putting distance back into their relationship. Space. Division. Her duties, his duties. It would make the parting that much easier, she knew. On both of them.

"Maybe I shouldn't take this job," he was saying. "Maybe I should just stay here, do what I do best, take care of cattle, hunt, fish. What do you think?" He turned toward her.

Yes, stay here. Stay here so I can come running back to a small space in heaven when things turn to hell in the office.

"Don't you think you can do the job?" she

challenged.

"Yes, I believe I can. I just don't know if I want to. It's a big change for me. And for the people in that company."

"I know exactly what you mean," she said. "I've been passed over for a position I believed I was right for. It hurts."

"Do you think you can't work with a person who's over you in the very position you wanted?"

"I try to get along with everybody, so I think I'll get along fine with him. It'll be a struggle, though. I'd have been good in that job."

"These things happen. Fair or not. What's this guy like?"

"Don't know. Haven't met him yet."

"Well, then, you just march right into his office and state who you are up front." Nick sat up straight and used his expressive hands to make his point. "That's what I do at a cattle sale. I say this is who I am, what I'm looking for, and I expect to play fair and be treated fairly. I know my work, so don't insult me or try to snow me. I'll give you a no-hassle fair deal, and I expect the same from you."

"Just like that?" Mary marveled at such a direct approach. It might work at a cattle sale, but in a sophisticated city office, it was doubtful.

"Yep."

"Does it work?"

"Most of the time. There's always at least one who won't make a square deal."

"What do you do then?"

"Don't deal with him again."

"Is that what you'll do in your new venture?"

"Only way I know how to be," he said simply.

"What about the women on the staff you were so worried about?" she chided him.

He stroked his beard. "I hope it can be the same way. Like you said . . ."

"They'll teach you."

"They'll teach me." He sighed.

They sat in silence for a long time together, yet separate, in their own thoughts. The room darkened and the fire died down.

Nick pushed himself away from the couch. "Well, enough gloom and doom. Let's start the Christmas festivities. Light the lanterns, stoke the fire, turn up the music, make the biscuits!"

"Hear! Hear!" Mary pushed off and set to work.

When Mary came down from the loft after

changing into a dark green turtleneck sweater and matching trousers, Nick had once again transformed the room and himself. Emotion rose in her and tightened her chest. He was making it very difficult for her to maintain their reconstructed distance.

He'd set the table, first covering it with a colorful quilt, set a bowl of pine greens and cones in the center, and candles in tarnished brass holders on either side. A couple of mismatched china plates with two green bandannas for napkins folded over them sat side by side, facing the fire.

And he'd changed into a cream-colored Irish fisherman's sweater and slim jeans, and looked enormously appealing. He continued to surprise her, delight her.

"I suppose we should have some wine, but would beer be all right?" He didn't wait for an answer, but went back to the kitchen and pulled two long-necked bottles from the refrigerator. "Can't find the corkscrew right now. I suppose Smokey was using it as an ice pick again, and I'll find it in the woodshed sometime." He flipped the caps off the bottles and handed one to her.

Mary took it slowly. Nick touched the top of his bottle to the top of hers. "Merry Christmas," he whispered, "if you don't mind too much. This is the best one I can remember spending in years." He tipped the bottle and took a long, obviously satisfying swig.

He held out a chair for her, and she sat down. His hand brushed the back of her neck and sent tingles down her spine. She tried to control their sensation but couldn't. She was starving.

Mary had to admit the stew was delicious, and once again the biscuits were cloud-light. When she looked over at Nick to show her appreciation for the meal, she noticed flour dust in his hair blending with the silver streaks at his temples. She had the strongest urge to blow on it and brush it away with her fingertips, but she managed to quell the desire.

"Got an idea," he said, and pushed away from the table.

He took the bottle of champagne from the refrigerator, sat down on the couch, and held the bottle between his knees. With careful turns and gentle pressure the cork slipped out with a healthy *pop*.

"*Voilà!* Real Christmas cheer!" he said, jumping up and smiling and heading for the kitchen. He grabbed a couple of tumblers from a shelf and poured the champagne.

"I'll make the toast this time," Mary announced. "To the finest Christmas meal I can remember." He started to drink, but she stopped him. "And to the talented chef who prepared it."

"I'll drink to that!" He lifted the glass to his lips.

"Wait!"

"You make long-winded toasts, ma'am. I'm thirsty. Get on with it!"

She raised her glass again and touched the rim of his. "To a most memorable Christmas," she said, and took a sip before her voice gave out.

He made no comment, but drank in thoughtful silence.

"What do you usually do after Christmas dinner?" he asked after they'd cleaned up the dishes together and finished the champagne.

"Sit around like a bunch of overweight, underslung toads and watch a video of *It's a Wonderful Life*. You?" Mary dropped down on the couch, pushed the coffee table aside, and stretched her feet out on the bearhide rug toward the fire.

"Not much. I've chopped wood, or read. Maybe carved a little."

Mary dropped her head to the side and regarded his profile. "Thank you for the carving of Blitzen. It's the first real piece of art I've owned."

He looked down at his hands. "It's hardly art."

"It's a treasure. I'll keep it always."

He looked at her and swallowed. "That's how I feel about your drawing."

"I wasn't sure you liked it."

"I do. I just couldn't say . . ."

She reached out and slipped her hand between his two, where they rested over his stomach.

"How fortunate we are to have hands that can express what's in our minds," she whispered.

He pressed his palms together, holding her hand fast. "Or in our hearts. Mary, something's happening to me. . . ."

She tried to extract her hand, but he wouldn't let her go. He held her gaze and wouldn't let go of that either. She sat up straight and drew her eyes toward the fire.

"All right," she sighed. "I didn't want to admit it. Something's happening to me, too, and I can't let it continue."

"Why not? Never mind. I think I know."

"It wouldn't work." She looked back at him.

He ran his fingers up her arm.

"We live in different places, live different lives. This was just a . . . I don't know, fluke or something." She moved toward him ever so slowly.

"Or something," he said quietly, and moved toward her smoothly.

"We had no control over it." Her gaze fell to his mouth.

"None whatsoever."

Mary saw his lips glisten in the firelight and felt a tightening below her stomach. His hand running up her arm inside the sleeve of her sweater made her shiver on one side while the fire was heating her on the other. His head dipped, his eyes closed, and her vision blurred as he fit his lips over hers and she felt again the light brush of his beard.

She gave back to him, and their kiss was even deeper, lusher than the one they'd shared on Christmas Eve. And then he was drawing her into his arms, she was sliding her arms around his back. They were sliding from the couch onto their knees on the bearhide rug. He turned her shoulders and lowered her onto her back while holding her lips fast with his own.

Mary slid her body under his length and entwined her legs through his. Nick plunged his hands into her hair and massaged her head with his fingers. Mary slipped a hand inside his shirt and ran her fingers over the smooth skin of his chest and the light dusting of hair. Nick slid one hand down the length of her body and around her hip to cup her buttock and pull her close to the burgeoning fullness in his groin.

And then they were all arms and legs and hands and lips and flying clothes and panting breaths. And naked, flame-baked skin. And champagne and lust-drugged senses. And long and languorous entwining of breasts to chest, and thighs to thighs, until everything between was buried and enveloped.

And they moved in mutual rhythm and sensual depth. Moved fast and hard, and demanded each from the other everything that had been held in check, everything crying for expression. And then they moved slowly, savoring, sensing, burning the memory into all their senses.

The last to part were their lips, swollen and moist. The last to subside was their breathing as they fell together in the deep sleep of satisfied lovers.

"But what a mischievous devil Love is."
                              —Samuel Butler

Sometime during the night Mary awakened and slipped out of his arms and up to the loft. Nick arose at first light, stoked up the fire, and made coffee. Only this time it wasn't like every other morning during the week. This morning was different.

He was different.

Mary was different.

She went through her morning ritual in near silence, engaging in minimal polite conversation.

"Mary," Nick started when he could stand it no more.

"Please, Nick, not now. I can't." She'd waved him away and retreated to the loft to finish packing.

From below the hill Nick heard Smokey's four-wheel grinding through the deep snow. He'd be here any minute, and he and Mary hadn't settled anything between them. She bumped her suitcase down the ladder, then packed her radio and tapes and books into the other suitcase. He watched her carefully wrap the elk carving in a bandanna and place it inside her flannel pajamas in her first case.

"Mary, please" — he crossed the room to her — "we have to talk. About last night, about this week, about the future."

She raised her eyes to his, and he saw them glassy hard from withheld tears, saw the storm brewing behind their green-gold depths.

"Nick, Chicago is a long way from here. Not just in miles."

"Chicago?" He swallowed hard.

"My family's there, my work is there. . . ."

"When is your next vacation or time off?" He rushed to interrupt her at the sound of Smokey's vehicle door slamming.

"Easter," she said. "Why? Anyway, I might not get vacation. The new vice president, you know. It's a busy time."

He nodded and looked down. "Easter's early next year, I think," he said.

"March," she added. "When will you get a break?" She said that without looking at him.

He looked up and brightened. "If I'm here, Easter's a good time for me. If I'm . . . somewhere else, well, I won't know. Maybe it won't look good if I take off so soon into the job."

She nodded and zipped her suitcase. "Maybe you could just tell them in advance you're taking that time off. Maybe you can get someone to cover for you."

"Maybe," he said. "Maybe you could do

the same thing. After all, you're a senior member of your department, right? You're going to need a break after all the stressful work you'll be doing. I mean, with the new vice president, and all."

"Maybe. If I did, I mean, if I came back here, would you be . . . ?" She couldn't finish.

"I'd consider that, I mean, if I could be certain you'd be here."

Smokey knocked on the door. Both Mary and Nick twisted their heads toward it.

"I'll speak to Mr. Robinson about the possibility," Mary said.

"I'll talk to Smokey," Nick said.

"Good luck," Mary said.

"You, too," Nick said. "Don't forget to tell him who you are."

"I won't." Mary swallowed hard, then lifted her gaze to Blitzen. He gazed back, unseeing, yet she thought seeing everything. "I never thought I'd miss a stuffed elk, but . . ."

"He'll miss you, too," Nick said. "Believe me, he'll miss you, too."

Full of courage and determination, and an exuberance and joy she hadn't felt since the first time she roller-skated around the block without falling down, Mary strode into her office. At her desk she pitched the pitiful philodendron, pot and all, into her waste can, and ripped every one of her positive-thinking sayings off her bulletin board.

Then she reached into her leather tote and took out the bandanna-wrapped treasure. Carefully she removed the yarn ribbon and opened the bandanna. With loving hands she lifted the intricately carved elk with its proud chest and display of superb rack, and set it in the middle of her desk. It inspired, moved, sent waves of courage and strength into her blood.

She was different now. Nobody, but nobody, was going to trample her. She was a team player, yet an individual, and as soon as the new man learned that, the better for both of them.

She squared her shoulders, took a deep breath, and started toward the new vice president's office.

Her secretary, Meg, greeted her in the same cheerful manner she had for seventeen years. "Welcome back, Mary. How was Christmas?"

"Terrific! Stupendous!"

"Wow! You must have received everything you asked for. Unlike me, who got a food processor instead of a white fox jacket."

"You bet I did! My stocking was full! So full, in fact, I feel like sharing it with our new vice president."

"Uh, Mary, wait a minute. Have I got something to tell you!"

"Hold the thought, Meg. I've learned how to handle an elk, antlers and all, and that's just what I intend to do with the new man."

"I can see that, but, be careful. He's the CEO's nephew."

"I don't care if he's the Pope's son! I just want to get a few things straight between us. No more wondering, no more misunderstanding. I'm good at what I do, and as Smokey Robinson was my miracle, I'm gonna state that loud and clear."

"But, he's . . ."

"All right, Meg, he's what?"

"Well, for one thing, he's drop-dead gorgeous. I was gonna stand up for my rights, too, but so much for premature New Year's resolutions. I started making coffee and bringing him a sweet roll even though he said he would do that himself. I'm even thinking of shining his cowboy boots."

"His what?"

"Cowboy boots. I tell you, Mary, we've got the King of the Cowboys in that office."

"Oh, great. Well, *I'm* going to tell *him*

something right up front. Watch my dust, pardner!"

Mary stalked to the office door. A smudged line was visible over the one that was still emblazoned in black block letters, VICE PRESIDENT, the same line where she'd hoped her name would appear. The sign painter hadn't been around to put the new name on yet. She knocked and didn't wait for an answer. She opened the door and strode in resolutely.

"Mr. Vice President," she said to the back of the high gray-tweed desk chair. The new man was seated in it, staring off across the Chicago skyline. Probably in awe of concrete, she thought. She noted the perfect haircut. It was so recent she could practically see the scissor cut in the thick crop of dark hair. No visible gray from where she stood. He's probably twelve, just like every other hotshot corporation exec, she fumed. And he didn't even have the courtesy to turn around and acknowledge her presence.

"Ah-hem," she said loudly. My name is Mary Madigan and I've worked here for seventeen years. Started in the steno pool and worked up to accounts manager. I run things my own way and I do a damned good job. I'm prompt, work hard while I'm here, don't conduct personal business during working hours. And I should have been promoted to this position. Oh, and I'm taking vacation during Easter week."

Nothing. No response. What had they done, put a yuppie robot in the VP slot? She saw the massive shoulders in the navy blue blazer shake. Was the lout laughing at her? Well, that's just what she needed to really show him a thing or two. She started to open her mouth and give him an earful of what female empowerment was all about, when she was stopped cold.

"Fine! I am, too," came a baritone voice, "and I want no arguments about it."

She waited, for what she wasn't certain. Nothing more came. "Excuse me?"

"I said, I am, too."

"Am what?" Mary was fast losing her steam. Something disturbed her deeply, and it wasn't just his interruption. What had Meg said? Something about the CEO and a relative?

A long pause caused her to feel even more tightly wound. Then he said, "All those things you are, except for the name." He chuckled low, and Mary frowned. That chuckle struck a chord of . . . what? Familiarity?

"And I'm also taking Easter week off," he added.

"Well, that's . . . fine . . . with me." Why did her pulse race so? "I'll be going now. I just wanted to get a few things straight." Odd how she'd had this confrontation, this faceoff, so to speak, without speaking to this man face-to-face, without even seeing his face.

"No, you're not."

"What?"

"Sit down."

"What?"

"Sit down . . . please." He drew the words out slowly. Why did it sound as if he were speaking into a wadded handkerchief? "There's one thing I want settled right now, Ms. Madigan."

Mary lowered herself into the chair opposite the desk. "Yes, sir?" She felt oddly benched. So much for team playing.

"That we have elk stew for Easter dinner. It inspires such interesting and exciting reactions in you."

"What!" Mary's eyes bored into the back of his head.

It was then that she noticed her drawing hanging on the wall next to the window. She stood up, leaned across the desk, placed both hands on the corners of the chair back, and gave it a mighty spin. It twisted easily until the cleanly-shaven new vice president faced her head-on, a warm smile spread across his face.

"What are you doing New Year's Eve, MOM? Oh, by the way, Blitzen sends his love!"

What Every Woman Knows

by Peggy Roberts

"Mom, I hope you understand."

"Of course I do!" Callie Hughes pushed away her disappointment and made her voice lighthearted.

"It's just that Ann and I didn't have a honeymoon, so we thought we'd make this first Christmas together special by going to Hawaii," Jim Hughes continued.

"That's a wonderful idea," Callie said warmly.

"It means leaving you alone on Christmas."

"Don't give it another thought. You know how much time the bed and breakfast takes. We're booked solid right up to the holidays. I'll be exhausted by Christmas. I'll probably spend the whole day in bed." She paused, making her voice gay. "We'll have our celebration when you get back."

"Are you sure you don't mind?" He sounded relieved and anxious at the same time, reminding her of when he was a little boy and needed reassuring.

"As sure as can be. Now, you and Ann go have a wonderful holiday and tell me all about it when you get back."

"I love you, Mom."

The warmth of his words stayed with her long after she'd hung up. Glancing around her cheerful, spice-scented kitchen, she tried not to let disappointment creep into her day. Actually, she'd planned on Ann and Jim coming home for their first Christmas. She'd fibbed about the bookings for the bed and breakfast. Deliberately, she'd turned people away so she would have time for her son and his new wife. Now the Christmas holiday stretched before her gloomy and lonely.

"None of that," she stated positively, and set about wrapping her famous fruitcakes in rum-soaked cheesecloths and putting them in specially made wooden rounds to age until the proper moment. They were prepared from an old recipe, handed down from her southern grandmother. Placing the cake boxes on shelves in the big old-fashioned pantry, Callie glanced around the kitchen. Modern ovens, freezers, and dishwashers, needed to meet requirements as a restaurant, had been discreetly built in so as not to detract from the natural charm of aged brick chimneys and rich oaken cabinets. When she'd first come here as Gerald's bride, he'd offered to put in a modern kitchen for her, but she'd refused, loving the authenticity and charm of the old house that had been in his family for three generations. There was a feeling of stability, of things never lost, of family and strength and security.

She'd had all those things, too. Gerald had been a successful lawyer. Their days together were golden . . . until Gerald died unexpectedly of a heart attack and everything changed. She'd been dismayed to find she was without money and Jim was soon to leave for his first year at Harvard Law School. She'd been hurt and angry with Gerald that he'd mismanaged their savings, even mortgaging the house to shore up his bad investments. Then she'd begun to understand how desperate he must have been. He would never have risked losing his beloved home or endangering their security. Understanding hadn't brought a solution, but it had helped her put away her bitterness over the turn her life had taken. With her own feelings resolved, she'd set about finding a way to save the house and put Jim through school. Gerald's insurance policy had paid off his business obligations and paid Jim's first year at school. It had been left to Callie to pay off the mortgage on the house and support herself. An outdated fine arts degree hadn't prepared her for a career.

Her hobbies and crafts had been a reflection of her creative needs as a housewife and mother. None of them had given her the skills to compete in the business world. She'd allowed time to pass her by.

"What on earth will you do?" her best friend Kitty had asked, shaking her head in disbelief.

"Something, I'll do something," Callie had said to hide her own fears. Slowly, through the long, sleepless nights, the answer had come: If she ware to keep the house, it must help pay for itself. She would turn it into a bed and breakfast. She'd tried not to think about Gerald's grandmother, who might be turning in her grave. Desperate times demanded desperate measures.

Some of their old friends had snickered at her plan, some, having long coveted the graceful old house, had tried to buy her out, but Callie had remained steadfast in her desire to keep the house. It was Gerald's legacy to his son. She wanted to see her grandchildren play here. So she'd closed her mind to the scoffers and set about turning the beautiful old house into a paying establishment. She'd catered fine meals to an exclusive group, limiting her luncheons and dinners to a fixed number. That alone had helped establish the Wainwright House's reputation. Businessmen could bring their clients there for lunch and be assured of a discreet private room, where they could conduct their affairs over tasty dishes of grilled salmon, marinated filet of beef, light fluffy soufflés with raspberry sauce. Elite dinner parties, small, elegant weddings, and family anniversaries were Callie's forte. All events were by reservation only. People who wanted something extraordinary came to the Wainwright House. Callie and her specially picked staff entertained each guest as if he were royalty. They came back; they told their friends. Now her reservation book was filled for months in advance.

She'd made a success and had gained a certain pride from it. She'd enabled her son to continue his education and now he was firmly established in a prestigious law firm in Chicago. Her friends no longer scoffed. Many of them were no longer her friends, but came as guests for her to serve them. Her life had changed and she'd changed with it. She was no longer the pampered wife of a wealthy professional man. Life had gone on and she'd caught up with it. She liked herself better and wondered what Gerald would have thought of her if he'd been there.

Well, he wasn't there and she was going to be alone for Christmas, and she still had a hundred things to do in the meantime. She couldn't stand around moping. She turned to the counter and began sifting flour for pie crusts. She couldn't help humming a little as she worked.

"Callie?" Judy, her day maid, poked her head around the door. "There's someone in the parlor who wants to speak with you."

"Who is it?" Callie asked, glancing up from her pie crusts.

"I didn't ask his name, but he's mighty good-looking." Judy wagged her eyebrows.

Callie couldn't resist a smile. "Couldn't you take care of him, Judy? I'm kind of tied up here."

Judy shook her head, her brown eyes

friendly but firm. "He asked to speak to you."

"All right," Callie sighed. She took off her apron, smoothed down her skirt and flecked an imaginary speck from her creamy lace blouse. Then checking the mirror to see if she needed to tidy her hair, she hurried to the front parlor.

He was a tall man, she could see that the minute she stepped into the room. He wore a handsome overcoat of a rich glen plaid and clasped a hat in one hand. Standing before the fireplace with his back to her, he appeared entirely engrossed in his study of the hand-painted mural over the mantel. Sunlight streamed through leaded glass windows on either side of the fireplace, creating a warm rich glow over the Oriental carpet. Callie always felt peaceful when she entered this room.

She must have made a noise, for the man swung around and fixed her with a keen eye. Judy was right. He was handsome, Callie saw, with the mark of a man used to shouldering authority. His eyes were a brilliant blue and his brown hair was silver at the temples.

"Ms. Hughes?" he asked, stepping forward and extending his hand.

"*Mrs.* Hughes," Callie said, taking his hand in a brief handshake. "And you are?"

"William DeWitt," he answered, drawing a business card from his coat pocket.

Callie took the card. It was elegantly simple, stating his position as a CEO for one of the large manufacturing companies back east. They had a branch here in Battle Creek.

"Yes, Mr. DeWitt. I spoke to your secretary a few days ago."

"That's right," he said brusquely. "She's the one who told me about this place. I see she wasn't exaggerating. It's beautiful."

"Thank you, Mr. DeWitt, but as I explained to your secretary, I can't accommodate you and your guests for the holidays."

"Marilyn gave me the message. I—just thought I'd come and talk to you personally." His smile was charming, erasing some of the fatigue on his face. The smile held something else as well. It said he was used to getting what he wanted and he was certain this would not be an exception. He glanced around the room as if appraising it, and nodded in satisfaction. "Marilyn thought it would be perfect for my needs and she's right."

"Be that as it may, Mr. DeWitt. We're all booked up until a few nights before Christmas and of course over the holidays we'll be closed."

"Why?"

"Why? Because it gives my staff and me a chance to rest and enjoy Christmas with our families." Callie was a little peeved at his persistence.

"Do you have a large family, Mrs. Hughes?" he asked, pacing about the room again.

"No, just my son and his wife." But Jim and Ann would not be coming for Christmas.

"I don't have a large family, either," William DeWitt was continuing. "Just a daughter I haven't seen in years. There's been an estrangement for some time. I haven't even seen my grandson. He's seven years old." He stopped speaking abruptly, pressing his lips together in a thin line as if to stop himself from revealing too much about himself and his family. Callie was at once intrigued. Why would a daughter be so estranged from her father that she'd deny him the chance to see his own grandson? William DeWitt swung back to face Callie.

"Whatever arrangements you've made, whatever the price involved, I'll double the money you're getting from someone else."

"Mr. DeWitt, I would never oust one of my

guests for the sake of money. I don't operate that way," Callie said in mild disapproval.

"You don't understand, Mrs. Hughes. I'm not interested in renting just one of your rooms. I want the whole house."

"It makes no difference," Callie said. "I've told you we can't accommodate you."

All the starch seemed to go out of him. His features sagged, revealing tired lines and haunted eyes.

"I'm sorry," he said softly, sinking down on a love seat and running his hands over his face. "It isn't fair of me to pressure you like this. It's just that my daughter has finally agreed to bring my grandson and her husband and spend a Christmas with me and I wanted it to be special. I guess I wanted to buy what I don't have to give her, a sense of warmth and belonging and family." He glanced around the room. "Something about this place conveys all those things I never gave her." He smiled, but it was only a mechanical twist of his lips and never reached his eyes.

"I'm sorry to have troubled you, Mrs. Hughes," he said, getting to his feet. His expression was resigned.

"Wait," Callie said, putting out a hand to touch his coat sleeve. "My son and his wife aren't coming for Christmas this year and I'd set aside several days to have them here. Perhaps we could work something out. Let me get my calendar."

His grin took twenty years from his face. His eyes warmed, grew hopeful. "The time might not be right for you," she cautioned him, not wanting to build up his hopes and then dash them.

"I'll make the time right," he said quickly, and she knew how important this was to him. Berating herself for her softheartedness, she hurried to her office and took up the ledger in which she recorded all her bookings. Carrying it back to the front parlor, she studied the openings.

"How many will be in your party?"

"Just five of us. My daughter, her husband and my grandson, my fiancée and me."

Callie glanced up at him. "And you want to rent the whole house?"

"Yes, I want this to feel like our home while we're here." He glanced away. "I—I never made much of a home for Nancy and her mother when we were all together. We lived in rented condos and hotel rooms. It was all rather impersonal, I'm afraid." She read the guilt he must have carried with him for some years.

377

"How many days would you want to be here?"

"As many as I can get," he said firmly.

"I have open rooms five days before Christmas. There are a few other guests, but everyone will be gone by Christmas Eve. I'll be short-staffed over Christmas, but the hostelry will be yours. I'll handle the meals and service for you and your family."

"Thank you, Mrs. Hughes," he said, gripping her hand. "You don't know what this means to me."

Her gaze was unwavering. "I think I do, Mr. DeWitt. That's why I've agreed to your coming here for Christmas."

"Please. Call me Billy. All my friends do." He smiled then, and she glimpsed the man behind the image, the man riddled with guilt and loneliness. Something inside her reached out to him. She wanted to smooth the creases from his forehead and around his eyes. She wanted to take off the expensive overcoat and brogans and seat him before the fire and bring him the paper and a whiskey and tell him funny things to make him laugh. She wanted to touch him as he seemed to have touched her.

Pulling a brisk professional air about herself, she closed the ledger and nodded. "I'll see you and your family on the twentieth, then," she said.

"The twentieth," he echoed, and turned toward the door. She wanted to tell him to button his overcoat before stepping out into the cold wind, but she refrained. William DeWitt wasn't a man one treated in such a familiar way.

Bemused, she stayed overly long in the parlor, reflecting on her Christmas guest, wondering about him. She was oddly moved by him. He'd awakened an old restlessness in her, one she'd thought long since buried. Finally, realizing time was passing and her luncheon guests would be arriving soon, she hurried back to the kitchen and her pies. But as she rolled and patted and filled and baked, she couldn't help wondering what kind of woman William DeWitt had chosen for a fiancée.

And that night she had strange, erotic dreams of a blue-eyed man named Billy.

"Mrs. Hughes? This is Billy DeWitt."

His tone implied she would surely know who he was without further explanation, and of course she did.

"Yes, Mr. DeWitt?"

"My daughter is arriving sometime today.

I'd meant to be there and greet her when she arrived, but some things have come up. I'll be delayed a couple of days."

"I shall convey the message to your daughter."

"Do that," he said crisply. "And, Mrs. Hughes?"

"Yes, Mr DeWitt?"

"Don't let her leave."

"I beg your pardon?"

"If she tries to leave, don't let her. Convince her to stay somehow. This delay can't be helped, otherwise I'd be there for her."

She'd meant to deny any such responsibility. It wasn't her place to detain her guests if they wished to leave, but something about his plea touched her.

"I'll do my best, Mr. DeWitt," she said instead.

"Billy," he answered. "Call me, Billy."

"And what is your daughter called, Mr. DeWitt?" Callie asked firmly. "So I'll know who I'm expecting."

"Nancy and Glen Simpson," he answered, and there seemed to be a touch of amusement in his tone. "My grandson is Maximillian, a hell of a name for a little kid." His voice was filled with laughter and eager anticipation. "I'm going to call him Max."

"I'll take care of them until you get here, Billy," Callie said. It wasn't until after she'd hung up that she realized she'd called him by his absurd nickname. Billy didn't fit him. He was a tough businessman, cold and centered on his career, so much so that he'd lost touch with his family. He was used to getting what he wanted; he probably even turned ruthless, if that was what it took. No, Billy did not suit him at all. William the Conqueror was more like it!

She put all thought of Billy "William the Conqueror" DeWitt out of her mind and went back to her task of working up menus for the holidays. She'd keep it fairly simple since she'd be manning the kitchen and the house by herself. She'd be concentrating her best efforts on a traditional Christmas dinner with turkey and all the trimmings.

It was late afternoon when Nancy and Glen Simpson arrived. Callie hurried to the foyer to greet them. Her first impression was of a young family very much at home with themselves. Glen Simpson was good-looking and dark-haired, as was Nancy. She possessed her father's brilliant blue eyes, but there the resemblance ended. What she had missed, her son had inherited. His resemblance to his grandfather was startling, even the sharp, piercing way he had of looking at people as if seeing far more than they were prepared to reveal. His smile was pure Billy DeWitt, charming and blatantly aware of its power.

"I'm Callie Hughes," she said, stepping forward to shake hands with each of them. "I'll be your hostess while you're here."

"We're happy to meet you, Callie," Glen said, stepping forward to shake her hand. "This is my wife, Nancy, and our son, Maximillian." His forthright manner was so sincere and friendly, she hadn't the will to establish a more formal manner of address. After all, they were going to spend ten days of the holiday season together. Perhaps it would be better if they were on a first-name basis.

"Is my father here?" Nancy asked abruptly, and Callie could sense the tenseness.

"He called to say he'll be delayed for two days," Callie said quickly. "He asked—"

"I told you it would be like this," she said to her husband. "I won't stay here like a little puppy dog, waiting for crumbs of his attention."

"Nancy honey," Glen said softly, taking hold of her arm in a protective gesture. "You've come this far. Give him a chance. Maybe this delay really couldn't be helped."

"You don't understand," she said sharply, pulling away from him. "He's left me waiting and hoping so many times. I'm not a child anymore. I can't—" She stopped as if her words were choked off by unreleased sobs.

Glen pulled her close. Even little Max moved toward her, taking her hand and holding it tightly, his eyes soft and wounded-looking.

"You want him to meet Maximillian," Glen reminded her gently.

She smoothed back dark hair from a pale oval face and forced a smile to her lips. "You're right, of course. I want him to see Maximillian. Maybe then he'll understand all he's missed." An old bitterness twisted her pretty features.

"Mr. DeWitt said the delay was unavoidable and he was most anxious you stay," Callie spoke up, wanting her words to give reassurance and comfort.

"The delays always were unavoidable," Nancy said. "But we'll stay, Mrs. Hughes. Will you show us to our rooms?"

"Please, won't you call me Callie, as your husband has?" Callie found herself saying. "As for your rooms, they're right this way." She picked up a suitcase and mounted the stairs. The three of them fell in behind, each bringing a bag.

"We'll have some other guests for the next few days," Callie explained, trying to fill the awkward silence that had fallen over them all. "But by Christmas Eve the house will be yours."

"It's beautiful," Nancy said stiffly, as if she didn't mean it. "Of course, Daddy always bought the best." She paused on the top steps and peered over the banister at the foyer below with its hand-stenciled canvas wall coverings and the hammered glass chandelier with Steuben glass shades. "It's rather humorous of him to try to buy something like this now."

"He wanted you all to have an old-fashioned kind of Christmas," Callie said from the landing above.

"As always, his timing's a little off, his efforts too late." Nancy joined Callie on the landing. Her smile was bleak. "As you may have guessed, Mrs. Hughes, we're not your ordinary Norman Rockwell kind of family."

"Few people are," Callie said gently. "Your rooms are this way." She swung open the door to the Victorian room and stepped back. "This one is for you. Through that adjoining door is the room for your son."

Silently, Nancy stepped inside the beautiful room and slowly looked around. When she turned back to Callie, her eyes held a grudging admiration. Callie had expected little else. A tall leaded-glass window cast a glow of color over the nine-foot-high mahogany headboard with its carved birds and flowers. Callie had hung her fan collection on one wall above a marble-topped walnut stand which held a pitcher and bowl. A Victorian settee and matching chairs had been placed before the marble fireplace. A nearby table held an electric teakettle, cups and saucers, crackers, and a selection of herb teas.

A door opened onto a private bath, its large ceramic tub resting on milk-glass legs and banked by large plants. Shelves of Gerald's collection of shaving mugs were flanked by framed family silhouettes. A sun porch also opened to the backyard overlooking the gardens, but would be of little use now, since the gardens were covered with snow.

"I hope you'll be comfortable here."

"I'm sure we will be," Glen Simpson said, his boyish young face looking more hopeful.

"Come on, Max," Callie said. "I'll show you to your room. It's the next one and there's a connecting door."

"His name is Maximillian," Nancy Simpson called after them.

"Darling," Glen Simpson chided.

"Well, it's true. We agreed no cute nicknames like Max or Billy." The door closed behind them.

"I like Max better'n Maximillian," the boy said gravely.

"That's what Billy said he was going to call you," Callie said, and silently berated herself for interfering in someone else's affairs, but suddenly she wanted more than anything for Billy DeWitt to be here and see his family.

"Who's Billy?" Max asked, pausing with his hand on the doorknob to his room.

"Billy is your grandfather," Callie said. "And he'll be here in a couple of days to spend Christmas with you. Isn't that wonderful?"

The boy stood solemnly, regarding her. "I don't know," he answered. "I've never had a grandfather before."

"Never?" Callie squatted so her eyes were level with his. She liked his intelligent eyes and sensitive face. "What about your other grandfather? Everybody has two, you know?"

Solemnly, he shook his head. "Grandpa Simpson died when I was a baby and Grandpa DeWitt was lost. I'm glad we found him again."

"I'm glad you did, too," Callie said, and

barely refrained from hugging the little boy. Her memory of boys his age was that they were embarrassed by such displays of affection and submitted to them only when tired and troubled. Straightening, Callie looked down at the solemn, far too self-contained lad. He seemed almost like a little old man, so serious was his demeanor.

"Go on, see how you like your room," she said a little more sharply than she meant to. Suddenly she didn't want the DeWitts and Simpsons here. She didn't want to get wrapped up in someone else's life. She had her own. Still, she waited as he pushed open the door to his room and looked in. Once this had been a child's nursery. Her own son had slept there and played in the sunny room. The walls were still lined with shelves and some of his old toys, though the trains and trucks and puzzles were a little more worn now from the rough handling of impatient little hands. Posters of astronauts and space-ships and old knights in armor still hung on the walls. Gravely, Max studied the room and looked back at her.

"I shall be quite comfortable here. Thank you," he replied with far more aplomb than some adults showed. He entered the room and closed the door behind him. Callie stayed where she was, thinking about Max and Billy and Nancy and Glen.

"He's a funny little kid, isn't he?" Glen Simpson said from the doorway of his room.

"He's quite intelligent."

"Too intelligent, if you ask me. Sometimes he scares me." He smiled to show he didn't really mean that as a criticism. A certain amount of pride and respect crept into his tone. "He's like his mother, quick to understand other people and their motives and quick to be disappointed. I just hope this—" He shrugged. "I'm sure you don't want to hear all your guests' family problems." He turned back into his room without waiting for an answer from her. Callie descended the stairs, her thoughts on her three new guests and Glen Simpson's unspoken wish. She understood what he'd been about to say and suddenly her hopes for this family Christmas reunion were as keen as theirs.

"What is there to see and do around here at this time of year?" Glen Simpson asked the next morning over a hearty breakfast of baked apples, oatmeal, poached eggs, and Callie's special hot muffins. They'd elected to be served in the sunny breakfast room with its small round ice-cream tables and chairs. The slotted dish rail running round the room held Callie's collection of hand-painted plates. Beyond the panes of the French doors, a new snowfall lay fluffy and sparkling and inviting. Callie sensed the restlessness that seized a man like Glen Simpson. He might enjoy the comfort and warmth of her home for a time, but he was a man given to action. Jim was like that, too.

"There are wonderful little shops around the town square," she said, replenishing his coffee. "We do have a new mall just at the edge of the city. If you follow the old highway north, you'll come to a park and zoo which you can visit even in the winter. They also decorate for the holidays, so it's become rather a grand affair. There's a skating rink in the town square, and north of town, about ten miles, are some fairly challenging ski slopes. They'll be in fine shape this morning after this snowfall."

"We should have brought our skis," Glen said.

"We had too many other things," Nancy answered with some detachment. Her face was paler today with dark circles about her eyes as if she hadn't slept well, in spite of her pert avowal of having done so.

"The ski shop would have rentals," Callie said helpfully.

"What about it?" Glen asked eagerly.

"I—not today, Glen," Nancy said. "I want to be here when—if he comes."

"Darling, you can't mope around, waiting for Billy to show up. He's said he'll be delayed for two days. Let's go skiing today and get your mind off things." Glen took his wife's hand and squeezed it encouragingly.

"Can you ski, Mom?" Max asked gravely.

"Can I ski?" Nancy said with a sudden laugh. Her pretty face looked younger without its perpetual frown. "Just come on and I'll show you," she cried, and threw down her napkin. Behind her back, Glen and Max signaled victory to each other. Callie's heart warmed at their harmless conspiracy. With a light heart she hummed as she cleared away the breakfast china and began preparations for lunch. The ringing phone interrupted her good mood.

"Is my daughter there, Mrs. Hughes?" Billy DeWitt said on the other end. His voice was husky and uncertain.

"They've just left to go skiing. I'll see if I can catch them." She put down the phone and hurried to the front parlor in time to see Glen's car easing into the light traffic.

"Sorry, they've already left," she said into the phone.

"Are you sure they're only going skiing?" he asked anxiously.

"Don't worry, Mr. DeWitt. Your daughter is waiting until you arrive." There was a long pause at the other end, and she wasn't sure if it was one of relief or further anxiety. "Your grandson is a delightful little boy," she said, hoping to dispel some of his worry."

"Is he?" His voice was full of emotion. "Does he look like Nancy?"

"He looks like you."

"Me?" There was another long pause. When he spoke again, his voice was cool and professional. "I'll be delayed longer than I'd thought," he said with implacable coolness. "I won't be arriving until Christmas Eve."

"Surely you don't mean that," Callie said sharply. She knew she shouldn't become embroiled in this family's problems, but she didn't want to be the one to see Nancy's expression when this new information was made known to her.

"I beg your pardon," Billy said on the other end. "Mrs. Hughes?"

Callie took a deep breath and counted to ten, but it didn't work. "Mr. DeWitt," she began crisply. "If you ever have hope of reconciling with your daughter, you mustn't delay any more than you have."

"What do you mean?"

"I mean your daughter is here, but if I tell her you're not coming until Christmas Eve, she'll leave. She's already expressed some exasperation over this first delay. Can't you get away? This is important to you both."

"You're right, of course," he said quietly and sighed. "I'd hoped to bring Novia with me, but she can't get away until then."

"Novia?"

"My fiancée."

"Can't she come later, by herself?"

"She says she won't." He paused, sorry he'd told her so much. She wanted to feel sorry for him, caught between the need to mend a rift with his daughter and the demands of a fiancée, but somehow she couldn't. She'd already witnessed Nancy's pain. Suddenly, Callie didn't like Billy DeWitt and his fiancée, Novia.

"It seems to me, Mr. DeWitt," she said coolly, unaware her voice held a hint of rebuke, "that you must choose."

"So it seems, Mrs. Hughes," he said impatiently. "Since you seem to be well aware of my family problems, have you any advice to add?"

"The problems are yours, Mr. DeWitt, and I wouldn't presume to interfere in any way."

"But you already have."

"My apology. "

"Unaccepted," he said, and she thought she heard that quick tinge of humor in his voice.

"What shall I tell your daughter, Mr. De-Witt?"

"Tell her nothing for now, Mrs. Hughes. Good day."

His completion of the call was crisp and impatient. Had she offended him? Well, no matter. She'd only rented him her home, not her advice or support for his wrong decisions. She went back to her chores in the kitchen. Judy had finished with her daily cleaning and Aggie had come in to help with the luncheon crowd. Callie was too busy greeting her guests, seeing them to the proper tables or small conference rooms and checking that the entrees of steamed vegetables and grilled almond chicken breasts were presented with the high quality the Wainwright House demanded.

After luncheon the Royal Doulton china was cleared, carefully washed, and readied for the special dinner party they were serving that evening. Following would be an evening of music, with a small ensemble of musicians. Her day was filled and busy and Billy DeWitt and his family existed only on the outer perimeter of her thoughts.

The Simpsons returned from skiing late in the afternoon, their cheeks reddened from wind and sun, their eyes glowing. Nancy looked happier, more relaxed than she had since she arrived.

"Did you hear from my father?" she asked the first thing after shucking off her coat.

"Yes, he called to see if you'd arrived and were comfortable here," Callie hedged.

"Did he say what time he'd arrive?"

"No, as a matter of fact, he didn't."

Nancy's face fell. The old pain was back in her blue eyes.

"I'm sure he'll be arriving at the time he said he would," Callie said, and hoped Billy DeWitt would live up to his word.

"What's for supper?" Glen Simpson said in an obvious attempt to distract his wife. "We're ravenous and something smells delicious."

"I'm serving an old-fashioned pot roast the way my grandmother used to prepare it," Callie said, "and fresh coconut cream pie."

"Made from scratch?" Glen Simpson asked with hopeful eyes.

"No other way," Callie answered with a laugh.

"Coconut cream pie from scratch. I can't remember having that since I was a kid," Glen said in wonder as he walked up the stairs beside his wife. "This is already getting to be one of the best vacations I've ever had."

Nancy placed a quick kiss on his cheek. "If I beat you to the shower, I get your piece," she challenged, and the two raced up the stairs like a couple of kids. Max shook his head as he watched them disappear. His manner was grave and far more adult than that of his parents.

"Did you have a good day skiing?" Callie asked him.

"It was an interesting distraction," he said solemnly, "but I hope Grandfather shows up. Nancy will be very disappointed if he doesn't."

"What about you?"

The thin shoulders shrugged. "I should like to see my grandfather, but if I don't, I shan't be hurt as my mother will be. I don't like coconut very much."

"Well, then I'll see you get a big piece of banana cream pie," Callie smiled at the youngster.

The dinner went well. The musical group was festive and appreciative of the meal. In anticipation of dessert, Glen Simpson had little dinner and devoured two large wedges of pie. His look of satisfaction brought laughter to Nancy and Callie. After dinner Glen and Nancy joined the guests in the parlor as the ensemble played a selection of classical music and Christmas melodies.

Callie oversaw the work in the kitchen as tables were cleared and dishwashers loaded. She was intent on folding napkins and setting the table for breakfast, when a small, dark head poked through the swinging doors from the parlor.

"Ah, you're not a Beethoven lover?" she said to the solemn boy with the intelligent eyes.

He shrugged. "I find Mozart more interesting and Tchaikovsky more engaging emotionally," he said nonchalantly. Once again Callie was stunned by his poise and knowledge.

"What do you intend to do when you grow up?" she asked, pulling out a dining room chair and patting its seat in an invitation to him to sit. He slid on the chair, composed himself, and fixed her with a steady gaze.

"I'm not sure yet," he said. "I've thought about being a chemical engineer, but then, I like computers, too. Maybe I can combine the two interests in some way."

"Perhaps you can," she answered, trying not to show her awe of him. Gifted or not, he was still a kid. "Computers are so much a part of everyone's life these days."

"Do you use a computer in your work?" His small head tilted to the side in curiosity.

"No, I do everything the old-fashioned way."

"Dad says old-fashioned is good, too," he acknowledged. He paused and then asked her the question she knew had been his reason for seeking her out. "You're the only one who's seen my grandpa for a long time," he said thoughtfully. "What does he look like?"

"He's handsome," Callie said, concentrating on folding the napkins into a fan pattern. "He seems very nice. I think you'll like him."

"I think I will," Max said confidently. "I think he'll like me, too."

Callie had finished with her preparations in the dining room. "Would you like to come out to the kitchen and have some cookies and milk?" she invited him. Max nodded and followed her out to the old brick kitchen. Seated on a stool at the counter, he munched on cookies and regaled her with stories of his days at school and camp. Callie found herself laughing often and realized he was every bit in control of their conversation as a charming adult would have been. She liked his company.

Suddenly the back door flew in, and amid a flurry of snow, Billy DeWitt entered.

"Sorry to come by the back door," he said, slapping the snow from his shoulders and meeting her startled gaze with his own amused one. "I saw you were having some sort of entertainment in the parlor."

"Yes, they're nearly finished," Callie said, and wondered why she felt, so happy at the appearance of Billy DeWitt. He'd slid out of his coat and looked around the room approvingly. His gaze came back to her.

"This house suits you," he said, then he turned to the small boy at the counter. "Is this your son?"

"No," she answered in some surprise. "This is your grandson."

He went deadly still, his blue gaze taking in the small boy who looked so like him. Max didn't fidget as he and his grandfather studied each other. Finally Billy reached out a hand, palm up.

"Hello, Max," he said with quiet dignity.

Callie wanted to cry out. Hug him, he's just a little boy for all his noise, but Max took hold of his grandfather's hand and shook it solemnly.

"Hello, Billy," he said with grown-up aplomb, "I'm happy to meet you. I've heard a lot about you."

Billy wrinkled his nose. "Any of it good?"

"That would depend on what you mean by good," Max answered.

"Billy?" The sound was small, nearly unheard. Nancy Simpson stood in the kitchen doorway, her eyes wide and wounded-looking as she gazed at Billy.

"Nancy," he said, and moved jerkily as if he wanted to hurry toward her but was afraid of her reception. "You look wonderful."

"Thank you. So do you," Nancy replied. "We weren't sure you'd make it what with all the snow."

"I wouldn't have missed this for anything," he said, still staring at her. "It's been a long time. You've become a woman."

"Yes, I have," Nancy replied stiffly, and Callie knew she was thinking about the years in between.

"You remember Glen, Billy," she said, turning to her husband as if for support. Glen sensed her uncertainty in meeting her father again after so many years. His arm went around her shoulder while he held out a hand to Billy.

"It's good to see you again, sir," he said

stiffly.

"The pleasure's mine, Glen." Silence fell over them, and Callie ached for them all.

"I have some fresh-baked cookies and hot coffee, if anyone would like some."

"No!"

"Yes!"

Everyone spoke at once.

"There's no one in the breakfast room," Callie urged. "Go on in and I'll bring the coffee."

"I'll help you," Nancy said quickly, and turned blindly toward the stove. Callie recognized her need for a moment's privacy.

"Pretty hard, huh?" she said to Nancy as she gathered a tray and cups and saucers.

"Harder than I thought," Nancy said in a low voice. "I didn't think it would still hurt after all these years."

"Must be you still care some for him." Callie handed her a cut-glass plate and pushed the cookie jar closer. Absently, Nancy began filling the plate.

"No, yes. As Glen says, he is my father and I can't just cut him out of my life like a—a—"

"I think the hardest thing for children to realize about their parents is that they're just human. We don't come with guarantees that we're always going to do things just right."

"Oh, I know that," Nancy said ruefully. "Maximillian is always telling me what I do wrong."

"Do you suppose when he's an adult he'll look back over all the years and remember the good and forgive the bad?"

Nancy glanced at her sharply. "You're a nice person, Callie. I'll bet you were a super mother to your children."

"Son. I had only one."

"I'll bet he doesn't have any bitter memories to look back on," Nancy persisted.

It was time for Callie to pause now. "I hope not. I hope he was forgiving of my shortcomings."

"Shortcomings! That's a good word," Nancy said. "I never really knew if Billy had any shortcomings or not. He was never around much. After Mom and he divorced, he came to see me at first, then the visits grew further apart, and finally, he just stopped coming. I'd get expensive presents and money for Christmas and my birthday, but no father."

"He's here now."

She laughed, a little sound that hardly counted. "He's here because I called him and asked to get together for the holidays. When

401

Mother died, I thought, well, it doesn't much matter."

"Of course it does," Callie said quickly. "I know it matters to your father. How else do you think I was persuaded to give up my own Christmas?"

"Oh, you must count us as ungrateful, hard-hearted people."

"Not in the least," Callie said, and picked up the tray. "I think you're people trying to find your way back to one another."

"Trying to find our way back to one another," Nancy repeated, then smiled. "That sounds far more hopeful."

"It's the season for hope," Callie said. "Shall we take them these goodies? I've always found something on the stomach does wonders toward mellowing a tense moment."

"In other words, the way to a man's heart?"

"Precisely. It's what every woman knows."

The talking helped, and Callie liked to think her fresh Snickerdoodles and almond spice tea helped as well. When she and Nancy entered the room, Max and Billy were seated beside each other, and Billy had caught hold of Max's hand as if he couldn't refrain from touching this young stranger who was his grandson. Glen was seated on the other side of the table, his smile easy, his eyes watchful and friendly. Callie wanted to hug him for the relaxed way he had of seating Nancy on the other side of Billy and helping to fill cups. She sensed he wanted the reunion to work for them as much as she did. Once she glanced up and caught his eye and he winked at her. They were conspirators in crime, he seemed to say, helping stubborn, wounded people to be well and happy again. Callie smiled her approval and turned away.

"Please, Mrs. Hughes, won't you stay?" Billy asked, and she paused, glancing around the table.

"I've had my tea for the evening, Mr. De— Billy," she replied. "I'll just be here in the kitchen, working on pies for tomorrow, if you need me."

She left them then, softly closing the door on the awkward silence that had fallen between them. Forcing her mind off the De-Witts, she set about making pie crusts. Soon she was so immersed in her work that she forgot about the time and was startled when she glanced at the clock. It was nearly eleven, and she'd heard nothing from the breakfast room. Putting away the prepared pie crusts, she tiptoed to the door and pushed it open a crack. The Simpsons were no longer there, but Billy DeWitt sat at the table with his head bowed. He glanced up and she saw his eyes were red-rimmed.

"Come in, Mrs. Hughes," he said, sitting back and wiping his eyes as if he had something in them. It was a purely masculine gesture and heartrending in its revelations. He'd thrown aside his suitcoat and tie and sat in shirt-sleeves. His attire made him appear more human, more reachable. Hadn't Nancy felt it?

"I didn't mean to disturb you," she said hesitantly.

He smiled wearily. "You aren't. In fact, you've been a godsend. Thank you for watching out for my family."

"They're lovely people."

"Have you and your husband children, Mrs. Hughes?"

"Please, call me Callie."

"Callie! It suits you. Pretty and homey in an old-fashioned way."

"Thank you." Callie couldn't stop the blush. She hadn't blushed since the first time she was kissed. Quickly, she began gathering up the cups and saucers. "As for my own family, there's just my son and myself and his

404

new wife. They're spending Christmas in Hawaii this year."

"No husband?"

"Gerald died some years ago of a heart attack," she said softly, and was surprised that the pain she usually felt at these words barely registered.

"And you've carried on with the hostelry on your own?" Billy reached for a clean cup, filled it and set it before her. Callie had no choice but to sit down with him. Billy refilled his own cup.

"Actually, when Gerald died I started the hostelry as a way to save the house," she said. "I couldn't bear to lose it. It had been in his family for generations."

"It would be a shame to lose a fine old place like this," Billy said. "You're a remarkable woman, Callie."

"Not really," she answered, trying to still the flow of heat rising at his glance. He's engaged, she kept telling herself, but she couldn't help noticing things about him. The high cheekbones from distant Slavic ancestors, the clear skin of clean-shaven jaws, the long-fingered hands, the broad shoulders hunched over the delicate Spode teacup. But most of all were the eyes, warm and caring, very direct and very, very blue.

The sonorous tones of the hall clock sounded throughout the still house. Saved by the bell, Callie thought, and jumped to her feet.

"Goodness, it's midnight and I have a big day tomorrow."

"I've kept you," Billy said regretfully.

"No, this has been a lovely chat."

"I'll help you with the dishes."

"That's not necessary. You must be tired from your trip."

"I insist." He carried the tray and helped place the fragile china in the dishwasher. Callie had to rearrange everything so the pieces didn't knock against each other and chip. She knew she must seem like a fussy old maid with her china, but when she dared glance up, his gaze showed no amusement or condemnation. He seemed to accept her care with precious things.

"Thank you for your help," she said, setting the dishwasher on a gentle cycle and wiping a counter that didn't need it.

"Are you going up now?"

"No, I have a room down here at the back of the house," Callie said, and polished the counter some more. She didn't see the frown that crossed his face.

"Thank you again for all you've done for

my family," he said.

"I've done nothing special, just what every woman does," she said, glancing up at last. She wondered how it would be to kiss a man like Billy good-night.

"But this time you did it for me," he said, taking hold of her hand. "Thank you again, Callie."

"You're welcome, Billy," she answered, and for a minute their gazes were locked as if neither could tear away. He collected his coat and tie and with a final salute he was gone down the hall to the front stairs. She stood listening to every creak until he reached the upper landing and the door of his room closed behind him. Then she let her breath out.

Whew! It might be a cold, snowy December outside, but in there it felt like an August heat wave! She made her way to her bed and lay thinking about Billy DeWitt. This time when she dreamed about him, he was far more real to her. She could smell his skin and feel the warmth of his big body next to hers. More than that, she was searching for and found his hard arousal, gripping it in her hand, guiding it toward her. So vivid was the dream, she woke up with a gasp and blinked at the sunshine glistening on new snow outside her windowsill.

What had happened to her mind? she wondered crossly. She hadn't had such erotic dreams since, well, not for a long time. At first, after Gerald's death, the nights had been unbearably lonely. Their love life had been easy and friendly and eminently satisfying. She'd taken it for granted until it wasn't there, then out of a sense of loyalty to Gerald she'd buried her needs. Now they'd come back full-blown and not to be denied. How on earth was she to face Billy DeWitt this morning after such a wanton dream?

Disgusted with herself, she got out of bed and dressed for the day. At last she stood before her mirror, wondering how Billy DeWitt saw her. Scoffing at such a thought, she turned away, but carried with her the image of a woman who had been no beauty in her youth and certainly wasn't beautiful in middle age. Her face was too round, her figure, though thin and firm from the demands of the hostelry, was too short. Her eyes were nice, her blond hair too fine. Her hands were dainty and she kept her nails neat. She wondered what Billy's fiancée looked like. Gorgeous, no doubt, and younger. Billy would be drawn to young, good-looking people, and they to him.

"Good morning, Callie," Aggie, the part-time cook, said when Callie entered the kitchen.

"Good morning," Callie said briskly. Deliberately, she pushed any thought of Billy and his family aside. A call from Jim and Ann at midmorning brightened her day. They were packed and ready to leave for Hawaii. Callie wished them a safe trip and promised to see them as soon as they returned. When she put down the phone, she stood thinking of what Christmas at the hostelry would be like this year with only Billy DeWitt and the Simpsons present.

In the afternoon she set about putting up the rest of the Christmas decorations.

"May I help you?" Nancy asked from the stairs, "The men have gone off and abandoned me for the day."

"Then by all means, I'd be grateful for the help," Callie said, thinking her gratitude was more for the fact that Billy was out of the house. "Come help me with these pine boughs," she asked, and Nancy eagerly lent a hand. Together they fashioned wreaths of box wood decorated with apples, red cedar, and hollyberries, hung garlands of white pine tied with crisp red velvet bows and pine cones, and arranged banks of poinsettias. The

Christmas tree in the main parlor was decorated with Victorian porcelain figures, candles, and bows. A painted porcelain Santa Claus collection adorned the mantels, and Gerald's collection of old soldier nutcrackers lined the stairway. Beneath the tree they placed old and new teddy bears and porcelain dolls from another century. Candles added soft light everywhere, and sprays of pine boughs spread their fragrance to hall and parlor.

As they worked, they talked, and Callie discovered a lightheartedness to Nancy that hadn't shone through before this.

"Have you and your father worked out some of your differences?" Callie couldn't help asking.

Nancy paused, straightening the lacy skirt of the porcelain doll she held. She was seated on the floor before the tree, her long, dark hair flowing around her shoulders. She looked like a young girl instead of the mother of Max.

"I want to think we have," she said. "But sometimes I still feel so much anger toward him. No matter what happened between Mother and him, he shouldn't have forgotten about me."

"I don't think he did, Nancy," Callie said.

"I think your father feels a tremendous guilt for those years. And he's trying so hard now to make things right again."

Nancy looked down at the doll that lay forgotten in her lap. "I know. I don't think they can ever be what we want them to be, what they might have been. Too much time has passed. There's too much hurt."

"Things may never be what you wanted them to be, but you and Billy can build something new. Maybe over the years you'll find it's even better than it might have been."

"You know, Callie, I do believe you're an optimist."

Callie laughed, caught off guard by Nancy's assessment. Suddenly, she felt young and gay again. The excitement of Christmas was in the air. For the first time since Jim's phone call, she felt it and was grateful to Billy and his family for being here.

"I think we've finished," she said, looking around. "Everything is beautiful, isn't it?"

Nancy nodded and stood staring at the tree with wonder. "I haven't seen a tree this big since I was a little girl," she said softly. "You know how big the trees seem when you're little, then you grow up and the trees have somehow lost their magic."

"I know what you mean," Callie said softly,

and couldn't help looping her arm over Nancy's shoulder. Nancy turned at once and gave her a warm hug. "You're a wonderful person, Callie. I wish—well, I wish Billy were bringing someone like you home as his fiancée."

"You mustn't make a prejudgment," Callie said. "Your father wouldn't choose anyone unsuitable."

"I hope you're right. I just wish she weren't coming for this first Christmas with us. Billy and I—need to get to know each other again. What if she—"

"Don't worry about what-ifs," Callie said quickly. "You'll drive yourself crazy. This is a season of hope and miracles. Believe in them and everything will turn out right."

Nancy smiled and clasped Callie's hand. "You keep saying that. I'm beginning to believe it a little bit."

"Good."

Nancy gave her a quick peck on the cheek. "I'd better go get dressed for dinner," she said quickly without meeting Callie's eye. The sudden shyness was endearing. Silently, Callie watched as the young woman climbed the stairs. Nancy and Ann would like each other, she thought idly, then understanding where her thoughts might be taking her, she clamped a lid on them and hurried off to the kitchen to oversee dinner preparations.

That evening the dining room was filled with the last of the hostelry's guests. Callie had made a point to remain in the kitchen and send Aggie and Judy out to serve dinner. Now she'd dismissed both helpers and was puttering in the kitchen, too tired to start another big project and too restless to return to her own tiny room and try to sleep.

"Callie?"

The sound of his voice cut through her like a flame, and suddenly she understood that she'd been waiting for this, for his appearance. Somehow she'd known he would come, and looking at his expression, she could tell he'd been certain she'd be there waiting for him.

"Are you alone?" he asked, and took a few steps forward into the room.

"Yes," she answered rather breathlessly, when she'd wanted to appear impersonal.

He walked closer, punching his hands into his pants pocket and jingling his change, not nearly as certain as he tried to appear. She felt better.

"I thought we might have some coffee and chat," he said diffidently. "I've rather gotten used to our talks."

"We've talked over coffee only once," Callie

413

said.

He grinned, and she was amazed to discover he had a charming dimple and his eyes sparkled with humor.

"See how quickly you become a habit?" he said.

She couldn't resist him. She made the coffee and drew out one of her rum-soaked fruit cakes. They sat at the wooden block she used for chopping and cutting. Its surface had been scrubbed clean and smooth. Balancing on an old bentwood chair, he sipped and nibbled and talked and dimpled, and all the time she fought not to evoke the images of her dream, the images of Billy in bed beside her, his hands doing wonderful shivery things to her while she explored his body.

He stopped talking and looked at her, his eyes going darker, his dimple disappearing as he grew serious. "You make a fine home for a man and his family, Callie," he said huskily. "You've made a world of difference in us all. At dinner Nancy could speak of nothing else but you and the way you both had decorated the house. It looks beautiful, by the way."

"Thank you." Callie had to look away from him. She couldn't reveal too much of herself now.

"You're beautiful, Callie," he said softly,

and somehow he'd taken hold of her hand. His clasp was warm and protective, making her feel very womanly. "Callie!" There was a slight impatience to his tone, an urgency. "Look at me."

"I can't," she said, and did anyway. There were things in his gaze that shouldn't have been there, unspoken desires, curiosity, and more she couldn't name for it had been too many years since she'd seen them in Gerald's glance.

"Callie," he said in a low, vibrant voice. It drew her into his arms. His arms were warm and strong around her, awakening old needs, bringing new desires. He held her first, as if cherishing the feel of her, then he raised her chin so he could stare into her eyes, then slowly he lowered his head and brushed her lips with his.

"More," she whispered, and his kiss deepened. Desire flooded her body like the heralding of a new morning, like a sunrise announcing a new day. There was music in her, in the flowering joy and passion of a body long unused now awakening to its natural course. His arms had tightened around her and she felt her full breasts flatten against his chest. His hands spread open on her buttocks, guiding her closer, bending her to his needs, too. She felt the pliant supplication of her body giving to him and drew a breath like sweet nectar, for it bore the scent of him.

She was young again, better than young, for now she possessed the experience and knowledge of a woman who had once been well loved and would be again. She never was sure who guided whom to her room behind the kitchen, to the big bed with its four-poster and ruffled comforter. The room was chilly, for she'd not been in it all day and was in the habit of turning down the old-fashioned corner radiator. They undressed quickly, facing each other, their eyes filled with laughter as they shivered in the cold room, then they were beneath the comforter, their heated bodies chasing away the chill of the sheets while snow fell quietly outside the window.

He was a thorough lover, taking time to know her body, caressing, teasing, arousing her to a breathless flush. He was experienced and understood the needs of women, the almost reluctant relinquishing of their very selves to a man's onslaught. He was gentle, yet never hesitant; undemanding, yet winning all he wanted from her. His hands stroked her to a near climax, then his teeth nipped at her chin and ear as she lay gasping with need. She searched for and found the object of her dream, finding the reality far more satisfying as she stroked him to a rigid hardness that brought a groan. When they could bear it no longer, he rose above her, his fit body stroking hers, lifting her to higher planes than she'd ever achieved before. She closed her eyes against all realities of the hostelry—her son, his daughter, their separate lives. They weren't separate now. They were one, striving for that sweet release that lay just a heartbeat away from them, tantalizingly near, yet not attained. When they reached it together, they knew this moment of sharing was special. They strained toward each other, holding the golden moment between them, sharing the rapture, crying out at its perfection, then sliding down the long silken passage of completion.

The next morning might have held recriminations, but didn't, might have been filled with regret, but wasn't. Billy had left sometime in the night, taking with him his warmth, his laughter, his magic. Callie woke and stared at the pillow which still bore the imprint of his head. She remembered the feel and scent and sound of him, and it all

417

seemed so right. But it hadn't been and it couldn't be. They were strangers, really. He had his family and his fiancée. She had her family and the hostelry. Their worlds were different. What had occurred between them must be no more important than if she'd poured him a cup of coffee or given him a friendly smile and a piece of rum-soaked fruit cake.

So saying, she rose and began her day. The last of the guests checked out. By noon the staff had the rooms cleaned and gathered in the kitchen for a final round of eggnog and holiday greetings. By two, they were gone. Nancy, Max, and Glen had gone off to the mall to do some Christmas shopping. Billy hadn't been seen, and Callie hoped he was out for the day as well. With a simple roast and potatoes in the oven for dinner, Callie collected the leftover food from the night before, several of her special fruit cakes, and a large turkey she'd bought especially for this occasion and carried them out to her car. The box was bulky and resisted her efforts to place it in the trunk.

"Need some help?" a voice asked, and strong masculine arms lifted her burden from her and settled it easily in the car. Callie stood silent as Billy closed the trunk and turned to face her, a slight smile on the face.

"All your staff has left," he said matter-of-factly.

"Yes, I had promised them a few days off before Christmas to prepare for their own families." She couldn't meet his eyes, so she pretended to be absorbed in tugging at her gloves. "If you're concerned about who'll serve you, why, you needn't be. I'll take care of everything."

"I wasn't worried," he said hastily, then his face brightened. "Do you mean you have no one else coming for the next few days. We'll be all alone here in this house like a real family?"

She couldn't help laughing. How could a man his age still be so boyishly eager? "You could have been that anyway," she said. "Just think of me as your cook and maid."

"Nonsense," Billy said. "You're part of our family, and we'll all pitch in and do our share."

"You needn't," Callie said with a start. "After all, you're paying to stay here."

"Yes, yes, but let's pretend for a little while." He caught hold of her hand and looked at her appealingly.

"About last night—" she began.

"It happened. I have no regrets. Let's not

mess things up by talking about them too much."

"I just want you to know, that sort of thing has never happened before with me."

"I know." One gloved hand cradled her cheek, and his eyes were dark blue and somber. "That's what made it so special to me. Let's not let it keep us from being friends."

"Friends," Callie repeated dryly, looking away from him. Somehow his words made her feel disappointed. "Well, friend, if you'll excuse me now, I have some deliveries to make."

"Need some help? That box was awfully heavy. Where are you taking all that food anyway? I'll come with you."

She stopped walking and he stopped talking. He stood regarding her over the roof of the car, his eyes twinkling like a child's, yet there was a blatant sexuality to him that never once made her think of mothering him. Her feelings were much more wicked than that.

"I'm taking the food down to the mission for the homeless," she said. "I don't really need your help. Someone will come out and take the box for me." His grin faded. "However, if you're hell-bent on coming, get in." His grin returned and was echoed in her heart. How could one person express such simple joy?

They drove down the snow-slicked streets to the old brick building where the mission was housed. The street outside the mission was empty now, but Callie had often passed it on her way to church on Sunday mornings when a line of ragged, despairing men waited for a hot meal. Father Cabot answered the door.

"Ah, Mrs. Hughes, you've remembered us for the holidays."

"Of course, Father. Did you think I could forget you now? I've brought you a special gift of my fruitcakes. I hope you'll save a piece or two for yourself."

"I'll be happy to. I see you have a helper this year." The tall, thin priest acknowledged Billy DeWitt as he carried the box indoors. Callie made the introductions, and the two men stood chatting about the work of the mission. Billy wanted to know everything about how it was run and how many people it helped. Father Cabot showed him the dormitory where simple cots were given to the homeless men on cold, windy nights and the kitchen with its faulty ovens and blackened grill. All had been donated to the mission. The dining room sported long tables and benches, and some men were already seated, quietly waiting until the evening meal was ready.

They stayed longer than Callie had intended, but she hated to hurry Billy along. He seemed so involved in everything Father Cabot said. Finally the two men disappeared into Father Cabot's study and Callie guessed Billy was making arrangements for a donation. He was strangely quiet on his way back to the hostelry. The falling snow, the warm hum of the car heater, all added to a sense of isolation, as if the two of them existed in a world apart. He said nothing until she'd pulled the car into the garage, then he reached for her hand.

"The more I learn about you, the more I'm touched by your generosity and warmth," he said softly. "You always think of others."

"You make me sound like a saint," she protested laughingly.

"Now, I know *that's* not true." His smile was roguish and she flushed, remembering how uninhibited she'd been in the night. Without returning his smile, she pulled her hand away and got out of the car. He caught up with her in the kitchen.

"Callie, don't be offended," he said, gripping her arm. His gaze was steady and filled with caring as he studied her face. "I'm sorry if I've said or done anything to hurt you."

She resisted for a long moment, then relaxed, no longer pulling against his hold, while a long sigh escaped her. "You haven't," she whispered. "It's just that—"

"Darling, there you are." The kitchen door swung open and a tall, slim woman with dark auburn hair swept into the kitchen and melted into Billy's arms. "We heard you come in and I just couldn't wait to see you." Callie saw the look of consternation on his face, and knew he hadn't quite expected this guest.

The woman laughed, a deep, throaty sound. "Darling, don't look so stunned. I know I said I wouldn't come here to this godforsaken town, but you should have known I couldn't stay away from my Billykins."

Callie couldn't hold back the sudden wild need to laugh. This must be Novia, Billy's fiancée. Her heart ached. Billy stared at her over Novia's shoulder.

Billykins? Callie mouthed the word at him and feigned laughter. Inside she wanted to cry. Billy waved a playful fist at her, but his eyes were devoid of humor. Novia pushed him away from her long enough to settle a bright red mouth against his. Her hands held him by his cheeks. When she finished with her greeting, his lips and cheeks were stained with the imprint of her red mouth. Nancy had

423

come into the kitchen as well, and stood watching the two people embrace. At last Billy drew away from the auburn-haired woman and patted her hand placatingly.

"Novia," he said hesitantly. "How—how did you get here?"

"I flew to Detroit and took the most miserable little plane from there. When I got here, I took a cab."

"You've met Nancy."

"We've had a long chat," Novia said lightly. "I think we understand each other quite well, don't we, dear?"

Nancy merely nodded, but Callie read the bleakness in her eyes. She must have known something about Novia before she arrived, Callie thought, and longed to put her arm around the girl, but Billy was introducing her now, and she turned to the woman who was Billy DeWitt's fiancée.

"I'm so happy to meet you," Novia gushed, holding out a slender white hand with long, tapering nails painted the same bright red as her lips. "What relation are you to Billy?" she asked brightly.

"None," Callie said flatly. "I'm the cook here."

"Oh!" Novia looked around, slightly nonplussed that Billy should have presented her to a mere cook.

"Callie owns Wainwright House. She's our hostess while we're here."

"I see." Novia's smile was tempered now. Previous charms were husbanded for more important people. Callie took off her coat, hung it in the back closet, and got a clean apron, tying it around her waist.

"If you'll excuse me now, everyone, I'll see to supper."

"What are you serving tonight?" Novia asked. "I'm famished. I simply couldn't eat that beastly fare on the plane."

"I thought we'd have a roast of lamb, roasted potatoes, and sweet baby peas," Callie said going behind the counter.

"Oh, darling, you know I abhor lamb," Novia said. "Can't we just go out tonight?" Callie picked up a carving knife.

"I—ah—I think that's an invitation to quit the kitchen," Billy said, herding them out. Novia's husky laughter could be heard as she clung to his arm and whispered in his ear.

Callie fully expected to see Billy's and Novia's places empty that night at supper, but they were present. Leaves had been removed from the Duncan Phyfe table, making it smaller and more intimate. Callie served the food beneath silver-domed covers, automatically adding elegant finishing touches to each course, while all the time her thoughts were on Billy DeWitt sitting so handsome and aloof at the end of the table. Novia dominated the conversation with light chatter about people and places none of the others seem to know or care about. Finally even she grew aware of the restraint in the air, and, casting an eye around the table, fixed on Max.

"Tell me, darling, what do you want Santa to bring you?" she asked with an indulgent tone.

"I don't believe in Santa Claus," Max said disdainfully. "Why do you talk so much?"

"Max!" Nancy cried, and Callie wondered briefly when she'd reverted to the nickname.

"Max, you know better," Glen chided. "Apologize at once, or go to your room."

The youngster rose, and, casting a baleful glance at the newcomer, walked out of the room.

"I don't know what's wrong with Max," Nancy said. "He's never acted like this before."

"No harm done," Billy said.

"No harm done? My dear," Novia exclaimed. "They were quite right to send him to his room. If a child can't behave himself, he shouldn't be allowed the privilege of eating with adults. Perhaps you should have him eat in the kitchen with the help for the rest of his meals."

Callie's head came up, and she longed to say something to the shallow, self-centered woman, but she drew a deep breath, removed the plates of barely touched food, and served a simple lemon cake dessert and fresh coffee. She could see Billy's scowling face and wasn't sure for whom the scowl was meant. Surely, not poor little Max and his honesty.

"You may take my dessert away," Novia said to Callie, wearily lighting a cigarette. "I simply don't eat such things, and my dear, if I might offer you some advice, you're unfashionably short. You should try abstaining from desserts yourself. A figure like yours can't take an extra pound without looking ghastly."

"Novia!" Billy's voice was sharp.

"Yes, darling?" Novia asked innocently, a smile lighting her flawless features.

"Perhaps you'd like to go to the parlor now?"

Novia looked around the table at them all, then shrugged her shoulders. "Well, if that's all there is to do, I suppose I must." Still smiling, she tossed aside her napkin and rose.

Trailing cigarette smoke, she followed Billy to the parlor.

Nancy and Glen looked apologetic. "I guess we'd better join them," Glen sighed, rising and holding a hand out to his wife.

"I'll stay and help Callie with the dishes," Nancy said, reaching for the plates.

"Of course you won't," Callie scolded.

"We've said we'll all pitch in and help around here during the holidays," Nancy insisted.

"If you really want to help me, go see about Max," Callie said pleadingly. "It breaks my heart that he's been sent to his room."

"Don't worry about it," Glen said. "He probably prefers it to spending his evening down here with us." He paused, and a sly smile grew. "On second thought, maybe I had better go see about him." He left the room, and Nancy stood staring after him, a slight smile curving her lips. Callie looked at her quizzically.

"I'm sorry," Nancy said. "It must be rather obvious that we've all had enough of Novia Gregory for one day. Now, please, let me help you with these dishes."

Callie made no more protests. The two of them worked side by side, as they had the day before decorating the house, chatting easily about things. When they were finished, Nancy hung up the dishcloth and glanced at the door leading to the dining room and the parlor beyond.

"Poor Daddy," she sighed. " 'Night, Callie." With a final wave she disappeared up the back stairs. Callie stood watching her, wondering if the girl had been aware that for the first time, she'd called Billy Daddy. Then her thoughts turned to Billy and Novia Gregory sitting in her front parlor, and she felt sad and lonely as she went alone to the big bed she'd shared with Billy just the night before.

Christmas morning dawned bright and sunny. Callie rose and dressed quickly, choosing a lace-embellished blouse of white silk and a black velvet skirt and black pumps. Casting a critical glance at herself in the mirror, she acknowledged she was a bit overdressed for kitchen duties, but she wanted to appear chic and sophisticated to Billy. Shaking her head in self-disgust, she fixed simple pink crystal teardrops to her ears and hurried out of her room. She should be ashamed, she chided herself. Billy was engaged to be married. This holiday was his attempt to reconcile his family and introduce Novia to its circle. Callie meant nothing in his scheme of things, simply an overly-accommodating hostess of a Victorian hostelry. Yet her heart cried out that it wasn't true. He'd come to her, seeking something she'd been all too willing to give. Theirs had not been merely a lustful melding of bodies, but of spirits as well. She'd missed this sense of oneness with another soul. Now that she'd known it, however briefly, through one glorious night, how was she to deny its power?

Sounds of merriment drew her from her melancholia. Setting the coffeepot to perk, she crossed the formal dining room to the door leading to the parlor. Pushing it open a crack, she stood watching the people gathered there. Nancy had placed their gifts beneath the decorated pine tree, gay, beribboned boxes that spoke of thoughtfulness and love. Max was occupied in one corner with a building set, while other toys and gifts sat temporarily forgotten. Novia, magnificent in a brilliant magenta velvet lounging robe, languished on the settee, her dark auburn hair a cloud around her shoulders, her makeup perfect even at so early an hour. She was no slouch, Callie thought grudgingly. She deserved to be beautiful because she worked at it. Even as Callie watched, Billy crossed to the settee and held out a foil-wrapped box.

"For me, darling?" Novia asked coquettishly, her red lips curving into a smile. "You didn't forget me." Her tone said she had never believed he would. Greedily, her red-tipped fingers ripped away the paper covering the velvet jeweler's box. With an excited, teasing glance at Billy, Novia opened the box and exclaimed.

"Billy, it's magnificent." She held up a wide bracelet glittering with diamonds.

"I hope you like it, Novia," Billy said, and bent to drop a quick kiss on her mouth. Callie could watch no more. Moving back to the kitchen, she set about stuffing the turkey, refusing to acknowledge the hot stinging behind her eyelids.

"Callie?"

Startled, she whirled, her hands messy with the remnants of oyster dressing. Billy stood in the doorway. His ready smile faded when he caught a glimpse of her face.

"You've been crying."

"No, I haven't. It was the onions for the dressing—" She paused awkwardly. He didn't believe her. "Maybe, a little," she acknowledged. "This is the first Christmas without my son being present."

"I'm sorry he couldn't be," Billy said gently. "But you have us, Callie. We could be your family." His voice was husky, his eyes caring.

She didn't want his caring, his pity. He had Novia. She had no one, but she wasn't to be pitied. Her expression hardened, and he sensed her feelings. He moved closer to her, his hands catching hold of her shoulders so she couldn't turn away from him.

"I've brought you a gift," he said softly. He reached into his pocket and brought out a small wrapped box.

"You needn't have," she said.

"I wanted to. Please, won't you take it?"

She couldn't refuse. She couldn't show the depths of her despair. If she did, he'd guess how important their night together had been, how important he'd become to her. Slowly, she wiped her hands and took the box. It was small and ring-size.

"Open it," he urged when she hesitated. His face was boyish, eager. Her heart quickened. Could this be? She let all expectation drain from her. Taking the gold foil paper from the box, she opened the velvet lid and stared at a gold engraved heart on a gold chain. Somehow, its simplicity and beauty made her cry. It was such a right gift between two close friends who valued each other.

"Do you like it?" he asked, and she was

forced to raise her face to his and smile through her tears.

"Thank you, Billy. It's lovely," she said.

"Like the lady herself," he said, and taking the necklace, fastened it about her neck. It lay against the lace of her blouse, just above her heartbeat.

"Thank you again," she said, and her gaze got all entangled with his. Quickly, she turned back to the half-stuffed turkey. "I'd better get this in the oven if we're to have Christmas dinner," she said with forced lightness. Billy stood nearby, waiting while her fumbling hands wrapped the turkey in foil. When she would have lifted the heavy pan, he quickly took it and slid it into the oven.

Turning back to her, his glance was thoughtful, somehow filled with regret. "We make a good team, don't we?" he said lightly.

She didn't know how to answer. All jest was gone from her. Finally, she turned back to the kitchen sink. "Perhaps you could tell everyone that waffles and strawberries will be served in the breakfast room in fifteen minutes."

"All right." The door swung closed behind him, and Callie reached for the rich warmth of the gold heart resting on her bosom.

Billy and Novia weren't present for coffee

and waffles. Nancy and her family made up for any absences, each having seconds. Afterward they carried their plates to the kitchen and insisted on helping clean up. Callie was grateful for their presence and their laughter.

Nancy presented her with a beautiful eelskin purse, and Max gave her a glass-boxed butterfly specimen, then he hurried off to set the dining table for the Christmas dinner.

"You've put out too many plates," Callie said when she'd been called to inspect his handiwork.

"No, I didn't," he replied, naming off each guest on his fingers. When he added her name, Callie shook her head.

"We insist," Nancy said quietly. "We want you there."

"But who will serve the dinner?" Callie protested.

"We'll serve ourselves. I'll help you and we'll put all the dishes on the table like a real family dinner."

Callie hugged Nancy. "I'm going to miss you when you leave," she said.

"I was hoping we might stay in touch," Nancy answered.

"Let's do!" Callie's smile was genuine now. She'd found a new friend in Billy DeWitt's daughter.

The rest of the morning passed in a flurry of activity, yet there was a relaxed, homey atmosphere to it all. Max retired to the parlor to play with his toys, Glen settled into a sofa to peruse a book about birds that Max had given him. Nancy stayed in the kitchen with Callie, helping put the last-minute touches on the holiday meal.

"I'd love to have your rum-soaked fruitcake recipe," Nancy said.

"It's an old family recipe," Callie answered, then, seeing Nancy's crestfallen face, she smiled and gripped her hand. "Of course I'll share it with you." Nancy's face brightened, and Callie knew it wasn't for want of the recipe, but because she, too, cherished this unexpected warmth that had grown between them.

Billy and Novia remained in their rooms, and Callie tried not to think of how they were spending their Christmas morning.

At two o'clock, complaints of hunger began to emanate from the front parlor. Nancy went off to warn everyone dinner would be served in a matter of minutes and they were to gather in the dining room. The table sparkled with crystal and silver and old china. Polished silver candelabra held lighted red candles at either end of the table, while a crystal-footed cake dish holding one of Callie's famous rum-soaked fruitcakes occupied the center of the table. Crystal bowls of vegetables, stuffing, cranberry sauce, and various side dishes filled the table. Near the head of the table sat the turkey in brown-roasted perfection. Billy entered the room at the last minute and automatically crossed to the head of the table. He looked incredibly handsome in a dark suit and white shirt.

His quick glance noted the number of place settings, and he nodded his head. "You've set too many places," he observed.

"We want Callie to eat with us." Max spoke up quickly, while Nancy and Glen looked at him in consternation. Callie's cheeks reddened. She would never have believed Billy would object to her joining them. She raised her head proudly, a tight smile curving her lips as she prepared to leave the dining room.

"I wasn't referring to Callie," Billy said, his glance warm on her face. "Of course we all want her here. I meant Novia won't be joining us."

"Is she ill?" Nancy asked quickly.

Billy shook his head, his smile growing, his enigmatic gaze settling on Callie's face. "Novia has left for New York."

"She's left?" Nancy repeated in outrage. "After that beautiful, expensive gift you gave her, she didn't have enough courtesy to spend the rest of the day with you?"

"That diamond bracelet was a going-away gift," Billy said softly. "Novia and I have decided not to marry."

"Daddy!" Nancy said wonderingly. "You're not getting married?"

"I hope that I am," he said, reaching for his wine goblet. "Kids, I want you to meet the woman I'd like to marry, if she'll have me." He held a glass out in a salute to Callie. His gaze was uncertain, yet hopeful, questioning and eager for her answer. All eyes turned to her. Faces were wreathed in smiles of approval and expectation. Callie stood speechless, then slowly her gaze locked with Billy's. She reached for her glass and silently, fervently, returned his salute.

Callie's Fruitcake

2 cups butter, softened
2 1/3 cups sugar
1 dozen eggs, separated
2 tablespoons lemon juice
3 tablespoons rum
4 cups flour
2 teaspoons baking powder
2 pounds candied fruit

2 pounds candied fruit
1 1/2 pound candied cherries, chopped
1 pound pecans
Dark rum

Cream butter and sugar well. Add egg yolks, a few at a time, to creamed mixture. Add lemon juice and rum. Add 3 cups sifted flour and baking powder. In an extra-large mixing bowl, coat candied fruit, cherries, and nuts with 1 cup of flour. After fruit and nuts are well coated, fold in cake batter. Beat egg whites until stiff. Fold into batter. Pour into greased and floured bread pans (6 small or 3 large) or 3 tube pans. Fill pans 3/4 full. Bake at 300 degrees for 1 hour and 10 minutes for small bread pans or 1 hour and 45 minutes for large bread pans; 60 minutes for tube pans. DO NOT OVERBAKE. Cool in pans 15 minutes. Remove fruitcakes. Cool on racks Soak fruitcakes with rum. Wrap in cheese-cloth and foil. Let set for 1 month. Soak weekly with dark rum to desired taste.

Smoky Mountain Magic

by Clara Wimberly

Susan Douglas stood back a few feet from the newly-decorated Christmas tree and frowned. At home they'd always had an enormous tree for Christmas, and those memories made this little spruce look inadequate by comparison.

She glanced at her watch thinking what a short time it had taken to decorate the tree. Supper was in the oven and she had nothing else to do until her son Todd arrived, which should be any moment now.

Susan felt only a slight momentary twinge of anxiety, thinking of his hiking trip and the cold, foggy weather that had moved in earlier in the afternoon. She knew he was an expert hiker and that he would be careful. Besides, he knew the trails in the Smokies as well as anyone, having grown up in Townsend at the edge of the park.

"Townsend," she whispered, frowning at the sound of the word in the quiet room. What poignant memories came, unbidden and unwanted, at the mention of that name. The small mountain community was where she had lived for the past twenty-four years.

And with those memories came the sharp, vivid image of Patrick, the man she'd married all those years ago. The man she'd argued with, fought with . . . the man who never seemed to understand that she had needs as an individual and not just as his wife. Patrick Douglas, whose green eyes had captured her heart and soul the first moment she met him.

Even at age fifty, those eyes were still clear and expressive, and still an odd green color, the color of glass. Someone had told her long ago that green eyes were a trait of the native mountaineer . . . something inherited from their Scottish and Irish ancestors.

Susan had seen passion in those beautiful eyes and she'd seen humor. She'd seen love there and awe when their son Todd was born twenty-two years before. And six months earlier, when Susan finally put her foot down and moved to Knoxville, she'd seen anger in those eyes such as she'd never seen in all their years together. Not even the tumultuous, passion-filled early years had created that much anger, when all they seemed to do was fight and make love.

She remembered the look in his eyes, and even now the pain that had edged into her heart was still there.

"You can't be serious," he'd said on that hot June day the previous summer. "You can't really intend to leave . . . leave our home, the orchards . . . all we've built here together."

"All *you've* built, Patrick! The apple orchard is not my life; it never was. That's your work, your family's work, but it's never been mine. If I ever intend to know what my potential is, I have to do it now . . . don't you understand? I'll be forty-nine years old in November, Patrick. Why can't you see—" She had stopped and looked at him with tears in her eyes, wishing he would come to his senses, wishing for the last time that he would finally begin to see her as an individual who had wants and needs of her own.

She didn't really want to leave him or their home in Townsend. All she wanted was a chance to go back to school, maybe get a degree. She could easily have done it all and remained at home. But Patrick was too stubborn. It had to be his way or nothing, and he couldn't seem to see that he was the one who had forced the issue of her leaving the mountains for good.

She remembered him raking impatient fingers through his graying hair as he whirled to stare at her. When he took a step toward her, she moved away, afraid he would touch her, afraid he would pull her into his arms and kiss her the way he always did when there was a confrontation between them.

"Is that what this is about, Susan? Your age? Is this some mid-life crisis we're talking about here? That worn old feminist war cry of 'I have to find myself'? God! I never took you for someone who thought that way. You seemed happy just being my wife. . . . You were always so practical, so—"

"Patrick," she sighed, shaking her head at him. "Why must everything with you be black and white? This is something I've thought about and wanted for a long time. We've discussed it before. But with you that's all it would be—a discussion. You never took me seriously, not about this or about anything."

"That's not true," he said, frowning, those green eyes troubled and wary. "I love you, Susan, and I thought you loved me. Why isn't that enough for you? You know I admire you. You're smart and pretty. You've been a wonderful mother. And I could never have asked for a better wife—never. Mom and Dad adore you—"

"Oh, Patrick, this has nothing to do with all that. And it doesn't mean that I don't love you and Todd . . . I do . . . more than anything. And you know I think of your parents as my own. But can't you see, I have to do something for myself now—before it's too late. I don't want to grow old, knowing I had this chance to learn and to grow and I never took it. I don't want to sit in a rocker on the porch, staring at the mountains and wondering what it would have been like—"

"I don't want to hear any more," he snapped. "I don't believe it has anything to do with any of that; this is something that's been coming for a long time, and you know it. You're not the same woman I married, Susan. You've become restless, critical even. Not only of me, but of the mountains and the simple life—"

"Oh, stop! The simple life . . . I'm sick of hearing about your so-called simple life. You can just save all that mountaineer propaganda for the tourists. You can dress in jeans and a plaid shirt, Patrick, and you can emphasize your southern drawl all you want to. But behind all that you're a shrewd businessman who knows exactly what he wants and what he has to do to get it. And I'm beginning to wonder if that really includes me at all unless it's on your own terms. Maybe what you want is an automated hillbilly robot, a sweet, compliant housewife who wears a print dress and sits out front at the apple barn, smoking a corncob pipe for the visitors. A mountaineer woman who submits to her husband in every way, just the way they did a hundred years ago in the cove." She stopped and took a deep, slow breath, and her eyes glittered at him. "I have always helped you gladly. But there's more to me than that, and if you had bothered to see who I really am, you'd know it by now."

"You've lost your mind," he said, staring at her with an odd expression. "And maybe you're right . . . maybe I never knew you at all."

Susan was lying back against the chair, her eyes closed tightly against the decorated tree in the corner of her tiny apartment. The lights that blinked so merrily lit the darkened room, and right now it was not something she wanted to see.

"Oh, Patrick," she whispered. "You were the

only man I ever loved . . . my first love. What happened to us along the way?"

Maybe the trouble had always been that she was just as stubborn as Patrick. That day in June when he'd stormed out, he saddled a horse and rode into the mountains, not bothering to explain where he was going or when he'd be back.

And when he came back two days later, Susan was gone.

She opened her eyes now, glancing around the apartment. She'd had a harder time than she ever dreamed, adjusting to life in Knoxville. Sometimes the small apartment closed in on her and the noises from the other tenants were distracting and bothersome. Hard to take, considering the most she was ever used to hearing at night was the sound of a whippoorwill or a horned owl that sometimes roosted near the old house in the cove.

But she loved the beautiful university campus that lay on the Tennessee River, and she loved her classes, even though they were harder than she'd ever imagined. Still, she was making good grades, and if she tended to shy away from making friends, she thought that would come in time, as her confidence in herself grew.

It was only on nights like tonight, or special occasions like Christmas, that she became homesick and nostalgic. Sundays, too, were hard; the day when everyone at home would be gathered for Sunday dinner. Todd would be there with his girlfriend; Patrick's brother and their children would come. Sundays were good days, a time for rest and family and in the mountains a traditional day for reflecting on one's blessings.

Susan frowned at the thought. Those blessings always included the exalting of the family.

She knew that was the one thing Patrick couldn't forgive . . . that rending of family ties that meant so much to him. And that was why he'd not contacted her once since she moved to Knoxville, why Todd would only shrug when she asked him about his dad.

"He's hurt, Mom," Todd would say, not quite meeting her eyes. "He thinks you've betrayed him and he's hurt."

Susan closed her eyes again, seeing Patrick's strong, handsome features and remembering how the pain in those green eyes seemed so out of place in such a masculine face.

There was a knock on the door. Susan's eyes flew open and she smiled, standing up to smooth her beige sweater down over her slacks before going to let her errant son in.

"It's about t—" She stopped, holding the door, her breath caught in her throat as she

446

stared into green eyes and the very face she had just been thinking of.

She had not seen Patrick since that day in June. And now, seeing him in her hallway with such a serious look in his eyes, she didn't stop to think why he was there. She could think of nothing except how he looked, how tall and handsome he still was, and how the sight of him still brought that undeniable tingle to the pit of her stomach.

"Patrick . . ."

"May I come in, Susan?"

He was just as impatient, just as matter-of-fact as always. And for a moment Susan chided herself for hoping that this most holy of seasons had brought him to make amends.

She stepped aside and motioned him in, watching as he moved past her in a cool, pine-scented breeze that instantly brought the mountains into her living room.

It was only when he turned to face her that she recognized the look of worry in his eyes and the tired, drawn look on his face. She felt her heart begin to race with fear even as she took a step closer to him.

"What is it? What's happened?"

Patrick took her hands in his and she felt the calluses, the coldness of his skin that seemed to move from his fingers into her heart.

447

"It's Todd," he said. "He didn't come home from the mountains this afternoon. We found his truck still parked at the trailhead long after dark." Patrick stopped for a moment. "We can only assume he's lost, Susan."

"Lost?" Susan whispered, staring at him as if his words made no sense at all. Her eyes immediately went toward the window of her apartment as she visualized the cold, shadowy mists that had darkened the earth in early afternoon.

For a moment the steeliness of Patrick's eyes wavered and he took a step toward her.

"Here," he said. "Let's sit down."

She did so, hardly aware of moving. She tried to visualize Todd's handsome face, so much like his dad's. Tried to hear his confident voice somewhere in her dazed mind. But all she could hear were her own words that went around and around in her head.

"Lost."

She lifted her eyes to Patrick, aware that he was sitting on the sofa beside her. It was the first time she'd seen him in months. Why did it have to be under these horrifying circumstances?

"He'll be okay, Susan. You know what a good athlete he is, and he knows the trails better than anyone."

"Where . . . where did he go?"

Only for a moment did Patrick's eyes look away from her searching ones. "To Spence Fields and Thunderhead."

"Oh," she said, thinking of the arduous and difficult trail that led to one of the Smokies' mysterious balds. "He wasn't alone, was he?"

Her heart sank when Patrick slowly nodded that he was. Then he stood up, moving restlessly around her small living room as his hand stroked his chin. He turned to her with a wry smile.

"Unless, of course, you count old Rebel."

"Rebel." Her voice sounded disdainful, but there was a crooked smile on her lips as the vision of the old hound came to mind. "That crazy dog probably got lost himself. That's probably why Todd hasn't come back yet . . . he's still looking for that silly hound."

Patrick smiled, and his eyes were sympathetic as he gazed down at his wife. She looked so small and helpless, so fragile sitting there on the couch, trying to appear brave and unworried.

All the animosity he'd felt for months had fallen away the moment he saw her in the doorway. His eyes had quickly taken in her tiny apartment, the sparsely decorated little tree in the corner. And he thought Susan looked tired with dark circles beneath her big brown eyes.

This wasn't right; she shouldn't be in this cramped little place, alone and isolated. She should be back home in the big farmhouse that she loved so much, working among the flowers while the sun made golden lights in her brown hair. He had visualized her there often, her face smiling up at him as they walked through the meadows in autumn or slogged through the snow on some quiet, secluded winter trail.

Even now, after all this time, he still had to fight the ache in his heart that he felt whenever he thought of her. How often he had wondered if she was lonely, or if she wanted to come back home but wouldn't because of some stubborn Yankee pride.

It was that same stubborn Yankee pride that had captured his attention twenty-five years earlier. Susan had come to the mountains with her family, and once he saw her, he had done everything he could think of to keep her there.

Had that been a mistake? One that perhaps Susan had resented all along?

"What are we going to do?" she asked, her voice shaking him from his thoughts.

"The rescue squad is organizing right now, so I suppose there's nothing to do except wait until morning. They can't go in until then."

"Oh."

The look in her eyes was reflected in

Patrick's own heart. He saw her impatience and worry, the dread of what this could mean. And he knew she felt the same as he did . . . Todd was their only child, conceived in the tempestuous love of their youth and adored throughout his life, not only by his parents, but by his grandparents, his aunts and uncles.

"I thought you should know," he said, realizing his words were unnecessary and made no sense. "I knew you'd be worried . . ."

"Are you going back to the cove?"

He nodded. "I'm sure Mom and Dad will be at our house now—" He hesitated, seeing her look away when he said the word *our*. "And if I know Mom, she's already brewing coffee and cooking."

Susan smiled at his words. Even in her anxiety the thought of Mom Douglas cooking and stirring about in the big kitchen made her feel warm and comforted.

"I'm going with you," she said, jumping up from the sofa and going toward her bedroom.

Patrick made no effort to argue with her.

"I thought you'd say that," he murmured to himself as she disappeared through a doorway.

Patrick paced the small room, letting his eyes move over the objects Susan had brought there. As he gazed at the pitifully small collection, he felt remorse for the first time. For the first time he allowed himself to admit that he was responsible for their painful separation.

But he had never been able to keep his stubborn pride from interfering in his decision making. A man had to have pride and Patrick's had come honestly . . . from generations of mountain men who had fought and died to clear the rugged Tennessee countryside and build homes for their families.

He stood before Susan's Christmas tree, and his hand went automatically to touch a heart-shaped brass ornament nestled in the top branches. His fingers moved over the cold metal, then turned it so the back was facing him and he could read the engraved lettering.

To Susan, my beautiful Yankee bride, on our first Christmas together. All my love, Patrick.

Patrick closed his eyes and took a step back away from the tree, frowning with pain as if the needled branches had pierced his skin.

God, he had almost forgotten the ornament, even though it had hung at the top of every Christmas tree since that first one twenty-four years ago. But this was the first year there was no huge, decorated spruce in the den of the farmhouse, so it was only natural he wouldn't miss this particular piece.

He was surprised that Susan had brought it

with her, thought of it, even, when she left that June day in the heat of summer.

Patrick took a long, deep breath, taking in the scent of the tree, and the other, more provocative, lingering scent of Susan's perfume that lay softly in her new home.

He turned sharply from the tree, going to stand at the window and gaze out at the streetlights that twinkled in the darkness.

It's over, he told himself, and there's no need dredging up old memories or wishing for something that could never be again. Susan had made her choice; this was what she wanted. Hell, she hadn't even bothered to come back to Townsend, not once. She hadn't called; her only contact was with their son, and then at Thanksgiving when she had called his mother.

It was only this concern over Todd that had brought Patrick to Knoxville. He would never have come otherwise. He was not the kind of man to beg, never had been, and, dammit, Susan knew that. If she had wanted to change things, she could have.

"Patrick?" Susan's voice was soft behind him. "I think I'm ready."

He turned to face her and saw that she had changed into jeans and a sweatshirt. She was pulling on a heavy quilted jacket as she looked his way.

"Good," he said, going to open the front door.

He watched as she turned to unplug the Christmas-tree lights. And as her hand went to touch the heart-shaped ornament on top, she glanced at him and her lips trembled ever so slightly before she moved away from the tree.

Susan looked at Patrick, wondering at the odd look on his face, feeling foolish. He probably didn't even remember the ornament, or what it had once meant to them.

They didn't talk as Patrick maneuvered the truck out of the parking lot and onto the wet streets of Knoxville. And by the time they left the lights of the city behind them, the truck's heater was purring softly as it quickly turned the air inside the cab to a cozy warmth.

Just before they turned onto the highway that led to Townsend, they passed several brightly lit fast-food restaurants and Patrick turned to Susan for the first time since leaving the apartment.

"Are you hungry? Would you like a cup of coffee, or—"

"No," she said quickly, her eyes anxiously scanning the darkness that lay before them. The mist that fell on the windshield seemed to contain bits of ice now, and she felt an overwhelming urge to hurry, to get to the house at Townsend. They might even find that Todd had miraculously come home.

"No," she repeated. "I'm not hungry."

"Todd had matches and food," Patrick said as if reading her mind. "If he managed to find shelter, he'll be warm and safe until morning."

Susan gulped and nodded, unable to answer for the lump in her throat. The horror of Todd's disappearance was just beginning to sink in, and the fear she felt was almost overwhelming. Nothing could happen to Todd, she prayed silently. *Please, just don't let anything happen to my son . . . he's the sweetest, most precious thing in our life.*

She turned her head toward Patrick, realizing she had used the word *our* just as he had earlier. But that was the way it had always been with them. Despite any differences or problems, Susan always knew that Patrick loved his son as much as she did. And she knew that now he was just as worried as she.

At twenty-two, Todd was independent, intelligent, and perfectly capable of making his own decisions, as he so often reminded them. And like most young adults, he was amused that she and Patrick still regarded him as their little boy, and saw him as that chubby, dark-haired little kid who was so tough, he rarely cried. He had been Susan's funny little angel, who liked to laugh and play jokes on anyone available. She could still see her son's handsome face and the look of amusement as he teased her about their protectiveness.

She was surprised at the quiet sob that escaped her lips and even more surprised when she saw the look of understanding in Patrick's eyes. She felt the truck sway as he pulled over to the side of the highway and into a vacant parking lot.

He switched off the engine and turned to her. Suddenly she was in his arms, allowing the tears to come and clinging to him as if he were her lifeline. And as she sought comfort against his chest, it seemed right and familiar; it seemed as if she had never left his arms.

"Hey," he murmured against her hair. "It's all right. You know what a tough kid our boy is; he'll make it."

She nodded, unable to speak for the tears that choked her throat.

"Just like his dad," she finally managed to say, finishing their old, worn litany.

"Yeah," Patrick said, his voice hoarse and scratchy. "Tough and stubborn, just like his dad."

"Oh, God, Patrick," she whispered against his shoulder. "What will we do . . . what will we do if anything happens to him? I don't think I could make it if—"

He took her by the shoulders and held her away, seeing the fear in her dark eyes in the lights from the passing traffic.

"We'll find him, Sue. You and I together, we're going to find our son and we're going to bring him home to the house in the cove. You have to believe that . . . and help me believe it." His hands tightened on her shoulders as he tried to convince himself as well. Then he pulled her against him, holding her tightly as if he needed her comfort as much as she needed his.

Finally he pulled away and Susan slumped back against the seat, watching him with dark, sad eyes as he started the truck and drove back onto the roadway.

She couldn't stop crying, and she covered her lips with her fingers, trying to think of something else . . . anything but the possibilities of what could have happened to Todd.

The emotions of their embrace caused an awkwardness that was palpable in the enclosure of the small truck as they drove through the night.

They had parted with such bitter words, with such anger. And now, six months later, when they finally embraced for the first time, it had not been out of love or passion, but for comfort. And that was something Susan found hard to believe.

Their relationship had been many things over the years. They had worked hard together in the orchard, building it to a nationwide business that promised security for the entire family. They had laughed together . . . fought each other. There had been periods of quiet when their lives consisted of months of sameness and monotony. But always there had been passion. No matter what happened in their lives their passion had never died.

And now Susan glanced at the man beside her and wondered if that, too, was gone.

She watched the road signs as they approached the small community of Townsend until finally she saw the one that read MILLER'S COVE. Her heart ached at the sound of it in her mind.

When they had first married, she had found all the names in the Smoky Mountains quaint and homey, delicious with atmosphere. How Patrick had laughed at her excitement upon learning she would be living in a place called Miller's Cove.

"It sounds like something out of a book!" she had squealed, her eyes bright with delight.

"Anything would sound like a fairy tale to

you, city girl," he drawled, pulling her into his arms and kissing her. "I just hope you feel the same enthusiasm after you've lived through your first summer season, when the tourists somehow manage to find their way right to your door and are disappointed if you aren't wearing a flour-sack dress and combat boots."

She had laughed at his nonsense. And through it all, through the summer invasion of tourists and the hard, icy winters that followed, she had loved it. Even when the rich mountain earth and summer sun turned the trees into a thick green jungle that obliterated the sun. She loved the wildflowers and the mountain laurel, loved the clear, cold streams and the flower-filled meadows that one came upon unexpectedly in the hazy blue-green mountains. She even loved the dark green shadows that shut out the light in summer and turned the mountains into a mysterious, isolated place.

She had never wanted to live anywhere else.

The farmhouse lay at the entrance to the cove and was surrounded by huge beech and oak trees. It was only past the house, toward the barn and other outbuildings, that the cove began to grow wide and spacious, and the distance between the mountains began to grow farther apart.

There were several cars and trucks parked in the short driveway. Lights blazed in the downstairs portion of the white two-story house, and Susan felt relief that Patrick's parents were already there.

The rain had grown heavier, and as they ran from the truck, Susan could hear the hiss of ice against the ground and against the roof of the house. Patrick carried her small bag onto the long, covered front porch and set it down, then turned to her.

"I didn't think," he said, glancing down at her bag. "If you'd prefer to stay with Mom and Dad . . ."

"No," she said, looking into his eyes as if she might see what he really wanted her to do. "If you don't mind, I'd prefer staying here. I . . . I feel closer to Todd and—"

"Of course," he said with a nod as he pushed open the front door and picked up the bag, then motioned for her to enter the house.

Susan had felt reluctant to see the house, afraid she might feel like a stranger in her own home. But stepping inside, she realized she needn't have worried; nothing had changed.

The familiar scents of the house—the smell of polished wood and spices, the pungent odor of burning wood from the fireplace in the den—all of it flew straight to her heart with a

460

pang so real that she had to stop for a moment and take a deep breath.

Patrick waited patiently while Susan stopped and looked around the entry hall, then moved slowly toward the den. Her eyes took in the gleam of polished wood floors and brightly colored rugs, the warm pine furniture and high ceilings with their exposed beams.

This is where you belong, Patrick wanted to shout. He wanted to pull her into his arms and kiss her until she was breathless, until she could not protest, until she finally admitted with that languid look in her eyes that she belonged here, too, that she belonged to him.

"Nothing's changed," she whispered, turning to look at him.

He stared at her for a moment before his dark lashes lowered and closed out whatever emotion had been reflected in his eyes.

"Everything's changed," he said, taking her bag and moving toward the staircase.

"Susan!" she heard, and turned to see Patrick's mother coming from the kitchen at the end of the hallway. "Oh, Susan, sweetheart . . . come here to me."

The small woman in the baggy corduroy pants and oversize shirt stood waiting, arms outstretched. And Susan practically ran to her, throwing herself into her arms.

"Nell," she whispered. She had not realized how much she needed comforting until she felt Nell's motherly hands patting her back. "Oh, Mom," she said, pulling away to look down into her mother-in-law's face.

"I know," Nell said. "I know how afraid you must be for our laddie. But he's going to be all right, you know." Even though she was smiling, the woman's eyes were bright with unshed tears.

"I was hoping there would be some word by the time we arrived," Susan said.

"No, dear. Nothing yet. But some of the men are staying in the parking lot at the trail tonight, just in case Todd finds his way out." She glanced away from Susan as she turned to watch her son coming down the stairs.

"Where's Dad?" he asked.

"Oh, he's here . . . he's upstairs, on the phone, I think, making arrangements for coffee and food to be taken out there."

"How's he feeling?" Patrick asked, watching his mother's face carefully. His father's bout with a heart condition last year made them all wary when he tried to do too much or when he grew tired.

"He seems fine," she said. "I made sure he took his medicine, and your brother Paul had a little talk with him when Dad insisted on going

462

out to help look for Todd. But I don't have to tell you how stubborn that man is. I probably would have been better off if I'd just let him go and be done with it."

"You're probably right," Patrick said with a wry grin. "I'll bring him down to the den and keep him company."

Susan felt a deep tug of disappointment when Patrick did not look her way. He turned and went upstairs, going past her as if she were nothing more than a shadow in the room.

Nell watched Susan, saw the look in her dark eyes, and she smiled. These two needed to be together; they were meant for each other, and she wondered how long it would take for them to finally see that.

"Come with me, dear," she said, tugging at Susan's arm. "You know me, I have to keep busy, and cooking usually seems to be the best way to do that."

The kitchen was bright and warm, filled with the scent of baking bread and hot coffee.

Susan looked at her mother-in-law with concern. She looked tired, and her small, graceful hands seemed hesitant and uncertain tonight.

"Nell, why don't you sit down awhile. I'll be glad to help if you'll tell me what you need done."

Nell slid with a sigh onto one of the kitchen

chairs and looked up at Susan with quiet, solemn eyes.

"I suppose the cinnamon loaf is done . . . if you'd like to have a look in the oven. And I was just about to take Dad a cup of coffee." She frowned in a distracted sort of way. "I usually make decaf for him, but he insisted on the real thing tonight. And you know how I am sometimes when he looks at me with that little-boy look."

"Oh, yes," Susan said, taking off her jacket and turning to the stove. "I can certainly relate to that." She smiled, thinking of how both Patrick and Todd had used those looks with her. "But I don't think one night's worth of caffeine is going to hurt Dad." She took a deep breath of the spice-scented bread, thumping her fingers against the golden-brown crust before setting it on a bread board on the cabinet.

"I hope not," Nell muttered.

Susan smiled at Nell and patted her arm, then she turned to pour two cups of coffee and rummaged through the cabinets for a tray. She placed a small pitcher of cream and some sugar on the tray and started toward the den.

"I'll be right back. You just sit there and rest."

As Susan stepped across the threshold into the den, she was struck immediately by the smell of hickory logs in the fireplace. She could hear the crackle of the flames and see the firelight's reflection flickering around the room in lamps and other glass objects.

Patrick and his dad were sitting on the sofa, neither of them speaking. They looked up when she entered the room, and the father, so like the son, stood up slowly.

"Sue," he said softly. "Our little Sue has come back home."

Susan frowned, wondering what they had told Dad about her leaving. Were they letting him think she would be staying now, that she had decided, because of Todd, to come back to the cove for good?

Looking into Patrick's warning eyes, she set the tray down on a coffee table and went to embrace her father-in-law. He was still tall, but his shoulders had grown stooped in the past few years. And as usual, he wore his ever-present denim overalls and flannel shirt. As Susan's face was pressed against his shoulder, she breathed in the familiar scent of smoke and old spice. She had loved this man and Nell like her own parents, and seeing them grow old and frail was as painful to her as it obviously was to Patrick.

She sat with them awhile, talking quietly and answering her father-in-law's questions as he sipped the coffee. Patrick was quiet, but watched her above his own cup, his eyes cool and unreadable.

He hates me, she thought. *I have finally made him hate me.* And the realization made her heart ache with grief, not unlike the pain of someone's dying.

"Dad, why don't you and Mom stay here tonight?" Patrick asked. "Go on upstairs and go to bed. There's nothing else we can do until daybreak."

His father looked at him skeptically, frowning with hesitation.

"Besides," Patrick continued, "if you stay up all night, you won't feel much like doing anything tomorrow."

"You're right," the old man said, his voice softly gruff. "You're right. Besides, your mama needs her rest. I'll go get her." He smiled at Susan and reached across to pat her head. "I guess whatever needs tendin' can be done by our Susan. After all, it's her house."

Susan's smile was tight and forced as she watched the old man walk slowly across the room and out toward the hallway. Then she turned to Patrick.

"He seems so frail . . . so . . ."

"He's getting old," Patrick said, his eyes filling with a kind of pain she had never

466

seen before.

"You're worried about him. . . ."

"Yeah." But as he did so often, Patrick managed to lose the emotion that had flickered in his eyes. He gazed at her steadily now, as if he dared her to find any sign of sentiment in him.

Awkwardly, she glanced around the den, trying to find some topic of discussion that would not touch a sore spot between them.

"You don't have a Christmas tree up yet," she said.

Patrick made a sound, a soft grunt of humorless laughter.

She turned and frowned at him, wondering at his cynicism and feeling herself beginning to grow impatient.

"I don't understand you," she said, frowning.

His lips smiled at her, but his eyes were cold and unfeeling. "So what else is new?"

She jumped up from the sofa, feeling her face grow hot and flushed, feeling the heat all the way to the pit of her stomach.

"Damn you, Patrick. Don't you do this . . . not now, not tonight. We shouldn't be arguing . . ." Her voice trailed away as she felt the trembling of her chin. She took a deep breath, trying to steady herself as she vowed silently not to cry in front of him. "I was only trying to make conversation, trying to think of something we could talk about that wouldn't—"

He looked away from her, dismissing her and her words.

"I know you're bitter, Patrick, but don't you sit there and deny that I was a good wife to you. Don't do that to me . . . to us."

Slowly Patrick stood up, moving within inches of her. He seemed to tower above her, and in the dimness of the room he even seemed to shut out some of the light.

"There is no 'us' anymore, Susan," he growled. "There is no more family. There's you and then there's me and somewhere in between there's our son, Todd."

She could feel the angry tension of his body as he leaned toward her. Suddenly his hand shot forward and he grasped her arm, pulling her against him. "Do you know what you did when you walked out on me? Do you know how long and miserable the nights were without you in my bed, how quiet the mornings were without the sound of your voice in the kitchen? You took the laughter out of this house when you left, and by God, now you have the nerve to ask why I don't have a Christmas tree?"

Susan stared up at him, stunned by the fury in him, and by the undeniable hint of hoarseness in his voice.

"God!" he said, turning from her with a violent jerking movement.

He ran his fingers through his hair, and she could see the movements of his shoulders as he took a long, slow, calming breath of air.

"Patrick . . ." she whispered, reaching her hand toward him.

"No," he said, whirling back around to face her with blazing, pain-filled eyes. "Don't. Don't try to console me, Susan. Don't be kind and humble and don't look at me with those big brown eyes as if you really care how I feel. I was just beginning to get on with my life. I need something that's real now, and I can't let myself think anymore that you're that something."

He stalked out of the room, leaving her stunned and silent. And as she watched him leave, she felt dead and lifeless, as if he had ripped out her heart and taken it with him.

Susan walked around in the den, touching different objects and remembering. She sat on the sofa, her chin propped in her hands as she watched the last flicker of the fire die away, leaving a bed of orange coals that winked and twinkled.

Finally she rose and went into the kitchen. Nell had gone upstairs with her husband, but the kitchen was neat and orderly. There was nothing to be done there.

She turned out all the lights except one small lamp in the den and the front porch lights. Gazing out the front door, she saw that the sleet still fell and now a heavy fog had moved into the cove, obliterating the security lights and everything else past the small front yard. She sighed, trying to fight the feeling of desperation that tightened her chest and stomach.

She turned toward the stairs; the moment she had been dreading couldn't be put off any longer. She didn't want to go up, past Todd's room, past the room that she and Patrick had shared for so many years. She had no idea which room she was to sleep in; Patrick had not bothered to mention that. She didn't suppose it mattered; she doubted she would be able to sleep anyway.

She stopped at the top of the stairs, then slowly walked toward Todd's room. She switched on the lights, smiling at the usual disarray and the colorful posters that still occupied most of the wall space. So sweetly familiar . . . and so painful.

She went into the room, breathing in the strange combination of scents — expensive shaving lotion, boot polish. And she stood for a moment, letting her eyes take in everything that was her son.

Without thinking, she began to pick up his clothes that lay scattered on the floor and across the bed. Her son was a man now, a tall, handsome man who could talk knowledgeably about any subject. He had grown into his own opinions and beliefs, some of them very different from those of his parents and grandparents.

Susan smiled, thinking of some of the arguments they'd had, none of them serious. It had been more a coming-of-age thing with Todd, and she suspected it was the same with most children as they reached adulthood.

But she had to admit that some of Todd's ideas had not pleased Patrick, while she, on the other hand, enjoyed hearing her son's opinions, no matter how far out they were. Marveled, in fact, that this person whom she had rocked and cuddled, the little boy they'd taught to talk, to play ball—he had changed before their eyes into an adult with a mind of his own, no longer dependent on his parents for much of anything.

She saw his face before her, and suddenly her vision blurred with hot, bitter tears that threatened to overpower her and make her forget all her vows to remain positive. She was afraid; she was so desperately afraid that she would never see her son again.

"Todd," she whispered, pulling his shirt from the bed and holding it to her face. She breathed in the fragrance of her son, letting it bring back everything she could remember about him, letting the pain swallow her up.

Still crying, she turned off the overhead light and switched on a small lamp near the windows. She had always left this lamp on for Todd when he was out. He had told her once that he liked seeing the small light burning in his window when he drove into the yard at night. It made him feel safe, he'd said. Safe and at home.

Susan took the shirt, holding it against her as if she actually held her son. Then she lay on the bed, allowing herself to feel all the grief and fear she'd tried to keep hidden until then. She fell asleep with Todd's shirt still in her arms.

She didn't know what woke her next morning. She sat up in bed, seeing Todd's crumpled shirt and feeling desperation hit her once again. Was this what it was like to lose a child? That gnawing, aching fear that never left, that was there constantly before you went to sleep and again immediately when you awoke. She

472

didn't know how parents stood it.

It was still dark outside, but she was sure she smelled coffee from downstairs. She swung her legs over the side of the bed and stood up, trying to allow her body to become fully awake before she staggered downstairs. She had no idea who, if anyone, would be there.

She went into Todd's bathroom and splashed water on her swollen eyes, then brushed her hair.

"You look awful," she muttered, her voice scratchy and hoarse.

Going downstairs, she heard voices from the kitchen. But she was relieved to see no one else in the house except Mom and Dad and Patrick. She wasn't sure she could deal with Patrick's brother Paul or his wife. She had no idea what they thought of her, but whatever it was, she just didn't want to have to face it now.

"Morning," she said as she walked into the kitchen.

Patrick, who had been facing the doorway, turned now and splashed his coffee into the sink. But not before Susan saw the look on his face. There had been a worried frown across his brow, and his mouth was set in a straight, grim line.

"What's wrong?" she asked, feeling her heart begin to pound. "Tell me." She heard her voice rising with fear and desperation. "Have they found him . . . oh, God, Patrick is he . . . ?"

Patrick turned immediately at that sound of fear in her voice, his brows lifting in surprise. But before he could speak, Nell had already come to put her arms around Susan.

"No, darling . . . no, it's nothing like that," she said. "Here, you sit down and let me get you a cup of coffee. Do you think you could eat something? I have ham and eggs and hot biscuits."

"No, nothing." Susan lifted her eyes questioningly to Patrick, feeling herself trembling with tension.

"It's just that they found Rebel early this morning. He wandered out of the mountains and ended up at the parking lot, looking for something to eat. Paul took him home with him."

Susan sensed that Patrick was trying to relate the story in a way that would not frighten her. But she knew him too well. He was as worried as she was, and this new bit of information seemed to have heightened his fear. She wondered why.

"But . . . but Rebel would never leave Todd. Would he?" Her eyes were large and shining beneath the kitchen lights.

"Now, Susan," Nell began, setting a cup of

474

coffee at her elbow. "We mustn't go borrowing trouble. You know how that old hound is. Doesn't have a lick of sense most of the time. He probably got to chasing rabbits and got lost from Todd."

"That's right," Dad said with a wise nod of his head. "That old blue tick's got a mind of his own. Don't know why the boy took him to the mountains in the first place."

Susan saw the look that was exchanged between father and son, and she saw how Patrick seemed to be avoiding her eyes.

"Patrick," she said, feeling as if they were the only two people in the room. "There's something else, isn't there? You aren't telling me everything."

"It probably doesn't mean a thing," he said with a shrug of his broad shoulders. He glanced toward his mother. "The dog has been hurt; he had a couple of slashes on his chest."

Susan took a long, shuddering breath, her eyes never wavering from Patrick's face. She knew how adept he was at hiding his feelings, and she wasn't sure she could believe anything he said at this point.

"What—what kind of slashes?"

"Hogs, most likely."

She felt her breath leave her lungs. "Wild hogs? Oh, Patrick . . ."

"Rebel might not even have been with Todd when he received these wounds, Susan. We just don't know. And until we do, I don't think we should make too much of it."

Susan stood up, feeling as if her lungs might actually explode if she didn't do something to use up the energy that had coiled in her muscles.

"I want to go out there."

She had expected Patrick to protest. But no one in the room said a word, and when she looked up into his eyes, she saw a look of acquiescence and understanding.

He nodded, then pushed himself away from the sink where he'd been standing.

"All right. Get your coat. I was just about to drive out there myself."

"Not before she eats something, she's not," Nell said. "Susan dear, you can't go all day long on two sips of black coffee. You have more sense than that." Her mother-in-law's eyes were dark with caution.

"Nell, I just can't sit here another moment," Susan said with an exasperated sigh. "I think if I do, I might explode."

"Well, now," Nell said with a wry grin. "We wouldn't want you to do that. Tell you what, it won't take a jiffy to open up some of these biscuits and put a slice of ham on them. I'll wrap them in foil and you two can be on your way." Nell glanced toward her son. "Patrick hasn't eaten much either since all this started."

Patrick smiled at his mother, nodding his head slowly, knowing there was no need arguing with her. Besides, he was surprised at how much better he felt having told Susan about the dog. And the fact that she had not gone completely off the deep end gave him confidence that Rebel's appearance meant nothing ominous. He wondered if she had any idea how much it always meant, talking things over with her. Had he ever told her that? He glanced at Susan now, seeing the tired look on her face and the way her eyes were red and swollen.

He had walked past Todd's room that morning and seen her asleep on their son's bed with her arms wrapped tightly around one of Todd's shirts. It had taken all the willpower he had not to go in and crawl into bed beside her, take her in his arms, and hold her.

Sometimes at night his body actually ached for the feel of her body snuggled up next to his. God, that was all he'd ever wanted, just to take care of her and their son. And her need for something more out of life, her leaving, made him feel betrayed and unneeded.

Susan was a good woman. And when she'd shouted at him last night in the den that she had been a good wife, he could not deny it. The only problem was that he had never been very good at sharing her, not with anyone except their son. That was one bond that had never made him feel jealous or insecure, that precious bond between the woman he loved and the son she had borne him.

Patrick shook his head and forced himself to stop looking at her. There was no time now for wondering what had gone wrong, or for wishing it hadn't.

"You'll need your boots," he said to Susan. "I'll get them from upstairs while you and Mom get the food ready. It should be daylight soon, by the time we get to the trail anyway."

Later, as they were going out the door, Nell handed Susan a small foil-wrapped package. Susan could feel the heat from the ham and biscuits that lay inside and suddenly she felt hungry. When Nell handed Patrick two cans of soft drink that glistened with cold moisture, Susan couldn't resist smiling at him.

She had always teased Patrick about his penchant for cokes, especially in the morning. It was something she'd never grown used to. She caught his eye and he smiled, handing her one of the cold cans with a teasing look.

"Want one?"

"Yes," she said slowly, taking it from his

hand. "Something cold sounds pretty soothing right now."

There was not much conversation as they drove through the darkness out to the main highway. Once the highway entered the winding, twisting area of the Little River Gorge, the light was beginning to break in the eastern sky. Patrick pulled the truck over to a wide space beside the river and glanced at Susan.

"I thought we'd stop and eat before going any further."

"Sounds like a good idea," she said, hearing the grumble of her stomach.

She stepped out of the truck, feeling the breeze of cold air from the river ripple her hair and sting her cheeks. It felt good. And for some unknown reason, just being out there in the mountains drew her closer to Todd. He loved it so much.

She stood near the truck, watching Patrick walk slowly down to the river. He gazed into the cold water as it tumbled over the rocks; sometimes he'd stop and throw pebbles into the clear stream. He was hurting and she wanted to go to him. It had always been so easy to love him, so natural to go to him and put her arms around him. And this feeling of holding back seemed strange and foreign to her, something that ate at her and made her arms actually tremble with her need to touch him.

Patrick came back to the truck; he seemed worried and tired. "Are you ready?"

"Yes."

It was a long drive into Cades Cove. When they finally arrived at Cable Mill, they saw several cars belonging to the park service, along with trucks with the rescue squad's logo on the side. Susan thought there was something strange and unreal about the entire scene. The men milled restlessly about, talking quietly, drinking coffee. The pale morning light, dimmed by fog and mist, made the atmosphere even more bizarre. She could hardly believe this was happening to them, or to Todd.

When she and Patrick got out of the truck, several of the men recognized them. Some nodded and touched the brims of their hats as they turned sympathetic eyes toward Susan. She had always been impressed with the gentlemanly manners of mountain men. And on this cold, empty morning, their concern touched and warmed her. It made her feel as if she'd come home.

Seeing the men and hearing their confident talk, Susan felt buoyed and hopeful. But the day passed slowly and despite the number of people combing the mountains for Todd, there was no sign of him. By afternoon a numbing

480

wind had moved over the mountains, a wind that set the huge pines and hemlocks swaying above them and threw a mournful sound into the air. Finally Susan went to the visitor center which was located nearby. But she found the atmosphere there sad and almost funereal until finally she felt desperate to get back outside. She stood in the wind, her eyes searching the crowd of men for Patrick.

When she found him, she went up to him and slipped her arm through his. He turned and gazed down at her with a look of surprise. But he didn't pull way.

"Can we walk somewhere?" she whispered, "I just have to get away from this for a while."

"Do you want me to take you back to the house. You'd be much more comfortable there—"

"No," she said with a shake of her head. "I want to be here. But I just can't bear the looks . . . the . . . the sad expression in their eyes. You'd think Todd was already—" She stopped, lips trembling as she gazed up at her husband.

"I know," he said, putting his hand over hers. "But they just don't know our son as well as we do." His smile was sweet and reassuring. "Come on, we'll take a good, long walk."

When darkness fell early over the mountains, Susan felt sick with disappointment. They had found nothing. Even the helicopter that had flown all day had not discovered anything new, and the crew came in early because of the weather. Susan could see the dejection in the slump of their shoulders as they stepped out of the helicopter. They knew, just as she and Patrick did, that time was running out. The weather was growing worse, and even if Todd had food and matches, he couldn't survive much longer in these conditions.

And now another long, sleepless night would have to pass before they could continue looking.

Patrick came to her, his eyes filled with anger and frustration.

"Are they quitting for the night?"

"Yes," he said quietly. Suddenly his fist slammed down against the hood of the truck. "Goddammit!"

"Patrick," she murmured. "Don't. Please, don't give up. I don't think I can handle this if you give up, too."

His head came up and his eyes met hers, eyes filled with pain and sorrow. Without a word he moved to her, pulling her into his arms and holding her against him. She could feel the trembling of his body and she knew, even though she didn't want to admit it, that they both should go home.

But for the moment Susan clung to him, reveling in the strong feel of his arms about her. And even in her sorrow she sighed with pleasure, with the relief of finally having him hold her this way again.

"It's going to be all right," she murmured. "Please . . . tell me you believe it will be all right."

"I do," he whispered.

He pulled away from her, looking down at her. In the growing darkness she could barely see the outline of his face, but she reached up to touch him.

"I haven't given up," he said. "I guess I'm just frustrated and impatient. I didn't want Todd to have to spend another night in the mountains. But I still believe he's alive, Susan. And I believe he's going to come back home to us, safe and sound."

"Good," she said. "So do I."

Both of them stepped apart, feeling the awkwardness separate them again, feeling the need to put distance between themselves.

Later, as Patrick maneuvered the truck out of Cades Cove and down the winding Little River road, he was quiet and thoughtful. He wondered what Susan would have done if he'd kissed her in the parking lot. Would she have pulled away, or would her eyes have grown dark the way they used to . . . would her mouth be as sweet and yielding as ever?

The truck skidded for a second on a small patch of ice. Patrick slowed down, telling himself he needed to concentrate on the road. And he needed to stop fooling himself about Susan. No matter how much he wanted her, or how much he might like to plead with her to come back into his life, he just couldn't seem to find the words. She'd often accused him in the past of being stubborn and unbending where his pride was concerned. And he had to admit, she was right. He couldn't allow himself to beg, only to see the rejection in her eyes, or, worse than that, to see sympathy there.

Susan glanced from time to time at Patrick as they drove silently. She could see the tension in him, in the hard grip of his hands on the wheel, and she wondered what he was thinking of.

Todd, probably, she thought. After what she had done to him, how could she expect him to be thinking of her? She had told herself time and again that Patrick didn't care, that her going to Knoxville had upset him only because he couldn't be in control. But now, seeing him this way, seeing the pain in his eyes, she wondered.

And she began to hope.

Patrick's mom and dad met them on the porch when they walked from the truck. Susan could see the hope in their eyes, then the slump of their shoulders when Patrick shook his head.

"Oh, son," Nell said, going to put her arms around Patrick.

They could hear the spatter of sleet on the bare trees around the house and on the fallen brown leaves.

Patrick's dad walked to the edge of the porch to gaze at the sky, shaking his head in dismay. "I hope the boy's found some shelter somewhere. It's going to be a long, rough night Weather service is predicting snow."

Patrick and Susan exchanged glances. *What next,* she wanted to scream. *Why does everything seem to be going against us and against Todd?*

Later, in the kitchen, the four of them ate silently as they listened to the low murmur of the radio. Nell had turned it on, hoping there might be news of Todd, or about the weather.

The phone rang several times, interrupting their dinner. So many people in Townsend loved Todd and the Douglas family. And many friends called just to say they were hoping and praying for Todd's safe return. The pastor at Miller's Cove Church called to say they had planned to incorporate a special prayer service in their annual Christmas Eve program the following night. And if the family felt up to it, he would like them to attend.

Susan nodded when Patrick held the phone away and asked her about it. It had been so long since she'd been to the little white church.

"Sure, preacher," Patrick said into the phone. "We'll try to be there. Thanks."

"That's very nice," Nell said quickly when Patrick sat back down. "But I hope it will turn out to be a thanksgiving service; I hope our laddie will be home before then."

"So do I, Mom," Patrick said, pushing his plate away as if he had suddenly lost his appetite. "I think I'll walk down to the apple barn, see if everything's battened down before the storm hits."

"Want me to go with you, son?"

"No, Dad. You stay inside."

His dad stood up and went to put an arm around him. "Me and your mama will likely be gone when you get back. I think we've decided to go on home for tonight. I need to see to the cattle, make sure they got plenty of hay."

"Your daddy didn't sleep good last night,"

486

Nell added. "We thought it might be better at home in our own bed."

"Sure," Patrick said with a shrug. "That's fine . . . you two go ahead. We'll see you tomorrow." He hugged his mother and turned to grab his jacket from the coat rack near the back door.

"Good night, son," Nell said, her eyes dark and worried as they followed him out the door. "Poor boy," she said after he'd gone. "He's worried sick about Todd."

Susan would have liked to talk to Nell for a while about her son, but she could see how eager they were to go home.

"I can finish the dishes," she said. "Besides, I need to keep busy. You two go ahead before the weather gets any worse."

She thought that both of them were relieved as they kissed her goodbye and hurried out to their truck. Nell turned once and blew a kiss to her where she stood watching from the doorway.

Susan walked slowly back down the hall into the kitchen, turning up the radio as she filled the sink with soapy water. The weather report didn't sound good. There seemed to be no doubt that they were going to get several inches of snow. Any other time she would have been ecstatic. How she loved snow at Christmas!

But now, for the first time in her life, she wished with all her heart that the snow would hold off for a couple of days.

When Patrick came back in, she was in the den, putting more logs on the fire that had burned down during dinner. She liked a fire; somehow it made a room seem cozy and comfortable. Besides, she needed a diversion tonight.

"Everything okay?" she asked.

"Fine," he said, pulling off his boots and placing them on the hearth to dry.

"Would you like a cup of coffee, or—?"

"I can get it."

She watched him leave the room and wondered what had happened to make him so withdrawn. For a while this afternoon she'd thought they were getting closer. When he pulled her impulsively into his arms, she'd even thought he was going to kiss her.

And she'd been disappointed when he hadn't.

But now he seemed angry again, withdrawn and angry.

She turned on the television, scanning the channels and finding only joyful reminders of the Christmas season. Finally, she clicked off the switch and went to the bookcase near the fireplace. After looking for a moment she pulled out a thick album and turned back to the sofa. She was looking at it when Patrick came back in, carrying a cup of coffee.

He didn't sit on the sofa beside her, but rather took a chair across the room, propping his ankle against his bent knee and looking at her solemnly over the cup of steaming coffee.

"What's that you have?" he finally asked as if only to be polite.

"It's one of our old albums," she said, looking up at him with a wistful smile. "Look," she said, holding the book toward him. "It's Todd's fifth birthday party . . . do you remember? You gave him a baseball glove, of all things. Look at this . . . the darned thing was bigger than he was." She laughed, then stopped, seeing the look that crossed Patrick's face.

She glanced back down at the book, turning the pages and wishing she knew what to say to him, wishing this awful strain were not here between them. She glanced at him again, and saw the blank look on his face, the look of indifference that he feigned when things threatened to become too emotional.

But for all his indifference, she thought he needed her probably more than he ever had in his life. And, dear God, she had to admit how very much she still needed him. But she had no idea how she could go about telling him such a thing.

She continued to turn the pages of the album. Somehow it made her feel better, seeing pictures of Todd and remembering all the scrapes and bumps he'd received growing up. He'd always been a tough kid, and these pictures helped reinforce that thought.

There were many pictures of Christmas, their favorite family holiday. The tree was always in the same spot in the den, and through the years one could see changes in the furniture, changes in their clothes and hairstyles. But always there was one thing that was constant, the happiness on their faces as they opened gifts or decorated the tree.

She glanced now at the empty spot where the tree always stood, and a thought began to germinate in her mind. She wondered how angry Patrick would be if she got a tree tomorrow and decorated it.

Patrick was still sitting in the chair across the room. His eyes were quiet and dark and he seemed lost in thought. Finally, feeling her gaze upon him, he glanced up, then his eyelids slowly lowered, closing out her view of his eyes and whatever lay in their depths.

He stood up suddenly. "I'm going up to bed. Make yourself at home, Susan."

His words did not seem calculated to hurt

her, but they did. His flat, polite statement flew straight to her heart like an arrow.

"Take any bedroom you like."

He turned then and left her sitting there, stunned and alone and unwelcome in the house that she still considered her home.

She sat for a long while, trying to concentrate on the pictures, trying to tell herself she could make it through this long, cold night, that there would be good news tomorrow. But finally she had to give up; she simply could not bear sitting in the big, empty room alone.

After turning out all the lights, she moved up the stairs, reaching the top step, and glancing automatically toward Todd's room. Thinking about turning on the lamp at the window, she walked across the hall and silently pushed open the door.

For a moment she could not understand why Patrick was in Todd's room, why he was standing so silently, gazing out the window. Then she saw the baseball glove in his hand that hung limply at his side. Her heart felt as if it actually stopped when she saw Patrick's shoulders shaking, and she had to put her fingers to her lips to quiet the sob that threatened to give her away.

Patrick was crying. It was the first time she had ever seen her husband cry. She had seen him grow sentimental at times, and she had seen his eyes darken with love and tenderness. She always suspected that hidden deep within his proud heart was that place soft as a child's. And that was what he always hid from her.

"Patrick," she whispered, feeling tears stinging her own eyes.

He turned and frowned, then turned back to the window. He lifted the ball glove and with his other fist, punched the soft leather pouch that had been made by years of use. She saw his shoulders lift, and her heart ached as she realized how desperately he was trying to conceal his feelings from her, those feelings that he considered weak and unmanly.

"I hardly ever told him I loved him," he whispered hoarsely.

"Oh, Patrick," she whispered. "He knows you love him."

"Sometimes when I was proudest of him, of his accomplishments, I couldn't . . . I just couldn't seem to find the right words to say . . . you know?" He turned, not trying to shield his tears from her, not bothering to pretend his heart wasn't breaking.

She went to him then and gently pulled the baseball glove from his hand, tossing it on Todd's bed. She put her arms at his waist and looked up into his eyes.

"Todd knows you're proud of him, darling. You've shown him that in so many ways. Sometimes it takes more than words to convey how much someone means to us. And Todd knows . . . he's always known that you love him . . . and he adores you in return."

Patrick's smile was weak. "You always seem to know exactly what to say, while I—"

"One of your worst traits, I always said."

His hand went to caress her cheek and she turned so that his fingers cupped her face. She felt as if her skin might actually drink in the warmth of his hand.

"Do you realize you called me darling just now?" he asked, his voice soft and quiet.

"You are my darling, Patrick. You have always been . . . my only darling. Through everything . . . through all the years, the disagreements and the bad times . . . the good times, you, Patrick Douglas, were my first and only love. Don't you know that?"

He frowned, wanting to believe her, wanting so much more. But as always, he was afraid to trust his heart too soon.

"I wish I could believe that."

"What would it take to convince you?" she asked as her fingers moved down to the buttons of his shirt.

She felt his hands on hers, saw the doubt in

his eyes and the confusion. Then his fingers gripped hers, pulling her hand away as he stepped around her.

"I don't want your pity, Susan. I've thought for so long that I would do anything to have you back in this house, back in my arms. But I can't do this if it means I just have to lose you all over again. I can't."

He turned and walked out of the room, leaving her feeling bereft and empty, making her want to shout and scream at him. He was as proud and unyielding as ever.

Susan stood for a long while, thinking about her life with Patrick, thinking about all the emotions, all the regrets she had gone through since leaving this house. She had never wanted to be away from him. He had forced her hand with his unyielding stubbornness . . . and she had let him.

She realized that had been a common pattern in their life. Patrick would withdraw from her emotionally and she would let him, never pursuing, but giving him space and time to work things out in his own way. Was that why he always assumed that her love was not as strong and committed as his?

Suddenly her eyes widened and she smiled.

"That's it!" It had to be . . . and yet in all the years she had never been able to see it.

"But I do now," she muttered, turning purposefully from Todd's room.

She marched down the hall and opened the door to the bedroom that she had once shared with Patrick. She heard the splash of water in the shower and hesitated only a moment before stepping into the bedroom and closing the door.

She could actually feel the pounding of her heart when moments later the sound of the shower stopped. And when Patrick walked from the bathroom, he was drying his hair and did not see her immediately.

She took advantage of the moment, letting her eyes move over him, taking in his tall, muscular frame and the towel draped around his hips. He was still the sexiest man she'd ever met, and she felt her pulse quicken at the thought of being in his arms and feeling those strong hands against her skin.

Patrick looked up, a glint of surprise in his eyes. The towel he'd been using to dry his hair was suspended in midair as he stared at her.

"Patrick Douglas, you're the stubbornest damned man I've ever known." She paused, lifting her chin and staring into his eyes, praying that she had made the right choice by barging into his room. "And I just realized tonight that I've let you put me off hundreds of times because of that stubborn pride. And I'm warning you that starting this moment, I'm never going to let you get away with it again."

"What are you talking about?" he asked, his eyes narrowed and wary.

"You know perfectly well what I'm talking about," she said, walking to him. She placed her hands on his bare chest, feeling with satisfaction the tension in him, the growing excitement that he was trying to hide. "I love you . . . and I know that you still love me, no matter how hard and gruff you try to be. You want me just as much as I want you and—"

His green eyes slid away from her gaze and he moved around her. "I've never denied that I still want you, Susan. That's not the point."

"Then what is the point? Is the point that I left you? That I wanted to go to school and accomplish something I never got to do because we married so young? If that's the only thing keeping us apart, then I relent . . . I'll quit school."

He whirled around, his brow wrinkled as he frowned down into her eyes.

"No," he said quickly. "No, that's not what I want. God, you don't understand at all." His hands reached for her, pulling her against his still-damp body. "If you'd just have given me a chance to adjust to the idea . . . Susan, I'm so proud of you, of what you've accomplished. Todd has told me about your grades and . . . no, I would never ask you to give this up. I just assumed it was more than that . . . that you needed . . . time away from me."

"Sometimes, my darling, you assume too damned much."

She smiled at him, surprised, and feeling foolish that she had waited so long to confront Patrick.

"Tell me what you do want, Patrick. Because at this moment . . ." She ran her hands over his chest and down to his waist, slipping her fingers beneath the top of the towel. "I'd almost be willing to promise you anything."

His eyebrow quirked and a slow smile moved across his face as he shook his head in bemusement.

"Susan Douglas . . ." he muttered, taking her hand and bringing it up to his lips. "You really mean it."

"Yes," she whispered. "I really mean it."

Slowly, very slowly, he bent his head toward her, teasing her with light kisses that made her lips reach for his, wanting more. Suddenly his arms tightened around her, pulling her roughly against him as he took her mouth in a long, deep kiss.

"I want you," he said when he finally lifted

his head. "Just you, Susan, in any way, under any condition you name. I want you as my wife, as the mother of my son —" His voice cracked, and he had to stop and take a deep breath. "All I've ever wanted is you, in this house . . . in this room."

"I'm here," she whispered against his searching lips. "And I promise, I'll always be here."

Her hands moved downward again, giving one deft pull at the towel and releasing it to fall to the floor. She heard Patrick's soft rumble of laughter as she quickly stepped out of her clothes and began to pull the shirt over her head. She thrilled at the feel of his hands against hers, as he helped her with her clothes and moved them both toward the bed.

There was no time for preliminaries; neither of them had the patience for further waiting. Patrick gasped at the feel of her body beneath his, at the feel of her soft breasts against his chest. His hands went to her hips, pulling her up to meet him as each of them reached desperately for the other, meeting and melding together with heated sighs of pleasure and passion.

Later, Susan lay in Patrick's arms, contented, feeling the confusion lift away from her mind. This was all that was needed: being together.

She lifted her face from his shoulder, trailing soft kisses along his neck. "I love you," she whispered. "And I've missed you so much."

Patrick's fingers moved through her hair and down the side of her face. The rumble of his voice beneath her ear sounded deep and warm. "I meant what I said earlier. I don't want you to give up school."

She pulled slightly away from him so she could see his face and his eyes. "I can always go to Maryville College, or Pellissippi State. That's only fifteen miles away, and I could easily make the drive every day."

Patrick frowned and his eyes narrowed. "But is that what you really want? Wouldn't you prefer the University of Tennessee?

"Not if it means being separated from you," she said, moving her fingers along the curve of his mouth. "Where I go doesn't matter; it has never really mattered to me. I just didn't like the idea of you telling me I couldn't do it."

He closed his eyes and sighed. "I behaved like a jerk, but then, I guess I don't have to tell you that. I don't know why, but all I could see was your pulling away from me. And I—I guess I was afraid of losing you. And I've never been very good at accepting changes."

"I know," she said lightly. "Dad says it's like pulling teeth to get you to use a new method in the orchard or at the apple barn."

He grinned and kissed her. "So, you believe what they say is true . . . that you can't teach an old dog new tricks?"

"No, I don't believe it. I'm pretty much of an old dog myself, in case you haven't noticed. And I've learned so much this past six months, Patrick, and I don't just mean school. I mean about myself and life—about us."

"So have I."

"Then it's settled," she said quietly. "I'll change to one of the schools in Maryville and you'll let me come back home."

There was the slightest whisper of a catch in his voice. "I don't even have to think about that one, baby. I want you back under any condition you can name."

"Just love me," she whispered, snuggling closer against him. "That's my condition."

"I do love you, more than anything. And your being here now is going to make things perfect when Todd comes home."

"Yes," she whispered, feeling her throat tighten. "We'll be a family again when he comes home."

It was sometime near dawn when she felt Patrick throw the covers back and get out of bed. He bent down to place a soft kiss against her bare shoulder.

"Hmmm," she murmured. "Where you going?"

"It snowed; I want to see how bad it is."

She was awake in an instant, throwing the covers back and getting out of bed to follow him to the window.

They could feel the chill through the glass panes. And even in the predawn hours the snow was like a bright blanket over the ground and trees. It seemed even to light the darkness.

Susan sighed, then felt Patrick's arm go around her as they stared helplessly at the snow.

"They have to find him today," he said almost to himself. "There's no more time."

While Patrick was in the shower, Susan huddled in bed beneath the quilts, thinking of his grim words and praying desperately. It couldn't be too late . . . it just couldn't. But she knew the snow took away some of their chances.

After she had showered and dressed, she went outside to the front porch, where Patrick was gazing hopelessly at the drifts of snow.

"I'm not sure I can make it to the main road," he said, stepping out into the snow that came almost to the tops of his boots.

"Can't we call the visitor center and see what they say?" She had never felt so helpless or so afraid.

"Yeah," he said, turning back to the house and stamping the snow from his boots. "I'll call right now."

"Do you feel like eating some breakfast?" she asked, linking her arm through his and looking up at him with a new tenderness.

"Actually, I'm starving this morning . . . how about you?" He kissed her mouth, trying to appear lighthearted.

"Yes," she said. "Me, too. I'll fix something while you make the call."

By the time Patrick got off the phone and came to the kitchen, Susan had sliced the cinnamon bread and was placing it on the table.

"I hope you don't mind oatmeal," she said, putting a steaming bowl before him.

"No," he murmured. "Sounds good."

"What did they say?" She sat at the table across from him and poured herself a glass of sparkling apple juice from their own orchard.

"Well, the sky's clear . . . that's good. The helicopter is going up in half an hour." He stopped eating and gazed solemnly at her. "They offered to fly here and pick us up. The pilot knows the area and he says it won't be a problem landing in the big pasture just past the apple barn."

"Oh," she said, feeling her stomach churn at

the thought of flying.

"If you don't want to go, baby, I'll—"

"No," she said. "Don't stay here because of me. I know how much you want to go and how much you need to be involved in finding Todd." She smiled at him and took his hand. "Would it bother you too much if I stayed here? Actually there's something I wanted to do."

He frowned at her and squeezed her hand. "Are you sure? You won't fret yourself to death, sitting here alone, worrying about Todd, or worrying about me in the helicopter?"

"Well . . ." she drawled, giving him a sheepish look. "Don't ask me not to worry; I can't help that."

He took a deep breath, and as he did, his eyes moved lovingly over her face and hair, then down to her lips.

"My beautiful little Yankee bride," he said, his voice soft and wistful.

She frowned at him. "How long do you have to live in the South to overcome that label?"

He laughed and leaned across to kiss her. "I'll let you know in another twenty or thirty years."

After breakfast Susan walked with him out to the apple barn where both of them cleared a space in the snow for the helicopter to land.

Then she waited there with him until they heard the roar of the engine coming over the mountains.

They turned to each other, and Susan threw her arms around his neck. "You have to find him, Patrick . . . you have to."

"I intend to." He kissed her again and turned to go, waving back at her. "I'll call you from the visitor center when we know anything at all."

Susan held her breath as Patrick ducked his head and ran to the helicopter. As soon as he was inside, the big blades began to pick up speed and the machine lifted slowly from the ground and glided away toward the mountains.

She went back into the apple barn and rummaged through the shelves until she found a small handsaw. Then, with determination she pushed her way through the heavy snow past the barn to the dense forest. By the time she found a spruce small enough for her to cut and drag back to the house, she was exhausted.

She stood for a moment in the stand of trees, listening to the birds and watching the way the sun turned the snow to glistening crystals as it floated from the trees around her. Finally, having caught her breath, she hauled the tree across the snow and back to the house.

After she had changed into dry clothes and

built a fire in the den, she called Patrick's mom and dad to tell them what had happened.

"And Patrick actually flew in that thing?" Dad asked.

"Yes, Dad," Susan answered with a smile. "And I think he loved it."

"That boy always was adventuresome," he said with a proud chuckle. "Next thing you know, he'll be wantin' one of those things for the orchard."

"Oh, dear," she said, hearing his teasing laugh at the other end of the phone.

"Don't you worry, Sue," he said. "Patrick knows the mountains better than any of those civil service fellows. If anybody can find Todd, Patrick can."

"I hope so," she said, trying to remain hopeful. "And you tell Nell not to worry about coming over. The roads are still too bad; I'll call you if I hear anything."

It took a while for Susan to find the box of tree ornaments and bring them all downstairs. By the time she had the tree in a stand and in its usual place in the den, it was almost noon.

With each hour that passed, Susan grew more tense. Her stomach churned, causing waves of nausea to move over her. Every time the phone rang she ran quickly to pick it up, hoping and praying it was Patrick.

Still, he didn't call.

Finally the tree was finished. Susan plugged in the lights and backed away from it to get the full effect. She sighed with satisfaction.

"Beautiful," she whispered.

It was small, much smaller than what they were used to. But if this was going to be a surprise, that couldn't be helped; it was the best she could do.

As the day dragged slowly on, Susan began to feel ill from anxiety. Perhaps it had been a mistake to stay home alone. Perhaps she should have swallowed her fear and gone with Patrick. At least she'd know what was going on.

She cleaned and vacuumed, straightened the furniture, made fresh coffee, and every time her eyes glanced toward a clock, she was amazed that the time was passing so slowly.

She glanced out the windows, seeing that the sun was very low in the west. She should have heard something by now. Surely Patrick would call her.

"He would have," she whispered worriedly. "If they found Todd, he would call."

And that thought made her heart ache.

"Please," she prayed aloud, feeling her heart

tremble with a quiet feeling of doom. "Please don't let this be happening."

She walked to the phone, thinking she would call the visitor center. But then she stopped, not sure she wanted to hear whatever news they had. She'd rather hear it from Patrick.

Finally she grabbed her coat and walked out onto the porch, leaving the door open so she could hear the phone if it rang.

It was going to be dark soon, and that meant another long, torturous night of worry. She felt the tears of desperation gather in her eyes as she placed her forehead against the cold wood of the porch supports.

Then she heard it — the sound of a helicopter somewhere far in the distance. The sound was a low drumming, a rhythmic roar that grew nearer and nearer.

"Dear God," she whispered, feeling her heart sink. "They've given up for the night. Oh, Patrick . . ." How he must be feeling after being so certain he would find Todd. But that was why he had not called; they hadn't found him.

Tears were streaming from her eyes as she stood on the porch and watched the helicopter hover over the pasture, throwing a cloud of snow into the air before slowly settling to the ground. Her hand went to her heart, wishing the pain were not so intense as she watched

Patrick step slowly from the helicopter. She watched when he turned back to the door and then — then she saw someone else step to the ground.

She took a deep breath and straightened, holding her body very still and staring hard into the distance. Who was it who stood beside Patrick?

"Todd . . . ?" she whispered. "Todd?"

She began to run then, not even noticing that she wore no coat or that the cold, wet snow filled her sneakers after the first few steps. She fell once, and jumped up, trying not to lose the two men from her sight and praying even as she ran. As they grew nearer, she saw the man beside Patrick begin to run, too. And she knew.

It was her son! He was safe. And he was home.

"Oh," she cried, stopping and watching him breathlessly as he ran toward her.

Todd grabbed her up in his arms, rocking her back and forth, both of them crying. In a few moments Susan felt Patrick's arms around them as they stood in the fading light of day, not speaking, but simply rejoicing silently in being together again.

Susan pulled away, reaching up to touch Todd's face as if to make sure it was really he.

His skin seemed red and chapped, but she thought he had never looked better. His bluish-green eyes looked brilliant, more like his father's than ever.

"What happened?" she asked breathlessly. "Are you all right? Are you hurt?"

"Nah," he said with a grin, shaking off her concern as if he had been on a Sunday afternoon stroll. "I was cold and hungry, but the guys back at the park made sure I got plenty to eat." He laughed and looked at Patrick, who nodded.

"We'd have been home sooner if it hadn't taken so long to get the boy's stomach filled."

"But, Patrick, why didn't you call?"

"I wanted to surprise you," he said, bending to kiss her. "I'm sorry . . . did I scare you?"

She stared at him, then sighed and shook her head.

"You men," she said with a teasing smile.

They began to walk back to the house, and Susan put her arm around Todd. "How did they find you? The snow was so bad, I thought . . ." She looked around Todd at Patrick, who was grinning at his son.

"Tell her, son."

"Actually, Mom, the snow was a blessing. Late in the afternoon, the first day I went in, me and Rebel ran into a pack of hogs . . . hungry, ill-tempered hogs." He grimaced and shuddered for effect. "Well, that's another story," he said with a wink at his dad. "But the gist of it is that I wound up off the side of the bluff on a wide ledge. Luckily there was a good overhang which gave me a little shelter. But the light there wasn't good so no matter how much I screamed or yelled, no one was ever able to see me. Anyway, after the snow I ripped up the red backpack and made a signal with it against the bluff. It showed up well in the white stuff. Old eagle-eye here spotted it right away." Todd grinned and grabbed his father's arm, shaking him like an affectionate puppy.

"You said you'd find him," Susan said, looking at Patrick with awe.

"Yeah . . . I did, didn't I?"

They walked arm in arm back to the house, laughing. She slipped off her snow-filled sneakers on the front porch and went inside, stopping at the den, wanting to share one last moment alone before she called the family to tell them their son was safe.

Todd glanced at his mother and father.

"Dad says you're coming home, Mom."

"I *am* home" was all she could manage to say.

"I'm glad . . . real glad."

"Come into the den," she said. "I have something . . . something for both of you."

They walked into the den, and Susan was pleased at the emotion she saw on Todd's face. And she was even more surprised to see the same emotion reflected on Patrick's. She smiled and went to put her arm around her husband, holding out her other arm for Todd.

"I think this is going to be the best Christmas of our lives," she whispered. "The very best."

KATHERINE STONE—
Zebra's Leading Lady for Love

BEL AIR   (2979, $4.95)
Bel Air—where even the rich and famous are awed by the wealth that surrounds them. Allison, Winter, Emily: three beautiful women who couldn't be more different. Three women searching for the courage to trust, to love. Three women fighting for their dreams in the glamorous and treacherous *Bel Air*.

ROOMMATES   (3355, $4.95)
No one could have prepared Carrie for the monumental changes she would face when she met her new circle of friends at Stanford University. Once their lives intertwined and became woven into the tapestry of the times, they would never be the same.

TWINS   (3492, $4.95)
Brook and Melanie Chandler were so different, it was hard to believe they were sisters. One was a dark, serious, ambitious New York attorney; the other, a golden, glamorous, sophisticated supermodel. But they were more than sisters—they were twins and more alike than even they knew . . .

THE CARLTON CLUB   (3614, $4.95)
It was the place to see and be seen, the only place to be. And for those who frequented the playground of the very rich, it was a way of life. Mark, Kathleen, Leslie and Janet—they worked together, played together, and loved together, all behind exclusive gates of the *Carlton Club*.

Available wherever paperbacks are sold, or order direct from the Publisher. Send cover price plus 50¢ per copy for mailing and handling to Zebra Books, Dept. 3979, 475 Park Avenue South, New York, N.Y. 10016. Residents of New York and Tennessee must include sales tax. DO NOT SEND CASH. For a free Zebra/ Pinnacle catalog please write to the above address.